DRAKE'S DRUM

(ARK ROYAL, BOOK XVII)

CHRISTOPHER G. NUTTALL

Text copyright © 2021 Christopher G. Nuttall

Printed in the United States of America.

ISBN: 9798505096963

Imprint: Independently Published

Cover by Justin Adams

http://www.variastudios.com/

http://www.chrishanger.net
http://chrishanger.wordpress.com/
http://www.facebook.com/ChristopherGNuttall
All Comments Welcome!

CONTENTS

PROLOGUE

FROM: Admiral Paul Mason, Director of Alpha Black, Special Projects
TO: Admiral Susan Onarina, CO Operation Lightning Strike

SUSAN,

Since your return to Earth after the successful completion of Operation Lightning Strike, my department has been studying the alien artefacts retrieved from Target One. I say studying, but the blunt truth is that we have drawn a blank. The artefacts are apparently beyond our current level of understanding, to the point we have been unable to identify the materials used to construct them or to determine precisely *how* the field they generate affects either infected zombies or uninfected humans. In desperation, we consulted with Tadpole and Fox specialists and they drew a blank too. The only detail we learned through their involvement was confirmation of our theory that the artefacts affect both intelligent races and their mechanical servants.

Certain things can be said with a great deal of certainty. To us, and other uninfected races, the artefacts are almost unfathomable. They appear to be something strange, almost mythical; a handful of my team noted that the artefacts felt like something put together by a god, something that honestly does not belong on our plane of existence. Other, more sober, specialists believe the effect to be artificially generated, in much the same way modulated sounds have been used to shape emotions and, in some cases, encourage or discourage certain types of behaviour. The apparent application of the field to all known races is curious, given the differences between them, but a confirmed fact. A handful of my researchers have even speculated that the artefacts are actively monitoring their surroundings, then tuning their field to influence newcomers as they enter their sphere of influence. We have been unable to determine if this is actually true and, if so, if the artefacts are intelligent—in some sense—or simply operating under a preset program. Our belief is that the field is designed to make it difficult for anyone to study the artefacts.

The effects on the infected, however, are very different. We took the risk of inserting an infected zombie into the artefact chamber and the results were dramatic. The viral matter within the host's brain went, for want of a better word, comatose. There was no sign of recovery until we removed the zombie from the sphere of influence, at which point the virus appeared to retake control. Further research proved that we could flush the virus out of the victim's system while it was comatose, although it was extremely difficult to save the victim afterwards. We tested the artefacts on four zombies, all in Level IV or Level V stages of infection, and only one survived and regained his independence. Two more died when we tried to flush the virus; the third was apparently too heavily infected to survive without the virus. Our preliminary analysis suggests that the virus had simply destroyed too much of the host's brain tissue. Further investigation is underway, hampered by the condition of the body. I'll keep you updated.

Our belief is that the artefacts, positioned as they were on an infected world, effectively numbed the virus's nervous system. The virus should have been aware of their presence, as we would become aware of a needle being stuck in our flesh, but the artefacts might have produced an anaesthetic-style effect. There was certainly no move to remove or destroy the artefacts from a distance, which should have been well within the virus's capabilities. We are uncertain, as yet, what it would actually take to *destroy* the artefacts, but the virus should have been able to hit them with KEWs or nukes. We do not believe it tried.

Unfortunately, while the existence of the artefacts has many interesting implications for the future, we fear they may be of little immediate help. The field they produce is very limited in range and we have been unable, so far, to determine how to take control. Nor have we been able to duplicate the effect. We are still working on the problem, and we have come up with some very interesting theories, but it may be decades—at best—before we have a practical breakthrough that leads to workable hardware. The artefacts do not represent a silver bullet, I'm afraid, and it is imperative you bring this to the attention of the PM and government ministers. (I have tried, but you know how little attention they pay to us boffins.) We know very little about the artefacts and their builders. We do not know where they live, nor their motives. The idea they may be willing to help us is tempting, but little more than wishful thinking. We cannot rely on it.

Therefore, as you have suggested, we must turn our attention to Operation Footfall. It is my belief that, in the aftermath of Operation Lightning Strike, we have rocked the virus back on its heels. I cannot believe, even with its warped (by our standards) economic and technical base, that losing the catapults, and then a handful heavily-industrialised worlds, did not hurt. It may take the virus some time to notice, given its nature, but notice it will. I believe that you are correct to say that we have a window of opportunity to put the boot in, before the virus rebalances itself and resumes the offensive. We may not have a better opportunity to win the war, or at least secure the uninfected worlds and deny the virus the chance to spread any further.

Accordingly, it is my very strong feeling that Operation Footfall should be launched as soon as possible.

CHAPTER ONE

CAPTAIN–LORD–THOMAS HAMMOND prided himself on being calm and composed, whatever the situation. It was a trait that had served him well throughout the years, as he joined the navy and commenced his slow yet steady climb towards flag rank. He knew, given his birth and family connections, that he would become an admiral—inevitably—unless he screwed up so badly that even *his* family's wealth and power were unable to keep the story from breaking into the media. It had birthed a sense of patience that had made him calm and reliable, a safe pair of hands for the Royal Navy's largest starships. He knew he wasn't flashy—he knew he wasn't bold enough to stake everything on one throw of the dice—but it didn't matter. It wasn't his job to take risks, merely to do his duty.

His calm fled as he stepped into his wife's bedroom and stared. She was on the bed, naked, with…his thoughts seemed to slam to a complete stop as he spied Captain Mitch Campbell beside her. No, *inside* her. The sight was so…so staggeringly insane that it was almost impossible to convince himself that what he saw was real. Charlotte was an aristocrat, married to a naval officer…she knew the sort of social opprobrium she could expect for betraying her husband, as well as her family. Thomas knew their marriage hadn't been the same over the last few years, as the stresses and strains of constant war and endless naval deployments had ground them both down, but...he'd never expected her to find a lover. Not like this. To be caught in bed with her lover, in the family mansion, with a party going on below...

"Get out!" Charlotte's voice rose, in anger and embarrassment. "Get out!"

Thomas felt his face grow hot. He'd never cheated on her. He'd never... and with a junior officer, with a man who was—technically—under Thomas's command? Red rage flared through him. He was going to be a laughingstock. He was going to be...he clenched his fists, thinking of his daughters. Their prospects were about to hit rock bottom because their mother couldn't keep her...he cut that thought off before it went any further, reaching desperately for his legendary calm. He expected surprises on the bridge of a starship, from orders from home that made no sense to enemy starships materialising out of nowhere and opening fire before his ship had even registered their presence, but here...? He'd expected life to go on as it always had, in the centuries between the Troubles and the Third Interstellar War. He had never thought...

He clenched his fists. It had been a long time since he'd fought hand-to-hand—he'd taken the required courses at the academy and then dropped it as soon as he could—but he wanted to smash Captain Campbell in the face. How dare he? How *dare* he? Thomas's thoughts ran in mad circles. God! He'd known the younger man was reckless, to the point Captain Campbell had buzzed an infected world purely for the hell of it, but he'd never dreamed the man would sleep with his wife! Or that...

Thomas's thoughts grew darker. Sleeping with Charlotte was one thing, but doing it so publicly was quite another. The cream of the cream were gathered downstairs, eating Thomas's food and drinking Thomas's wine. It was just a matter of time before the tabloids broke the story. His family had enough enemies to make damn sure of it.

Captain Campbell sat up, clearly bracing himself. Thomas glared at him, too angry to feel intimidated. The younger man had grown up on the wrong side of the tracks—his academic record was a mixture of genuine achievements and countless disciplinary reports—and he was one of the navy's foremost unarmed combat experts…Thomas wondered, with a flicker of bitter amusement, if Captain Campbell realised how badly he'd fucked up his career. It was quite possible he hadn't been thinking at all. Campbell didn't seem to give much of a damn about the future. It was why the Royal Navy had never trusted him with a ship it couldn't afford to lose.

Charlotte held up a hand. "Thomas, I…"

"Don't hurt her," Captain Campbell said. "It was…"

"Shut up." Thomas slapped the caller on the wall, ignoring his wife's gasp of horror. "Just…shut up!"

The butler materialised behind him. "My Lord?"

Thomas almost smiled at the man's dry tones. The butler had worked for Thomas—and his father before him—for decades, long enough to have seen everything. He was loyal to the family…Thomas cursed under his breath as it dawned on him that the remainder of the servants might be more loyal to Charlotte than himself. It was *Charlotte* who'd run the household, supervising the staff even as she tended the family's interests and business holdings. And some of them *had* to have known what was going on. The maids might have said something—would have said something—if they'd thought Charlotte hadn't wanted it. Paranoia washed through him. If his wife had cheated on him once, so blatantly that there was no way word *wasn't* going to get out, had she cheated on him a dozen times? A hundred? A thousand? His heart sank. She could have gotten away with a great deal, as long as she was discreet. The staff knew who signed their payslips. They'd keep their mouths firmly closed.

If only because they'd never be able to find another job if they were dismissed for talking to the gossipmongers, he thought. *No one would hire someone known for telling tales out of school.*

"Escort Captain Campbell to his bedroom, see that he gets dressed and then evict him from the grounds," Thomas ordered. The nasty part of his mind was tempted to insist that Campbell be thrown out stark naked, but it would just make matters worse. The mansion was quite some distance from the nearest town. Campbell would have to use his wristcom to call a taxi and then…Thomas didn't give a damn. The younger man could probably find a hotel or simply drive straight to the nearest spaceport. "Now!"

"You can't," Charlotte said. She clutched a pillow to her chest. "Thomas…"

"Escort him out," Thomas ordered, ignoring his wife. "And then go tell the guests the party is over."

"Thomas," Charlotte said. "If you send them away…"

"Shut up," Thomas growled. Charlotte had pulled out all the stops for the party, inviting guests from all over the country…including some names who would not, normally, have been caught dead in the mansion. She'd gone to all that trouble, striking deals with the rest of polite society, and then betrayed him? She'd betrayed herself! "Shut up!"

The butler beckoned to Captain Campbell, who stood and marched out of the room with all the dignity he could muster. Thomas would have laughed, if the situation hadn't been so dire. A naked man could hardly muster any dignity…ice washed through him as he realised Charlotte had assigned Captain Campbell to a bedroom very close to her own, close enough to allow them to slip into each other's room in the middle of the night. How long had they been sleeping together? They hadn't even *known* each other for more than a year, perhaps…they'd first met when he'd invited Captain Campbell to the mansion, after their first joint operation. Or had they known each other for much longer? Had they been laughing at him all along? Thomas ground his teeth in fury. He could have taken it calmly, he thought, if they'd been discreet. It wouldn't have been that hard.

He closed the door, hoping and praying the servants had the sense to get well clear of the bedroom. They'd be heading downstairs, telling the guests the party had come to a sudden end…it was going to be the talk of polite society, he knew, and not for a good reason. The last time a party had been terminated, it had been when the Tadpoles attacked Earth. And he'd been told that other parties had just gone on and on, even when the rocks were falling and thousands of people were dying.

His fists clenched, again. Charlotte had betrayed him, betrayed their daughters, betrayed their entire family and their network of allies and clients...he forced himself, carefully, to unclench his fists. He couldn't afford to give in to his anger, not now. And yet, he needed answers. He just wasn't sure he wanted to hear them.

"Why?" Thomas could *hear* his voice shake. "Why...?"

The words seemed to stick in his throat. *Why did you betray me? Why did you betray me with him? Why did you do it in such a public place? Why...?*

Charlotte stood and glared. "Because I was *sick* of staying here."

Thomas stared. "You were sick of staying *here*?"

"I have been your wife for an eternity," Charlotte snapped. He heard a wealth of pain and long-buried resentments in her voice. "You left me behind, managing the estate, while you tended to your career. You had a life of your own, while I raised *your* children and handled *your* estate..."

"*Our* children," Thomas replied. A sudden flash of paranoia ran through him. His daughters...were they *his*? Everyone said his girls had his eyes, but...that could be just wishful thinking. Elizabeth and Lucille had always taken more after Charlotte than himself. He'd thought that was because they were girls, but...what if they weren't *his*? What if...he wanted to know and he didn't want to and...raw anger surged through him. How could he trust her, ever again? "And this is *our* estate."

"No, it isn't," Charlotte corrected. "It is *your* estate, held in trust for the girls. I'm just a glorified manager."

She leaned forward, dark eyes burning with unshed tears. "I don't ask for much, do I? I just wanted you there, being...being part of my life. Instead, you just walked in and out of the mansion as if you...as if you didn't give a damn about me."

Thomas glared back at her. "You're the one who wanted separate bed-rooms," he snarled. "How many armies of lovers have you brought to this house? How many?"

Charlotte flinched, as if he'd hit her. "Just him."

"Why him?" Thomas heard his voice shake and gritted his teeth. "Why him?"

It was hard to resist the impulse to grab Charlotte and shake her. He knew Charlotte was about as civilian as they came, but even she—surely—should have understood the problem. God knew there were countless soap operas where military wives lost everything through cheating on their husbands. The government pumped them out constantly, hiring hack writers and worse actors to ram the point home time and time again. Perhaps the propaganda had backfired. It wouldn't be the first time telling someone not to do something had encouraged them to do it. There'd been no shortage of examples in his schooling and naval career of people breaking rules merely because they were there.

"Because he was there," Charlotte said, echoing his thoughts. "And because he's everything you're not. Brave and bold and *exciting* and…"

"And what?" Thomas forced himself to take a step back. It wasn't easy. "Do you think he can give you…what? Happiness? A life of…of what?"

He stared at her, trying to understand her thinking. Captain Campbell had once told Thomas, a few months ago, that he was blind to his privilege, but it wasn't true. Thomas *knew* how lucky he'd been to be born into an aristocracy with real power. He knew his path from birth to a command chair on a starship's bridge, where every child wanted to be, had been smoothed by his family. And Charlotte had been lucky, too. She'd had the best of education, the best of opportunities…she'd *chosen* to marry him, knowing that she'd be moving to his family estate and helping run the family. She'd been good at it. She had no reason to feel discontented. She could even have had a discreet affair…

… And yet, she'd set out to deliberately hurt him.

It was hard to keep his churning thoughts under control. She'd had an affair…but she'd been so indiscreet that the entire *world* would know the truth. She was looking social death in the face. She was…he couldn't believe it had been an accident. Making love to Captain Campbell in the middle of a party, a gathering she'd planned, a gathering she was expected to coordinate…she was mad. She had to be. She might as well have detonated a nuke under the family's prospects. Thomas *knew*, with a certainty that could not be denied, that word was already flashing through the datanet. His enemies would make sure of it. Of *course* they would. And they'd gloat his wife had humiliated him in front of both his naval and aristocratic superiors.

"You could have done it in private," he said. His anger faded, to be replaced by a numbness that made it hard to think. "You could have…"

Charlotte crossed her arms under her breasts. "What do you care?"

Thomas found himself lost for words. It was the family. It was their daughters. It was a career and a life, and a position in society…it was everything. They were all at risk, thanks to Charlotte's actions. And… he wanted to believe she was crazy, that it was a moment of insanity…he needed to believe. It was impossible. It was…

"I care about our life," Thomas said weakly. "And about the world…"

"You don't care about me," Charlotte said. "Or our children. You just care about your career."

Thomas was too tired to feel angry. "You knew you were marrying a naval officer," he said, numbness spreading through his mind. Too much had happened, too quickly. "You *knew* what it would mean for our life together."

"*Together?*" Charlotte snorted. "How often have we been *together* in twenty-four years of marriage?"

She went on before Thomas could think of an answer. "I have sacrificed my life, for yours. I have given up all hope of a career of my own, to run your family interests. I have placed the interests of my family—and yours—ahead of my own, to the point I agreed to a match I didn't particularly want just to please the old biddies who think blood and breeding is so much more important than anything else. I have given birth to two children and supervised every aspect of their lives, from supporting their schooling to fighting for them when they needed me to drop everything and help and…"

The resentment in her voice was almost palpable. "And what have I gotten out of it? Nothing!"

"You have a life far beyond the ordinary," Thomas pointed out. He waved at the nearest wall, covered in paintings of distant ancestors. "Do you think Captain Campbell's sister"—he couldn't remember if the bastard *had* a sister, but the point stood—"wouldn't swap places with you in a heartbeat?"

Charlotte ignored him. "I have served you faithfully ever since we got married," she said, coldly. "The children are adults now. I want a life of my own."

Thomas found himself lost for words. If she'd wanted a divorce…it wasn't *that* uncommon, when children reached adulthood. Charlotte had had the very best of medical care, along with everything else. She was looking at another fifty years of reasonable health, barring accidents. He wouldn't have begrudged her a separation, if she'd wanted to go. He wouldn't have tried to keep her on the estate. God knew, they'd planned for his career to end when he reached flag rank…

She stood and reached for her clothes. "I'm leaving," she said. "Don't try to stop me."

Thomas sat on the bed, his thoughts churning. Charlotte wasn't penniless. She had a dowry as well as a salary, paid to her personally as part of a tax rationalisation scheme. He assumed she had savings, although he wasn't entirely sure it was true. She'd certainly crammed her bedroom and adjoining chambers with expensive coats, handbags and jewellery. Her relatives might try to cut her off from the trust fund, when they realised what had happened, but…Thomas didn't think they'd succeed. There'd be too much opposition from everyone with the sense to realise just what sort of precedent they'd set for the rest of the aristocracy.

His heart sank as he watched Charlotte zipping up her fur coat. She looked like a stranger, not the woman he'd married. Pain gnawed, deep inside; pain and anger at the betrayal. She could have talked to him. She could have made a life for herself, if she'd been discreet. No one would have cared, if she'd been…he shook his head. He knew, without having to check, that the guests were already wittering to their relatives. The news would be all the way around the world before breakfast. He said nothing as Charlotte pressed the buzzer, ordering the servants to bring the car around to the main entrance. He could have cancelled the order, but… what would have been the point?

Charlotte didn't even *look* at him as she stalked out. Thomas felt a flicker of anger, mingled with a bitter numbness. Too much had changed, too quickly, for him to feel much of anything. And yet…he wanted to scream and shout and lash out at Captain Campbell for seducing his wife. Thomas couldn't believe the younger man was innocent. He should have had the sense to say no.

Bastard, Thomas thought. *What the hell were you thinking?*

CHAPTER TWO

CAPTAIN MITCH CAMPBELL KNEW, without false modesty, that he was brave and bold and willing to risk his life—and everything else—on one throw of the dice. His childhood had taught him there was nothing to be gained by waiting, that patience was not always a virtue. He'd grown up in a place where everything could be taken from you in the blink of an eye, where seizing every opportunity that came your way was pretty much the order of the day. The idea of waiting one's turn was absurd. One's turn would never come unless one reached for it.

His heart was still pounding as the taxi carried him towards the nearest town, a dear little place that he'd seen in passing when he'd been driven to the mansion. It looked like a town from three centuries ago, the halcyon days when Britain ruled the waves and the sun never set on the British Empire. And, like those days, it was a veneer that masked an ugly reality. They might be held up as long-gone wonderlands, before liberals and socialists and weak-chinned men had ruined everything, but Mitch knew better. The British Empire had rested on the exploitation of the subject races, eating its own seed corn instead of thinking about the future; the modern-day town had been designed to follow a pattern, rather than developing naturally into a genuine settlement. He wondered, as the taxi passed into the town and stopped in front of the hotel, if it was little more than a giant theme park. Victorian and Edwardian nostalgia had been part of the post-Troubles world for far too long.

He paid the taxi driver, then walked into the hotel and pressed his military ID against the scanner. The average hotel chain would make room for a military officer or, if it couldn't clear space for him, find another room somewhere in the town. Mitch didn't really care, as long as it was somewhere he could sleep. It had been a long day, even before Captain Hammond had caught Mitch in bed with his wife. He suppressed an urge to giggle as the machine bleeped, an urge that would probably land him in more trouble. Sleeping with a superior officer's wife was probably a court-martial offense. If it wasn't, it soon would be.

His feet ached as he made his way up the stairs and down the corridor to the room. The hotel was surprisingly automated, given its location. There would be maids and a bellhop, unless he was mistaken, but they wouldn't show themselves until morning. He pushed open the door and stepped into the room, looking around with relief. It was small and snug, but he'd slept in worse places. He dumped his bag on the bed, silently congratulating himself for not bringing more than a simple knapsack. Captain Hammond had promised him he'd be able to source whatever he needed at the mansion.

And you slept with his wife, Mitch reminded himself. *He didn't like you before. What do you think he'll think of you now?*

The thought mocked him as he undressed and stepped into the shower. It was hard not to feel a twinge of guilt for leaving Charlotte with her husband, even though he knew there'd been no choice. There was no way he could have picked a fight with the butler, not without making things far too easy for Captain Hammond. The man could have pressed assault charges…no, he could have had the manservants take Mitch into custody and hold him until the police arrived. The fix would have been in, well before Mitch posted bail. Leaving had been the only logical option. And yet, he'd had to leave Charlotte behind. He cursed under his breath, torn between anger and a certain awareness it had been his fault. He hadn't *had* to let her seduce him. He should have known it would end badly.

He closed his eyes as water sluiced over his body, washing away the signs of their lovemaking. It hadn't been the first time he'd been caught in a compromising position—he'd spent most of his free time since puberty trying to get laid—but it was certainly the most outrageous. An angry father or brother was *nothing* compared to a cuckolded husband, a husband tied to the most powerful families in the land. Mitch scowled as he scrubbed himself down, all too aware he would have to fight or lose everything. And yet, he didn't know *how* to fight. Captain Hammond was probably already calling the Admiralty, loudly demanding Mitch be reassigned to an asteroid mining complex in the middle of nowhere. The Royal Navy wasn't short on dead-end postings to send officers who couldn't be summarily dismissed...

Fuck, Mitch thought. He clenched his fists as he turned off the water, then dried himself with a towel. *What the fuck do I do now?*

He wrapped the towel around himself, stepped back into the bedroom and stopped. Dead. Charlotte was sitting on the bed, waiting for him. She wore a long fur coat that probably cost as much as a gunboat, perhaps more. A pair of heavy bags sat by the door. Mitch stared at her, awareness coming in fits and starts. He'd never really expected to see her again, not after they'd been caught. Captain Hammond would have all the excuse he needed to seek a divorce. Cheating on one's husband was bad under any circumstances, but cheating on a serving officer was the worst...

"Mitch." Charlotte smiled at him. "It's good to see you again."

Mitch gaped at her. "How did you...?"

"Find you?" Charlotte smiled. "It wasn't *that* hard. You used your military ID to book the room. I had no trouble tracing it."

"Right," Mitch repeated. "No trouble."

He stared. Charlotte had never been his usual type—she was older, for a start, with a body that suggested she was permanently on the verge of letting herself go. Normally, he admitted in the privacy of his own mind, he would never have paid more than a second's attention to her. And yet, there was something about her that called to him. She was a confident woman, in touch with her own sexuality…someone who knew what she wanted and was willing to do whatever she had to do to get it. She'd made the first move. Mitch acknowledged to himself, if no one else, that it was one hell of a turn-on.

And yet, she'd followed him.

"What?" He swallowed and started again. "What happened? I mean… what happened after I left?"

"Thomas and I exchanged harsh words," Charlotte said. "A lot of old resentments came bubbling up. We…snapped and snarled at each other. We…eventually, I left. I came to find you."

Mitch nodded, torn between a certain pleasure she'd come to him and a gnawing fear his life was about to turn upside down. Charlotte had cheated on her husband. He feared it was just a matter of time before she cheated on him too. And yet, he found it hard to believe *that* of her. He had no doubt there *had* been a lot of old resentments, between her and her husband. A person wouldn't cheat on their partner unless the marriage had been on the rocks for years…perhaps decades. Mitch cursed under his breath. Charlotte could have had a discreet affair with him, or anyone, without doing something her husband couldn't overlook. Why…?

He put it into words. "Why did you let us get caught?"

Charlotte frowned. "Because…"

He saw a wealth of emotion wash across her face. He thought he understood. Common sense was often pushed aside, when someone wanted to just lash out at the object of their resentment. He'd seen men take horrible beatings—or worse—just to hurt someone they hated. Charlotte might have arranged for them to be caught, without admitting—even to herself—that that was what she was doing. Letting her husband catch them would have brought all the buried resentments into the light, without…

"We need a plan," Charlotte said. "Right now, the tabloids are already catching wind of what's happened."

Mitch blinked. "Do you really think they'll care?"

"They will," Charlotte said. "They dedicated several dozen articles to the dress I wore to the Queen's Gala, last year. A complete waste of electrons, you might think, but they did it. Countless society commenters babbled nonsense about how my dress showed support for this political faction or that political faction…some complete pervert even had the nerve to suggest I was hinting I was pregnant, again, because I showed some cleavage. And if they made a mountain out of that molehill, what do you think they'll make of this?"

She smiled, rather coldly. "It will be a big scandal. Everyone will want a say in how it goes—the less involved they are, the more they'll want it. They'll think having their say will make them important. By this time tomorrow, there will be a hundred different narratives of the story, ranging from nearly-true bullshit to *complete* bullshit. People who want a distraction from their own affairs will promote the story, in hopes it'll consume all the attention; people who want to conceal awkward facts and bad news will use the story to hide it. You and I—and Thomas—are about to be at the centre of the greatest scandal since Princess Felicity was caught in bed with two of her maids."

"Oh." Mitch felt his heart sink. "Was that story actually true?"

Charlotte shrugged. "You'd be surprised how much never makes it into the tabloids," she said. "Lots of secrets never see the light of day. Point is, I'm the wife of a wealthy and powerful nobleman and you're a famous naval hero. They'll seek to destroy your reputation, in order to discredit you, but that'll be difficult because of all the time they spent boosting it in the first place. That gives us time to go on the offensive. We need to push back hard before Thomas manages to get the narrative on his side. Once that happens…"

Mitch grinned. "It's like a military campaign, isn't it?"

"Yes." Charlotte smiled back. "Our objective will be to make it impossible for them to crush us. If we can get the power of public opinion on our side, we will be untouchable."

Mitch considered it for a long moment. Like most military officers, he detested reporters even though he admitted they had their uses. He'd certainly been quite willing to hire PR experts to put his name before the public, in a desperate bid to ensure he was ranked with Nelson, Cunningham and Theodore Smith. And yet…he shook his head in frustration. He'd gotten caught in a trap. His only real options were to play the game to the bitter end, all too aware of the risks of losing, or surrender and hope he'd *merely* be exiled somewhere light-years from civilisation. There was no way in *hell* he was going to surrender his command. If fighting was their only hope, he'd fight.

"I see," he said. He knew he should worry about the future—he certainly had no idea if they even *had* a future—but training and inclination told him to deal with the immediate problem first. Advanced planning was the Admiralty's job, not his…his lips quirked at the thought. The REMFs weren't *that* good at their jobs. Their track record was pathetic. "So…where do we begin?"

"I've already spoken to my contacts," Charlotte said. She stood and began to disrobe. "They'll be putting out stories already, shaping the media battleground for our interviews tomorrow. And then we keep running until we get what we want."

Mitch felt himself stiffen as she removed her underwear. "And what do we want?"

"You want to keep your command, I assume," Charlotte said. "Right?"

"Yes."

"Yes," Charlotte echoed. "And I want to secure my place in society."

Mitch doubted it would be easy. Charlotte had cheated on her husband. Even if she was allied with a *bona fide* naval hero…it wasn't the sort of thing society would forgive and forget. And yet…he frowned, remembering what he'd read when he'd looked Thomas and Charlotte Hammond up in *Who's Who*. They were wealthy and powerful enough to bend society to their will, if they worked at it. Charlotte might believe she could come out of the storm with wealth, influence and power intact. He had no idea if she was right.

He met her eyes. "You could have organised a separation without all this"—he waved a hand around the room—"strife."

"I have been married to him for *centuries*," Charlotte said. She knelt and pulled his towel away. "During that time, I have handled the family affairs while he spent his time flying starships around the cosmos. I controlled the estates. I controlled our industrial interests. I handled the land distribution. I made sure our daughters had a quality education, then were presented at court when they reached the right age…I did all that for him, all of it. And he couldn't even be bothered to stay with me."

Her hand gripped his manhood. "I want something for myself, just once," she said. "Is that wrong?"

Mitch had no time to think about it as they made love, with a passion and vigour that surprised him. Charlotte seemed a different person, determined to lose herself in passion. He wasn't sure, as he opened his eyes the following morning, quite when they'd slipped into the bed and had sex there. His body ached, in a good way. The events of the previous night seemed almost dreamlike. If Charlotte hadn't been lying beside him, snoring loudly, he would have wondered if it had all been a dream. His wristcom—placed by the side of the bed—was blinking. Someone had sent him a message. No, hundreds of messages.

He sat upright and reached for the device, opening his secure mailbox with his thumbprint. A stream of message headers flashed in front of his eyes, each one requesting—sometimes demanding—an interview. There wasn't anything from the Admiralty, something he couldn't help finding a little ominous. The Admiralty wasn't known for moving quickly—it delegated such tasks to its junior flag officers—but he'd expected Captain Hammond to start lighting a fire under their collective behinds. On paper, Captain Hammond was a mere starship commander; in practice, his aristocratic title and connections gave him one hell of a lot of clout. And yet, he'd never used it. Mitch guessed Charlotte had been the one who'd handled such matters.

Charlotte groaned and sat up. "What time is it?"

"Ten in the morning, give or take a few minutes," Mitch said. They *had* been busy, last night. Normally, he woke up early even if he was on leave. "Do you want to see what this place does for breakfast?"

"There'll be somewhere in town that delivers," Charlotte said. Her bare breasts bobbled as she pushed herself up, shakily. "Get something sent up here, if this place doesn't run to room service."

"It probably doesn't," Mitch said. He was surprised she thought food could be delivered, although he supposed he shouldn't have been. This far from the big cities, the risk of viral contamination was minimal. He keyed the room terminal and was unsurprised to discover there was no room service. "Do you want to order anything in particular?"

"Anything," Charlotte said. "I'm not feeling fussy."

She stumbled into the bathroom. Mitch watched her naked behind until she closed the door, then keyed his wristcom to search for a suitable local restaurant. The online menus were surprisingly detailed, as were the charges. He gritted his teeth as he ordered a handful of pastries and coffee. The hotel hadn't so much as bothered to install a coffeemaker, let alone a kettle and fridge. There wasn't even a minibar. It struck him, suddenly, that Charlotte was slumming it. She might decide to go back to her husband, and her comfortable life, for lack of servants. The thought made him smile. Captain Hammond wasn't likely to take her back.

Charlotte emerged, moving with a complete lack of concern about her nakedness. Mitch found himself staring as she picked up her wristcom and terminal, then started tapping on them without even bothering to get dressed. He hoped no one could see her, through the terminal's camera... he knew, from grim experience, how easy it was to give someone an eyeful. He'd made that mistake himself, as a young man. Someone tapped on the door. Charlotte didn't seem inclined to move as Mitch opened the door just enough to collect the pastries, then pay the delivery man. Mitch hoped the younger man hadn't seen anything of interest.

"We'll hit the noon media cycle," Charlotte said, as she took a pastry and bit into it with every evidence of enjoyment. "I've already got a dozen interviews lined up."

"Good, I think," Mitch said. "What do you want us to tell them?"

"The truth," Charlotte said. "Our truth. And make sure the story gets out before Thomas starts blabbing."

Mitch glanced at the time. "He could have been talking to the media for hours."

"No, he won't," Charlotte corrected. "He was—is—always very old fashioned about this sort of thing. He relied on me to handle such matters for him. He'll need someone to take my place and…"

She shook her head. "We have an edge," she insisted. "And we cannot afford to give him time to collect himself and strike back."

"Got it," Mitch said. "It's *just* like a military operation."

CHAPTER THREE

"MY LORD?"

Thomas stirred, unsure—just for a moment—where he actually *was*. His memories were a jumbled mess. He'd been at a party...no, he'd hosted a party. Charlotte and he had invited the great and the good and...his eyes shot open as he remembered the rest of the night. He'd caught his wife in bed with his subordinate, which would be quite bad enough, but it had been so *public* that there'd been no hope of quashing the scandal before it spread from one side of the country to the other. He'd sent his guests home early...he forced himself to sit up, rubbing sleep from his eyes. There was no getting around the simple fact he was going to be at ground zero of a major scandal.

"Fuck," he grumbled. The butler was standing at the door, his face carefully blank. "Bartleby? What is it?"

"My Lord, there is a small army of reporters at the gates," the butler said. "What would you like us to do?"

Tell them to fuck off, Thomas thought. *Turn the hoses on them. Send out the game-beaters with whips and flog them.*

He cursed under his breath. "Keep the gates closed," he ordered, finally. "They are not to be permitted entry. Anyone who tries to get over the walls is to be held, pending the arrival of the police. They are *not* to harass anyone on the grounds. Is that understood?"

"Yes, My Lord," the butler said. "I'll see to it at once."

"Please," Thomas said. "And have some breakfast sent up here at once."

Bartleby bowed once and withdrew, closing the door behind him. Thomas stared at the blank wood, wondering how his life had come crashing down so quickly. He'd thought Charlotte understood the demands of naval service. He'd thought she understood that the navy was all that stood between the human race and a fate worse than death. He'd thought... he swallowed, hard, as he forced himself to stand. There was no point in worrying about it now. He needed to shower and eat something and then decide what to do. Cold anger rushed through him as he stepped into the bathroom. Charlotte could hardly deny adultery, not when there were so many witnesses. She could be cut out of his life completely...

He groaned as he realised the full scale of the brewing scandal. There was no hope of keeping it quiet, which meant the case would be decided by the court of public opinion. He could win the battle in the courtroom, but lose it in the streets. Charlotte's family would have to rally around her, just to ensure the safety of the rest of her clan. And...he scowled, remembering just how much Charlotte had *done* for him. She could do a lot of damage if she sold his secrets to the highest bidder. The thought mocked him as he showered, dried and dressed himself. There really *wasn't* any hope of keeping it quiet.

A maid stood by the table when he re-entered the bedroom, holding a tray of food. Thomas eyed her narrowly, wondering if she was loyal to him...or to Charlotte. His wife had done most of the hiring, which meant the staff might believe she was their true mistress. The maid might be her eyes and ears...Thomas sighed inwardly, wondering if he was just being paranoid. The maid was younger than his daughter. She didn't deserve to be swept into the midst of a political scandal.

"Thank you," he said. He couldn't remember the girl's name. "I'll ring when I'm done."

The maid placed the tray on the table, bobbed a curtsy and retreated in a manner that suggested she wanted to flee. Thomas didn't really blame her. It wasn't easy serving one's commanding officer, even when there were strict rules governing how the senior officers were supposed to relate to their juniors. The maid had fewer protections, whatever might be said on paper. Thomas had a distant uncle with a habit of trying to grope the maids and the bastard had pretty much gotten away with it. He shook his head. What did a man like that care about society's feelings?

He sat at the table and removed the covering, then poured himself a mug of coffee and tucked into the kedgeree. Someone had placed a copy of the morning newspaper beside the plate, a luxury when most newspapers were exclusively electronic, but he couldn't force himself to open it until he felt almost human again. His head pounded as he finished the first mug of coffee and poured himself another one, hand reaching for the terminal by the bedside. The lead story was a lurid description of the previous night's events. Thomas wondered, idly, who'd given the reporter his information. The bare facts were there, but buried in so much nonsense it was hard to believe anyone would take the story seriously.

Not that it matters, he thought, sourly. *There are people who'll take anything seriously.*

He forced himself to skim through the remaining newspaper stories, then the messages in his inbox. The stories were all the same, to the point he wondered which of his enemies was calling the shots. They certainly got the basic details correct. The messages ranged from demands for interviews to updates from HMS *Lion*, readying herself for her next deployment. Thomas hoped he'd be allowed to return to his ship. His XO could go on leave instead, while Thomas took care of the repairs. It wasn't as if he couldn't handle them himself. He'd have to go through everything as soon as he returned anyway, just to make sure he knew what had been done in his absence. A commanding officer's job was never done.

There was a tap on the door. Thomas looked up. "Yes?"

A maid—a different maid—opened the door. "Lady Elizabeth's

compliments, My Lord, and she hopes you'll join her and Lady Lucille in the conservatory."

Thomas sighed, inwardly. "Please inform Her Ladyship that I will join them shortly," he said. "And ask Bartleby to attend upon me first."

The maid curtsied and withdrew. Thomas finished his coffee and stood, brushing down his shirt and trousers. He'd have to see about leaving the estate and travelling to his ship…he sighed, again, as he realised he'd have to make arrangements for Charlotte's absence. She really *had* done a lot for him…he'd have to put matters in his eldest daughter's hands and hope for the best, unless he resigned his commission and devoted himself to the estate. He doubted *that* would go down well. The House of Lords might refuse to seat him if the House of Commons threatened to *impeach* him for gross misconduct. It would be another scandal at the worst possible time.

Bartleby stepped into the room. "My Lord?"

"Contact Mr. Gleeson," Thomas said. "I want him here as soon as reasonably possible."

"Yes, My Lord," Bartleby said. "That will be at least an hour, assuming he leaves at once."

Thomas nodded. "Encourage him to be here within two," he said. The nasty part of his mind was tempted to threaten to ditch the lawyer, if he didn't get to the mansion within two hours. "And inform me the moment he arrives."

"Yes, My Lord."

"And one other thing," Thomas added. "Inform the staff that"—he paused, unsure of the right words – "inform the staff that they are not to contact Lady Charlotte, or share anything with her without my prior permission. If they do so, they will be sacked and blacklisted. Is that clear?"

Bartleby showed no visible emotion. "Quite clear, My Lord."

"Good." Thomas nodded, curtly. "You may go. Send a maid to collect the tray."

He headed to the door himself as soon as the butler left, making his way through the corridors to the conservatory. The giant chamber had always been a refuge, even though he'd been worried when he'd realised one of his ancestors had imported plants from a dozen different worlds and planted them in his flowerbeds. The permits to do *that* hadn't come cheap. Too many people had worried, back then, about what would happen if alien ecologies got loose on Earth. Thomas didn't blame them, although the worries had been overblown. Earth's biosphere was tougher than any other known world, save perhaps for the other planets that had birthed intelligent life. The plants in the conservatory would die within weeks if the windows shattered, allowing them to mingle with the outside world.

"Dad," Elizabeth said. She sat on a bench, next to her younger sister. "What happened?"

Thomas took a moment to study them both, unsure of what to say. They'd both taken more after Charlotte than him, although there was enough of him in their faces for him to be sure they were his. Not, he supposed, that there'd ever been any real doubt. He and Charlotte had planned both pregnancies carefully, ensuring their unborn children received the very best start in life. Neither of them had known humanity was about to run into an alien virus, bent on turning the entire galaxy into host bodies…

"Your mother and I had a fight," he said. He wondered, suddenly, how much they already knew. The maids weren't scared of them. Charlotte would never have let her daughters bully the maids. They might never be friends—they couldn't be—but they weren't enemies either. And that meant they might have gossiped…"She's left us."

He felt a pang of guilt at their shock. Charlotte had been right to say he hadn't spent anything like enough time with his daughters. He'd missed just about every major event in their lives because of his career. He hadn't accompanied them to school, he hadn't discussed their education with their teachers, he hadn't watched with pride as they were formally presented to the Queen…Charlotte had asked, once, if he'd even have time to walk them down the aisle when they married. In hindsight, perhaps that had been a sign of trouble in their marriage. It hadn't been *him* who'd gone to the headmistress and made the case for their younger daughter *not* being expelled…

Elizabeth exchanged glances with Lucille. "Dad, what happened?"

"It's a long story," Thomas said. He didn't want to discuss it. Anger washed through him as he realised the girls would hear a distorted version of the truth, first from the maids and then from the media. Charlotte could have been discreet…he gritted his teeth. God knew there were plenty of aristocratic matches that were marriages in name only. He would have turned a blind eye…probably. "I…

He found himself unable to speak. The words refused to come. He knew how to handle military operations, from attacking a planet to defending a convoy, but how could he address this problem? What could he say? He didn't want to pour poison on their mother and…no, that wasn't true. He did want to. He just knew he shouldn't.

"We have parted," he said, finally. "I want you two to know that, whatever happens, you are my daughters. I wouldn't trade you for the world."

Lucille smiled. "Does that mean we don't have to go back to Hanover Towers?"

"I'm already out," Elizabeth said, with all the smugness an older sibling could muster. "You have only one more year to go…"

"I could leave now," Lucille said. "Mum said I had to stay, but I don't *have* to."

"Yes, you do." Thomas forced himself to meet her eyes. "If you leave early, you may not be able to find a career or land a good husband."

Lucille stared back at him. "And if I don't want a husband?"

"Then you need a career," Thomas pointed out, evenly. "And besides, at Hanover Towers, you will be protected from the media."

"Yeah, I saw the army outside," Elizabeth said. "Are they going to storm the walls?"

"I certainly hope not," Thomas said. "It would be…awkward."

Elizabeth looked downcast. "Mum promised me that we could…Dad, can I email her? Call her?"

"Yes," Thomas said. It would be cruel to say no. Besides, any military officer worthy of the name knew better than to give an order that wouldn't be obeyed. "Just be…just be yourself."

He sat back, bitterly frustrated. There was so much he'd have to do, just to clear the decks before his next deployment. He'd have to make sure Elizabeth was ready to take over managing the estate, at least on paper; he'd have to hire and vet managers to assist her, knowing that it would be all too easy for her to let them handle everything. Charlotte had been meant to teach her how to run the estate, now that she'd graduated. It wasn't going to be easy to learn on the job. Thomas considered, not for the first time, simply resigning his commission and taking the consequences. His daughters—and his family—came first.

The door opened, behind him. He turned to see Bartleby. "Yes?"

"My Lord, Mr Gleeson has arrived and is waiting in the Green Room," Bartleby said. "He was apparently already *en route*."

Thomas frowned. It hadn't been an hour since Bartleby had placed the call. It couldn't have been. And that meant…he stood and headed for the door, without a backwards glance. His lawyer wouldn't have been on the way, before he'd even been called, unless he'd thought he'd be needed. Had he heard the story? Or…had Charlotte called him? Thomas ground his teeth as he made his way down the corridor. It was all a horrible, tangled mess.

He pasted a calm expression on his face as he stepped into the Green Room. He'd never understood why it had that name—the only green thing in the room was a simple emerald vase—but it hardly mattered. Some long-dead ancestor had turned it into a private discussion room, lining the walls with all sorts of equipment to make it difficult—if not impossible—to spy on the proceedings. Thomas's wristcom bleeped an alert as he closed the door behind him, warning him that it was cut off from the mansion's private intranet, the civilian datanet and the military communications network. Bartleby would call him, if something happened that required his urgent attention. He knew it and yet…he still felt trapped.

"My Lord," Mr Gleeson said. He was an older man, wearing a suit that had been fashionable well before his birth. "I heard the news. I assumed you'd wish to speak to me."

Thomas nodded. Gleeson—and his firm—had been the family lawyers since the Troubles had catapulted them back to prominence. They were smart, well-connected and—above all—discreet. Gleeson Senior had once told him, before his untimely death, that he felt old money was the best. Thomas wasn't sure how he felt about *that*, but it was the clearest possible sign—in his view—that the lawyers wouldn't switch sides. They'd destroy their own reputation if they tried. Whatever clout Charlotte might have had with them would have vanished, the moment she left the family.

"My wife has committed adultery," he said, bluntly. It felt odd to put it into words. "What are my options?"

Mr Gleeson leaned forward. "How much are you prepared to spend to get rid of her?"

Thomas frowned. "I ask again," he said. "What are my options?"

"You have several," Mr Gleeson said. "From a legal point of view, given the lack of doubt over what actually *happened*, you should have no trouble securing a divorce. She cheated on you, as you said, and that is grounds to end a match. However, you also have a very tangled family situation. She brought a sizable amount of money, and a number of properties, to the marriage. You would have to separate her possessions, and whatever wealth may have accumulated through them, in order to return them. And *that* doesn't include any custody issues."

Thomas scowled. "Lucille is seventeen," he said. "She's hardly a *child*."

"No," Gleeson agreed. "However, she is still underage. It would complicate things."

He paused. "I think you would win, from a legal point of view. She cannot deny her adultery, nor can she accuse you of being actively abusive. That would destroy her case overnight, perhaps even leave her open to counter-charges. However"—he held up a hand - "from a PR point of view, it would be a great deal harder. It might be better to simply offer her a large sum of money to disappear."

Thomas stared at him for a long moment. "She humiliated me in front of the entire world and...you expect me to just pay her off?"

"It might be better, in the long term." Gleeson said. "A protracted argument over which of the family assets are rightfully hers would result in a great deal of mud being hurled around the world. So would a dispute over custody, which would put a great deal of stress on both of your children. I know they're adults, or close to it, but...they would still be in some trouble."

"And she could have avoided it if she'd been a little more discreet," Thomas snapped. "I think she isn't going to take the money and run."

He forced himself to think. "Inform her lawyers that I want a divorce, on grounds of adultery," he said. He wanted to lash out at her. He wanted it to *hurt*. "And we can start calculating how much is rightfully hers."

"She may not accept whatever offer you make," Gleeson said. "And public opinion may not be on your side."

"Of course not," Thomas snarled. "It never is."

He shook his head. "Send word," he ordered. "I want the matter resolved as quickly as possible."

CHAPTER FOUR

ADMIRAL LADY SUSAN ONARINA allowed herself a scowl as she studied the tablet, noting just how many *important* matters had been kicked off the front page and relegated to the rear of nearly every newspaper she followed. The Hammond-Campbell scandal had been trending for the last few hours, pushing editors to ensure that *everyone* saw their breathless coverage before shoving it aside to get to the meat of the matter. Susan found it hard to suppress the urge to call both Hammond and Campbell and give them both a chewing out, even though they were—technically—not under her command any longer. People who played with fire—or the media—always got burnt.

And wind up smelling like roast shit, she thought, reflecting on something her father had said years ago. He'd been asked to do an interview, after Susan became famous, but he'd flatly refused. *One cannot rely on the media to be honest about anything.*

She lifted her head as the car turned the corner, making its way past a pair of military checkpoints and down towards Downing Street. It felt as if there were more soldiers on the streets every time she visited, a situation that seemed certain to end in disaster. The news from Jamaica—her father's homeland—had made that clear. The soldiers had shot infected zombies, then people they believed to be infected, then just people...and then civil war had broken out, giving the infected all the time they needed to slip into position to infect the entire country. She wanted to think it couldn't happen in Britain, or America or France or one of the other major powers, but she feared it could. There were so many armed men in position that a single cough might be enough to start something violent.

Best not to worry about it, she thought. The military might fear they were making things worse, by stationing armed guards around the centre of government, but the public needed reassurance. *It isn't as if you can change it.*

She took one last look at the tablet and sighed. Captain Campbell and his lover had gone on the offensive, filling the datanet with stories about their love, while Captain Hammond was taking the slightly more sedate path of filing for divorce. Public opinion looked to be slanting towards Captain Campbell, although it was hard to be sure. He was a naval hero, as the papers openly admitted, but he had also aided and abetted an act of adultery. Susan had the nasty feeling *no one* was going to come out of the affair looking good…she shook her head. Banging their heads together wouldn't accomplish much, beyond making her feel better, but…it might teach them a lesson. Their boat was sinking fast and, instead of bailing out the water, they were actively drilling holes in the bottom.

And the media will turn on them eventually, she reminded herself, as the car pulled to a halt outside Ten Downing Street. *They'll rue the day they threw fresh meat at a pack of charging hyenas.*

She picked up her briefcase as a policeman helped her out of the car, then stepped through the door into Downing Street. The days when someone could just *walk* into the building were long gone. She gritted her teeth as the guards took blood samples, then tested her clothes and breath for signs of alien biological matter. The virus was bizarre by human standards, with a mentality that was completely alien, but it couldn't be underestimated. They still didn't know how it had managed to get so many zombies onto the planet before the security forces had cracked down, let alone remain undetected for so long. She feared they might never be able to lift the state of emergency. God alone knew how much damage it was doing to the economy.

"Admiral," Samuel Hallow said. "Welcome back."

Susan nodded as she shook the civil servant's hand. She didn't remember him, but it wasn't surprising. The Prime Minister rotated assistants on a regular basis, making sure he never got too comfortable with any of them. Susan didn't understand the logic, but it was his choice. She would sooner deal with one person, someone she knew well enough to trust they could make decisions if necessary. But it wasn't *her* office.

She retrieved her briefcase, then followed him up the stairs. The interior looked duller than she recalled, a grim reminder that most of Downing Street's functions had been outsourced to a government command centre somewhere to the west of London. Susan hadn't been told the full details—no one who might be captured and infected had been trusted with information that could lead to the bunker's discovery—but she'd heard enough to read between the lines. The Deputy PM would be there, along with the heir to the throne and enough trained and experienced personnel to run the country if something happened to London. It was quite possible. The virus might tire of probing the defences and try to use a nuke instead...

The thought faded as she was shown into the Prime Minister's office. Prime Minister Arthur Harrison rose to greet her, holding out a hand. Susan shook it tightly, then sat on the proffered chair. A young woman in a simple black outfit delivered a tray of tea and biscuits, then retreated as silently as she'd come. Susan knew the maid probably held a higher security clearance than she did, even if the maid wasn't assigned to any specific departments. No one could afford to overlook the help. The maid had a pair of ears and the wit to use them.

"Susan," Harrison said. "Thank you for coming."

"Thank you, sir," Susan said. The PM's accent had always put her teeth on edge—he reminded her of the snooty girls she'd known at school—but he'd never been anything other than good to her. He was certainly a lot more respectful than some of her fellow officers. "I'm glad you found the time to see me."

"If much less time than I would have wished," Harrison said. He sat back in his chair, sipping his tea. "I understand you wanted to brief me personally?"

Translation, get on with it, Susan thought, with a flicker of humour. It hadn't been easy to convince the PM to see her, even after the successful completion of Operation Lightning Strike. She wasn't blind to the political dimension, nor to the fact they'd come within bare seconds of total disaster. *I'm lucky he agreed to meet me in the first place.*

She opened her briefcase, removed a datachip and inserted it into an isolated terminal. A starchart appeared over the table, each star covered with tactical icons. Earth and the surrounding systems appeared to be crammed with starships and defence platforms. Susan knew better. There were vast reaches of interplanetary space that were completely undefended. It would be easy for the virus to get a fleet into striking distance without being intercepted. The Tadpoles had done it, back during the First Interstellar War. Earth had yet to recover from *that* disaster.

"Operation Lightning Strike succeeded better than I dared hope," she said. "First, we captured and then destroyed the alien catapults. It is unlikely the virus can afford to replace them in a hurry. In any case, we don't have any indications it is currently rebuilding and powering them up. Second, we hammered a number of infected worlds with both conventional weapons and biobombs. We believe we took a serious chunk out of the virus's infrastructure."

"It can rebuild," Harrison pointed out. "And reallocate resources to patch the cracks in the supply chain before it rebuilds the destroyed shipyards."

"Yes," Susan agreed. The virus would probably have an *easier* time of it than its human enemies. It didn't have to worry about international rivalries, or jockeying to secure one's place in the post-war world. "However, even under the worst-case scenario, it will take months—if not years—for it to regain its balance."

She paused, keying the terminal to display the next image. "Third, we acquired a more detailed understanding of infected space. In particular,

HMS *Unicorn* stumbled across a far more industrialised world. We've given it the provisional title of Virus Prime. Given the sheer number of industrial stations surrounding the system's planets, we think it is one of—if not *the*—major industrial nodes. It may even be the virus's original homeworld. Prime Minister, we believe that—if we can take the system out—we can finally start putting an end to the war."

The Prime Minister studied the image for a long moment. "Are you sure this world is as vital to the enemy as you believe?"

"No, sir," Susan said. There was nothing to be gained by suggesting otherwise. "However, the sheer size of the system is clear proof of its importance. We also believe that the alien fleets that nearly trapped us, two systems short of New Washington, were deployed from Virus Prime. At the very least, taking the system out will make it even *harder* for the virus to rebalance itself."

"Point," Harrison said. His eyes never left the display. "It doesn't look like an easy target."

"It isn't," Susan conceded. "*Unicorn* didn't have enough time to carry out a full planetary survey, Prime Minister, but she logged the presence of hundreds of orbital weapons platforms, thousands of remote platforms, dozens of ground-based defence installations and enough mobile units to pose a serious threat to Earth. It wouldn't be an easy system to crack even if we deployed every starship in human service, and our allies, to the mission. I think it wouldn't be easy to even get a BioBomb into the planet's atmosphere."

Harrison frowned. "But wouldn't that work? If the system is as heavily infected as the others, surely the counter-virus would spread rapidly?"

"Yes, but we think they would isolate their space-based installations from the world below," Susan said. "We'd kill billions of host-bodies without really damaging the system's ability to make war."

"That would be awkward," the prime minster observed. "Do you think it can be done?"

"My staff and I have been drawing up a concept under the provisional title of Operation Footfall," Susan said. "Given the sheer size of the system, we think the virus will feel compelled to defend it…perhaps even to the point of recalling ships from the border systems to stand in its defence. That alone would be of great value to us, as we need to resupply and reinforce a dozen systems before the virus breaks through and continues the offensive against Earth."

She tapped the terminal, switching the display. "The first part of the plan focuses on a small task force, centred on HMS *Lion*. They will enter the system, set up a base within the asteroid field and commence bombarding the planet with ballistic projectiles. The virus will have to either come after our ships, allowing them a chance to weaken the enemy fleets with missile and gunboat combinations, or let us rain rocks on their homeworld with impunity. The odds against us scoring a hit are pretty high, but we only have to be lucky once.

"In the meantime, we will assemble a fleet here"—she pointed to New Washington—"and proceed up the chain to the alien homeworld. We will use decoys to lure their fleet out of position, using the flicker network to coordinate a pincer movement, and then move in for the kill. If we can destroy their remaining mobile units, we can close in on their homeworld and bury it in kinetic projectiles. It will take time, Prime Minister, but we believe it can be done."

Susan allowed herself a tight smile. "If Virus Prime is the last of their major industrial nodes, Prime Minister, the war will be effectively won. If it is not, we will still have grievously weakened them, buying time to continue working on new weapons while readying ourselves for the final offensive."

"And then the *second* final offensive," Harrison said, essaying a weak joke. "Admiral, how sure are you of *any* of this?"

"As sure as we can be," Susan said. "With all due respect, Prime Minister, there are always unknowns surrounding *any* military operation. A great deal of our assessments are based on hard data, but far from *complete* data. We think we have a rough idea of how many ships the virus has left, yet…we just don't know. We've done what we can to avoid wishful thinking, but…for all we know, we're still scratching the surface of a much bigger volume of occupied space. The virus may regard us as little more than a painful irritant, as we regarded Ulster during the Troubles. Unpleasant, but not exactly a lethal threat."

"Except we designed and deployed BioBombs," Harrison mused. "Biological weapons have always been regarded as an obscenity. Even the virus must regard the BioBombs as a major threat."

"We hope so, sir," Susan said. "We think the virus is actually starting to expend more resources on planetary defence. There were more remote sensor platforms, as well as defences, around the worlds attacked during Lightning Strike and Virus Prime is clearly heavily defended. Our best projections suggest it will be very difficult, if not impossible, to sneak a missile through their defences, even on a wholly-ballistic trajectory. We have been looking at ways to do it anyway, but anything likely to reach the atmosphere is almost certain to burn up before it can deploy the counter-virus. If nothing else, we have taught it a lesson."

"Good." Harrison looked up at her. "What about the alien tech?"

"The latest reports suggest we cannot hope to duplicate it, not yet," Susan said. "The knowledge gap is just too wide. We simply don't know how they do what they do. We might as well send a modern-day carrier back to the Troubles and expect our ancestors to instantly understand and duplicate it."

"We know a great deal about how the universe works," Harrison said, dryly. "I suppose it's a reminder that there is always something more to learn."

"Yes, sir," Susan said. "Our ancestors didn't know about drive fields, or artificial gravity, or the tramlines. They had the concept of starfighter carriers, but not the ability to actually build them. It would take them years to understand what they were seeing, if they could even do that. The gap might be too wide."

She rubbed her forehead. She'd heard a theory, once, that there were limits to how much change a person—or a society—could embrace. The Troubles might have stemmed from change after change, with society never being allowed to take a breath and absorb the last change before the *next* change appeared. Her ancestors might have agreed, when they'd moved from being African tribesmen to suddenly becoming slaves in a much wider world...she wondered, idly, what the Britain of 2050 would make of a modern-day carrier. Would they accept the advanced technology? Or the news of alien life and alien wars? Or...

The Prime Minister cleared his throat. "I assume you have provided complete copies of your assessments?"

"Yes, sir." Susan popped the datachip out of the terminal and passed it to him. "That's everything, from preliminary post-battle assessments to the final reports."

"I can authorise *our* role in the operation," Harrison said. "What I cannot do is speak for the other Great Powers. They'll need to be consulted, if we want them to lend us ships for the operation. They may hesitate to gamble on another thrust into enemy territory."

Susan took a breath. "Sir, there is no way we'll win this war by standing on the defensive."

"Not until we develop a vaccine," the Prime Minister agreed. He paused, thoughtfully. "Here's another question, one you should perhaps consider. The race that built the artefacts you found might well have *also* created the virus. They might have designed it as a weapon and then built the artefacts to keep it under control."

"It's a possibility," Susan agreed. "The idea crossed our minds, but there simply isn't enough data to say. The virus doesn't appear to be under anyone's control. The artefacts neutralise the virus, but only within a few metres of the artefacts themselves. So far, we haven't been able to scale up the effect either. It's a mystery, sir, one we may never solve."

"A society capable of building those...*things*...isn't going to vanish completely," the Prime Minister said. "Where have they gone?"

"Unknown, sir," Susan said. She'd read a dozen papers suggesting everything from transcendence to simply being destroyed by someone more powerful than themselves. Or the virus, if they'd made it. "I can give you the speculation, but it is nothing more than wishful thinking. It cannot be taken too seriously."

And there were a bunch of people who claimed to have discovered alien artefacts on the edge of explored space, she thought, grimly. *It might be time to start taking those stories a little more seriously.*

The Prime Minister nodded. "Make your preparations, Admiral," he said, a clear sign the discussion was over. "I'll discuss the matter with my advisors, then the rest of the Great Powers. If they agree to go along with it, we can act as soon as possible."

"There are other options," Susan said. She disliked the concepts—they struck her as sacrificing long-term gains for short-term advantage—but there might not be a choice. The virus was powerful—and dangerously unpredictable. "Even a handful of ships might keep the virus focused on home defence, giving us time to rebalance ourselves and resume the offensive."

"We'll see," the Prime Minister said. He made no sign, but the door opened. "Good luck, Admiral. Keep me informed."

Susan stood. "Yes, sir."

CHAPTER FIVE

MITCH COULDN'T HELP FEELING under siege as they left the hotel long enough to go for dinner—at the most expensive place in town, naturally—before returning to spend the night together. The hotel was surrounded by reporters, baying for stories like rioters bayed for blood. It had been two days since the news had broken and, somehow, public interest had yet to fade. It was hard not to feel slightly ridiculous, as if they'd walked through the looking glass into a very different world. Mitch had never even *considered* being at the centre of a national scandal before he'd found himself in one.

Absurd, he thought. It felt decidedly unreal. *Maybe I'll just wake up and it'll be all a dream.*

He checked his wristcom automatically as soon as they reached their room, but there was nothing beyond a hundred requests for yet more exclusive interviews. Mitch suspected it was a curious definition of *exclusive*, given that clips from their earlier interviews had been pirated almost as soon as the interviews had gone live and had been widely shared across the datanet. It would have been easy to remove them, suggesting—to a suspicious mind—that they'd been simply *given* to the pirates. Charlotte seemed to be having the time of her life, steering the ship of public opinion to her chosen destination. Mitch was tempted to just hold on tight and enjoy the ride.

His lips tightened. The Admiralty hadn't contacted him, something that bothered him on a very primal level. There were no messages from his superior officers, nothing beyond standard updates from his XO on *Unicorn*. The ship was ready to depart again, apparently. It was probably just a matter of time before they received orders to leave…Mitch wondered, suddenly, if Captain Hammond was burning the midnight oil, trying to get Mitch removed from his command chair. It wouldn't be easy. Charlotte's PR team had worked overtime to present Mitch as a naval hero, hinting that Mitch—and Mitch alone—had kept Operation Lightning Strike from turning into a complete disaster. It wasn't entirely untrue. The cynical side of Mitch's mind noted that *had* to be a first.

Charlotte waved her hand in front of his face. "Do you have time for one more interview?"

Mitch blinked, then checked the time. It was only seven in the evening. He'd thought it was later. Much later. Long duty shifts were hardly unknown to him—like most naval personnel, he'd long-since mastered the art of catnapping whenever he had a chance—but moving from interview studio to the next, time and time again, was uniquely draining. He knew what his XO would say, if she was looking over his shoulder. His lips quirked at the thought. Commander Staci Templeton wanted more command experience for herself and sending her captain to his bunk was one way to get it…

She might get the formal promotion sooner rather than later, thanks to this, he thought, sourly. *And who knows how that will play out?*

He glanced at Charlotte. It had been a long day for her too, yet somehow she managed to look cool, collected and strikingly glamorous. She looked like a creature from another world, a fairy princess…Mitch shook his head in amusement. It was strange to watch her put on her mask, with as much skill and care as a commanding officer preparing himself before stepping onto the bridge and taking command. Mitch had never really cared about how aristocrats presented themselves to the world, but…he had the sudden feeling that Charlotte would have made a decent naval officer. She had the same attention to detail, and the ability to present a calm face even if she was screaming on the inside, that the navy valued in its senior officers. If things had been different, she could have gone far…

"One final interview?" Mitch tried not to groan. Self-promotion was part of the job, when one's family didn't have a PR team to do the dirty work, but it was often tedious. There was a fine line between talking about your achievements and bragging to the point everyone decided you were an ass. "Just one?"

"Just one," Charlotte confirmed. "It's with Monica Rotherham."

Mitch nodded, thoughtfully. He hadn't known any of the society reporters he'd met over the last two days, men and women with an unhealthy interest in the aristocracy, but even *he* had heard of Monica Rotherham. She was one of the country's top independent reporters, crafting her own stories and uploading them onto the datanet. Mitch was surprised she was interested in their story. Her work was normally focused on serious matters, not discussing the aristocracy. But then, her viewers had probably pushed her to address the issue. He wondered, idly, if she intended to be friendly or hostile. A handful of society reporters had been openly hostile to them.

"If we must," he said. "Where'll we meet her?"

"Downstairs." Charlotte gave him a faint smile. "The hotel kindly put a conference room at our disposal."

Mitch rolled his eyes. The hotel had lost a number of paying guests when the story broke and reporters started blockading the entrances, shouting questions at everyone trying to enter or leave the building. It didn't matter, to them, that most of the guests didn't have the slightest idea what was going on. A couple of guests had amused themselves by giving completely nonsensical answers—Mitch had been amused to see a gossip page proudly proclaiming him to be a distant descendent of the House of Stuart, which wasn't remotely true—but the rest considered it a nuisance. He was mildly surprised the hotel hadn't asked them to move somewhere else. Charlotte was shelling out cash at a terrifying rate, but it would—eventually—come to an end. The guests might not return after the media circus left town.

Charlotte fussed around him as he changed into his dress uniform—she'd purchased one from London and had it shipped north, then tailored to him—and checked his appearance in the mirror. It was commonly believed naval dress uniforms had been designed by sadists—they were hot and uncomfortable, designed for form over function—but he had to admit he looked good. The medals on his breast were copies of the originals—he'd left them with his family when he'd assumed command of *Unicorn*—yet he had every right to wear them. The reporters could look up the records, if they wished. He wondered, idly, if any of the bastards would accuse him of being a Walt. *That* would put the cat among the pigeons.

And give me grounds to sue, he thought, snidely. *We'll probably need the money.*

He composed himself, as best as he could, as he followed Charlotte down the stairwell and into the tiny business section. The hotel apparently hosted corporate meetings that, for one reason or another, couldn't be held in the bigger cities, but not enough to justify devoting an entire floor to the job. The conference room was clearly designed for multiple roles, the wooden walls concealing everything from a display projector to a minibar and fridge. The lights were bright enough to make Mitch feel exposed, even though he knew there was no physical danger. He'd spent too much of his career sneaking up on bigger ships, enemy starships that could blow his ship to atoms if they got a clear shot, to be entirely happy about being in the open. It struck him, as Monica Rotherham rose from her chair and held out a hand, that that was precisely what they were doing. Charlotte was trying to land the killer blow before her husband—her estranged husband—could divorce her, cutting her off from her children and family resources. It was just a matter of time.

"Captain Campbell," Monica Rotherham said. She was a tall woman with long dark hair that reached all the way down to her rear, wearing clothes that hinted at her shape without actually revealing anything below the neckline. "It's a pleasure to meet you at last."

"Thank you," Mitch said. As far as he knew, Monica Rotherham had *never* expressed an interest in meeting him. "It was a pleasure to receive your request for an interview."

"Quite." Monica waved them to a chair. "It's been two weeks since the completion of Operation Lightning Strike. Since your return, there has been a great deal of debate over the mission's outcome. Some people have even argued that the mission was a failure. Do *you* agree with that assessment?"

Mitch took a moment to consider his answer. He wasn't fool enough to assume they weren't being recorded. There were no obvious cameras in the room, but that was meaningless. The jewels in Monica Rotherham's hair could easily conceal a dozen pickups…hell, it would be *very* easy to conceal a tiny camera within the light fixtures or wooden panelling. Mitch had never been a spook, but he'd attended cautionary briefings before visiting foreign parts. The counterintelligence officer who'd given the briefing had been a paranoid sod, but he'd made his point. It was very easy to say—or do—the wrong thing and have it come back to haunt you.

The Admiralty won't thank me for contradicting the official line, he thought, wryly. *And, for once, the official line isn't* that *inaccurate.*

He took a breath. "The operation succeeded in its objectives," he said, firmly. "The fleet defeated an enemy attempt to outflank our defences, smashed a handful of enemy targets and made its escape from enemy territory. By any reasonable standards, it was a successful operation."

"The fleet was nearly ambushed and destroyed by the enemy ships," Monica said. She sounded calm and composed, but Mitch could hear an edge in her voice. "Do you not feel the operation came very close to disaster?"

Yes, Mitch thought. It was true. True *enough*, at least. *And yet we escaped disaster by the skin of our teeth.*

He leaned forward. "War, if I may resort to cliché, is a democracy. The enemy gets a vote too. We knew, from the moment we jumped into enemy territory, that they would do everything in their power to destroy us. They certainly gave it their very best shot. It was just not enough to defeat us. The operation was a success, in that it hit the enemy where it hurts and then allowed us to escape their ships and make it back to New Washington. It was not a disaster."

"It could have been a disaster," Monica pointed out. "There are people who believe the operation should never have been attempted."

Mitch had to smile. "And who are they?"

Monica smiled back. "People."

"People," Mitch repeated.

He felt a flicker of irritation. It was easy enough to take criticism from his fellow naval officers, people who'd been there and done that, but not from anonymous civilians who simply didn't understand the realities of naval combat. Their opinions were worthless. The operation had been extensively wargamed, prior to departure, then thoroughly analysed by people who actually knew what they were doing. An opinion from someone who didn't was worse than useless.

"Risk, in the words of a very famous captain, is our business," Mitch said. "There are always risks inherent in anything, from asking a girl out on a date to leading a fleet of warships straight into the teeth of enemy defences. You do all you can to mitigate the risk and it *still* threatens to overwhelm you. The girl may laugh in your face and tell you she wouldn't date you if you were the last man on Earth. The enemy defences might be stronger than you thought and chew your ships to ribbons. Every operation carries the risk of failure, from a retreat in the face of superior force to complete disaster. The fact remains that *this* operation was a success. We got in, we hurt the enemy, we got out again."

"And we are all very grateful," Monica said. "How do you feel, as a naval hero, about the government's current policy?"

"It is generally a good policy," Mitch said. It was true. Besides, even if he had disagreed, it would be unwise to say so in public. People would raise eyebrows if he so much as spoke a word of doubt. "The virus cannot be allowed to get into bombardment range of our homeworld."

Monica nodded. "Do you believe there *is* a risk? Do you think Earth might come under attack?"

Mitch hesitated. The virus had been reluctant to drop weapons of mass destruction on planetary targets. It made sense—the virus wanted to infest the entire biosphere, which wouldn't be possible if it reduced a planet to radioactive ruins—but he was all too aware that policy might have changed. The virus needed to teach the human race a lesson, after BioBombs had been deployed against its worlds. It was impossible to say for sure, but Mitch feared it was just a matter of time before the virus hit back hard. And that was something he couldn't say publicly either.

"The risk is ever-present," he said. "All we can do is try to mitigate it."

The interview went on and on, with questions ranging from the sensible to the thoroughly bizarre. Mitch had the oddest feeling that Monica Rotherham was merely marking time until she edited the recordings into something more palatable, then uploaded them onto the datanet. There would be limits to how much creative editing she could do—Charlotte had made it clear she was recording the interview herself as well—but... Mitch hoped his support of naval policy would win him some support. By the time it was finished, he was tired and drained and barely had the energy to shake her hand before they returned to their bedroom and went to bed. He was too tired to make love.

But it was no surprise, the following morning, to discover a recall message in his inbox.

"The Admiralty wants me in London," he said, tightly. "I think they saw the interview."

"You looked good," Charlotte assured him. "When do they want you?"

"This afternoon," Mitch said. "We'll have to take the monorail."

Charlotte snorted. "I'll hire a hopper," she said. "We'll be back in Central London before you know it."

Mitch blinked. "You're coming?"

"I have lawyers to see," Charlotte said. "And a few other things, too."

She waved a hand at the walls. "I can't stay here, can I?"

"No," Mitch agreed. "I guess you can't."

• • •

"It is vitally important that we concentrate our efforts on both defending our homeworld *and* building up the forces to take the war deeper into enemy space," Captain Campbell said. His image looked perfect, the very picture of a resolute naval hero. "We must never lose sight of our enemy's nature. We cannot come to terms with a force that is literally incapable of recognising our right to exist as independent, uninfected people. The virus must be destroyed or it will destroy us."

Thomas growled as he watched the interview. It was bad enough watching his family life being splashed across the society gossip rags, but that was containable. He could afford to play a waiting game, to watch them carefully and pounce the moment they said something actionable. But this? An interview with Monica Rotherham was a step into the mainstream media, a step towards enlisting the entire country against him. Thomas felt his fingers clench around the tumbler, silently cursing himself for pouring the glass. He'd never realised just how much Charlotte resented him until now. If she'd talked to him...

"It is true an extensive program of naval construction will be expensive," Captain Campbell said. "But it is cheaper than surrendering ourselves to infection."

"Fuck," Thomas swore. He wondered, sourly, if the Admiralty would rein Captain Campbell in before it was too late. Some prick who'd never commanded a starship in his entire life would probably argue that the whole affair worked in the navy's favour, that Captain Campbell was arguing for higher budgets and more naval construction and everything else the Admiralty wanted. Or needed. "Fuck it!"

He turned off the viewscreen and paced his office. It had been *Charlotte's* office, in her role as estate and business manager. It might belong to him, and legally entailed so he *had* to pass it and the mansion down to his eldest child, but he'd always considered it hers. It felt as if he was trespassing, as if he was intruding somewhere he shouldn't…he clenched his teeth in bitter frustration. If Charlotte had talked to him, they could have worked something out. It would have hurt, but it could have been done. She could have had a covert lover and…he wouldn't have cared, as long as it stayed private. He really wouldn't have cared.

Yes, you would, his thoughts mocked.

His wristcom bleeped. He pressed his finger against the scanner, then scowled as the secure message decrypted itself. He was being recalled, to London. He wondered, idly, if it was a new deployment or if someone intended to read him the riot act. His stomach burned as he called the butler to make arrangements, then left the room. He'd worry about his estate later, when things settled down. If the navy wanted to send him back to space, ahead of time…

It'll be better than hanging around here, he told himself. He hadn't done *much* in the last two days, beyond giving orders to the lawyers and spending time with his daughters. He'd been too depressed to muster the energy to go riding, walk the estate, or even pay a call on his neighbours. *And it'll buy time for everyone to forget what happened here.*

CHAPTER SIX

IT FELT WEIRD, GUNBOAT PILOT RICHARD Tobias Gurnard thought, to be returning to HMS *Lion* without Marigold. His girlfriend had had to attend a medical clinic for a check-up before she boarded a shuttle herself and, in the navy's infinite wisdom, it had ordered Tobias to take an earlier shuttle instead of waiting for her. Tobias had tried to argue, but the dispatcher had told him to shut up and get onto the shuttle in time or be forced to explain the delay to a *very* unsympathetic commanding officer. Tobias thought, as the shuttle made its steady way towards the battlecruiser, that the dispatcher was one of the staff officers who considered the gunboat program to be nothing more than a waste of government money… and the gunboat pilots geeks and nerds pretending to be naval officers. He'd never realised just how difficult it had been to get the program into production, even though the concept had proved itself right from the start, until he'd spent four days going through the mission logs and explaining, in great detail, what had worked and what hadn't.

Which was a pain in the ass, he thought, as a dull thump echoed though the shuttle. *The staff officers made it clear they didn't trust* my *judgement.*

He sighed as he stood, collected his carryall and made his way to the hatch. The gunboat program had recruited pilots who *hadn't* applied to the Luna Academy, pilots who'd never dreamed of being officers, enlisted men or starfighter pilots. Tobias knew—his instructors had never made any bones about it—that the policy wasn't entirely good-hearted. It was true he'd had less to unlearn than a regular spacer, but it was *also* true that he and his comrades were expendable. The Royal Navy would sooner lose an entire squadron of gunboats than a single starship. Tobias could understand the math—gunboats were relatively cheap, to the point they could be churned out in vast numbers—but he didn't like it. He supposed it would be a little easier to take if he hadn't been one of the gunboat pilots in question.

The gravity flickered, just slightly, as he boarded HMS *Lion*. UV lights burned down on him, his skin tingling under the glare. A pair of suited marines, faces hidden behind tinted masks, blocked his way. Tobias held out an arm, allowing them to press a bioscanner against his bare skin. He didn't blame them for being paranoid. There'd been a spate of viral outbreaks right across the world in the last few days. Hell, Tobias himself had been far too close to one only a few short months ago. The government *still* didn't know how that outbreak had even started, let alone how it had spread so far without triggering alarms.

Tobias sighed, inwardly. He'd spent some of his leave on the dark web, the network of computer servers and hidden datanet sites that was—supposedly—a gateway into a very different view of the world. There'd been a great deal of speculation, from a modern-day Benedict Arnold—someone working for the virus, willingly—to a government plot to keep the public under control. That, Tobias reflected, would have been a great deal more convincing before he'd joined the navy. The government, he'd learnt, was too inefficient to conceive of such a plot, let alone carry it out. Simple incompetence was much more likely, if boring. No one was interested in logic and reason when they could argue the world was controlled by lizard-people instead.

The marines nodded and waved him through the hatch. Tobias allowed himself a sigh of relief. He wanted to believe he wasn't infected, but it was impossible to say for sure. A zombie who hadn't yet *realised* he was a zombie would spread the infection far and wide, in perfect innocence. The hatch closed, leaving the marines waiting for the next set of crewmen. Tobias didn't envy them. If a zombie went active when his true nature was exposed, the marines would be its first victims.

He felt oddly unsure of himself as he made his way down the corridor to Gunboat Country and stepped through the hatch. The compartments were completely empty. The majority of the squadron had been killed during Operation Lightning Strike, the remainder being reassigned to different ships and squadrons. Tobias was surprised he and Marigold hadn't been reassigned too. The idea that he represented a priceless resource was hard to swallow—not least because he was also considered expendable—but there was some truth in it. He'd spent far too long detailing everything that had happened to him, ever since the fleet had set out. He knew he was damn lucky to be alive.

His heart twisted as he stepped into the sleeping compartment and placed his carryall on the nearest bunk. The bedding had been nicely made up by the caretaker crew, somewhat to his surprise, but it was so blandly done that he *knew* he was the first person to set foot in the compartment. There were no more pilots…the silly part of his mind wondered if he was going to be the only pilot. It was possible, in theory, for a single pilot to fly and fight a gunboat, but in practice…he shook his head. It wasn't something anyone would do if there was any other choice.

He sat on the bunk and keyed his wristcom. The orders that had sent him hurrying back to the ship were clearly visible, but there was nothing else. The navy was very fond of making its personnel run from place to place, then wait for hours before they received the next set of orders. He snorted at the thought as he brought up the latest set of gunboat manuals and scanned through them, looking for changes. His name wasn't anywhere on the latest manuals, he was sure, but he'd helped write them. Thankfully, whoever had taken his rambling comments and smoothed them out had done a good job. The manual was neither loaded with naval technobabble nor crammed with bullshit that made it impossible to read properly. But none of it was really *new*.

I could probably make use of the simulators, he thought. *No one would complain if I spent the next hour training for war.*

He heard a hatch open and looked up as footsteps echoed down the corridor. They sounded oddly familiar...the gunboat CAG? Or one of the old pilots, someone who might be reassigned to the ship? Or Marigold? He shook his head at the thought. Marigold moved quietly, as quietly as a mouse. The newcomer walked as if he didn't have a care in the world, as if...Tobias kept his face impassive as Corporal Colin Lancaster stepped into view. His heart clenched, torn between old and new feelings that made little sense. Colin had been a bully, then...it was hard to say. They weren't quite friends, yet they weren't enemies either. It helped, he supposed, that they'd each saved each other's life.

I could have killed him, he thought, numbly. It would have been easy to make it look like an accident. So many missiles and beams had been flying about, during the first major engagement, that no one would have thought twice about it. *And he could just have left me to die.*

"Tobias," Colin said. "Did you have a good leave?"

"It was...interesting," Tobias said, neutrally. "I had to spend a chunk of it at the Admiralty."

"Ouch," Colin said. "I had to spend some time in Portsmouth, explaining to all and sundry what happened when we added an alien to the roster."

Tobias raised his eyebrows. "How did it go? I mean...really?"

Colin said nothing for a long moment. "After some weeks on the job, it was easy to forget he wasn't human," he said. "But there were...issues... that need to be addressed. I don't know if they'll allow him to rejoin us, let alone invite more Vesy to join the marines. It might be better for them to have their own units. The logistics would be a great deal easier."

"Even though they can eat our food," Tobias said. He was surprised *Colin* was capable of putting together such an argument. He'd never struck Tobias as being particularly reasonable. He had always been the kind of person who'd pick on someone for the colour of their skin or their genitals or…Tobias decided the asshole he'd known had grown up a little. "Or were there other issues?"

"I think the issues would need to be uncovered, then fixed," Colin said. "There was nothing *easy* about it."

He grinned, suddenly. "Have you heard the gossip?"

Tobias frowned. He didn't follow gossip. And yet, it had been hard to miss the story shaking the world. "The gossip about George Mole running away with Ivan Braithwaite?"

"What?" Colin stared. "What is that?"

"The stars of *Starship Wars*," Tobias said. He would have been surprised if Colin had ever heard of it. *Starship Wars*, a rip-off of *Cosmic Wars* which had been a rip-off of *Star Wars*, had been decidedly uncool when they'd been kids. "Mole dumped his wife and ran off with a male co-star."

"No, no," Colin said. "About the Captain. And his wife. And Captain Campbell."

Tobias shook his head. "No, why?"

"Well, the official story is that Captain Campbell ran off with Captain Hammond's wife," Colin said. He grinned, mischievously. "But the unofficial version of the story is that they were having threesomes, or that the two men became lovers, or the whole story is just something to distract the proles from the budget announcement next week."

"Oh." Tobias shook his head. He never paid any attention to society gossip. Captain Hammond and his family were so far above him they might as well be on the moon. "Does it really matter?"

"It might, if we have to sail in partnership again," Colin pointed out. "You think they can be adults about it?"

Tobias winced. He'd seen his fair share of adults acting like children. Hell, their children had shown a great deal more maturity. And…he had to admit he'd acted poorly as well, when he'd discovered Colin was on the same starship. He'd believed, in his panic, that Colin had done it deliberately, that he'd been intent on chasing Tobias across interstellar distances. It had been hard to comprehend, let alone admit to himself, that it had been a coincidence. The navy had neither known nor cared about their prior relationship. Why should it?

He considered the point for a long moment. He'd met Captain Campbell once and hadn't enjoyed the experience. The captain hadn't been *unpleasant*, but he'd come across as the kind of person who enjoyed a charmed life. Dashingly handsome, endlessly successful with the ladies, a tactical genius and master at self-promotion who would keep climbing the ladder until they made a new rank just so they could promote him into it. He was the sort of person Tobias had learnt to loathe, as a child. The sort of person who would happily destroy a marriage just so he could get laid.

You don't know him that well, Tobias reminded himself. *For all you know, he's kind to his mother and always helps old ladies cross the road.*

Colin cleared his throat. "Well?"

"I'm sure they'll be fine," Tobias said. He made a mental note to do his best to avoid learning the details, although he was sure he'd hear about them anyway. "And it isn't our problem, is it?"

"No," Colin said. "But it could affect our mission and…"

"And it is well above your pay grade," a new voice said. "You're far too close to speaking ill of a pair of superior officers."

Colin jumped and spun around, falling into a combat crouch before relaxing. Tobias peered past him and saw Colonel Richard Bagehot leaning on the hatch. The gunboat CAG looked bone-tired, as if he'd just spent the last few hours in a cockpit—or, more likely, an endless conference that went around and around in circles, with no one willing or able to take control and actually make some decisions. Tobias had heard enough about *them* to know he didn't want to become a staff officer himself, even though he had *real* experience. He intended to serve his term and get out. Marigold and he could move to the asteroids or a distant system and leave the past behind.

"Sir," Colin said. "We were merely…"

"You have duties to attend to," Bagehot said, firmly. "I need to speak to Tobias."

Colin nodded, saluted and left the compartment. Tobias watched him go, then looked at Bagehot. The older man entered the compartment and sat on one of the bunks, resting his hands on his lap. Tobias had grumbled about losing some of his leave to brief the senior officers, but Bagehot might have lost *all* of his leave. The navy was supposed to make sure they took it, yet…there *was* a war on. The needs of the country came first.

"A word of advice," Bagehot said. "Gossiping about one's superior officers is a good way to wind up in hot water."

"Yes, sir," Tobias said. It was hard not to be irritated. It wasn't *him* who'd brought the subject up. "I'm sorry, sir."

Bagehot shrugged. "Do you know why you were recalled early?"

"No, sir," Tobias said. "I had the impression we had two more days of leave."

"The navy needs you," Bagehot said. "You're going to take over as squadron commander."

Tobias frowned. "Does it come with a pay raise?"

"And a hefty increase in responsibility," Bagehot said. He grinned, humourlessly. "You'll be leading the squadron from the front. I considered suggesting you take my place, but we're far too short of experienced pilots. Your maggots will need to see you set a good example by taking the lead. Of course, this could end badly."

"Yeah." Tobias didn't need to calculate the odds. There weren't many gunboat pilots who'd survived so many encounters with the enemy. It was strange to realise he had more experience than many of the starfighter pilots he'd loathed and envied as a young man. In fact…he frowned as something occurred to him. "Why not Marigold?"

"As a commanding officer?" Bagehot shrugged. "She's a pilot, not a gunner. We thought it would make sense for you to take the lead, rather than her. We also may want to move you sideways, into my role, if things work out well. In that case, she'll take your role."

Tobias hesitated. "Sir…I don't know how to command."

"You are an experienced pilot, compared to the newcomers," Bagehot said. "They'll look up to you. All you have to do is build on it. Make it clear you know how to handle yourself, and that your advice is good advice, and they will follow you anywhere. And don't show fear. They can smell it."

"Sir..." Tobias winced. "I hope that's a joke."

"They're not monsters," Bagehot assured him. "Most of them are just like you were, a few short months ago."

"I'm doomed." Tobias wasn't sure he was joking. "If I fuck up..."

Bagehot met his eyes. "There isn't a single commanding officer worthy of the name who hasn't fucked up, once or twice," he said. "You'll make mistakes. Some of them will be bad ones. Some of them will be court-martial offences. Others...you learn from them and move on. I don't blame you for being nervous. But you cannot allow fear to bring you down."

Tobias made a face. Fear had been a constant companion, ever since he'd realised he was right at the bottom of the social hierarchy. He'd been picked on by Colin and his cronies, time and time again, but he'd also been picked on by the kids who were picked on themselves. He'd been at the bottom. There'd been no one for *him* to pick on...he knew he should be relieved he hadn't become a shithead, like so many others, but it was hard not to resent it, too. It had been so hard to force himself to do anything...

... And yet, he'd built a career for himself. He knew his endeavours didn't *have* to end in failure. He didn't *have* to wallow in his own resentments until they curdled and turned to poison. He didn't have to...

A thought struck him. "How green are they?"

"They've had the modified training program, which was based on experience from Thunder Child and Lightning Strike, but they've never seen real action," Bagehot said. "They're just like you were when the test squadron was taking shape. You'll understand them, Tobias. I thought, often enough, that I didn't understand you and your comrades."

"Because we weren't typical military recruits," Tobias said. "Right?"

"Right," Bagehot said. "The average starfighter cadet is a cocky ass who needs to have his ass beaten, repeatedly, before we can risk putting him in a cockpit. There's no shortage of fools who think that dressing like that twat from *Stellar Star* and snapping off witty one-liners is a substitute for training and experience. But the gunboat pilots were drawn from a very different spectrum of society. They didn't need to be broken down. They needed to be built up."

He reached out and clapped Tobias's shoulder. "You know what your people need," he added. "All you have to do is do it."

Tobias nodded. "I'll do my best, sir."

"Good," Bagehot said. His lips curved into a humourless smile. "Just don't picture them in their underwear. That never helps."

"And now I'm not going to get that out of my mind," Tobias said, with a grimace. "Thanks."

"You're welcome," Bagehot said. "Good luck."

CHAPTER SEVEN

MITCH HAD EXPECTED, when he arrived at the Admiralty and passed through a series of increasingly intrusive security checkpoints, to be shown directly into a briefing hall. The last operation had involved hundreds of ships from a dozen nations—as well as humanity's alien allies—and the early briefings had been more like giant rallies than anything else. Now...he tensed, feeling his heart start to pound as he was escorted into Admiral Onarina's office. The admiral wasn't alone. Captain Hammond was seated facing her. His eyes narrowed as he looked at Mitch. From anyone else, it would have been a glare.

"Be seated," Admiral Onarina ordered. Her voice was calm, perfectly composed. She looked as if she'd spent the last few hours running tactical exercises. "We have much to discuss."

Mitch sat, resting his hands on his lap. He'd expected *some* kind of response from the Admiralty after the interview had gone live, even though he'd toed the party line. The navy had encouraged him to promote himself as a hero, expecting him to also do his level best to convince the public that the Royal Navy knew what it was doing. Mitch privately considered it a hard sell, even though the navy hadn't done badly. There were just too many loudmouths who didn't know what they were talking about, but never let it get in their way as they fought for public attention. He would sooner listen to Captain Hammond's dry tones than a naval expert who hadn't so much as stepped onboard a warship, let alone taken her into battle.

Admiral Onarina looked from Mitch to Captain Hammond and back again. "We have much to discuss," she said, coolly. "But there is one topic we have to cover first."

She leaned forward. "I understand you've had...*issues*," she said, with a hint of very British understatement. "The newspapers are taking sides, as is most of the general public. I don't give a damn. I expect the two of you to put your differences aside and work together as professional naval officers, or the two of you will be removed from your posts and placed on the bench. Do I make myself clear?"

"Admiral," Captain Hammond said. "I..."

"Do I make myself clear?" Admiral Onarina's voice hardened. "I don't care about your problems. I don't care about your issues. I neither know nor care about the truth. You signed up to protect and defend the country and you will do it or you will be put on half-pay for the rest of eternity. No fighting each other on the country's time! Do I make myself clear?"

"Yes, Admiral," Mitch said.

Captain Hammond shot him a sharp look. "Yes, Admiral."

"Good." Admiral Onarina tapped a hidden console. A holographic star system appeared over her desk. "Captain Campbell will recall this system, of course. We've designated it Virus Prime."

"And it might be the virus's homeworld," Mitch said. "Or at least a very powerful industrial node."

"There's no doubt about that, I'm afraid," Admiral Onarina said. Tactical icons flowed around the holographic planets. "The system is perhaps the most heavily-defended collection of worlds in known space. If you tried to convince the beancounters to build so many fortresses orbiting Earth..."

It would give them a heart attack, Mitch finished, silently. The sheer level of orbital firepower was staggering, even by the virus's standards. There were so many remote platforms that it was easy to believe someone could just walk around the entire planet, simply by jumping from platform to platform. *The cost would be as far beyond us as building a Dyson Sphere.*

"My staff and I have drawn up a plan to attack and reduce the system, provisionally entitled Operation Footfall," Admiral Onarina informed them. "The GATO Council is currently debating the concept, trying to determine how many ships can be detached from home defence duties and reassigned for the offensive. It isn't going to be easy. Despite the success of Operation Lightning Strike"—she shot Mitch a sharp-edged smile—"losses were quite heavy. It may take weeks, if not months, before GATO is convinced to gamble again."

"Admiral," Mitch said. "If we give the virus time to get back on its feet…"

"I am well aware of the risks," Admiral Onarina said, cutting him off. "However, the virus remains a powerful threat and, as I believe you were *kind* enough to remind the world, has a motive for trying to lay waste to our planets instead of merely infecting them. GATO believes it is just a matter of time before we face retaliatory action. The virus doesn't think like us, it is true. But if *we* were attacked with such force, we would seek to strike back as hard as possible. We dare not assume the virus doesn't agree with us on this, if nothing else."

Mitch let out a breath. Every instinct he possessed was screaming for the human race to go on the offensive, to put the boot in before the virus managed to pull itself together and launch a counterattack. He was all too aware that the only good enemy was a dead one…and yet, he was also aware that Admiral Onarina, an experienced officer in her own right, would be doing everything in her power to speed things up. GATO would talk and talk and talk, until the window of opportunity slammed shut. And if he was any judge, it was *then* they'd be ordered to try to make the operation work.

"The Prime Minister and the War Cabinet have authorised the navy to move ahead with preparations for both Footfall-I and Footfall-II," Admiral Onarina continued. "Captain Hammond—who will be breveted to Commodore for the duration—will assume command of Footfall-I. Captain Campbell will serve as his second. Like I said"—her dark eyes hardened—"I expect you to work together. Or else."

"Admiral," Captain Hammond said. "I really don't think…"

"I wasn't offering you a choice," the Admiral said, icily. Her tone brooked no contradiction. "I need you. The *navy* needs you. And if you cannot leave your personal issues behind, when you are called back to the flag, you can leave your resignations at the desk. Is that clear?"

Mitch nodded, forcing himself to think. The operation had clearly been in the planning stage well before the scandal had broken. He was an expert at throwing operations together on the fly, but never with more than a handful of ships under his command. Deploying a far larger fleet required weeks of planning, if only to get the logistics sorted out so the ships didn't run out of supplies light-years from home. But now…he wondered, suddenly, if someone from the Admiralty hadn't backed the operation in hopes of getting both him and his rival away from Earth. It would certainly buy time for everyone to take a deep breath and calm down.

"I can handle it," Captain Hammond said.

"Good." Admiral Onarina altered the display. "Your formal mission outlines and operational orders, such as they are at this point, have already been uploaded to your inboxes, but the basics are fairly simple. *Lion*, *Unicorn* and a handful of support ships are to lay siege to the system. You are to snipe their facilities from interplanetary space, hurl missiles and rocks into the teeth of their defences and wear them down. Ideally, you are to insert biological weapons into the planetary atmosphere, in hopes of killing the virus's collective awareness. You are to force them to put planetary defence first. If they come after you, and they will, you are to harry their ships with long-range missile fire and deploy drones to make them waste their time chasing ghosts.

"In the meantime, we will be putting together a fleet to crush the world and its mobile defenders once and for all. And, if we're lucky, it will be the first step towards ending the war."

"Apart from the infected worlds," Captain Hammond said. "We may never be able to free them."

"No," Admiral Onarina agreed. "But if we can trap the virus on a planetary surface, we can and we will hold it down long enough to find a vaccine—or a permanent cure. If we can free the zombies..."

Mitch nodded in grim understanding. There were millions—perhaps billions—of humans who'd been infected, who'd been infected long enough for the virus to gnaw into their brains and effectively kill them. The minds were already dead. Their bodies wouldn't live long without the virus. And if the virus was removed...he shuddered, trying not to think about the death toll. It was a grim reminder that human navies had failed to protect their populations. The final death toll might be more than anyone could bear.

And if we slaughter every last member of their host races, he thought, *we'll have committed genocide several times over.*

"It sounds like a workable plan," Captain Hammond said. "What assets will be placed under my command?"

"We're still putting the squadron together," Admiral Onarina said. "It looks as if you'll have six destroyers, plus twelve bulk freighters crammed with supplies and perhaps a mobile asteroid factory. And, thanks to the RockRats, a secret weapon."

Mitch smiled. "A planet-killer?"

"In a manner of speaking," Admiral Onarina said. She tapped a switch, revealing a device that looked like an old-style rocket booster. "There's a highly-technical name for this, but the RockRats just call it the *pusher*. It's a rather unusual variant on a standard drive field node."

Captain Hammond leaned forward. "What does it do?"

"We've been trying to find a way to improve upon drive field performance for decades," Admiral Onarina said. "The catch, as you know, is that we have to balance the speed with the compensator or the crew would be smashed against the far bulkheads as soon as they turned on the drive. The pusher imparts a vast amount of speed in a very short space of time, at the cost of overwhelming the compensator and becoming very difficult to steer. In a sense, unlike normal drive fields, the velocity remains constant even when the drive field is deactivated. "

"But you couldn't put it on a starship." Mitch felt a flicker of glee. "You *could* put it on a missile!"

"Or on an asteroid," Admiral Onarina said. "You can review the technical specs at your leisure, but you can basically put it on an asteroid, shove it at the target at a sizable percentage of the speed of light and take the pusher off again. By the time it slips into enemy missile range, it'll just be a hunk of rock. And they'll *have* to blow it apart because they won't have time to try to nudge it away from their homeworld."

"Assuming it is their homeworld," Captain Hammond said.

"Yes." Admiral Onarina grinned. "I won't pretend this is a silver bullet, captains. It has its limitations. The NGW project believes it can work through the problems and start putting pusher-type drives on missiles, which will reshape the face of warfare. Again. But, for the moment, it'll force the enemy to concentrate on home defence."

Mitch nodded, considering the options. No planet-bound industrial society could survive a mid-sized asteroid striking the surface. The devastation would be so intense that even orbital installations wouldn't be safe. He'd have to read the technical specs to confirm the device lived up to its promise—it wouldn't be the first time something had worked in the lab, but not in the field—yet if it did it would change everything. He frowned as a thought struck him. There had to be some way to take advantage of the technology, some way to cripple the enemy…

Read the technical specs, he reminded himself. *And then see if you can actually make it work.*

"Your ships have been given priority for repair and reloading," Admiral Onarina said. "I want you and your squadron ready to depart within two weeks. You'll take with you enough short-term flicker stations to allow us to remain in contact and keep you posted on developments with Footfall-II. In the event of GATO deciding against the operation, you may have to take out Virus Prime yourself."

She looked at Captain Hammond. "I won't attempt to determine your deployments for you, Commodore," she cautioned, "but I meant what I said. I expect you to be professional. Kill each other on your own time."

"Yes, Admiral," Captain Hammond said, curtly.

"Captain Campbell, remain behind," Admiral Onarina ordered. "Captain Hammond, we'll speak before departure."

Captain Hammond stood. "Yes, Admiral."

Mitch said nothing as he heard Captain Hammond leave the room, closing the door behind him. God alone knew what his rival was thinking. He hadn't expected to be summoned to the Admiralty, let alone to be put in command of an operation that could make or break the war. Mitch wondered, idly, what sort of high-level discussions there'd been over the last few days. Charlotte had insisted the scandal would be allowed to continue, if only to give the government a chance to bury bad news. Mitch had seen enough of how the government operated to suspect she was right.

"Captain," Admiral Onarina said. "Do you know what they used to call me?"

Mitch frowned, caught by surprise. "No, Admiral."

"The Nubian," Admiral Onarina said. "I was famous, for my service on *Vanguard*, and the media loved me. They had an odd way of showing it. They talked endlessly about the colour of my skin, praising me and my family and insisting, in a manner calculated to speak to their own prejudices, that I was a credit to my race. Never mind my father came from Jamaica. Never mind that I'd been born and bred in Britain. Never mind..."

She shook her head. "The media builds heroes, Mitch. It can tear them down just as easily. One moment, they were hailing me for winning battles; the next, they were making snide remarks about the size of my breasts or whining that I'd cut my hair into a decidedly mannish style. I went from being the greatest of the great to a low-born guttersnipe who should be grateful for what she was given, then fuck off before the public tired of her."

Mitch was genuinely shocked. "Admiral..."

Admiral Onarina held up a hand. "The media doesn't give a damn about you. Or me. Or Captain Hammond and his estranged wife. Their approval and outrage are always feigned. The *Morning Mule* spent years complaining about my time on the Admiralty Board, then published a series of stories suggesting I'm a direct descent of Lord Nelson himself after Operation Lightning Strike. Give them a few weeks and they'll be suggesting I step aside to let someone younger have a go."

Her lips twisted. "You'd be better off with a racist bastard who makes horrible jokes about the colour of your skin than someone who has no convictions at all. They'll build you up, when it is convenient, and then tear you down when the winds change. Don't expect them to love you. They don't love you and they don't hate you. They'll do whatever they think they have to do to get their stories published."

"I see," Mitch said.

"I doubt it." Admiral Onarina met his eyes. "Right now, you're basking in their praise. You and your"—her eyes narrowed—"lover are enjoying their plaudits. But that will change soon enough. You'll go from hero to zero so fast your head will spin."

She sighed. "You want my advice? During the mission, spend some time thinking about what you *really* want to do. Stay with her? You'll have very little privacy if you do. Or run far away, perhaps taking her with you? She might not want to go."

Mitch said nothing for a long moment. "I don't want to lose my ship."

"And you've made a bunch of enemies, thanks to you not keeping your pants on," Admiral Onarina snapped. "Would it have been *that* hard to find a discreet hotel?"

Her voice softened, slightly. "I know, naval service puts one hell of a strain on personal relationships. I've lost partners who…who couldn't take long separations either. I don't know what's going through Lady Charlotte's head and I don't much care. The aristocratic world has no room for me, even after I was admitted to the Order of the Garter. I don't care about the scandal. What I care about is winning the war."

She met his eyes. "I want you to be clear on this, and I will say it to

Captain Hammond too, as many times as I must. I don't care about your problems. I expect you to work together long enough to deliver victory. If I can get Footfall-II launched, we might win the war—or at least eliminate the threat to our worlds. *That* is the priority. Do you understand me?"

"Yes, Admiral," Mitch said. He didn't know what to say. Admiral Onarina was his hero. The thought of someone saying such things about her made him want to hunt down the reporter, drag him into the nearest alleyway and beat him to death. There wasn't a jury in the world that would convict him. "I...why were they so horrid to you? You saved an entire fleet!"

"It isn't about *me*," Admiral Onarina said. "And it isn't about you either. It's about selling garbage to the general public. They'll kiss your ass one day and kick it the next, whichever sells. Go back to your ship tomorrow and concentrate on your job. If the two of you want to build a life together, you can do it after the war."

Her eyes hardened. "And remember," she added darkly, "those who play with fire often get burned."

CHAPTER EIGHT

THOMAS HAD HEARD, ONCE, that Lord Nelson had forced his wife to host a dinner with Lord and Lady Hamilton, when Lady Hamilton had been Nelson's mistress and Lord Hamilton apparently turning a blind eye. It had struck him, at the time, as an unbelievably cruel thing to do even by the standards of the Napoleonic Era. And dangerous too, when Lord Hamilton could have sued Nelson or worse…he gritted his teeth as he strode through the Admiralty, wondering just what had got into the admiral. He'd heard the operation was being planned, but…

She probably wants to get both of us off-world before the scandal gets any worse, he thought, sourly. *She might even be right.*

The thought gnawed at him as he stopped in the lobby and ordered a car to take him to the spaceport. There was nothing to be gained by going back home, not since he'd received his marching orders. The Admiralty wouldn't be amused if he didn't report for duty on time. He waited for the driver to bring the car around to the door, then climbed in and activated his terminal as the car glided away from the complex. He'd have to call his daughter and tell her she was in charge of the estate, at least until he returned home. He hoped Charlotte wouldn't try to return. It would be awkward, to say the least, if their daughter had to tell her mother she wasn't welcome.

He scowled at the display as the latest email from the lawyer popped up in front of him. He had a fairly solid case, the man insisted, but the court of public opinion was in full session. It wasn't hard to see what Charlotte was doing—smearing Thomas in a bid to distract attention from her own behaviour—but there was nothing they could do, save for waiting it out. The public would lose interest sooner or later, perhaps sooner now both Thomas and Captain Campbell were leaving Earth. Thomas gritted his teeth. Charlotte could take the settlement and fuck off, as far as he was concerned. She could do whatever she liked, as long as it was a long way from him.

His heart clenched. He'd...he hadn't really *loved* her, not in the sense of grand passion and midnight flights to Gretna Green and all the other clichés of romance novels and flicks throughout the ages, but...she'd been part of his life. She'd shared his home, his bed...they'd raised two daughters together. She wasn't *love*, but...she was comfortable. No, she'd *been* comfortable. He scowled as he remembered what she'd said, in their final argument. He'd thought she was happy with the arrangement. He'd missed the signs suggesting she wasn't even *remotely* happy. And that meant...

I could send Captain Campbell to his death, he thought. It slipped into his mind as though the devil himself had whispered the suggestion, an idea so horrific and yet so tempting that he couldn't simply dismiss it at once. He would be in command, when the squadron departed. It would be easy to send *Unicorn* into danger, into certain death...he shook his head in horror. There were over fifty spacers on the frigate. *I can't send them all to their deaths.*

The thought mocked him as the car sped past the barricades, and the lines of reporters laying siege to the Admiralty, and slipped onto the road to the motorway. There were shuttles leaving regularly from Heathrow Spaceport to Nelson Base. He'd have no trouble boarding one, then arranging a flight from Nelson Base to the Hamilton Shipyards. There were supply runs going back and forth all the time. Thomas forced himself to sit back and relax as the car raced on. There would be a complete lack of formality—and no reception, when he reached his ship—but he didn't care. He'd never needed a formal ceremony to welcome him to his command.

London looked…faded, somehow. The city had barely recovered from the First Interstellar War when the virus had taken root on Earth. Half the shops had closed down, perhaps permanently. Clusters of wealthy and powerful people—and their partners and mistresses—moved along the streets, keeping their distance from the others. Charlotte would have been one of them once, welcoming people she wanted to favour and cutting everyone else dead. She'd have a hard time adjusting to life as a divorced woman. She'd still have her title—she couldn't be stripped of *that*, as long as her daughters remained alive—but she wouldn't have the wealth and power that came with it. Thomas wondered, idly, if Charlotte was hoping he'd die in interstellar space. It would be interesting, from a legal point of view, if he died before they were formally divorced. It would certainly make a great deal of money for the lawyers.

Thomas put the thought out of his head as the car raced through the checkpoints, slipped into the roads leading up to the spaceport and stopped in front of the military terminal. There were fewer visible civilians, almost all colonists leaving the planet in hope of a better or more secure life. In theory, it was easier to defend an asteroid colony against infection. In practice, a nuke would crack the asteroid open like an egg. And no one was *quite* sure how the RockRats had managed to lose a pair of asteroids to creeping infection. Thomas suspected—and he knew MI6 shared his suspicions—that someone had been careless at the worst possible time. The grey market that dominated most of the asteroid belt didn't welcome questions, let alone biological sampling. Who knew what'd happen to the blood and DNA records?

He thanked the driver, then walked through the checkpoint and into the terminal. The staff checked his card, booked him on a shuttle leaving in thirty minutes and directed him into the officers' lounge. Thomas ordered a mug of tea, then sat down to wait. It wouldn't be that long, unless he got bumped. If someone turned up with priority orders, they'd be put ahead of him. He snorted as he keyed his wristcom and started to read his orders properly. The admiral might have been keen to get them off-world as quickly as possible, but she hadn't bothered to cut them priority orders. It might have been difficult to explain. Operation Lightning Strike had come too close to disaster for the admiral to feel completely secure in her position. Her allies wouldn't go out on a limb for her. Thomas rolled his eyes. There was never any shortage of bastards willing to put the boot in, when their target looked vulnerable.

Wankers, he thought, as he drank his tea. *You can't trust anyone these days.*

The shuttle departed on schedule, taking him to Nelson Base. Thomas passed the time downloading the newest briefings from the datacores and skimming them, one by one. It was hard to be sure—political infighting had been worse than usual, after the fleet had made it back from Lightning Strike—but it looked as if GATO wasn't keen on sending another force deep into enemy space. There were just too many vulnerable stars, too many planets and their populations open to attack. Thomas understood the logic—it wasn't as if the worlds could be liberated, at a later date—but it was still frustrating. The virus was steadily grinding them down. They wouldn't win by standing on the defensive. They'd just give the virus all the time it needed to muster the force to crush them and effectively exterminate the human race.

He passed through a series of checkpoints on Nelson Base—two more than he remembered from his last visit—and boarded a shuttle to the Hamilton Yards. The pilot offered to take him there directly, as the senior officer on the flight, but Thomas declined. There was no need to hurry. Besides, someone might take note and use it against him in the court of public opinion. And who knew what'd happen then? Great Britain respected her aristocrats, he'd learnt as a child, but she also watched for signs of entitlement and arrogance. An aristocrat who misused his rank and title was not likely to be popular, or to command any public support if he wanted a political career.

Perhaps I should go into politics, he thought. It was an unpleasant concept—he wanted to stay on the bridge as long as possible—but he knew it might be his duty. He'd seen the elephant, unlike far too many politicians. *They'd find it harder to cut the naval budget if I was on the committee.*

He sighed, closing his eyes in a fruitless bid for sleep. His stomach churned with anger. His life had turned upside down, leaving him a laughingstock. And he had to work with the asshole who'd slept with his wife... not, Thomas had to admit, that it had been anything but consensual. Charlotte could have summoned help in an instant, just by saying the right words, if Captain Campbell had tried to *rape* her. She certainly hadn't tried to claim she'd been forced into bed when he'd caught them...

She wanted to hurt me, Thomas reflected, bitterly. In hindsight, the signs had been all too clear. The indicators had been blinking red. *And that was why she let herself be caught.*

• • •

Tobias had heard, long ago, about something called imposter syndrome. It was the belief that one did not hold the title one held, that one didn't have the objective right to call oneself...whatever. He had never really understood it, if only because he'd never really had a position of power. He'd never been a Prefect, let alone Head Boy. The idea was laughable. He couldn't have made anyone do anything. And yet...

He felt like a fraud as he stood in the briefing compartment and watched the younger pilots flow into the room. They looked so...so *young*, so innocent. It was hard to believe the oldest of them was actually two years older than Tobias, not when they didn't even have their space legs yet. Tobias glanced at Marigold, seated at the rear of the compartment, and felt another flicker of guilt. It should have been her in command of the squadron. She had as much experience as him, with slightly more composure. It should have been her.

And yet, she didn't object when she was told I'd take command, Tobias thought. His girlfriend had returned to the ship twelve hours ago, barely long enough for them to catch up before the maggots arrived. *What does she know that I don't?*

It was hard not to turn and run—the urge was overpowering—as he surveyed the newcomers. Twelve pilots, men and women, wearing uniforms so fresh and clean they looked neater than dress uniforms. They looked childish…Tobias had the sudden urge to check their records, to make absolutely sure they were of legal age. It was rare for anyone to join the navy before they turned eighteen, although he'd heard there were a handful of academy cadets who'd joined at sixteen and graduated at nineteen. He felt old, despite his own youth. He'd seen and done things…he shook his head. The maggots would catch up soon. Too soon.

He cleared his throat, then kicked himself an instant later. It made him sound weak. And yet, they quietened down and looked at him with… *respect?* Tobias had the uneasy sense someone was playing a joke on him, a very nasty joke. The only time anyone had pretended to like him at school was when they'd been trying to lull him into a false sense of security, to make him stick his head into the noose—metaphorically speaking—before they closed the trap's jaws. Tobias told himself, firmly, that the navy wasn't a badly-run school. He could rely on the captain and command staff to back him up if the shit hit the fan.

"Welcome onboard," he said. His voice sounded odd, even to himself. He wished he'd had more time to practice. Marigold would have listened to him repeat the speech time and time again, patiently correcting him until he had it down pat. "For those of you who don't know me, I am Tobias Gurnard, Squadron CO. I was one of the first pilots to join the gunboat program and take a gunboat into action against enemy ships. My experiences, and those of my comrades, helped to shape your training sessions. You have the great advantage of learning from our experiences."

He forced himself to keep his voice steady. "I don't know how much you were told, beforehand, about life on a starship. HMS *Lion* is currently preparing to depart. You—we—will spend most of our time in Gunboat Country, when we're not taking our gunboats out on live-fire training exercises. Our days will be filled with simulated engagements, followed by post-battle discussions and assessments of what went right—and wrong. We will try to get all the mistakes out of the way in the simulators, before we take our craft into battle. We can learn from our mistakes, in the simulators, without anyone actually getting killed."

His words hung in the air for a long moment. "Three other things to bear in mind," he added, after a moment. "Before departure, I expect you to remain in Gunboat Country unless you are specifically asked to go elsewhere. You are not trained starship personnel, and you will simply get in the way while the crew prepares the ship for departure. There will be time to explore the rest of the ship later, once we are under way. Second, if you haven't already done so, I suggest you write your wills before we cross the tramline. There is no guarantee you'll survive your first mission. You need to bear that in mind."

He kicked himself, mentally, as he saw their faces pale. He'd told himself that the engagements weren't quite real often enough, before he'd finally come to terms with the reality of his new life. He'd done it to keep his fears under control...he cursed under his breath. He'd yanked away their illusions as surely as Colin had yanked away his towel, back in the bad old days...

Tobias pushed the thought to the back of his mind. "Third, I don't expect you to *like* each other. You did not train together as a group. Some of you will have become friends, or more than friends, during your time at the academy. Others are currently in a room full of strangers. I do not expect you to like each other, as I said, but I expect you to *respect* each other. We are all in this together, as we are regularly reminded on the nightly news. Show a little consideration. Respect property. Don't hog the washrooms. And so on."

He paused, significantly. "Naval regulations are a little vague on sexual relationships between starfighter and gunboat pilots. The general feeling is that pilots live fast and die young, so officers often turn a blind eye to relationships as long as they don't cross any serious lines. There's a bunch of legalese about it, if you read the regulations, but it all boils down to a flat ban on relationships between people of different ranks. You are not allowed to have a sexual relationship with someone higher or lower than you in the chain of command.

"I don't care what you do on your time off, but I expect you to be professional when you're on duty. If you can't handle that, in this environment, I'll arrange for you and your partner to be separated. Don't try me on this. We cannot afford suggestions the gunboat pilots are more interested in fucking than fighting."

Even though it's true, Tobias added, as the newcomers chuckled. *It's certainly true for starfighter pilots.*

He made a show of checking his wristcom. "If you haven't already claimed your bunks and freshened up, go do it now," he said. "Report to the simulators at 1430. We'll start running through the basics, to make sure we're all on the same page, and then we'll move into the more advanced simulations. And if we're lucky, we'll be able to take our gunboats out for a spin in a few days. Any questions?"

A newcomer held up his hand. "Sir? When are we leaving the shipyard?"

Tobias blinked. *Sir?* "As far as I know, our orders have not been finalised. I've been told to have the squadron ready for deployment in a fortnight. That could mean anything from a hard deadline for departure to wishful thinking on someone's part. We will, for the moment, treat it as a hard deadline. It is quite possible we'll be told to leave early."

He cleared his throat. "No more questions? Dismissed."

The compartment emptied, leaving Tobias and Marigold alone. He glanced at her. "How did I do?"

"Well…" Marigold pretended to think about it. "I think you did fine. It helps that this is their first shipboard deployment. They'll start questioning you more once they get used to being onboard ship."

"Thanks," Tobias said, sourly. "Any words of advice?"

"Don't let them catch us in the privacy tubes," Marigold said. She grinned at him. "You do realise you outrank me now?"

Tobias blanched. "Uh…technically…"

Marigold snorted. "Try using that excuse on the CO," she said. "See what it gets you."

"A kick up the backside, probably," Tobias said. He headed to the hatch. "Come on. We'll set up the simulators, then put them through their paces."

And make sure they lose a battle, just to teach them a lesson before the missiles really start flying, he thought. He remembered some of his own experiences and cringed. *If they go into battle overconfident, they won't come out again.*

CHAPTER NINE

IT HAD BEEN A STRUGGLE, Charlotte had said, to book a hotel room in central London. It wasn't that she couldn't afford it—she could—but the hotel managers had been reluctant to appear to take sides in the ongoing public divorce. Mitch feared, reading between the lines, that the various managers would have denied her completely if he hadn't been sharing the room. He *was* a naval hero, after all, and it would have been very bad publicly if they'd turned him away. But he wasn't sure that would have been enough to allow them to keep the room if Captain Hammond and his allies started pressuring the hotels to kick them out.

They lay on the bed, spooned together. Mitch had returned to the hotel as soon as the admiral had dismissed him, where they'd spent the last hour making love. It astonished him just how adventurous Charlotte was, although he supposed it made a certain kind of sense. She was not only old enough to know what she wanted, she was also throwing off the shackles of her former life. Mitch wasn't sure there'd been many shackles, sexually speaking, but it didn't matter. He knew he'd have to make his way back to his ship soon enough.

And the admiral made it clear I'd better return victorious, he thought, grimly. It was easy to laugh at the admiral's warnings, but…looking at the media coverage, he was inclined to think she might be right. The media had made him. It could tear him down just as easily. *If I fail, I'll be torn down in an instant.*

Charlotte shifted, her bare breasts pressing against his back as she moved. Mitch felt himself stiffen, again. It felt odd to be so...*taken*...with her, with anyone, and yet he knew he'd be heading back to space within a few hours. There wouldn't be any sex on *Unicorn*. The frigate didn't have room for an artfully-disguised captain's woman, even if he'd thought he'd get away with it. There'd been an admiral who'd kept his wife on his flagship, an incident that had turned into a major scandal when it had finally burst into the light. Mitch smiled at the thought. Captain Hammond was probably wishing he'd kept his wife on his ship now, too.

"I wish you could stay," Charlotte said. She straddled him. "Life will be dull without you."

"You'll find it easier to get a separation if you're just arguing with his lawyers," Mitch pointed out. "And you'll be able to spend more time with your daughters."

Charlotte nodded, tartly. Mitch wondered, not for the first time, if there was anything binding them together beyond lust and shared adversity. What sort of future did they have, if he returned in glory? Would Charlotte be happy to be the wife of a naval hero? She'd *already* been the wife of a naval hero. Mitch had no illusions about Captain Hammond's shortcomings, and his excessive caution when faced with a chance to *really* hurt the enemy, but there was no doubting his competence. Would she stay with him? Or would she slip off into the countryside and forget him? He wasn't sure he wanted to know.

His thoughts fled as Charlotte pressed down on him, breasts bouncing as she rode him like a pony. Mitch felt himself moving in time, hands reaching up to play with her breasts as she moved faster and faster. Little mewling noises escaped her lips as she leaned down to kiss him, an instant before he exploded. She smiled, rolled off and stood, heading for the shower. Mitch followed. There'd be time to play in the water before he had to take his leave.

"I might run for parliament," Charlotte said, as she turned the water on and stepped inside. "My local MP is standing down this summer and the chairman of the local party owes me a favour or two. Do you think I'd convince people to vote for me?"

Mitch frowned. "I thought you needed to give up your title if you wanted to run for office."

"Only if I wanted a seat on the cabinet," Charlotte corrected him. Water ran down her body and pooled around her feet. "If I just wanted to be an MP, I wouldn't have to give anything up."

"Good luck," Mitch said. "Just remember to vote for higher naval budgets."

Charlotte's face darkened. "That'll be a hard sell," she said. "Right now, we're eating our seed corn just to meet the demands of the war. People are tired of it."

"They'll be a great deal more tired of being zombies, when the virus infects the entire planet," Mitch pointed out. "Or they would be, if zombies could think."

Charlotte nodded, pressing against him so they both got wet. "I take your point," she said. "But there are limits to what we can do."

Mitch kept his thoughts to himself. Charlotte wanted something for herself…a seat in parliament? It would be an interesting campaign. On one hand, she'd cheated on her husband; on the other, she was the lover of a naval hero. The local party would be unsure if it should support her or tell her to join the *other* party. Mitch had heard stories about local parties, particularly ones in rural areas. They were effectively single party counties, to the point the old rotten boroughs had practically been resurrected. Charlotte might just have enough influence to ride roughshod over all opposition.

Unless her husband takes a public stand against her, he thought. *That should make for an interesting time.*

He pushed the thought out of his head as he stepped out of the shower, dried himself and changed into a basic uniform. One advantage of the whole affair, he supposed, was that he had relatively little baggage with him. Charlotte had urged him to make a visit to London's famous tailors, to place orders for clothes he didn't need and probably couldn't afford, but he'd been insistent on carrying as little as possible. She could afford a private aircraft to carry her back home, wherever it was now. Mitch knew he didn't dare get into bad habits.

"I'll see you when you return," Charlotte said. "Don't let Thomas get you killed."

Mitch scowled as he called a cab. Captain Hammond could send Mitch and his ship into danger...the Board of Inquiry would be suspicious if *something* happened to *Unicorn*, under the circumstances, but it was possible Captain Hammond could avoid any blame for the incident. Mitch would just have to check his orders carefully, pushing his authority to the limit to avoid certain death. It wasn't as if he had to slavishly follow every order he was given. By long custom, a captain had wide latitude to determine how best to complete his mission.

"I'll be back," he promised. "Good luck."

Charlotte nodded and gave him a quick kiss, just before the terminal bleeped. There was rarely any need to wait for more than a few minutes for a cab in London. Mitch picked up his bag, kissed her one final time and headed down to the lobby. The bellhop held the door open as he stepped outside, his face completely unreadable. Mitch frowned, feeling uncomfortable. If he'd grown up in a world where servants bowed and scraped and did everything he wanted, would he be deeply weird too?

The very rich are different from you and me, he thought, wryly. *And it isn't just because they have more money.*

Mitch put the thought out of his mind as the cab glided onto the street. There was no point in dwelling on Charlotte, and their affair, now he was on his way back to his ship. His terminal bleeped, reporting it had received messages from the Admiralty. Mitch scanned his orders quickly, then read them more carefully to be sure he'd hit the high points. The Admiralty was pulling out all the stops to make sure Mitch—and

Captain Hammond—were dispatched on their mission as soon as possible. Mitch understood, all too well. The Admiralty was caught in a bind. If the Admiralty sought to punish one or both of the captains, there would be political and public outrage. And yet, the Admiralty couldn't have them hanging around the solar system either. Getting them both out of the system as quickly as possible was the best of a bad set of options.

But it's still pretty damn bad, Mitch thought. *They must be pissed.*

The cab reached the spaceport, allowing him to jump onboard a shuttle heading directly to the Hamilton Yards. He was aware of eyes following him as he was shown to the craft, spacers torn between admiration for his deeds and contempt for his role in the affair. Mitch had always sought the limelight, but...he wondered, as he boarded the shuttle, if he'd made a mistake. It was one thing to play to the media as a naval hero with a genuine record of success. It was quite another to help a woman cheat on her husband and start the scandal of the century. If he'd known she intended to use him to hurt her husband...a grin spread across his face as he remembered his first time in her bed. He suspected he would have done it anyway.

He spent the flight reading through the technical specs, noting how military technology had advanced. Again. It was odd to realise that *Unicorn* might be obsolete even before the tactical concepts behind her had truly matured, although he was fairly certain his ship would never be scrapped. There was no shortage of work for smaller ships...he wondered, suddenly, if Captain Hammond would have the patience to wait until the frigate could be downgraded to patrol duties, ensuring the end of Mitch's career without ever doing anything too overt that might get the public on his side. It would be a great deal more satisfying than a demented Uriah Gambit and much less likely to lead to a court-martial and the hangman's noose.

And he might think of it too, Mitch thought. *It certainly plays into his strengths.*

He dismissed the thought as HMS *Unicorn* finally came into view. The frigate looked crude, compared to some of the more elegant civilian ships that plied the spacelanes in happier times, but she had a certain presence that never failed to thrill. He drank in the details as the shuttle glided closer, until the frigate—tiny compared to a fleet carrier—dominated the porthole, then collected his carryall and made his way to the hatch. A low thud ran through the shuttle as it docked, the hatch opening to reveal a pair of suited men. Mitch allowed them to test his blood without protest. They were only following orders. There was nothing to be gained by reprimanding them.

"Welcome home, Captain," one of them said. "The XO requests your presence in your cabin."

Mitch blinked. His cabin was also his office—there were no ready rooms on tiny *Unicorn*—and his XO had every right to use it, but it was still a surprise. He'd been sure to send Commander Staci Templeton a message, informing her he was returning to the ship. They would have to have a long talk, just to make sure he knew everything that had happened in his absence…Mitch felt a sudden pang of guilt. He hadn't been keeping up with her messages and he was fairly sure she knew it. He'd known better. God knew his stint as an XO had been marred by a captain who hadn't paid attention to his officers.

He walked through the ship, silently noting the open hatches as the crew readied the frigate for departure. A handful of crewmen were strangers, newly assigned to his ship. Mitch made a mental note to find time to speak to them, just to impress upon the newcomers that the frigate's crew was a family. There was no room for anyone unwilling or unable to pull his weight. The newcomers saluted as he passed, a clear sign they'd never served on a frigate before. Their commanders didn't demand salutes, not when there was work to be done. The formalities were saved for visits from flag officers and reporters.

The hatch hissed open, allowing him to step into his cabin. It was the largest personal compartment on the ship, although it was barely large enough to swing a cat. His XO—a tall woman with short dark hair and a fiery disposition—sat at the desk. She stood as he entered, her face grim.

Mitch felt his heart sink. If something had happened that required his personal attention…no, he knew that wasn't the problem. Staci would have sent him an urgent message if there was something she couldn't handle.

"Captain," Staci said. "Permission to speak freely?"

Mitch frowned as he dropped his carryall on the bunk. Staci *always* spoke freely. It wasn't a trait that had won her many friends, not on the bigger ships, but it was something he'd come to value. Mitch had a high opinion of himself, like all frigate commanders, yet he was all too aware he could make mistakes. Better to have Staci question his decisions—in private—than to lose his ship and crew. And yet…why was she *asking*? She knew she could speak freely.

"Yes," he said, flatly.

"With all due respect, Captain," Staci said, "what the hell were you thinking?"

She went on before Mitch could think of an answer. "I know, being on leave is a chance to leave the uniform behind and…and have fun," she snapped. "But being caught in bed with a fellow officer's wife? Are you out of your mind?"

"No," Mitch said. "I…"

"Captain, the media will tear you apart," Staci said, cutting him off. "And if you and your career survive that, the Admiralty will finish the job. What the hell were you thinking?"

Mitch felt a hot flash of anger, which he forced himself to suppress. "I thought…"

He *hadn't* thought, he acknowledged ruefully. It would have been easy enough to turn Charlotte down. It wasn't as if he hadn't *known* she was the wife of a fellow officer. It wasn't as though he couldn't have insisted they kept it discreet, that they only met in hotels with a reputation for privacy. Hell, it wasn't as if he'd been desperate. He wasn't short of female company. He could have visited the red-light district or travelled to Sin City. It would have been a quick transaction, not something that would come back to bite him.

Staci met his eyes. "Yes, I get it. I know how it feels to want something. I know how it feels to go without. But do you think Captain Hammond is going to let this pass? Do you think all the other captains are just going to…let you anywhere near their wives? You are going to be involved in the worst scandal…no, you're *already* involved. And your career is going to hit an asteroid at near-light speed."

"I know," Mitch said. "But I…"

"You're not sixteen," Staci said. "Did you really have to let your small head do the thinking for you?"

Mitch flushed. "Staci, I…"

"You could have gone to Sin City and paid for a simulation of the aristocratic life," Staci pointed out. "Or you could have just kept it discreet. Instead, you've started a fight you can't win."

"I have to fight," Mitch said. "If I don't, my career goes straight into the crapper."

"And if you do, your career goes straight into the crapper anyway," Staci countered. "Is she really so fantastically stunning that you lost the ability to think straight?"

She shrugged. "She's a dangerously reckless aristocrat who just wants to have fun. I guess the two of you are pretty well matched."

"Thanks," Mitch said, sourly.

Staci smiled, humourlessly. "I get it. I really do. But you're going to spend the rest of your life paying for this mistake. The minute you expose yourself, someone is going to ram a sword into your career and that will be the end. I doubt your mistress gives much of a damn about you and, even if she does, she doesn't have the clout to save you. You might find yourself on an asteroid mining colony, once the shooting stops. Or simply discharged as part of the post-war military rationalisation."

"That's why I have to fight," Mitch said. "If I keep my name in front of the public…"

"This would be the same public that often shuns women who cheat on military husbands?" Staci snorted. "I seem to recall some poor bitch getting stripped naked, shaved bald and kicked out of her job for fucking another woman. Do you *really* think Lady Whatever will be able to keep her reputation? Her husband is already preparing to divorce her."

Mitch winced. "She'll be fine."

"I doubt you will be," Staci said. "Do you think she loves you? Or that she thinks of you as anything more than a glorified sexbot?"

She met Mitch's eyes. "Captain, you're in an untenable position," she said. "And that is the blunt truth."

"We'll see," Mitch said. He hoped she was wrong, but feared she was right. "Now, what's been happening since I left the ship?"

"The crew has been bombarded with interview requests," Staci said, flatly. "I've told them to keep their mouths shut, for the moment, but you should speak to them too. At the very least, you should reassure them their careers are not in danger."

"Understood," Mitch said. "Now, how soon until we can leave the system?"

CHAPTER TEN

"SO," THOMAS SAID, once the steward had poured tea and with-drawn as silently as he'd come. His senior officers looked back at him with varying levels of attention. "Where do we stand?"

He'd hoped, he reflected as he leaned back in his chair, that the media circus would die away once he—and Captain Campbell—were on their respective ships. The Admiralty hadn't made a public announcement that they'd resumed their roles, but somehow—he suspected Charlotte—the media hyenas had learned the truth and started requesting permission to dispatch reporters to the shipyards. And when that had been refused, the media had started all kinds of gruesome speculations about what Thomas and Captain Campbell would do to each other. It was just a matter of time, from the growing racket, before questions were asked in the House.

And that would really put the cat amongst the pigeons, he thought. *The MPs wouldn't be amused if they were forced to waste time discussing the scandal instead of turning their minds to weightier matters.*

Commander Shane Donker took a sip of his tea, then smiled. "The vast majority of our repairs have been completed," he said, shortly. "The Admiralty was kind enough to give us first call on the shipyard's resources, which ensured we were able to replace the damaged components and patch up the holes in the hull. There are a handful of sections that probably need to be replaced completely, after the pounding we took, but there's no way we can handle the task without taking the ship out of service for several weeks. Even with priority, it isn't something that can be handled overnight."

Thomas grimaced. "How bad is it?"

"It depends," Commander Donker said. "The engineering team think it'll be fine, as long as we don't take a direct hit or two on that part of the hull. The heavy armour should be enough to ward off anything below a focused nuke or a bomb-pumped laser, and if we take that sort of battering we'll have worse problems to worry about, but we've taken the precaution of securing the inner hull anyway. If they get a nuke through the outer armour, the blast will hopefully be contained and redirected out into space. We've gone as far as we can without adding to our overall mass."

"Which would make life difficult, if we have to play tag with a fleet of enemy ships," Thomas said. "We don't want to let them get into firing range."

He scowled as he studied his teacup. The Royal Navy's first spaceborn carriers had been heavily-armoured behemoths that, in the words of the legendary Theodore Smith, wallowed like pigs in muck. Their acceleration curves had been so low that practically *any* enemy ship could escape, if it had a head start. The second generation had traded armour for speed and flexibility, a concept that had looked good on paper but failed utterly when the fleet had to go to war. Later generations were designed to combine speed with protection, trying hard to balance both sets of requirements. *Lion* had been built to snipe the enemy from a safe distance. Thomas had no illusions about the outcome if the enemy brought their big guns to bear on his ship.

"No, sir," Donker agreed. "We have received a full load of the latest missiles, as well as everything else we requested when we were given priority. I've had the crew practicing replenishment while underway, as we dare not assume we'll be assigned purpose-built fleet tenders. Our order of battle has been changed so many times I'm unwilling to commit to anything until we actually cross the tramline. If we have to resupply while we're deep in enemy space…"

"We'll handle it," Thomas assured him. "And the gunboats?"

Colonel Richard Bagehot grinned. "Young Gurnard had a rather shaky start, not helped by chunks of bad advice from his marine friend, but he's doing well. It helps that pretty much all of the newcomers have zero experience, allowing him to impress them. He's had the wit to let them get their mistakes out of their system too, before they start flying *real* gunboats. I think the squadron will shape up fine, given time."

He made a face. "Realistically, they're not going to work up as I might wish. The entire program was started well after the war began, ensuring that no one involved had the time to take a leisurely approach. There simply wasn't time for a proper shift to a new duty station, let alone a steady program of gradual acclimatization. The upside is that it will sort the men from the boys, as we know. The downside is that tiredness will start taking a toll sooner rather than later."

"Ouch," Thomas said. "Keep an eye on them. Inform me if you feel they need additional support or some quiet mentorship."

"Aye, Captain," Bagehot said.

Thomas took another sip of his tea. Command—starship command, squadron command, departmental command—was never easy. It was hard to make a good impression if one was young and green and completely ignorant of how the *real* world worked. And it was *very* easy to make a mistake that would have a senior officer write *not recommended for independent command* in one's file. A young man who had *that* following him would have to work very hard to overcome it. He doubted Gurnard intended to stay in the navy—the youngster's file suggested a very unmilitary bearing—but it might change. Thomas made a mental note to keep an eye on the matter. If Gurnard started making mistakes, he could be corrected before it got out of hand.

He looked at Major Chuck Craig. "And with the bootnecks?"

"We have embarked two oversized companies, as you know," Craig said. "Our alien bootneck has been detached and reassigned to Portsmouth while the head sheds discuss progress and decide what to do with him next.

My personal recommendation is that we continue the program, but with due care and attention to biological and cultural issues that might—that will—cause problems. Corporal Lancaster has been placed in command of a semi-detached platoon, which was the simplest solution. We don't have time to reassign him to one of the new companies."

"And besides, he might be recalled to Earth at any moment," Commander Donker said.

"Yes," Craig agreed. "However, I do believe he's told the head sheds all he *can* tell them. He accepted an alien into his unit and tried to treat him as any other bootneck. His reports were very detailed and quite, it should be noted, self-critical. Mistakes were made. That is undeniable. But he also recovered from them."

"The matter is now out of our hands," Thomas said. "Do you foresee any problems with your department?"

"No, Captain," Craig said. "There will be a modest amount of pushing and shoving, as having two companies allows us to run one against the other, but I don't anticipate any real issues. Given the importance of the mission, Portsmouth made sure to assign experienced men to the ship. There will be bumps along the way, as always, but a few weeks of exercises will smooth them out. Right now, the only real problem is minor grumbling about leave being cut short. I'd like to arrange a handful of leave slots, if only to the shipyard facilities. It won't be much, but it'll be better than nothing."

"True," Donker agreed. "Leave was cut short because of the post-mission debriefings."

"Yes," Thomas said. He considered it for a moment, although he already knew the answer. "Assign the leave slots, but make sure they know we may be ordered to depart on twelve hours notice. I want everyone back on the ship at least two hours before departure. We *don't* want to slow departure because of a missing crewman."

"No, Captain," Craig said.

Thomas nodded. "Are there any other matters of import, before we proceed to the mission overview?"

"I don't believe so, Captain," Donker said. "The reassignment and reallocation program worked fairly well. Morale is high amongst the old hands, after we gave the virus a thrashing, and they're taking good care of the new hands. Some minor friction, as is to be expected, but nothing too serious. Departmental heads seem to have it under control. I don't envision any real problems."

"And there's probably already a bunch of illicit stills in hidden places," Craig teased.

"There are, yes," Donker agreed. "I'm keeping an eye on them. I won't interfere as long as they keep themselves under control. If someone turns up on duty dead drunk, that policy will change overnight."

Thomas nodded. It was incredibly hard to keep naval personnel from distilling their own alcohol. The military moonshiner had been part of naval tradition for hundreds of years. It was far from uncommon for the command staff to know *precisely* who was involved, but turn a blind eye as long as matters didn't get out of hand. If they did…Thomas kept his face under tight control. A moonshiner who poisoned someone, or let them drink too much, would spend the rest of his life wishing he'd never been born.

"There is one issue," Donker added. "The news about…ah…"

"I know," Thomas said. He'd never doubted the gossip would have reached his ship. The reporters trying to get to the shipyard would have sent messages to his crew, begging for background interviews and other crap. There was no point in trying to forbid it, if only because trying would make it worse. "My wife and I."

"Yes, sir," Donker said. "I can put a lid on it."

Thomas shook his head. There was no point in trying. A rumour could spread from one end of a ship to the other faster than the human mind could comprehend. Trying to stamp on the rumours would only make them worse. The only thing he could do was to ignore them, rather than treating them as threats to his position. The scandal would fade, sooner or later. Besides, the crew would have worse problems when they entered enemy space. One look at the defences orbiting Viral Prime would be enough to concentrate their minds.

"No," he said. He tapped the table. "Have you all had a chance to review the technical specs for the pusher?"

"Yes, Captain," Donker said. "The records are quite interesting."

"I suppose that's one way of looking at it," Bagehot said. He didn't sound so pleased. "You *do* realise that, if something goes wrong, the asteroid will fly around like a balloon? It could easily become as dangerous to us as the enemy."

"If the drive field destabilizes," Donker said. "If it doesn't, the problem shouldn't arise."

"Under normal circumstances, deactivating a drive field means an immediate drop in velocity," Bagehot pointed out. "We discourage pilots from trying because the sudden change could easily induce the compensator to fail, killing the pilot instantly. Even on a full-sized starship, which would have far greater power reserves, cutting speed so radically is asking for trouble. We'd put so much wear and tear on the drive nodes that we'd cut years off their projected lifespan. But this is different. The velocity will not be lost, if—when—the drive field is deactivated."

"Which will allow us to reuse the pusher," Donker said. "All we have to do is keep shoving asteroids towards the planet. They need to be lucky all the time. We just need to be lucky once."

"Yes, but the drive field will have to be deactivated carefully," Bagehot said. "Or the asteroid might come at us instead."

"We'll keep our distance," Thomas said. He'd seen the records. The pusher had more than lived up to its name. The asteroids had been pushed so hard that they'd arrive hard on the heels of any warning of their coming. It was unlikely one of their asteroids would come right at them, but... he shrugged. There was no point in taking chances. "We'll make sure we have enough time to get out of the way before it's too late."

"Yes, sir," Donker said. "Combined with the overpowered mass drivers, we should be able to give the virus fits."

Thomas nodded. There'd been a time, he recalled vaguely, when he would have been horrified at the mere *idea* of indiscriminately bombarding a planet. The BioBombs had struck him as genocidal weapons, merciless killing machines. The whole concept of letting the demon of biological weapons out of the bottle—again—had kept him up at night. And yet…he shuddered, inwardly. The war was wearing them all down. He'd seen the reports. A dozen infected worlds had been hit with BioBombs, their populations—zombies now—exterminated for the greater good. The thought made him sick. By the time the war was over, uncounted millions—perhaps billions—would be dead. God alone knew how many races had run into the virus and been infected, their cultures destroyed and replaced by a sick shadow of what they'd once been…

"*Unicorn* will spot for us, as we take up position," he said. He swallowed a surge of hatred and bitter resentment, reminding himself—sternly—that *Unicorn's* crew were blameless. "And we'll snipe at their positions with ballistic missiles as well as rocks and asteroids."

Donker nodded. "You know, we could change the face of missile warfare if they manage to make the pusher a little smaller."

"Assuming the target didn't move," Thomas countered. "They used to randomly alter course to protect ships from mass driver projectiles. It's a little harder to move a whole planet."

"Not really, not in theory," Bagehot commented. "You'd just need to scale the pusher up by a factor of ten or so."

"There's a wild idea," Craig agreed. "Set up a planet-sized pusher and shove the entire world into the sun."

"The movement alone would be enough to render the planet lifeless," Donker said. "It might even shatter the entire globe."

Thomas shook his head. There was no shortage of suggestions for mega-projects, from blowing up Mercury for raw materials to constructing a giant ring around Earth linked to space elevators to allow rapid travel between the surface and low orbit, but none of them had ever gotten off the drawing board. The practical problems of turning the dream into reality were just too difficult to solve. Besides, he doubted the virus would let them land long enough to set up the pusher. If they could do that, they could just blast the planet from orbit without wasting time on the surface.

"I think we'll focus on the practical options," he said. "It will not be that difficult to set up shop in their asteroid belt, then rain debris on them. We'll be ready for them when they come after us—and they will. And hopefully we can win time to put together a fleet to crush the rest of the defences and put an end to the war."

"Hopefully," Bagehot echoed. "Nothing is ever going to be the same again, is it?"

Thomas finished his tea. "They said the same when the First Interstellar War broke out," he said. "And they were both wrong and right. The discovery of alien life, intelligent alien life, changed a great many things. We were no longer alone in the universe, even though some of us wished we were. The bombardment changed too many things down there"—he nodded towards the bulkhead—"but other things stayed the same. The world didn't change that much."

"It will change now," Craig said. "We can eliminate the spacefaring threat, if we kill their ships and destroy their shipyards. We can obliterate their worlds from orbit. There'll be no need for a planetary landing that will bleed our forces white. But Earth itself has been infected. We will be fighting the war for a very long time to come."

"I hope you're wrong," Bagehot said. "I don't know how much longer we can take this."

"It isn't as if we have a choice," Craig pointed out. "It's fight, or die."

Thomas nodded. "We'll assume we'll be departing as planned, although that may change. Commander Donker, I want you to put the tactical staff to work, drawing up a rough plan for entering the alien system and setting up a base in the asteroid fields. Major, I want you and your men drilling to resist boarders and—if we have no other choice—boarding their craft and stations. CAG, I want you…"

The alarms started to howl. "Captain to the bridge! Captain to the bridge!"

Thomas stood, grabbing his jacket as he hurried to the hatch. The battlecruiser was technically on standby, not part of the formations deployed to defend the solar system, but they couldn't sit around doing nothing if Earth came under attack. The virus had probed the system before, at least twice. He dreaded to think what would happen if it tried again, this time with far greater force.

"Report," he snapped. Red icons dotted the display. "What do you have?"

"Captain," Lieutenant Commander Sean Sibley said. "We have at least two enemy fleets within detection range. The first one is heading straight for Earth. The second is coming here!"

At us? Thomas's mind raced as he took his chair. *No, not at us. At the yards.*

He forced himself to think. The yards were heavily defended, but most of the mobile units had been called away. The virus had either been monitoring the system or had simply gotten lucky. It didn't take a genius to work out that humanity would sooner defend its homeworld than a free-floating shipyard. And if the virus wanted to take on the fixed defences, it could blast most of them to atoms from a safe distance.

"I want full military power, as soon as you can get it," he ordered, curtly. The rest of his crew were hurrying to their stations. They were lucky most of his crew had returned from leave before the shit hit the fan. "And prepare the gunboats for immediate deployment."

"Aye, Captain."

CHAPTER ELEVEN

SUSAN FELT HELPLESS as she hurried down the stairs to the COBRA bunker, deep under London. She'd been in a meeting with the Prime Minister, briefing him on progress, when the alarms began to howl. His security team had whisked him—and her—into a concealed elevator, then pushed them down the corridor and through a pair of heavy armoured doors. The designers had claimed, from what she'd heard, that the bunker would remain intact, utterly undamaged, even if the planetary surface above was scorched clean of life. She muttered a prayer, as she followed him into the command centre, that today wasn't the day that theory would be tested. The living would envy the dead.

Ice washed down her spine as she caught sight of the holographic display. A cluster of red icons was advancing on Earth with murderous intent, while a second was heading directly towards the shipyards some short distance from the planet itself. Susan cursed under her breath as the enemy tactics became clear. By threatening the planet, they forced the defenders to stand in its defence…leaving the shipyards wide open. There was nothing she could do. She was just a helpless spectator, watching as orbital commanders mustered their fleets and organised the defence. Thankfully, ten years of constant war had ensured that incompetent or nationalistic officers had been quietly sidelined before their ships were hurled into the fire. There would be none of the friction, she hoped, that had given the Tadpoles a chance to hurl missiles and kinetic projectiles at Earth.

She took a seat and looked around the chamber. No expense had been spared to craft a compartment that was both efficient and photogenic, although the media had never been allowed in the bunker. A team of operators manned the consoles, absorbing information from right across the country—and orbital installations—and placing it on the big board. It was hard to believe they were accomplishing anything, save perhaps for making the politicians feel a bit better. A state of emergency had already been declared. The Regional Commanders had taken control of their districts. Civilians had been ordered to stay in their homes...Susan feared, as she waited, that many civilians wouldn't listen. The days when the automated traffic control system could simply deactivate every car on the road were long gone. Too many people had learnt the wrong lessons from the bombardment. One had been that the government couldn't be relied upon in a crisis.

And that staying near the water is asking for death, if the virus bombards the oceans again, she thought. The virus might not *want* to carry out a major planetary bombardment—there was no point in slaughtering prospective host bodies—but once missiles started exploding in orbit it would be just a matter of time before debris started raining on Earth. *Anyone with a car and some common sense will be trying to make their way to higher ground.*

She forced herself to pay attention as the display constantly updated, notifying her that defences were online—soldiers had been hastily recalled to their barracks, then deployed away from prospective targets—and that pre-recorded messages had gone out, time and time again, on the datanet. The datanet itself had been hardened, in the years since the bombardment, in hopes of preventing panic by keeping the civilian population informed. Susan doubted it would work—the blunt truth was that the government might not know what was going on, either—but it was worth a try. If the civilian population blocked the roads in large numbers, it would rapidly become impossible to move troops. The virus would have all the time it needed to land their own troops and begin infecting the local population. And once it got a firm beachhead, it was all too likely it would be impossible to stop.

The PM said nothing as he sat next to her. Susan was mildly impressed. In her experience, politicians *liked* to pretend they were in control. They struck poses that wouldn't have been out of place in a secondary school play, overacting to the point it was difficult to believe anyone would take them seriously. But there were no cameras in the bunker, no audience to play to. The only witnesses were the bunker's staff, the close-protection detail and Susan herself. None of *them* would talk if the PM did nothing during the crisis. It wasn't as if there was anything for him to do.

He cleared his throat. "Explain it to me," he said. "What's going on?"

Susan took a moment to carefully consider her words. The giant status display was almost childishly simplistic, from a military point of view, but it was still hard to follow if one didn't know how it worked. The lack of detail wasn't always an advantage. She studied the icons, silently tracing the alien fleet back to the tramlines. It might well have been dispatched, given the timing, before Operation Lightning Strike had punched into enemy space and forced the virus to defend itself. That would have galled her, if she'd been in command of the enemy fleet. It was quite possible the advancing fleet had intended to use the catapults to attack the homeworld, but simply adjusted the plans after the catapults had been captured and destroyed. The alien ships might not even *know* their systems had come under attack. They were well outside the virus's flicker network.

"One fleet is boring straight towards Earth," she said, finally. "Our defences are assembling to meet it. The second intends to take out the shipyards."

She frowned as the vectors continued to update. It was difficult to get hard data on the alien fleet—it was flying in close formation, harmonised drive and masking fields blurring together until they seemed a single, oversized starship—but it was clearly large and powerful. There were no starfighters, which suggested the virus was waiting for the range to close before it deployed them. She doubted the fleet would have been dispatched *without* starfighters. The virus's pilots didn't have the flexibility of their human counterparts, but quantity had a quality all of its own. And there was almost certainly at least one brainship in the fleet to handle command and coordination.

An officer hurried over to join them. "Prime Minister, the regional command posts are up and running," he said. "We have a direct link to the secret bunker, which stands ready to take command if this location is compromised."

Taken out, Susan translated, wryly. *Anything powerful enough to cut the command links will certainly do one hell of a lot of damage to the city above, as well as the bunker itself.*

The PM frowned. "What about the people?"

"The majority appear to be heeding the warnings and staying put," the officer assured him. "The remainder are being steered off the motorways to make room for military convoys."

Susan winced. A short emergency—a few hours or so—wouldn't be a major problem. The country could handle it, particularly if the alien fleet was beaten back before it managed to target Earth itself. But a long state of emergency...? The general public had long been advised to keep at least a week's worth of food in their homes, along with emergency supplies, but Susan was painfully aware that not everyone would have complied with the instructions. Her father's apartment had been so small that keeping a supply of canned food and ration bars would have stretched him to the limit. And with the shops shut, and orders being sent out to keep them shut until new rationing procedures could be sorted out, it was just a matter of time before people started to starve.

The PM looked at her. "There's nothing we can do, is there?"

"No." Susan shook her head. "All we can do is wait."

• • •

"Report," Mitch snapped.

Staci looked up from her console. "There is a sizable enemy fleet approaching the shipyards," she said. "It's impossible to pick out details at this range, thanks to their masking effect, but I'd say there's at least four battleships and two fleet carriers within the haze."

Mitch frowned as he studied the display. The virus could have sneaked a great deal closer before revealing its presence and opening fire, although there were so many sensor platforms surrounding the shipyards—both British and allied installations—that the chances of detection would have been quite high. He stroked his chin, wondering if the virus was up to something. It might have been trying to draw the defenders out of position…which might have worked, if there had been more defenders. The Hamilton Yards relied on their fixed defences. There were only nine mobile units—counting *Lion* and *Unicorn*—attached to the yards.

"Cloak us," he ordered. *Unicorn* was tiny, compared to the cluster of free-floating installations. The shipyard pumped out so many emissions that the virus must be a bit blinded. It was possible the virus hadn't even *noticed* his ship. Not yet. "Establish a laser link to *Lion*."

"Aye, Captain," Staci said.

"Helm, take us out of the shipyard," Mitch ordered. "And steer us on an angular course towards the alien ships."

"Aye, Captain."

Mitch felt the tension as the frigate hummed to life. She'd be obliterated in an instant if a single battleship drew a bead on her…and they were about to fly directly towards four of them. At *least* four, he reminded himself. The alien drive signatures were overlapping to the point it was hard to be sure there weren't more. *Lion* would need targeting data before she opened fire, data only *Unicorn* could supply. The only upside, as far as Mitch could see, was the simple fact the shipyard's emissions would be overlapping, too. The virus would have problems picking its targets.

It might also find it difficult to pick *Lion* out of the haze before the battlecruiser started shooting.

Although it might have had the system under covert observation for quite some time, he thought, grimly. *It couldn't have picked a better time to attack.*

The display sharpened as *Unicorn* glided through the outermost defence ring and headed towards the alien fleet. Mitch felt sweat prickling on his back as more and more starships came into view, passive sensors revealing no less than *five* battleships, one brainship, and a dozen smaller ships. They didn't appear to have any carriers, something that puzzled him. The virus was going to need them when the shipyard's squadrons came boiling towards the alien fleet, baying for blood. There were nearly a *thousand* starfighters assigned to the defenders...

"Captain," Staci said. "There are two ships of unknown configuration within the alien fleet. I cannot determine their purpose."

Mitch scowled as he examined the live feed. The alien ships were bulky, little bigger than *Lion*, but they didn't look like warships. And yet, who'd throw freighters into the teeth of enemy defences? Freighters weren't warships, a lesson the Royal Navy had learnt during the First Interstellar War. The virus was either desperate—and he wanted to believe it was desperate—or it was up to something. It certainly didn't *seem* to have brought enough guns to the coming gunfight. The enemy force was powerful, but nothing the defenders couldn't handle.

Tearing the shipyards apart would cripple us, he reflected. *You'd think they'd place more insistence on doing it.*

His scowl deepened as the situation continued to develop. The alien fleet was launching starfighters, readying itself to engage the planetary defences. Mitch contemplated, for a moment, the prospect of the invasion fleet being little more than a diversion, then shook his head. He'd taken part in training exercises, back before his assignment to *Unicorn*. The defenders wouldn't let themselves be drawn out of position, even if there was a chance of destroying the entire alien fleet. The virus wasn't human. It wouldn't hesitate to sacrifice entire fleets if it advanced its overall goal.

And yet, he had the feeling he was missing something.

"Launch probes on ballistic trajectories, then alter course randomly," he ordered. It was possible the virus would detect the probes launching, particularly given there was a brainship in command of the fleet. "Direct them to skim past the unknown ships."

"Aye, Captain," Staci said.

Mitch silently counted down the seconds as the probes raced away from his ship. They were barely moving, compared to the alien ships, but the range was steadily closing. The live feed grew sharper, allowing him to study the unknown ships. They really *did* look like freighters, although someone had installed military-grade drives. Mitch didn't understand what he was seeing and he didn't like it. The virus wouldn't have risked purpose-built fleet tenders unless it had a very good reason.

It's being stupid, he thought. *And we know it isn't...*

His mind raced. The virus was practically charging right into the teeth of the shipyard's defences. It was going to lose a lot of ships even if it managed to ram right through the outer layer and bring its weapons to bear on the shipyard itself. And...even if it didn't know about *Lion*...

It hit him, suddenly. "Priority signal, to *Lion*," he snapped. "Those freighters are missile carriers!"

He had no proof, but he knew he was right. It wasn't easy to reconfigure a battleship to carry internal missile tubes, certainly not in vast numbers. *Lion* had been built from scratch and *her* designers had had to argue with naval officers who feared she'd be nothing more than a paper tiger, her unusual design suggesting her internal backbone could be broken by a single missile hit. The virus certainly had enough missiles to fill a battlecruiser, and it could easily have copied *Lion's* design, but if it hadn't had the time...

"Captain," Staci said. "The enemy ships are scanning us."

"Evasive action," Mitch snapped. He'd hoped to get closer, but the virus had picked them out against the haze. "Deploy drones, prepare them to go live on my command."

"Aye, Captain," Staci said. "I…"

The display sparkled with red light. Mitch sucked in his breath. He'd been right. The freighters *were* missile carriers. They'd just launched a massive barrage at the shipyard. He guessed a number of missiles had been launched on ballistic trajectories, relying on their faster peers to draw attention while they sneaked through the defences and went active when they reached point-blank range. The enemy fleet was adjusting its position, deploying more and more sensor drones and decoys. It looked, very much, as though the virus had learnt from its previous engagements. It had not only copied the Royal Navy's tactics, he noted, but improved upon them.

"They have target lock," Staci snapped. "They're launching missiles at us."

"Overkill," Mitch noted. The virus didn't *have* to blow them to hell. Perhaps it thought *Unicorn* was the sole source of targeting data. If they were lucky, it would miss the sensor probes before it was too late. "Send a final update to *Lion*, then activate the decoy drones."

"Aye, Captain."

And hope to hell Captain Hammond is on the ball, Mitch thought, with a flicker of gallows humour. The irony of relying on the man he'd cuckolded would have been amusing, if there hadn't been a tidal wave of death roaring towards the shipyard. If they lost the shipyard, the war might be lost with it. *If he can't keep them away from the yard, we're doomed.*

• • •

Thomas had expected that, sooner or later, the virus would deploy its own missile-heavy battlecruisers. It had seen the concept in action, during Operation Thunder Child and Operation Lightning Strike; it certainly seemed to favour the idea of using wave upon wave of missiles to overwhelm point defences and slam into enemy targets. And yet, he had to admit the virus's trick had caught him by surprise. He'd assumed the virus would want to construct something akin to *Lion*. The idea of putting missile tubes on freighters had never occurred to him.

But it does make a good stopgap solution, he thought. The freighters were still pumping out missiles at a terrifying rate, but once they shot themselves dry they were effectively worthless. They'd be blown away within seconds if they tried to remain in the line of battle. And yet, he had to admit the concept worked. *They caught us with our pants down.*

He pushed the thought out of his mind. "Tactical, do we have updated targeting data from *Unicorn*?"

"Yes, Captain," Sibley said. The display updated, showing the live feed from the frigate. The enemy fleet was clearly visible, no longer a mystery. "We have solid locks on all enemy targets. The gunboats are moving into position now."

"Order the gunboats to counter the enemy missiles," Thomas ordered. The shipyard *had* to be protected, even if it meant allowing the enemy fleet to retreat unmolested. He might have to risk leaving his own ship uncovered, just to keep the rest of the facilities safe. "On my command, open fire."

He braced himself. A vast salvo of missiles was roaring down on the shipyard's defences. They would be easy targets, but there were just so *many* of them. They had to stop them all before it was too late. Nuclear explosions within the shipyard would do a great deal of damage even if they didn't actually *hit* something. The blasts would blind sensors and make it easier for the follow-up missiles to get through the defences…

"Open fire," he said.

CHAPTER TWELVE

"I THINK I'M SEEING THINGS," Gunboat Pilot Tully said. "*How many missiles are there?*"

"Keep the channel clear," Tobias ordered, sharply. He understood the urge to chat—God knew, he'd spent hours chatting while playing online games—but the more transmissions they made, the greater the chance of being detected and blown away. There were so many missiles roaring towards their position that he honestly feared one of the gunboats would collide with a missile. "Focus on your job."

He gritted his teeth. He'd hoped to have longer before the squadron actually went into battle. He'd hoped they'd have time to practice more… he scowled, dismissing the thought with a flicker of irritation. The planned departure schedule had changed three times—at least—over the last week, convincing him that no one knew when they'd be *actually* leaving. He had no doubt his pilots knew how to fly—they wouldn't have graduated if they hadn't passed the tests—but none of them had been in a fight before. They'd needed more time.

They're not going to get it, he told himself, savagely. *And you have to do everything in your power to keep them alive.*

The display updated time and time again, alien missiles blurring together until it looked as if a solid wall was bearing down on him. Tobias *knew* there'd be gaps between the missiles and yet it was hard to escape the impression they were doomed, that there was nothing they could do to avoid certain death. He heard someone whimper over the communications link and deliberately didn't look to see who it was, knowing he hadn't felt much better during his first real engagement. He'd thought Bagehot had just watched and shouted advice from the sidelines. He'd never realised just how much work the CAG had put into his job, or how badly it had cost him when a handful of pilots were killed in action...

He forced the thought out of his mind as his hand danced across the console, preparing the gunboat's point defence. Their only advantage, as far as he could tell, was the lack of enemy starfighters. It was unlikely the missiles were specifically targeted on the gunboats. The enemy planners—he grimaced as the brainship continued to lumber towards the shipyard—might not even have realised the gunboats were there. If they were lucky, they'd thin out the wave of missiles enough to give the remainder of the defences a chance to stop them completely. The incoming ships would notice the gunboats the moment they opened fire, but they'd still have to close the range to bring their point defence to bear. Tobias hoped they'd have enough time to escape before they were picked off one by one.

"Fire at will," he ordered. "I say again, fire at will."

The channel crackled. "Who's Will?"

Tobias rolled his eyes—the joke had stopped being funny years ago—as he tapped the firing key. No human mind could cope with the sheer *speed* of the engagement, even though most of the missiles were flying on very predictable trajectories. They had to rely on the computers to pick their targets, spot openings and take shots...he was all too aware, after countless exercises, that the risk of accidentally hitting another gunboat or a friendly missile was terrifyingly high. Even the computers didn't have time to be *entirely* sure of their targets. He didn't know how he'd live with himself if he accidentally killed two of his fellow pilots...

Your subordinates, he reminded himself, as enemy missiles started to vanish. *You're responsible for them.*

Time seemed to slow down as the wall of missiles raced up to the gunboats and swept past them, continuing towards the shipyard. Tobias watched dozens—hundreds—of missiles fall to the gunboats, vanishing from the display as they were picked off, only for hundreds more to rush out of range before they could be targeted. The enemy fleet slowed, as if it had no interest in challenging the defences directly. Tobias thought they were waiting to see if the missiles did any real damage, before pushing on or simply withdrawing. Their point defence was going online too, ready to defend the fleet against *Lion's* missiles. Tobias gritted his teeth. The gunboats were too far from the missiles to provide accurate targeting data. They'd just have to hope they could get through the enemy formation on their own.

Marigold cleared her throat. "How many did we lose?"

Tobias looked down at his console. "None," he said. "We...we survived."

He felt his heart clench. He'd known the names and faces of everyone on his first deployment—and it had hurt, more than he cared to admit, when they'd died. He'd known enough about them to feel they were real people, rather than just...names. He'd made a point of learning as little as possible about the other pilots on his second deployment, of thinking of them as nothing more than shadows rather than real people. And now... he'd had to read files and match names to faces and know, deep inside, that his subordinates were real. They had names and faces and lives and family histories and...he shook his head, trying to push the thought out of his head. It was just a matter of time until someone died. He almost hoped it was him. He had no idea how he'd cope with losing a subordinate.

"I'm linking to the active sensor platforms," he said. The odds were good the virus had hurled a handful of ballistic missiles as well as the tidal wave of active missiles, relying on the lack of sensor emissions to hide them from the defences. "If there are any more missiles coming our way, we have to find them."

"Got it," Marigold said. "And now we wait for orders."

. . .

Thomas made a mental note, if he survived the next few hours, to make it clear to the Admiralty that Commodore Dursley should have been reassigned long ago. The man was a gifted administrator, and smart enough to allow his design and construction teams to have a certain degree of independence, but he was no combat commander. He'd dithered a little too long when the enemy fleet arrived, then overreacted by launching his starfighters immediately and bringing all his defences online. Thomas didn't blame him for being seriously concerned, given the importance of the shipyard, but a more measured response might have given the enemy considerably less information. The active sensor platforms were already being targeted for destruction.

He watched, grimly, as the enemy missiles roared through the defences. They were making no attempt to hide their targets, throwing themselves straight at the construction slips and fabrication nodes instead of the defending battlestations or personnel quarters. The virus seemed to have gained some inside information, he noted; the targeting pattern had skipped over a handful of facilities that looked impressive, but didn't matter too much in the greater scheme of things. A zombie, he guessed; someone who'd been so thoroughly infected that the virus had been able to draw information from their brain. The defences were breaking down the missile formations, slicing through the onslaught like a knife through butter, but there were always more. It looked as if the entire shipyard was doomed.

A missile slammed into a construction ship, triggering off a series of explosions that consumed a half-built battleship. Another struck a nearly-completed carrier, although most of the blast was wasted on the armour. Four more lanced into a fabrication node, vaporising it and setting off another set of explosions. Thomas cursed under his breath as a second node exploded, silently calculating how long it would take to replace the destroyed facilities. The shipyard was going to need months, at best, assuming they had time to do anything before the virus resumed the offensive. Replacing the destroyed ships was going to take even longer.

Hell, replacing the dead personnel would take years. It would take...

He pushed the thought aside and watched as his missiles tore into the enemy formation. The targeting patterns had been good, practically perfect, but the enemy ships were still crammed with point defence. The brainship staggered under his fire, yet somehow managed to remain underway. A lone battleship fell out of formation, its drive field wallowing out of control; the remainder seemed unharmed by the bombardment. Thomas snapped orders, directing his ship to keep firing. They couldn't risk allowing the alien fleet to close with the shipyard.

"Signal from Earth, sir," Lieutenant Cook said. The communications officer sounded grim. "Home Fleet has engaged the alien ships. They cannot spare any relief for us."

Thomas had expected as much—Earth *had* to be protected—but it was still bad news. The fleet attacking the shipyard was waiting, assessing the damage...the only upside, as far as he could tell, was that it had apparently shot itself dry. God, he *hoped* that was true. The virus had fired so many missiles in its first volley alone that it was impossible to see how they'd stand against a second wave, unless it was significantly reduced. The railgun sniping was a pain—he cursed Dursley under his breath for revealing too many prospective targets to the enemy—but it wasn't going to be fatal. If the alien fleet decided to engage the shipyard directly...

He frowned. "Signal *Unicorn*," he ordered. "Order Captain Campbell to deploy Ghost Fleet."

"Aye, Captain."

• • •

Mitch kept a wary eye on the display as the range between *Unicorn* and the alien fleet continued to widen. The virus had lost its sensor lock some time ago—and it had other problems, as *Lion's* missiles were tearing into its defences—but Mitch didn't feel reassured. The alien virus was dangerously unpredictable. It might be concentrating on the shipyard, which had to be the primary target, but it might also have something nasty up its sleeve. The thought of a giant blob wearing a shirt made him smile, even though he knew it wasn't funny. The virus was so alien it wasn't clear if it had ever been *inside* the box.

"Signal from *Lion*, sir," Midshipman David Culver reported. "Commodore Hammond's compliments, sir, and he wants you to deploy Ghost Fleet."

Mitch nodded, curtly. "Tactical, deploy Ghost Fleet drones."

"Aye, Captain," Staci said.

Mitch frowned. The virus's ships had almost come to a halt, relative to the shipyard. It was impossible to tell what they were intending to do. If they'd wanted to break through the defences, they should have been speeding up...he glanced at the long-range display and scowled as he realised the truth. The virus was waiting for the first fleet to complete the destruction of Earth, then join the remainder of its ships before finishing the job. He had to admit it was a neat solution to its tactical dilemma. If the first fleet won, they could destroy the shipyard; if it lost, the second fleet could withdraw without further ado. And if it could be driven away...

It might not fall for the same trick twice, he told himself. *It must have realised we fooled it during the last operation.*

"The drones are in place," Staci said. "Ready to go active on your command."

"Go active," Mitch ordered. "And steer them right towards the alien position."

We mustn't give them any time to think, he thought, although he doubted it was possible to force the virus to panic. The xenospecialists had produced a whole series of speculative articles on the capabilities of the brainships, each more alarming than the last. There was certainly no doubting their tactical acumen or their sheer alienness, their utter lack of concern for their own skins. *If we can't force them to panic, they'll just stay where they are and keep sniping.*

The display sparkled with hazy icons. Staci had done a good job, angling the drones so the Ghost Fleet appeared to have come directly from the asteroid field. There would be a ready-made answer if—when—it occurred to the virus to ask why the relief fleet hadn't headed directly to Earth. And yet…he gritted his teeth. If he'd had a fleet of ten battleships— ten *real* battleships—under his command, he might just have headed to Earth anyway. The homeworld wasn't as important as it had been, a few short decades ago, but it couldn't be abandoned. The idea of simply allowing the virus to devastate Earth was horrific.

He waited, watching grimly as the seconds ticked down to zero. They had a very short window of opportunity for the virus to alter course and retreat before the ghostly ships closed the range to the point they needed to open fire. They couldn't, of course. The virus would *know* they were sensor drones, the moment they didn't fire. Mitch silently braced himself, hoping the analysts were right. If the virus was showing a new sensitivity to losses, it might just decide to quit while it was ahead…

"Captain," Staci said. "The enemy ships are altering course."

Mitch breathed a sigh of relief. The virus's ships would escape—there was no hope of catching them and no hope of actually killing them if they did—but at least the remnants of the shipyard would remain intact. He silently congratulated Hammond for thinking of the tactic, even though he knew the battle wasn't over yet. The alien ships could simply lurk on the edge of the system until their fellows retreated from Earth, or circle around the shipyard to head to Earth themselves. It wasn't a pleasant thought. Earth's defenders were already fighting for their lives. They didn't need more enemies.

Nor do we, Mitch thought. *Nor do we.*

• • •

The battle—or at least their section of it—was over as soon as the alien ships broke contact, running from a relief fleet that simply couldn't exist. Tobias wondered, as the gunboats swept the space around the shipyard for other threats, if the virus had been fooled or if it had simply decided it had done quite enough damage for one day. It had certainly dumped hundreds of makeshift mines and stealthed sensor platforms in the vicinity, a tactic that would normally be worse than useless. It had worked here. There was no way to avoid steering hundreds of shuttles and starships through a relatively small region of space, giving the mines a chance to actually *hit* something...

He breathed a sigh of relief as they received the recall order, then commanded his squadron to return to their mothership. The engagement felt as though it had taken hours, perhaps days, although he knew it couldn't have been more than an hour or two at most. Repair crews were already swarming the shipyard, trying to sort out what could be patched up in a hurry and what needed to be left for later, when the navy had time to do it properly. It was a chilling sight. Tobias was no expert on naval logistics, but he'd played enough online games to know what happened when a player lost his industrial base. The end simply could not be delayed for very long.

"We got lucky," he said, as they docked. "We could have lost everyone."

"Better not to dwell on that," Marigold advised. "They did well. None of us expected to be pitched into battle here, did we?"

Tobias shook his head, releasing himself from the chair and standing on wobbly legs. His shipsuit was drenched. He needed a shower...he checked the tactical display and decided, after a moment's thought, that the squadron would have at least an hour before the next engagement. The maintenance crews would need that long to check the craft and prepare them for redeployment. He tapped his wristcom, ordering the squadron pilots to make their way to the briefing room, then glanced at Marigold. He wanted to take her in his arms and kiss her and...

There's a battle going on, he reminded himself, curtly. *It would be a very bad time for us to be caught with our pants down.*

He smiled at her, then clambered through the hatch and walked into the briefing room. His pilots looked as if they'd been through hell. Their faces were streaked with sweat, their hair was a mess—he reminded himself to suggest that some of the pilots get a haircut—and one had even wet himself. Tobias pretended to ignore it and hoped everyone else would have the sense to do the same. It was hard to blame the poor bastard when he'd done it himself, back at the academy. It seemed to be a rite of passage for pilots.

"Get a shower and grab something to eat, then wait in the squadron room," he ordered. There was no point in trying to give an inspirational speech. It would fall on deaf ears. "Try to relax, but don't go to your bunks. You might be needed again."

He winced, inwardly, as they shuffled towards the hatch. They looked as if they'd been beaten down and battered, repeatedly...a failure on his part? He shook his head, although part of him felt responsible anyway. Perhaps it would have been better to mingle new pilots with experienced hands, rather than...he sighed. It hadn't been his decision.

Marigold entered, looked surprisingly perky. "What did you say to them?"

"Shower. Relax. Be ready." Tobias grinned at her. "Were we ever that young?"

"I think we looked worse," Marigold said. "At least these pilots are not charging headlong into the unknown."

Tobias checked the console. "The battle is still going on," he said. "If we're called to join the defence of Earth..."

Marigold nodded. "We'll see," she said. "Take it as it comes."

CHAPTER THIRTEEN

SUSAN RUBBED HER FOREHEAD as she passed through the security checkpoint, made her way through the corridors and stepped into the Prime Minister's office. She'd spent the last three days in the bunker, without even the slightest exposure to the outside world, but the PM's close-protection detail had insisted on everyone going through the standard security checks anyway. It was irritating, particularly when they insisted on checking and rechecking her blood to make sure she was not infected, but she couldn't blame them for being paranoid. A handful of zombies had appeared at the worst possible time, doing a great deal of damage to the defenders before being shot down. The virus's fleet had been beaten off, and forced to retreat, but it had left a shattered world and a number of ruined installations in its wake.

She winced, inwardly, as she saw the Prime Minister. He looked as haggard as she felt. He'd spent two days speaking to the country, trying to reassure people who were in no mood to listen, and another day having high-level discussions with a number of other world leaders. It was rare for them to handle such matters themselves—normally, they were left to diplomats who could be quietly disavowed if necessary—and mistakes could have deadly consequences. The aftermath of the brief but savage engagement had reminded the planet of the need to hang together or hang separately, yet there were just too many humans who were incapable of working together against a common foe.

At least the military worked in perfect unison, she thought. The engagement had been shorter than she'd feared, the virus probing the defences and bombarding the orbital installations before retreating again, but it had been a close-run thing. *If we hadn't managed to hold the line, all of Earth could have been infected by now.*

"Admiral," the PM said. A steward poured coffee for them both, then retreated. "I'm afraid I have bad news."

Susan kept her face expressionless. It was unlikely anyone could blame *her* for the engagement. She hadn't been in tactical command. Admiral Northgate had handled the defence and done about as well as could be expected, under the circumstances. The American had done a good job, from what she'd seen. The post-battle assessment teams—and entire armies of armchair admirals—might disagree, but that wasn't her problem. No, she wasn't in trouble personally. She had a nasty feeling, though, that it might have been preferable. She feared she knew what was coming.

"GATO has refused to supply ships for Operation Footfall," the PM said. "They feel that we need to concentrate on home defence."

"To stand on the defensive permanently is effectively conceding eventual defeat," Susan said, feeling her heart sink. She'd heard the arguments through the flag officer networks, listened to discussions of how best to proceed…she wondered, sourly, which of the old women of both genders had bent GATO's ear. "We have only a short window of opportunity to carry out the operation."

"Regardless, GATO is unwilling to supply the ships," the PM said. "And the Royal Navy is also reluctant to make a significant contribution."

Susan tried not to show her dismay. Politics had always cast a long shadow over military operations, but she'd thought *this* war was different. She kicked herself, mentally, as she hastily reassessed what she knew of the current situation. Several MPs were due to stand down at the next elections, while several others were in shaky seats. If three or four seats were to be flipped, the PM would find himself in an untenable position. The war cabinet would have to change to reflect the new balance of power... she recalled, suddenly, that Lady Charlotte had already announced her bid for election. If she became an MP, it would definitely put the cat amongst the pigeons.

She took a breath. "With all due respect, Prime Minister, we cannot afford *not* to launch the operation," she said. "We still don't have a solid damage assessment, but even in a best-case scenario we're looking at a severe drop in industrial production for at least nine months. Really, sir, that is the ludicrously optimistic scenario. We might not be able to rebuild for at least five years, by which time the war might have ended badly."

"I understand your argument," the PM said. "But the fact remains that we simply don't have the international or interplanetary support to launch the operation, nor do I have the political backing to mount the operation on our own. Parliament is hearing from the voters, Admiral, and the voters want to be safe. They don't want to watch helplessly as the Royal Navy sails off to a distant star, leaving them on their own."

"The remaining navies would protect them," Susan pointed out. She knew she was going to lose the argument, but it wasn't in her to simply give up. "It isn't as if we'd be leaving ourselves naked."

"Not in any real sense, no," the PM agreed. "But in a political sense, I'm sorry to say, that is exactly what we *would* be doing. We cannot afford to risk a major governmental upheaval, which is what *will* happen if we try to mount the operation alone. We can—and we will—reach out to the Tadpoles and our other allies, but even so we would be short on options and we certainly wouldn't be calling the shots."

Which wouldn't make the operation any easier to sell to the rest of the government, Susan thought. *The thought of us not being an equal partner wouldn't sit well with them.*

She composed herself. Her old mentor—Prince Henry—had once explained that politics was just like war. The written rules weren't any good as long as they weren't enforced across the board. Political figures would do anything, in a world where everything was perfectly legal as long as they didn't get caught. Even then…exposure didn't always mean the end of a career. Someone with the ability to talk the hindlegs off a donkey, or call in favours from other political figures, might be able to remain in power long enough to escape the scandal. It was a rotten system, he'd explained, but it could be manipulated. The secret was to always bear in mind that people were always self-interested. A good political bargain ensured that everyone got what they wanted.

"Without GATO, it is clear we cannot launch Footfall-II," Susan said, calmly. "However, we can still proceed with Footfall-I while working to build up political support for Footfall-II."

The PM eyed her thoughtfully. "It would still mean sending ships away from home defence."

"Two ships, the *Lion* and the *Unicorn*, aren't going to make much difference, not if the virus returns in force," Susan said. The analysts were arguing—loudly—that the alien fleet had been on its way before the Lightning Strike fleet had returned home, but the timing didn't quite work out. "And if we can cripple the virus's efforts to rebuild its fleets, we can keep it off balance long enough to repair the damage here and go on the offensive."

"If," the Prime Minister said. "What if you're wrong?"

"If the plan works, Virus Prime will be destroyed and the virus will be crippled," Susan said, flatly. "If the plan fails, because there are more infected worlds on the same scale, we'll still have thrown a spanner into the virus's works. And if the plan fails with both ships being lost, sir, it won't make any major difference. They don't represent enough mobile firepower to save our homeworld."

"Or doom it, by not being there," the Prime Minister said. "I take your point."

Susan watched him carefully. She could practically *see* the thoughts swirling through his mind. His career had been dented, even though nothing that had happened in the last few days could be reasonably blamed on him. His ambitious subordinates were already sharpening their knives. The general public would vote for whoever promised them safety, for whoever promised to bring the navy home to stand in defence of the planet from all possible threats. The Leader of the Opposition wouldn't find it easy to *keep* those promises, if he became PM, but by then it would be too late. The Prime Minister's career was doomed unless he did something brilliant. Deploying a pair of ships on a low-risk, high-reward mission might just work.

She felt dirty, even though she could justify—rationalise—everything she'd said, everything she'd thought. She knew she was taking a risk, that she was urging the PM to send two ships and over a thousand spacers against an entire system that was so heavily defended it might be impossible for her ships to get into position to start the bombardment. She knew it would be hellishly dangerous, even if Captains Hammond and Campbell didn't hate each other…she knew she'd never feel clean again, even though she couldn't think of an alternative. The war had to be won. If they gave the virus a chance to recover, the war might be lost instead.

And that will be the end, she reminded herself, again and again. *The end of everything we hold dear.*

The Prime Minister met her eyes. "What are the odds?"

"Not great," Susan said. "But better than doing nothing."

She paused. "And we can work on freeing up additional ships to support the operation once they are on their way."

"I see." The Prime Minister seemed to hesitate. "If the operation fails…"

Susan said nothing. All of Earth – plus the entire human race—was staring complete and total destruction in the face. They *had* to gamble. If they bought time…it would be enough, she hoped, to save the human race. It had to be.

And your career is roundly fucked, she thought, coldly. *You have to roll the die, too.*

"Very well," the Prime Minister said. "Footfall-I is authorised. The two ships are to depart as soon as their magazines are replenished, then proceed straight to the target. You and I"—his lips curved into something that might, charitably, have been called a smile—"will do what we can to get them some support."

"Yes, sir," Susan said. "With your permission, I'll get started at once."

"And try and keep the operation a secret as long as possible," the Prime Minister added. "We don't want someone getting in the way."

Or launching a bid to get you on the wrong side of a vote of no confidence, Susan added, silently. She understood…she just detested it. *That cannot be allowed to happen until the operation is well underway.*

• • •

"Captain," Lieutenant Cook said. "Admiral Onarina is calling on a priority channel."

"I'll take it in my ready room," Thomas said. "Commander Donker, you have the conn."

"Aye, Captain," Donker said.

Thomas nodded as he stepped into the ready room, relaxing slightly as he heard the hatch close behind him. It had been a hard few days, even after the alien fleet had withdrawn to the tramline and vanished. The shipyard had been devastated, forcing his marines to evacuate injured men from damaged sections while his gunboats swept local space for mines, sensor platforms and other unpleasant surprises. Mines were so rare, in space warfare, that no one had ever seriously expected to see them outside mission simulations. The gunboats simply hadn't trained to hunt for mines. In hindsight, he reflected, the assumption that mines were useless would have to be revisited. It had clearly been proven badly flawed.

He pressed his hand against the terminal as he took his seat. The screen blanked, a handful of icons flashing in and out of existence to remind him that the call was on a priority channel and that anything spoken was, legally, a state secret. It struck him as extreme—anyone who had access to priority channels should damn well *know* they were top secret—but it made the bureaucrats feel important. Besides, the system might not be foolproof. In his experience, there was always someone dumb enough to break the rules for a reason that made sense to them, if no one else.

"Captain." Admiral Onarina's face appeared in front of him. A moment later, the screen split in two and Captain Campbell appeared beside her. "Captains. I'm sorry I don't have time to call you back to Earth."

"We understand," Captain Campbell said. "How bad is it?"

"Bad enough that I have to speak freely," Admiral Onarina said. "There are a number of details we have to go through, quickly. You'll receive your formal orders later. The bad news is that Operation Footfall has changed…"

Thomas listened in disbelief as Admiral Onarina outlined the change. The idea of taking a handful of ships into the very heart of the virus's empire and raining death in its homeworld was bad enough, but going without any kind of support…even Captain Campbell looked daunted. Thomas would have found that amusing, if he hadn't been so tired and worn down. It was…it was going to be difficult. Very difficult.

"You'll have a small fleet train attached to your command," Admiral Onarina concluded. "I think it would be best if this wasn't discussed openly, although—with the majority of the fleet remaining here—fast fleet tenders can be reassigned without impeding operational requirements. You are to get your ships ready as quickly as possible, then depart without fanfare once your orders arrive. I won't give you specifics. I believe you two can be trusted to determine how best to proceed, once you reach the target system. Do as much damage as you can."

Her dark eyes narrowed. "The odds are not in your favour. Two warships may not be enough to bring down the system, let alone remain uncaught long enough to do real damage to the planetary installations. It is not easy to send both of you—and your ships—on a mission that could easily result in utter disaster. I have never"—she paused, clearly rethinking what she was about to say—"I want you to bear in mind that everything you do to buy us time will help save the human race."

And even if we die, it will be worthwhile if the human race as a whole survives, Thomas thought. He'd known the risks, even before the plan had changed. He had accepted them. It would have been easy, very easy, to avoid any real danger, when he'd started his military service. Instead, he'd chosen a career in which the risks of a violent death were quite high. *We knew the job was dangerous when we took it.*

"We knew it was a dangerous job when we took it," Captain Campbell said, echoing Thomas's thoughts. "And we know we're expendable."

The admiral grimaced. Thomas felt a flicker of pity. The admiral would have to live with the guilt if neither of them, and their ships, made it home. She was hardly an uncaring calculator, hardly unwilling to accept her subordinates were living people. She knew she was sending them into grave danger, perhaps straight to their deaths. Thomas understood. She wanted to come with them. And yet, there was no figleaf they could use to allow her to join them. It wouldn't look good.

And what does it matter, he asked himself, *if the mission fails and the human race dies?*

"You are to do everything in your power to hurt the enemy, but you are not to throw your lives away," Admiral Onarina said. "I don't want you dead."

Captain Campbell grinned. "It is sweet and fitting to die for one's country," he said, "but it is even more fitting to make the other bloke die for *his* country."

"That will do," Thomas snapped. Resentment bubbled up within him. "You…"

"*Enough.*" Admiral Onarina raised her voice, making them both jump. "I know you have your differences, but I need you to put them aside. You can kill each other after the war, if you want. Now…work together. Or else."

"Yes, Admiral," Captain Campbell said.

"Get your ships ready to depart," Admiral Onarina said. "Once your orders arrive, you are to take possession of the fleet train and leave as soon as possible. And just remember…"

She paused, looking down. "If you do this, it will save billions of lives," she said. "Good luck."

"Thank you, Admiral," Thomas said,

The channel closed. Thomas sat back in his chair as the other two vanished, feeling torn between excitement and a dull deadening numbness. He'd seen the mission plans, but…he shook his head, firmly. He had his orders and he had to carry them out, even if he felt they were…unwise. And if they failed…

"Failure is not an option," he muttered. He keyed his terminal. "Communications?"

"Yes, sir?"

"Contact Captain Campbell," Thomas said. It gnawed at him to extend any sort of olive branch to the man who'd seduced his wife, or been seduced by her, but he had no choice. "Invite him to a private dinner, this evening. And then inform the command crew that we'll be meeting at 1500 in the conference room."

"Aye, Captain."

CHAPTER FOURTEEN

IT WAS HARD, MITCH DECIDED as the shuttle glided towards HMS *Lion*, not to giggle at the sheer insanity of the situation. It was like a ridiculous period drama, in which modern-day sensibilities and shameless nudity collided with aspects of the past that made no sense to modern man. A society in which women had the same rights as men, but were also married off to the highest bidder or placed under the control of evil stepmothers or creepy uncles? It had made no sense to him, when he'd been a child. He'd certainly not felt the urge to linger in the past. Besides, as hard as life had been for the aristocracy, it had been a great deal harder for the working class.

He schooled his face into impassivity, calming his mind. He was going to have dinner with his lover's husband…he was going to sit down and plan a mission with him, even though Mitch was grimly sure Hammond wanted to call him out or simply send him to certain death. Or something. The last note from Charlotte had hinted her push to be nominated as a prospective MP had gone well, particularly after Mitch's role in the recent battle. He hadn't been anywhere near the *real* fight, he'd pointed out, but she'd ignored him. The truth was always flexible in service of a greater good.

The gravity field flickered as the shuttle docked. Mitch stood, brushing down his uniform as he made his way towards the hatch. It was a simple dinner, he'd been assured. They would be alone. There was no reason to wear his dress uniform. And yet, the paranoid side of his mind wondered if he'd been tricked. He'd met enough aristocratic bastards, men and women raised in the highest levels of society, to know they were experts at weaponsing society's rules against interlopers. The Admiral had said as much, he recalled. He'd checked her service record. Reading between the lines, it was clear she'd had enemies who'd sought to bring her down.

He braced himself as the hatch opened. A pair of suited marines stood in the airlock, one holding a bioscanner. Mitch was tempted to point out that he'd passed through a dozen checkpoints in the time since he'd received orders to return to his ship, but there was no point. The marines were only following orders. And no one, not even an admiral, could override them. There was no way to be sure the admiral wasn't a mask worn by an implacably hostile alien entity.

Commander Donker met him as he stepped through the second hatch. "Captain Campbell. Welcome onboard."

"Thank you," Mitch said.

He kept his face under tight control as they walked through the corridors. He didn't know Commander Donker that well, although it was clear the man was not a fan of his. It was hard to blame him for being wary. Showing more than bare professionalism might draw the ire of his commanding officer, the man on whom his future career depended. Captain Hammond could easily write a report that, on the surface, praised his XO while subtly putting him down, ensuring he never held a command of his own. It was disgusting, but it was a reality of naval life. An XO could not be seen to stand openly against his captain, unless the captain's guilt was beyond question.

Lion thrummed with activity, her crew preparing her for departure. Mitch stepped to one side as teams of crewmen rushed past, shoving pallets of weapons and supplies along the corridor. A handful of yard dogs were talking loudly to the ship's engineers, arguing over precisely how many components needed to be replaced from scratch. They looked as if they feared the ship would leave at any moment, taking them along for the ride. Mitch's lips quirked. There was an episode of *Stellar Star* where she practically kidnapped yard dogs to carry out repairs while her ship was underway, although anyone who tried that in real life would be in deep shit. He could understand the impulse—he wouldn't have cared to take a damaged ship into battle—but he knew better than to give in to it. The general public might approve. The Admiralty would not.

He frowned. The battlecruiser was just too *big*. It was impossible to believe her captain—and his senior officers—knew *everyone* on the ship. Her interior was a maze of compartments, each a world unto itself. Captain Hammond would never know the names and faces of the men under his command, the men who might die...Mitch wasn't sure if that was a good thing. It felt disrespectful to read a man's record, in preparation to writing home after his death, but he had to admit it had its advantages. He knew everyone under his command. Their loss would hurt.

They stopped in front of a simple hatch, which hissed open. Commander Donker looked at him. "The commodore will see you now."

And you're not going to announce me? Mitch found it hard not to smile. *How rude.*

He put the thought out of his mind as he stepped through the hatch, finding himself in an officer's dining room. It was the sort of compartment that had always struck him as wasteful, when the space could be used to store weapons or supplies or even provide more accommodation to junior crew. He dreaded to think how much of the Royal Navy's budget had been wasted, just so captains and admirals could feel important. It would be a tiny drop in the ocean, he conceded, but it was still irritating. The money could have been better spent on more missiles and starfighters.

Captain - technically, *Commodore*- Hammond sat at a small table. He stood as the hatch closed behind Mitch, his hands resting at his sides. He made no move to shake hands. The tension in the air was almost palpable.

Mitch nodded politely, forcing himself to remain calm. It was hard, again, not to giggle. He pushed the impulse down, out of his mind. The admiral would kill the pair of them—perhaps literally—if they allowed their personal issues to get in the way of completing the mission.

"Captain," Captain Hammond said. His voice was flat, emotionless. He'd donned a simple uniform, rather than a dress outfit. "Welcome onboard."

"Thank you," Mitch said. He had the feeling Captain Hammond had practiced what he wanted to say. "We have a lot of work to do."

"Correct." Captain Hammond studied him for a long moment, then indicated the chair. "Please. Be seated. The steward will bring dinner shortly."

Mitch sat, placing his hands in his lap. He wasn't sure what to say. He knew how to handle his ship in combat, and he knew how to argue for whatever he wanted, but…here, he wasn't sure *what* he wanted. In hindsight…he shook his head. There was no point in dwelling on the past. What was done was done.

"I don't like you," Captain Hammond said, bluntly. "I think you're irresponsible, reckless and *dangerous*." His lips twitched. "I thought that before you slept with my wife, by the way. But we have to work together."

"If I wasn't inclined to take chances, secure in my own expendability, you would be dead," Mitch said, equally bluntly. "The fleet was caught in a trap. If I'd made my way to New Washington, you would be dead. If I hadn't deployed drones to trick the alien fleet, you would be dead."

He met Captain Hammond's eyes. "You would be dead," he repeated. "How many times do I have to say it? You would be dead."

"I am aware you saved the fleet," Captain Hammond said, stiffly. "However, your recklessness could easily have gotten you killed instead."

Mitch felt his temper flare. "The navy needs people like me, people willing to risk everything on one throw of the die," he snapped. "And, like I said, without me, you would be dead."

"I got the message," Captain Hammond said.

He keyed a switch. A holographic starchart appeared over the table. Mitch studied it, keeping his face blank as his eyes glided over the alien system. It was a daunting target, even if it was the virus's homeworld. Mitch wasn't sure what he'd do if he discovered it was only one of many such industrialised systems. There was no proof it wasn't, he reminded himself. For all they knew, the virus could be fighting on multiple fronts against a multitude of alien enemies simultaneously. There was no way to know.

We'll find out, he promised himself. *And then we'll put an end to the war.*

"I believe we should start by setting up a base here," Hammond said. "You can carry out a tactical survey while we establish the mass drivers..."

Hammond had given the matter a great deal of thought, Mitch noted, as the older man outlined his plan. He'd taken the vague concepts the planning staff had put together and turned them into a decent operational plan. It was a little *too* precise for his peace of mind—there was no way to be *sure* of what they'd find—but the basic concept was sound. Set up a base, set up the mass drivers, start locating asteroids that could be shoved towards the alien worlds...

"It seems workable," Mitch said, when Captain Hammond had finished. "However, we cannot afford to get too wedded to a single plan."

"Unless someone invents a nova bomb, we may not have a choice," Captain Hammond said, dryly. "Do you know how to make a star go supernova?"

Mitch shook his head. He'd heard there were top-secret projects underway to turn radical concepts like supernova bombs into reality, but none of them—as far as he knew—had produced any reliable hardware. It might not be a bad thing, he reflected. The tramline network depended on stars. If a star exploded, if it blew off much of its mass, it was impossible to say what it would do to the tramlines. They might shift or simply snap out of existence. Interstellar travel—and warfare—would suddenly become impossible. He'd read quite a few horror stories that suggested losing the tramlines would trigger a galaxy-wide disaster.

"We also need to prepare for them coming after us," he said. "They'll have no difficulty tracing the mass driver projectiles back to their source."

"I was thinking we'd mount the mass driver on a freighter," Captain

Hammond said. "And we can simply move it between shots."

Mitch nodded. "Good thinking."

They discussed a handful of other concepts as the steward entered, pushing a trolley of food. Mitch was mildly disappointed it wasn't a grand meal, although he figured that might have been asking a bit much. The ship's crew was too busy to do more than prepare a simple dinner for their commander and his guest. Mitch wondered, as he helped himself to the pie, if someone had spat in it. There were people in *his* crew who would have thought that the height of humour. And they wouldn't have thought past it to the inevitable court-martial or beasting.

"We should be ready to leave tomorrow," Captain Hammond said. "Ideally, I'd like a couple more days to get everything ready, but it shouldn't be a problem."

"Take the time," Mitch advised. "We're going to be on the clock as soon as we pass the New Washington system."

He scowled, cursing under his breath. He was used to operating on a shoestring, to falling back on whatever his ship could carry and nothing else, but it wouldn't be easy to harass an entire system without a steady flow of supplies. Armchair admirals might talk of the wonders of automated factory ships, and in theory they were nothing less than a boon to all mankind, but he knew better. They would be burning through their supplies faster than they could replenish them. And the factory ship couldn't replenish *everything*.

"Point," Captain Hammond said. His gaze hardened, suddenly. "Is your ship ready to depart?"

Mitch felt a flicker of dull anger. Captain Hammond might be in overall command of the operation, but looking over Mitch's shoulder was a severe breach of naval etiquette. He was in sole command of his ship, Master under God. He could be removed from his post, but he couldn't be micromanaged. And yet...

"We can depart now, if you feel it wise," he said, crossly. "A couple of extra days will make no difference to us."

"Good." Captain Hammond looked irked, just for a second. "We'll depart in two days, unless the Admiralty wishes us to leave sooner."

"Which it might," Mitch said. "The mission is a political *footfall*."

Captain Hammond didn't smile at the weak pun. Instead, he gave Mitch a calculating look. It made Mitch feel uncomfortably exposed. Charlotte had kept him informed of political developments on Earth, telling him how the Prime Minister was on the verge of losing his majority—and, worse, his seat in the house. It would be difficult, even in wartime, to serve as PM without also being an MP. Charlotte's last message had included the suggestion that the party bigwigs would put pressure on some poor unsuspecting MP, urging him to give up his seat to the PM. Or simply advise the PM to resign before he was fired.

And that isn't something I would have cared about, Mitch thought. *He knows it comes from her.*

"Tell me something," Captain Hammond said. "Why did you sleep with her *there*?"

Mitch frowned, inwardly. It was a decidedly odd question. He'd grown up in a rough and ready environment, where a man who let himself be cuckolded had to either kill his wife's lover or be seen as a wimp. The thrill of forbidden love was made even spicier by the knowledge he couldn't afford to be caught, that being caught would mean being thrust into a fight for his life. It was hard not to feel a certain degree of contempt for the older man, even though Mitch knew Captain Hammond had grown up in a very different environment. He hadn't been raised to settle his disputes through violence.

"It seemed like a good idea at the time," he said, finally. He'd been too horny to care. And besides, he'd assumed they were safe. "Why did you come looking for her?"

Captain Hammond scowled. "It was her party," he said. "She had to be there."

"I guess she didn't consider it all *that* important," Mitch said. "Or... does it matter?"

"If the two of you had been discreet, it would have been a very different story," Captain Hammond said. "You really *are* reckless."

"Yes," Mitch said.

"Where did I go wrong?" Captain Hammond looked at him, without quite seeing him. "Why didn't she tell me…?"

Mitch shrugged. "It is never easy to look one's partner in the eye and discuss how unhappy one is," he said. He'd never married, but he'd seen marriages torn apart by issues that had remained buried until they'd come burbling into the light. "I guess what she got wasn't what she *wanted*."

"And she resented me enough to smear both me and my daughters—*our* daughters—in a manner no one could ignore?"

"Who knows?" Mitch rolled his eyes. No one with half a brain would blame Captain Hammond's daughters for their mother's conduct. Or their father's. Guilt wasn't something that was passed down the family tree, not like an entailed estate. "If you get angry or bitter enough, you'll find yourself doing things you wouldn't normally condone."

He grimaced. "Perhaps she wanted to make damn sure those bridges were burned to ashes," he said. "Or perhaps she was too far gone to care."

"We shall see," Captain Hammond said. He looked Mitch in the eye. "I don't like you. I think I detest you. And while you may believe that being a hero will get you whatever you want, I think the lustre of being a hero will fade soon enough. Whatever promises she made to you, they will fade, too. Her hopes of a political career are unlikely to be realised. Too many people will look at her as someone who cheated on her husband. Her integrity will be forever suspect."

Mitch's eyes glittered. "Is that all?"

"I will work with you, to bring down the common enemy," Captain Hammond said. "After that, you can do whatever the hell you like. The longer you live, the more people will forget the heroics and dwell on the rest of your conduct. I think you'll wind up penniless and alone, remembering a life that once was yours."

He smiled, suddenly. "But until then, we'll work together."

"Oh, *thank you*," Mitch said, with heavy sarcasm. The older man was making a quiet declaration of war. He was entirely sure Captain Hammond would work to block his promotion—and political career—in the post-war world. If, of course, they lived to see the end of the war. "I will work with you, *Commodore*. We have a job to do."

He allowed his voice to harden. "Afterwards…well, we'll see."

"Indeed we will," Captain Hammond agreed.

He poured them both a glass of shipboard rotgut. Mitch suspected that was intended as a subtle insult, although it was lost on *him*. He'd grown up drinking bathtub whiskey his uncles had produced, a drink that was noted more for its alcoholic content than its resemblance to *real* whiskey. The shipboard moonshiner was infinitely better than the old men's, he decided. He'd certainly not made the mistake of drinking his own supply.

"Confusion to the enemy," he said. "And victory to us."

"Quite," Captain Hammond said. They drank. "You'd better get back to your ship. I'll be in touch once the departure time has been finalised."

"Yes, sir," Mitch said. "I look forward to it."

CHAPTER FIFTEEN

"ALL THINGS CONSIDERED, our first engagement went very well," Tobias said. He stood at the front of the briefing compartment, feeling *slightly* less out of place. "We did quite a few things right. But... what did we do wrong?"

He surveyed the pilots, wondering if any of them had realised the truth. It was something of a trick question. Given that there'd been no reason to expect a massive alien fleet to appear out of nowhere and lay siege to the system, they'd done very well. It had been sheer luck, he supposed, that they hadn't been running an exercise—and draining their life support systems—when the enemy ships arrived. And yet, they'd done something wrong.

"It is a trick question," he admitted after no one, not even Marigold, said anything. "And it isn't entirely a *fair* point. We followed orders. We did what we had to do. But that meant we missed something."

Tobias keyed the terminal, bringing up an image of the battle. "*Lion*"— he waved a hand at the bulkhead—"opened fire, launching a dozen salvos of missiles into the enemy formation. We were not in position to provide targeting data to the missile seeker heads, which made it harder for them to strike their targets. Post-battle analysis has made it clear that the missiles could have hit more targets. They did not."

He held up a hand. "Make no mistake. I am not saying we had any choice. Our orders were to protect the shipyard, and we did so, but our principal role is to provide updated targeting information to the missiles. And in that we were unsuccessful."

"Sir," one of the maggots said. "Surely, it was not our fault."

"It wasn't," Tobias said. "But we have to bear in mind that our next set of missions will be very different."

He allowed his voice to tighten. "We were not priority targets, last time. The virus paid us no heed. It made no attempt to swat us, even after we started shooting down the incoming missiles. The virus simply had more important targets. Next time, things will be different. We will be seen as a very serious threat, one that simply cannot be allowed to continue to exist. And it will do everything it can to blow us out of space."

There was a pause. Tobias allowed his eyes to wander over the compartment, wondering how many of his pilots would actually understand. None of them had died. Not yet. Their first mission looked like a complete success...hell, in many ways, it *had* been. Tobias knew they weren't in any trouble. It wasn't as if they'd taken one look at the alien ships, reversed course and fled. But it hadn't prepared them for what was going to come, either.

He found it hard to believe, deep inside, that he and Marigold had ever been so young. The men and women in front of him looked like... he shook his head. It wasn't as if they were *that* much younger than him. The navy hadn't resorted to recruiting *children*. And yet, they felt young. It was hard to believe *he* was the shell-shocked veteran. He wasn't even in his goddamn twenties!

"We are scheduled to depart this evening," he said. He made a show of checking the time. "You have five hours. I suggest, if you haven't already, that you make a final call to your relatives, that you check your wills and get a little sleep. We might run into trouble the moment we cross the tramline. Dismissed."

He sagged, slightly, as they fled the compartment. They might not take the suggestion—it wasn't quite an order—seriously. It was easy to become disassociated, to believe that the world wasn't quite real. Tobias understood, all too well. He'd spent most of his life playing video games. One could lose, one could be blown to pieces…and step away from the computer, as hale and hearty as one had ever been. That wouldn't work in the real world. He needed them to remember that the missiles and plasma bolts were real, that they could get people killed…that it could get *them* killed.

Marigold grinned at him. "You're getting better at making long speeches."

"I think I repeated myself a couple of times," Tobias said. He had no idea how Bagehot had managed to keep the pilots paying attention. "Do you think they'll listen to me?"

"I don't know." Marigold affected a thinking pose. "Did *you* bother to write a will?"

Tobias nodded. He'd left everything to his mother and sister. He didn't have any other close relatives and, until he'd joined the navy, he hadn't had any close friends. Or a girlfriend. His heart clenched for a second as he remembered, again, that Marigold and he would likely die together. There'd been girls at school who'd insisted a shared death was romantic. *He* thought it was fucking stupid.

"And written messages for everyone who's likely to care if I die," he said. It wasn't as if there were many people who'd even note his death. His old headmaster wouldn't even bother to add his name to the list of honoured dead…probably. God knew Tobias had never been one of his favourites. "And all we can do now is wait."

He stepped off the podium and came to join her. It would have been a great deal easier, he reflected, if he'd had more pilots. There was no technical reason they couldn't rotate gunboat crews to ensure everyone was well-rested, when they encountered the enemy. But the pilots just weren't available. The training program hadn't been anything more than an experiment until the gunboats had proved their worth. It was being scaled up now, he'd been told, but it would be quite some time before more pilots started flowing out of the academy.

And something will be lost, when more regular recruits start applying to join, he thought, wryly. *I wonder if it will make any real difference in the long run?*

"We do have time," he said. "You want to head to the privacy tube?"

Marigold winked. "And get caught by the rest of the squadron? Don't you think that'd look bad?"

Tobias hesitated. Marigold and he shared the same rank. Or at least they had when they'd started sleeping together. He just had more responsibilities. They wouldn't be breaking any regulations if they went to bed together. And yet, he was the squadron CO. He commanded Marigold, even though he felt he *didn't*. He felt torn between duty and a grim awareness that, once they were underway, there wouldn't be much time for anything beyond training and fighting.

"I think we'd better be careful not to get caught," he said, finally. "The other option is sitting around and feeling sorry for ourselves."

"That"—Marigold giggled—"is the single worst chat-up line I've ever heard."

She caught his arm and pulled him towards the hatch. "Come on."

Tobias smiled. "It worked, didn't it?"

• • •

"The flight path looks reasonable," Staci said. "But you do realise it'll add an extra ten days to our journey?"

Mitch nodded. Captain Hammond had drawn up the plan. Mitch had been tempted to object, pointing out the importance of launching the operation as quickly as possible, but he had to admit they needed to remain stealthy until they reached their target. The virus had had centuries to monitor the infected systems, to determine what was—and what wasn't—normal for their region of space. The slightest flicker of energy, if it was out of place, might be enough to bring an enemy fleet down on their heads. Better to take longer to complete the voyage than to be intercepted and destroyed before even reaching their target.

"It can't be helped," he said. "We could cut a week or so off the transit time without being detected, but the fleet tenders aren't really designed for stealth work."

"True," Staci agreed. "We could go ahead."

"I raised the possibility," Mitch said. "Captain Hammond believes we should remain together until we reach the target."

"He wants to keep an eye on you?" Staci raised her eyebrows. "Or does he fear being unable to link up with us when he reaches the target?"

"That's the official justification," Mitch said. He hadn't seen any point in arguing, beyond a *pro forma* objection. Captain Hammond would insist, perhaps correctly, that a handful of days wouldn't make much of a difference. *Unicorn* wasn't going to be able to take on the entire alien system by herself. "And it will probably hold up if anyone asks a bunch of questions."

He sighed. Hammond had insisted they could work together—neither of them wanted to face the admiral's wrath—but it was hard not to check and recheck each other's work for possible trouble. And that meant...Mitch wondered, idly, if one or both of them should request reassignment. He was too stubborn to leave his command—he wouldn't get another one—and he feared the brevet commodore would feel the same way as he did. God knew the media was still doing its level best to talk the story up...

And they're probably being encouraged by people who don't want to discuss more weightier matters, Mitch thought. *Our little scandal provides cover for far greater scandals.*

"We shall see," Staci said. She cleared her throat. "The ship is ready to depart. We have integrated most of the newcomers into the crew, with training sessions still underway to ensure they're ready to fight when we finally see action. We have crammed the hold with supplies, to the point we've actually had to take over a handful of cabins. There should be nothing standing between us and departure."

"Good." Mitch sat back in his chair. "Get some rest. I'll see you on the bridge when we depart."

Staci nodded. "Have you decided what you're going to do about *her*?"

Mitch hesitated. Sheer bloody-minded stubbornness insisted that he and Charlotte were going to stay together, the media and the aristocrats and everything else notwithstanding. Common sense suggested the affair was doomed, whatever happened. It wasn't as if they had much in common, beyond lust. Charlotte and Captain Hammond had had a *lot* in common and look what had happened to them! He was tempted to take advantage of the departure to call it off and yet...

"I don't know," he said.

"Then you'd better decide, before the shit hits the fan," Staci said. She stood. "It isn't easy to keep a relationship going at the best of times and these, sir, are more like the *worst* of times."

Mitch nodded as his XO left, the hatch hissing closed behind her. Deployment placed one hell of a lot of stress on even the *strongest* marriages, where one partner was away for long periods and the other was forced to take care of the children alone. Staci had told him, once, that she had no intention of getting into a permanent relationship with *anyone* until she was more settled, if only to avoid the emotional storms that would come with each farewell. And Charlotte and he...

He stared down at his hands, wondering if he should record a message for her. If he didn't come back...he wondered, morbidly, if she was already planning to dump him. Or if she thought she could ride his coattails... he shook his head. There was no difference between riding his coattails and what she'd done for her husband, although he supposed it might be a great deal more exciting. She could *lose*. Mitch understood the thrill that came with gambling when you couldn't afford to lose—he'd done it himself—but she still had a safety net. He didn't.

She used me to get back at her husband, to confront him with a situation he could not ignore, he thought. It made sense. Charlotte wouldn't have had any trouble arranging a more discreet meeting, if she'd wanted to avoid trouble. *And that means she now has to decide what she wants to do next.*

He shook his head. Right now, it wasn't his problem. He liked her, but he wasn't attached to her. If she decided to strike out on her own, to build a career for herself that didn't involve him, that was her right. If she dumped him…Mitch shrugged. He'd been dumped before. It hurt—it always hurt—but there were plenty more fish in the sea. He wasn't going to waste his time chasing someone who'd decided she didn't want him. Charlotte could go back to her husband and…who cared?

Her, he reflected. *And him. And me.*

He stood and headed for the hatch. It was traditional for a captain to tour his ship before departure. It would give him one final chance to check on his family, to make sure his ship was in perfect condition and his crew were ready to leave. He made a mental note to check his inbox an hour before they left, just to be sure he hadn't missed anything. The ship was too small for an elaborate chain of command, the kind of ladder that had always annoyed him as a young officer. If someone had a problem, they didn't *have* to take it to the XO first.

Of course, on a bigger ship, there would be too many problems for the captain to handle them all, he reminded himself. Personnel management was the XO's job. *But I'm not going to be in command of one of them, am I?*

• • •

"Admiral?"

Susan looked up from her terminal. "Yes?"

"Admiral, you requested to be notified when *Lion* and *Unicorn* were cleared for departure," Midshipwoman Nancy Ryland said. "System Command just cleared them to leave at 1900."

"Good." Susan frowned. "Inform me when they've left the system."

"Yes, Admiral," Nancy said.

Susan nodded, dismissing the younger woman with a wave. It was hard to believe she'd ever been *that* young, although her memories were clear. Hanover Towers—she'd been a scholarship girl—the Luna Academy, her middy cruise, the climb up the ranks…she shook her head as the hatch closed behind the midshipwoman. She loved the navy, but it might be time to start thinking about retirement. It was unlikely she'd ever rise any higher. The politics wouldn't let her become First Space Lord...

I can still command a fleet, she thought. *And I can move sideways into diplomatic service or even the GATO bureaucracy...*

Guilt gnawed at her as she sat back in her chair. She wanted to accompany the two ships and their tenders, as they set out to Virus Prime. She wanted to share the risk. She'd sent them into danger...it was hardly the first time, but it felt wrong to be sending them into danger without sending herself too. She stared at her hands. She'd never liked or respected officers who stayed behind, in safety, while sending their subordinates out to die. It was the heart of irony, she thought, that she'd unwillingly *become* one of the bastards. She hoped—she prayed—she'd never lose sight of the realities of naval life. It would be all too easy to start thinking of spacers as nothing more than numbers, to add up the victories and defeats and calculate outcomes as if space battles were nothing more than games of chess. She liked to think it wouldn't happen. She wondered if the admirals she'd detested had felt the same way.

They know what to do, she told herself. *And they have everything I was able to give them.*

She keyed her terminal, wincing inwardly. Two days of negotiation, haggling and downright arguing hadn't convinced anyone to deploy a fleet to the alien homeworld. If, of course, it *was* the alien homeworld. Too many people believed the virus was just biding its time, gathering the firepower to crush Earth once and for all; too many people feared the alien homeworld was just another trap, a hammer and anvil waiting to crush the human fleet. It was starting to look as though no government was prepared to take the risk. And that meant there'd be no support for Hammond and Campbell.

I should have gone with them, she thought. The navy expected its officers to work together, even if they disliked each other, but adultery was more than mere dislike. *I could have kept their noses to the grindstone and forced them to cooperate...*

The terminal bleeped. She opened the message without really seeing it. Politics had always been the bane of her existence, but…she shook her head in frustration. Last time, she'd been in a position to do something about it. And she'd been too junior to bring anyone else down with her, if it had all gone to hell. And…this time, it wasn't the same. She could hardly order a fleet to the alien homeworld on her own authority. The captains would refuse to follow her and…

Her console bleeped. "Admiral, Lady Charlotte Hammond is requesting a private link," her aide said. "She would like to speak with you immediately."

Susan frowned. She'd met Lady Charlotte a couple of times, but they weren't exactly *friends*. They certainly hadn't moved in the same circles. Susan was unsure what, if anything. Commodore Hammond's estranged wife wanted to discuss. It wasn't as if Charlotte Hammond was on the Royal Navy Oversight Board. Talking to her could easily lead to Susan being in trouble too, and yet…she felt a flicker of the old excitement. She was certainly curious to hear what Charlotte Hammond actually *wanted*.

"Put her though," she ordered.

"Aye, Admiral."

Lady Charlotte's image appeared in front of her. "Admiral," Lady Charlotte said. She looked older than Susan remembered. "It's been a while."

"Quite," Susan said. It had only been a few weeks—it felt longer—since the affair had exploded into the public's eye. "What can I do for you?"

Charlotte smiled. "I have a proposition for you."

CHAPTER SIXTEEN

IT WAS HARD TO EXPLAIN TO A CIVILIAN, but a capital ship was something akin to a country. The hull encompassed a number of departments, from Life Support and Engineering to Tactical Analysis and even Personnel. The departments were both independent and part of a greater whole, their occupants trained to think of themselves as both individuals and a collective. It was strange, Thomas had often reflected, to realise there were parts of his ship that were largely unfamiliar to him. He was her commander, but he was also part of something greater. *Lion* would survive long after he moved on to greener pastures.

He started at the prow of the vessel, where the sensor officers manned their equipment, and walked slowly towards the stern. The crew stopped to salute him as he passed, a handful of familiar faces mingled with the multitude of strangers. He showed no reaction, knowing he had to treat them all equally. A small ship could afford—it could not avoid—relationships that crossed ranks and positions. A capital ship could not. He returned the salutes, listened to departmental briefings by officers who'd had plenty of warning to decide what they wanted to tell him, then continued on his way. He was relieved nothing had gone wrong. It would have been embarrassing if he'd had to explain a delay to the admiral.

And the officers would have told me if there was a danger something would *go wrong*, he told himself. He couldn't be a *friend* to his subordinates, but he'd worked hard to make sure they knew they could come to him if there were any problems. *They know where we're going.*

He felt a glimmer of excitement as he completed his inspection tour and made his way back towards the bridge. The thought of taking his starship away from Earth, so far away the Admiralty couldn't look over his shoulder, had never lost its thrill, even though he knew they were heading straight to the enemy homeworld. The operation was chancy as hell and yet...he sobered as he remembered the admiral's grim tones. Risking both ships and their tenders was acceptable, if it gave the human race a chance to rebuild and resume the offensive. It would hurt to *lose* them—and it would be fatal for him personally—but the situation was dire. The risks had to be run.

You knew the job was dangerous when you took it, he thought, again. He would have preferred to operate as part of a far larger fleet, with enough mobile firepower to destroy everything orbiting the alien homeworld, but that wasn't on the cards. *And you can't back out now.*

He took a breath as he stepped onto the bridge. The display was already lit, showing *Unicorn* and the six fleet tenders holding station with the battlecruiser. A seventh ship—an isolated medical vessel built on a destroyer hull—brought up the rear. Thomas wondered what her original crew thought of what she'd become—a mobile biological warfare laboratory, capable of producing vast quantities of counter-virus—and then shrugged. There would be no complaints, none that would be allowed to become public. After the attack on Earth, the general public would support *anything* as long as it removed the threat. It would take years—centuries, perhaps—before history's revisionists started arguing that perhaps genocide had been a little extreme...

And you thought it was genocide, when you first heard of the concept, his thoughts mocked him. It wasn't a happy memory. There was simply no way to avoid the fact they were planning to commit mass slaughter. *How far we have fallen in the last few months.*

He sighed, inwardly, as he took his chair. History would judge. Academics who'd never been in a fight in their lives, who had no true comprehension of the times they studied, would argue there should have been another solution. Perhaps, from an objective point of view, they were right. But that assumed a hindsight that was sorely lacking. The people on the spot had to make the best decisions they could, based on what that knew at the time, and live with them. The revisionist academics were just...*academics*. The only reason they had the freedom to pass judgement on their ancestors was that their ancestors had fought and died to ensure their survival. And their freedom.

"Captain," Commander Donker said. "All systems are green. We are ready to depart."

Thomas let out a breath. "Communications, signal the squadron," he ordered. "Confirm they are ready to depart on time."

"Aye, Captain," Cook said. He worked his console for a long moment. "All ships report ready to depart."

Thomas allowed himself a smile. "Helm, power up the drive," he ordered. "Take us to the tramline."

"Aye, Captain," Lieutenant Fitzgerald said. A low hum ran through the ship as the drives came online. "Powering up...now."

Thomas felt his smile grow wider as his ship started to move. It was always a special moment. The display changed, the shipyard icons falling behind them as the squadron picked up speed. *Unicorn* and the fleet tenders kept pace effortlessly. Thomas reminded himself not to fall into the trap of assuming the tenders could keep up over the long run, even though they had military-grade drives. They certainly didn't belong in the line of battle. It might be better to keep them powered down and cloaked when they reached the target system.

He leaned forward as the display zoomed out. Earth was surrounded by a small galaxy of tactical icons, from giant battlestations and industrial stations to fleet carriers and destroyers ruthlessly sweeping space for enemy mines and surveillance platforms. There were so many icons that they blurred together, reminding him that he and his tiny squadron were setting out alone. He wished, suddenly, that the admiral had been able to put together a bigger fleet. It would be more noticeable, true, but capable of doing a great deal more damage.

"Captain," Fitzgerald said. "We are currently headed straight for the tramline and will make transit in four hours."

"Good." Thomas knew they could reach the tramline quicker, but only by leaving the tenders behind. "Tactical, take us into cloak five minutes before we cross the tramline."

"Aye, Captain," Sibley said.

Thomas forced himself to lean back in his chair as the seconds ticked on. The jump *would* cause the cloaking field to fluctuate, giving any watching eyes on the far side of the system a chance to get a solid lock before the ships vanished again. He wanted to believe they were not being watched, or at least not being shadowed so closely the watchers might be able to get a solid lock, but it was impossible to be sure. There had been so many ships in the enemy fleet—and the formation had been so tight the signatures had overlapped—that it was quite possible an enemy ship or two had broken off when the fleet retreated. The long-range sensors on Terra Nova had revealed nothing, but that was meaningless. Thomas wouldn't have trusted Terra Nova's disunited military to tell him anything.

He keyed his console, checking the reports from the different departments. Engineering was reporting all systems nominal, much to his relief. The tactical staff were running tracking exercises on ships passing through the solar system. The gunboat crews were in their craft, carrying out exercises of their own. Bagehot had reported that the new Squadron CO was working out well. Thomas hoped that would continue, as they came to grips with the realities of naval life. It wasn't for everyone, he knew, and most of the gunboat pilots hadn't intended to join the military at all.

It beats stamping around with the Home Guard or digging ditches with the Land Brigades, he reminded himself. *And even if they did their best in the latter, they'd still be mocked as cowards.*

"Captain," Fitzgerald said. "We will cross the tramline in ten minutes."

Thomas looked at the display. There was no sign of *anything* near the tramline, save for a handful of early-warning satellites. They'd been worse than useless during the last engagement. The virus had crossed the tramline so far from Sol that their transit had gone undetected. The lack of warning had lulled the defenders into a false sense of security...he sighed, grimly, as the cloaking device came online. *That* wouldn't be a problem, not for the next few years. The various governments would be reluctant to assign any ships on missions that would take them a long way from Earth.

Like us, he reflected.

"Helm, take us across the tramline," he ordered.

The bridge seemed to fade, just for a second, as the ship made transit. Thomas braced himself as the display blanked, all too aware that any waiting ambushers would never have a better shot at his ship. It lit up again a moment later, as data flowed in from the sensors. The system had practically gone dark, half the installations he remembered either powered down or destroyed. It was a miracle the virus hadn't taken root on Terra Nova. The disunited world would be easy prey.

"Transit complete, Captain," Fitzgerald reported.

"No enemy contacts," Sibley added. "We haven't even been pinged by the local defences."

"Good," Thomas said. It was good for them, he supposed, but not for the defenders themselves. "Helm, take us on our planned course."

"Aye, Captain."

Thomas stood. "Mr. XO, you have the bridge. I'll be in my ready room."

"Aye, Captain."

• • •

Tobias had never thought, as the squadron steadily made its way up the tramlines towards Virus Prime, that he could be bored. There was always something to do, from endless simulations to simple paperwork...hell, he'd never realised how much *paperwork* the squadron CO had to do. He'd

155

wondered, more than once, why Bagehot didn't fly a gunboat himself, but after looking at the paperwork he was starting to get a pretty good idea. The poor bastard simply hadn't had the *time*.

He rubbed his forehead as he tried to force himself to read and sign off on one more report from the maintenance crews. Nothing had changed, if only because the gunboats weren't deployed while the ship was under cloak, but apparently it didn't count until he read and signed the fucking document. He'd always loved reading—books had taken him to worlds he knew he'd never see—and yet, just looking at the wretched documents gave him a headache. Gunboat maintenance records. Personnel files, including detailed historical and medical logs that made him feel uncomfortably like a voyeur. He'd never realised—either—just how much data the navy collected on its personnel, even the ones who were unlikely to stay in the service for more than a few years. He hadn't dared look at his file. He didn't want to know what it said.

His head ached. How long had it been since they'd left Earth? He knew the answer, but he honestly couldn't swear to it. Days? Weeks? Months? He'd spent the mornings in the simulators and the afternoons in his office...that was weird. He had never thought he'd ever have an office. All the horror stories he'd heard about employment had argued that sadistic managers forced their workers into open plan offices, just to keep an eye on them...never mind the damage to productivity. And...

"Hey," a quiet voice said. "What's up?"

Tobias didn't look up. "Marigold?"

"I think your eyes need checking," a distinctly male voice said. "It's me."

"Colin," Tobias said. "Are you here to put me out of my misery?"

"You have an office," Colin said. He stepped into the compartment, the hatch hissing closed behind him. "I suppose you don't have room for more than a handful of marines in full kit, but it's still better than any-thing I have."

He winked. "Have you and her had some fun in here yet?"

Tobias shook his head. "It's an office!"

"You've never even thought about it?" Colin winked, again. "Do you remember when Joan and I were caught behind the bike sheds...?"

Tobias snorted. He'd never believed that story, any more than he believed the other wild tales of sexual exploits. His classmates had bragged endlessly about their sexual conquests, all of which made porn movies look tame, but he was fairly sure most of them were nothing more than complete bullshit. In hindsight, he was also sure most of his fellows had been virgins. He supposed it explained the endless nonsensical bragging.

"This is an office," he repeated. "What do you think would happen if someone came in and caught us?"

"You tell them to fuck off while you're busy fucking," Colin said. "Come on. You've never even thought about it?"

Tobias snorted again. "Colin, I don't have the time!"

"That's bad," Colin said, a deadpan look on his face. "You need better time management skills."

"Right now, I need a painkiller and an uninterrupted night's sleep," Tobias said. "Do you know how much I have to do, every day, just to keep this job?"

"Do you know how much of it you actually *need* to do?" Colin looked serious, just for a moment. "You may not need to do *all* of it."

Tobias stared. "I do have to do it all."

"I don't think so," Colin said. "You could talk to the XO. I'd be surprised if he wasn't already keeping an eye on you. Get him to confirm how much you actually need to do during the voyage. And see what support network you have in place."

"I don't have a support network," Tobias said. "I'm the only one."

"Yes, you do," Colin said. "Who do you report to?"

"Colonel Bagehot," Tobias said. "I...he was the one who promoted me."

"So ask him," Colin said. "Yes, there's a lot that has to be done, but there's also stuff you can leave until we return to Earth. Or there's shit you can pass on to someone else. Tactical analysis, for example. There's a whole tactical department that handles that sort of thing. Just ask them to help you. They'll probably pay *you* for it."

Tobias stared.

Colin looked back. "What?"

"I'm trying to process the fact *you're* giving me good advice," Tobias said. "You."

"I've been in command of a platoon," Colin reminded him. "And I had to write a shitload of reports myself. Apparently, writing *everything is fine, nothing to see here* is not acceptable. Who knew?"

"Oh, dear," Tobias said, dryly. "Colin, how did you cope? I mean, when you lost someone under your command?"

Colin hesitated, visibly. "It's never easy to handle," he said, finally. "I know everyone under my direct command, such as it is. I wouldn't find it easy to lose any of them. But you can't wrap them in cottonwool, either. You have to accept that yes, some people will die. And then move on as best as you can."

Tobias scowled. "Is it really that easy?"

"No." Colin shrugged. "Anyone who tells you it's easy is a lying little gobshite or a complete sociopath. It's hard to lose anyone you know, even if you hate them. And you never really get used to it. You just have to move on, complete the mission and mourn later."

There was a time I would have cheered if you'd died, Tobias thought. He'd loathed the old Colin. He still wasn't quite sure what to make of the new one. *And I doubt you would have shed a tear if I'd vanished from your ken, too.*

Colin smiled. "You want to know something dumb? I got roped into an exercise a year ago, involving a lot of daredevil stunts and shit like that. The guy who planned the deployment was either addicted to complexity or a complete idiot. His plan involved a fifty-mile march to an enemy-held airport, a quick assault and capture of an enemy aircraft, a hasty flight to the next target, a parachute drop into complete darkness…"

"It sounds like an online game," Tobias said. "Were there boxes of ammunition just littering the landscape?"

"No," Colin said. "The CO took one look at the plans, said *fuck this*, and marched us five miles to the final target instead. The whole operation was completed in less than a day."

Tobias frowned. "Was the planner an idiot or was the *real* purpose of the exercise to see if your CO would actually try to carry the plan out?"

"I don't know," Colin said. "Point is, it's very easy to say that something is easy if you haven't already done it. Or to load someone who's already overburdened down with more crap. You want my advice? Go check with your CO, find out how much you actually have to do and then go get some sleep. Seriously."

He grinned. "Or you can come shoot a few rounds with me."

"I have a headache," Tobias said. "I can't take any banging right now."

Colin smirked. "Poor Marigold."

Tobias gave him the finger, then sobered. "What if he takes it as proof I can't handle the job?"

"I think he might be waiting to see what you do," Colin said, calmly. "Or he might be giving you enough rope to see if you manage to tie it into a knot or hang yourself. It wouldn't be the first time some commander gave a promising young officer just enough power and authority to see what he does with it. I sometimes wonder about my career."

"You're a trained soldier," Tobias pointed out. "There'll always be work for you. Me…? I don't know if my people take me seriously…"

"You're the survivor of two successive deep-strike missions," Colin countered. "Of *course* they take you seriously. To them, you're a hero."

Tobias smiled. "Very funny."

"I'm serious," Colin said. "And it's time you realised it."

CHAPTER SEVENTEEN

MITCH FELT, UNCOMFORTABLY, as though he was being watched.

It was an illusion, of course. *Unicorn* had slipped through a dozen tramlines and sneaked through five enemy-occupied star systems. There was no sign that either the frigate or the rest of the squadron had been detected. And yet, the sensation of being watched—of being played with, as a cat might play with a mouse—refused to go away. Perhaps it was the grim awareness that humanity had finally discovered evidence of a far more powerful and advanced race, or perhaps it was something deeply buried in the human psyche. They were deep within enemy space, far closer to the virus's homeworlds than anyone wanted to be. It was hard not to feel as though they were flying right into a trap.

He sat on his bridge and watched as his crew made the final checks. The tiny squadron had put weeks on its journey, just by making transit along the edge of each successive star system, but he had to admit there was no choice. Hammond had been right. They couldn't afford to be spotted, not now. It was going to be hard to carry out the mission even if they slipped into the alien system without being detected. The virus might miss their arrival, but it couldn't possibly miss the first asteroid hurtling towards their homeworld at a fair percentage of the speed of light. And it would have no trouble tracing the asteroid back to its source.

And we'll be gone by the time the virus's ships arrive, Mitch told himself. *We'll keep playing cat and mouse until the virus runs out of luck and its system dies.*

"Captain," Staci said. "We are ready to make transit."

Mitch nodded. "Signal the flag, inform them that we are ready to make transit as planned," he ordered. "Helm, start the countdown."

He tensed as Lieutenant Sam Hinkson started counting down to zero. There was no reason to think they would be spotted, the moment they jumped through the tramline…there was no reason to think the virus even knew the human scouts had reached so far into their territory. And yet, if there was any power that could line the entire tramline with scansats, it was the virus. It had deployed mines near the shipyard, a few short months ago. Why would it not expend the resources on keeping its homeworld safe?

If it truly is the virus's homeworld, he reminded himself. *We still know so little.*

His imagination filled in the details as the countdown reached its final stages. The virus might have been born on a very different world, infected unwary star travellers as they set up a colony and taken their bodies before they realised the danger. It was hard to believe a race that could traverse the tramlines would be unaware of the risks, although humanity hadn't discovered any disease that could spread amongst multiple species until it encountered the virus itself. Technically, he'd been told, the virus didn't so much kill its hosts as merely take root in them…a piece of medical technobabble that had never made much sense. A zombie was a dead man walking, as far as he was concerned. The precise mechanics of the poor bastard's demise didn't matter.

"Jumping…now," Hinkson said.

Mitch forced himself to project an air of calm as the display blanked and hastily started to reformat. They were a *long* way from the primary star, a long way from enemy installations that might be able to detect their passage…he told himself, firmly, that the odds were so much in their favour that there was no point in betting against them. And yet, it was hard to escape the sense they'd just flown into a trap. The display came to life, hundreds—thousands—of energy signatures appearing right across the system. Probability cones formed a moment later, showing rough locations for enemy warships and freighters. Mitch had seen the system once before, but it was still awesome—and terrifying. The entire system teemed with life. *Infected* life. Sol was the most heavily industrialised system in the human sphere, and even *it* didn't have so much activity...

"Captain," Staci said. "I am not picking up any signs of enemy activity within engagement or detection range."

"Good." Mitch allowed himself a moment of relief. Unless the virus had some weird detection system the human race had never imagined— and there'd been no sign it did—they'd made transit undetected. "Helm, hold us here. Tactical, record everything and upload to the drone. I want as complete an assessment as possible before we head in-system."

"Aye, Captain," Staci said.

Mitch felt sweat on his back as more and more data flowed into the holographic display. There were nine planets in the system, five rocky worlds and four gas giants...all clearly highly-developed. The energy signatures surrounding the rocky worlds were off the charts, while the gas giants were clearly orbited by hundreds of cloudscoops and mining stations. He guessed there were also layers of defences, just in case someone hostile came knocking. Mitch had never backed away from a fight in his life, but he was starting to feel intimidated. It was small consolation that the virus didn't know they were there. He had the feeling that attacking the system, with his small ship, would be about as effective as throwing eggs at a tank. The tank might not even notice.

He frowned as more starships and interplanetary craft were picked out by the sensors. It looked as if the virus was mounting a major building program, devoting the system's entire resources to churning out more starships and starfighters to fight the war. Mitch shuddered. The tactical analysis was very weak—it would take days for *Lion's* tactical staff to go through the data and turn it into something useful—but it was obvious the system was controlled by a single will. The virus didn't have to argue with bureaucrats or watch its allies for signs of betrayal. It didn't even have to churn out consumer goods to keep the home front happy. Communism had never worked for humans—it struggled against human nature—but it worked here. Mitch found it hard to calculate just how much the system could produce, yet…he shook his head. It was starting to look as though they *would* need a supernova bomb to take out the system.

And while you're wishing, he told himself sardonically, *why don't you wish for force shields, FTL drives and a planet-sized planet-killer, too?*

"Tactical," he said. "Have you located a handful of possible asteroids?"

"Yes, Captain," Staci said. She indicated a handful of icons on the display. "I think those asteroids should be suitable. There's no indication the virus is interested in them."

Mitch nodded. The system was littered with asteroids and other pieces of space junk. The virus had been working for years, mining the asteroid belts and clusters for raw materials, but it wasn't even *close* to running out of resources. The system was just too immense. His lips twitched as he realised the virus's communistic nature had actually worked against it, for once. *Humanity* had settled randomly, scattering small asteroid colonies throughout the solar system to the point where *no one*, not even the RockRats, knew how many settlements there really were. One could arrive at an asteroid, intent on turning it into a colony, only to discover that someone else had gotten there first. The virus probably wouldn't have that problem. And that meant, hopefully, there'd be no risk of being caught until the rocks started to fall.

"Prep the drone," he ordered. "Launch on my command."

He braced himself. The drone was as close to undetectable as anyone could make it, without installing a cloaking device. The designers had gone so far as to fit the drone with gas jets, rather than rockets or fusion plumes or drive fields or anything else that might be detected at a considerable distance. The virus shouldn't be able to so much as catch a sniff of its presence. And yet, he felt uneasy. He was tempted to take his ship back through the tramline himself. The cloaking device wouldn't fluctuate for more than a second or two...

"Launch the drone," he ordered. They'd hashed it out, time and time again, during the long flight to the enemy system. "And keep a close watch for any sign we've been detected."

"Aye, Captain," Staci said.

Mitch winced, inwardly. Her voice was carefully controlled, but... Mitch knew her well enough to catch her irritation. If they'd been detected, there would be *no* visible signs until it was far too late. The virus wouldn't tip them off until it got its ships into position to open fire. Hell, a single passive sensor platform—invisible against the sheer vastness of space—would be enough to signal a warning to the inner system's defenders and then quietly monitor the human intruders from a safe distance. He told himself, not for the first time, that the odds of them being spotted were infinitesimal. It helped that the drone was largely invisible even to *his* sensors and *his* crew knew what to look for. The virus shouldn't have a clue.

He waited, counting down the seconds, as the drone vanished. There'd barely even been a *flicker* as it made transit. Mitch breathed a sigh of relief. The one-shot pusher drive had been experimental. It would completely revolutionise interstellar survey missions when it went mainstream, if the boffins managed to work out all the glitches and produce something reliable. And cut the cost down to a few million apiece. Mitch's lips twitched at the thought of asking the government to finance a small flotilla of drones. It wouldn't be easy. The government would insist it would be cheaper, in the long run, to finance a few frigates instead.

A new icon appeared on the display, wrapped in a green haze. Six more appeared a moment later, holding position even further from the system primary. Mitch grinned. Captain Hammond and his crew must have been deeply concerned, unsure of *what* they were going to find on the far side of the tramline. They had to have feared the worst. The virus had proven it *could* take over a starship, infecting the crew and using them to sneak an attack force into point-blank range. The deceptions never lasted long—and humanity had developed procedures for verifying a newcomer's *bona fides* before letting them into engagement range—but they'd been quite successful. It was hard to be sure who you were dealing with when someone was just a face on a screen.

Nothing can ever be taken for granted, Mitch thought. *And there are no security precautions that cannot be circumvented, if one has access to the minds of the original crew.*

"Open a laser link," he ordered. "And transmit a complete starship diagnostic."

"Aye, Captain," Culver said.

Mitch nodded to himself. It felt odd to be shooting so much data at another ship, but starship diagnostics were hard to fake. Anything could be faked, given time, yet…he'd been assured it would take weeks, perhaps months, to fake a complete diagnostics log. Captain Hammond's crew would be checking the new log against the old, trying to determine if something had changed…something that might indicate the entire ship and crew had been infected. It was unlikely, but the possibility had to be taken seriously. They didn't dare let an infected ship into engagement range.

And Captain Hammond might be hoping for a chance to take a shot at us, he thought, morbidly. Hammond wasn't *that* type of person—Mitch would concede that, if asked—but it was still something to bear in mind. *Blow away his wife's lover and claim he was infected…*

"Signal from the flag, sir," Culver said. "They're authorising us to commence stage two."

"Signal our acknowledgement," Mitch ordered. "Helm, have you updated our course plan against the tactical sensors?"

"Yes, Captain," Hinkson said. "We should remain at a safe distance from any known enemy positions."

But not any unknown positions, Mitch added, silently. Humanity had emplaced passive scansats all around its core systems, in hopes of spotting any unwelcome guests. He refused to believe the virus hadn't done the same. *We might avoid a visible sensor platform and steer straight into an invisible one.*

"Good," he said. "Take us out."

He stood, ordering the beta crew to take the bridge while the alpha crew got some sleep. It would be hours before they neared their first target, unless they wanted to throw caution to the winds and charge at the enemy position. Mitch's lips twitched at the absurd thought. A lone frigate couldn't do anything more than die bravely, if it did. The virus would blow the frigate out of space, before it could do anything. Better to take the time to do it properly than risk detection.

Staci joined him as he stepped through the hatch. "We might need a few more mass drivers," she said. "Like a few...thousand."

Mitch grimaced. Mass drivers had been effectively outlawed, at least as weapons, until the First Interstellar War. Even now, they weren't *that* common outside the asteroid mining industry. The mass drivers the Belt Alliance had loaned the Royal Navy hadn't really been designed as weapons...or so he'd been told. Mitch had his doubts about *that*. The schematics suggested the designers had certainly kept military applications in mind, to the point they could be turned into weapons at a moment's notice. They were useless for engaging starships, unless the ships were crewed by idiots, but not for raining death on immobile targets.

He pushed the thought out of his head. "They promised they'd send us more, when they had them assembled," he said. The admiral had made it clear she intended to fight for a relief fleet, but he doubted one would be thrown together on the fly. No politician in his right mind would leave Earth uncovered so quickly, not after the virus had tried to punch through the defences. "Until then, we'll just have to make do with what we have."

Staci nodded, curtly. "Yes, Captain."

Mitch opened the hatch to his cabin and stepped inside. The compartment looked the same as always, but it felt oddly fragile...he shook his head in irritation. He had no illusions about how long his ship would survive, if an enemy squadron had her in their sights, yet...the odds of being detected were extremely small. He stripped off his jacket, then lay on the bunk and closed his eyes. It was important he be well-rested, by the time they reached their first target. If they were detected…

The alarm rang, seconds later. Mitch stumbled out of bed, feeling as though he hadn't slept at all. He was halfway to the hatch when it dawned on him that it was his personal alarm. The ship wasn't under attack. He checked the live feed from the bridge, just to be sure, then stepped over to the dispenser and poured himself a cup of coffee. There were no stewards on *Unicorn*. He had to fetch his own coffee.

And that makes me horrifically deprived, he thought, as he drank the hot liquid without waiting for it to cool. *Captain Hammond would probably faint at the thought of getting his own coffee.*

He snorted, then remembered Charlotte and felt a sudden flare of lust. It wasn't uncommon, he'd been told, when someone went into danger. The body wanted a last chance to mate, to pass on its genes, before death finally came. He controlled himself with an effort, reminding himself that he was the ship's commanding officer. There was too much else for him to do and besides…Charlotte was hundreds of light years away. It wasn't as if he'd been able to bring her with him.

The intercom bleeped. "Captain, we are approaching Virus-5," Hinkson said. "The planetary defence network looks solid."

Mitch glanced at the display. "Hold position here," he ordered. There was no point in sneaking closer, not yet. They'd learn all they could from a safe distance first. "I'll be on the bridge in a moment."

He scooped up his jacket, wishing he had time for a shower. Sleeping in his uniform might not have been a bright idea, but there hadn't been any choice. He might have been summoned to the bridge at any moment and…he shook his head as he donned his jacket and made his way through the hatch. If they ran into trouble, it was quite likely the bridge crew would either manage to evade it before he reached the compartment, or they'd be blown to atoms within seconds. Either way…

"Captain," Staci said. She stood in front of the display, hands clasped behind her back. "The gas giant will not be easy to attack."

"No," Mitch agreed. If anything, that was a colossal understatement. The gas giant was orbited by a cluster of moons, all radiating betraying sensor emissions. There were hundreds of installations surrounding the planet, from immense mining stations to industrial facilities and orbital defences. A handful of mass drivers sat in high orbit, looking like guns pointed into interplanetary space. As he watched, one of the mass drivers launched a projectile into the inner system. He guessed it was frozen HE3. "I wonder…"

He paused. "Record for the flag," he said. The message would be tight-beamed to a relay station, then forwarded to *Lion*. There would be no reply, not until they returned to the platform, but it didn't matter. "I've just had an idea."

CHAPTER EIGHTEEN

THOMAS HAD SEEN THE SENSOR RECORDINGS during the return from Operation Lightning Strike, but the sheer *size* of the alien system hadn't really sunk in. Sol was huge, in material terms, and yet it wasn't even remotely politically united. The plans to unite the entire human race under a single government had been going slowly, with the Belt Alliance and the RockRats making it clear they would never subordinate themselves to a planetside government in which they would never hold the deciding vote. There was no way in hell that the entire human race—and its industrial base—would become a finely tuned machine, one committed to winning a war that *must* be won. Human nature would never let it happen.

And yet, he couldn't deny that the virus had made it work. The analysts had told him things he didn't want to know about the system's industrial potential, their calculations veering on the side of caution and yet…he had the nasty feeling they'd underestimated just how much the virus could produce. The virus didn't have to worry about human nature, about the desire to crush one's rivals or lie to one's superiors to avoid punishment for something that wasn't one's fault. The virus would coolly adapt to any production shortfalls, fine-tuning the system to crank out some more of whatever it needed. Thomas had heard, once, about a human experiment in which corporate departments had been ordered to compete with each other, rather than their outside rivals. It had been a complete disaster. But the virus wouldn't have that problem. It was, in a sense, a single entity that came in many different bodies.

He sat on his bridge and watched, grimly, as *Lion* and one of her tenders made their slow way towards the asteroid cluster. The system was *full* of space junk, to the point that—if the system had been uninhabited—it would have been a prize catch. The survey crew that laid claim to the system would have been richly rewarded…he shook his head. The system *was* inhabited—infected—and it couldn't be put to any better use until the virus was wiped from existence. He was starting to believe it wasn't possible. The virus was just too widespread. They might have to simply abandon the infected worlds, if they didn't come up with a vaccine. Hell, given how quickly the virus adapted, there was no guarantee they'd *ever* come up with a workable vaccine.

His console updated as more reports flowed in from the analysts. Some of them were already picking the system apart, trying to determine the weak points that could be targeted to throw the entire edifice into chaos. Thomas doubted there would be many point failure sources within the system. The industrial base was just too large, with multiple redundancies built into the network. It was nice to think there was a single target that would cripple the entire system, if it was taken out, but he doubted there'd be one.

And if it did exist, it would be heavily defended, he mused. *We'd need the entire fleet behind us to take it out.*

He grimaced. He'd seen the sensor records, but…somehow, they hadn't conveyed just how much effort the virus had put into developing and defending its core system. He hoped—he prayed—it *was* the core system. He saw layer upon layer of orbital battlestations, remote weapons platforms and free-floating missiles, backed up by a sizable fleet. It was no real consolation to note that the fleet was largely comprised of cruisers and destroyers, orbiting a hard core of battleships, carriers and brainships. He knew that meant the enemy fleet was off wreaking havoc elsewhere.

They hadn't seen any signs of trouble, as they slipped through the New Washington system, but that was meaningless. For all he knew, the enemy had resumed their attack on Earth.

"Captain," Fitzwilliam said. "We are approaching the asteroid cluster."

Thomas glanced at Sibley. "Tactical, are there any signs of an alien presence?"

"None, sir," Sibley said. "The cluster is silent."

"Good." Thomas glanced at his XO. "Helm, hold us here. Tactical, deploy ballistic drones."

"Aye, Captain," Sibley said.

Thomas forced himself to wait. The urge to get on with it, to set up the first pushers and the mass drivers, was almost overwhelming, but he dared not let the tiny squadron be caught so quickly. Deploying the missile pods *might* give them a fighting chance, if the enemy came into view, yet even his most optimistic simulations suggested otherwise. They *had* to remain unnoticed until they were ready to hurl rocks towards the enemy planets. He could sense his crew growing impatient, wondering why they hadn't already gotten to work…he ignored it. There was no point in taking foolish risks. That was Captain Campbell's job.

The asteroid cluster grew sharper on the display as the drones glided onwards, lasers tight-beaming their sensor reports back to their mothership. There were nineteen large asteroids in what looked like a formation, although Thomas knew it was just his mind seeking to impose order on chaos. They were huge, the type of rocky asteroids that would have made excellent colonies back home. Now…he eyed an asteroid that looked vaguely like a club and grimaced. He was going to use it to smash the alien homeworld beyond repair.

Assuming it gets anywhere near its target before it gets blown to dust or simply deflected, he reminded himself. The pusher couldn't ram the asteroid all the way up to 0.99C. The virus would have enough time to save its world, if it reacted quickly. *In other times, we would be grateful for the limitations on the tech.*

"Captain," Sibley said. "The drones have reported no trace of alien presence."

Thomas nodded, curtly. It felt unnatural. Back home, such an asteroid cluster would certainly have drawn a great deal of attention. There were more than enough raw materials in front of him, from metallic chunks of rock to water-ice asteroids, to provide everything a civilisation needed to keep going. The RockRats would have turned it into paradise. Or a religious colony would have sought to turn it into a new world, separate from the tyranny of Earth. Or...he shook his head. The virus wasn't human. It had probably marked the asteroids for later attention and then dismissed them from its thoughts.

"Deploy remote platforms, then contact the tender," he said. "The crews can begin operations at once."

He felt a prickle of ice run down his spine. *Lion* was fast. The tender had been built on a warship hull. They could evade contact, unless the enemy managed to sneak very close before they opened fire, but...once they started deploying their crews and equipment, they ran the risk of losing everything when the enemy backtracked the asteroids and sent a fleet to stomp on them. Thomas had few illusions. The crews had practiced packing up and running for their lives, with the enemy breathing down their necks, but...he feared the worst. They hadn't really had time to do *enough* drills for his peace of mind.

Not that it would have been that reassuring, he thought. *Emergency drills always leave out the emergency.*

He studied the in-system display as more and more data flowed into the sensors. It was hard to grasp the sheer scale of the system. *Unicorn* was somewhere closer to the primary, carrying out her tactical survey...he tried not to hope she'd trip a sensor network and get caught by the virus. He loathed Captain Campbell, but his crew didn't deserve to die. They hadn't asked to serve under an adulterer...Thomas ground his teeth. Captain Campbell had worked with him, had planned the mission with him...*that* had been an awkward series of discussions. God! Thomas felt a flash of rage. It was easy to feel that Captain Campbell's weaknesses would drag him down one day, but…why did they have to drag so many down with him?

You should probably have paid more attention to Charlotte, he told himself, sharply. He'd known there would come a time when he'd have to make the switch from naval officer to politician, but he'd fought to put that day off as long as possible. *Or tell her you didn't mind what she did as long as she was discreet.*

"Captain," Donker said. "The asteroid crews report it will take at least two days to set up the pushers, then calculate the correct trajectories."

Thomas nodded, unsurprised. He'd expected as much. The simulations had been vague on what would happen when two or more pushers were activated at the same general time. It shouldn't have made any difference, but the modified one-shot drive fields were likely to interact in unpredictable ways. The asteroids might fly straight to their targets or they might swoop around randomly, like leaky balloons. And then…he shrugged. It didn't matter if the drive field imparted any actual velocity. The asteroids wouldn't be going in the right direction.

"Continue to monitor the situation," he ordered. "Alert me if they release even a flicker of energy."

"Aye, Captain."

Thomas stood, trying not to let his worries show. The virus had infected the system for hundreds, perhaps thousands, of years. It had had plenty of time to become intimately familiar with every energy surge or gravitational eddy that might briefly flicker through the system. It would have an excellent idea of what should and shouldn't be there, of what could be explained away by rogue bodies passing through or distortions from the tramlines and what merited inspection. He found it hard to believe the virus wasn't keeping a wary eye out for intruders. Hell, it would have no trouble collating reports from all over the system. God knew humanity had had problems with that, back before the First Interstellar War. The threat of being crushed by an alien enemy had convinced everyone that it was better to hang together than be hung separately.

"You have the bridge," he said. "I'll be in my ready room. Alert me if anything changes."

The hatch hissed open to allow him to enter, then closed behind him. Thomas sighed as he walked over to the desk, suddenly feeling a great deal older. It was hard not to think of himself as a sitting duck, tied to the asteroids just long enough to let the virus take a clear shot at his hull. Cold logic told him the odds of detection were small, but it was hard to convince himself. The mission had seemed like a much better idea before they'd crossed the tramline into the enemy system. He sat, trying to ignore the constantly-updating feed from the analysts. It was never good news.

And if you insist on only getting good news, people will stop telling you the bad until it bites you, he reminded himself. *You cannot afford to refuse to listen to the truth, or it will catch you by surprise.*

He glanced at the long list of department reports, wondering if he could afford to lose himself in them. There were no real problems, nothing that could threaten the mission. They'd have been brought to his attention long ago, if they existed at all. And yet…he keyed his inbox, noting the last set of messages from home. His oldest daughter was taking over her duties, aided by the family lawyer and a handful of distant relatives; his youngest daughter had gone back to school, where she was safe from the horde of reporters camped outside the walls. And Charlotte appeared to have political ambitions. Thomas was almost curious to see if she could pull it off. It wouldn't be *easy* for a known adulteress to win election…

Don't be silly, he told himself, with a flicker of humour. *She's going to be an MP. The lack of a criminal record would probably bite her. What's adultery compared to fraud and sexual deviancy?*

He ran his hand through his hair, dismissing the joke. It wasn't funny. Not really. The MP selection was largely in the hands of the local party. Charlotte might have enough influence to get herself put forward as a candidate, then get elected. Perhaps. Would dating a naval hero make up for adultery? Or would voters look at her record and note she was almost terrifyingly efficient? She would be one hell of an MP, if she got elected. If nothing else, she would shake the Houses of Parliament up.

"And this line of thought is unproductive," he muttered. "By the time we get home, the whole affair will be decided one way or the other."

The terminal bleeped. "Captain?"

"Speaking," Thomas said. The alarms weren't howling, which meant they weren't in immediate danger. "Go ahead, Commander."

"We've just received the latest datapacket from *Unicorn*," Donker said. "Captain Campbell has had an idea."

"Forward it to me," Thomas ordered. No one doubted Captain Campbell's tactical skill. His ideas couldn't be dismissed, not without a fair hearing. "Where is he now?"

"The update said he was making his way to Virus-3," Donker said. "Based on general projections, he'll be within observation range by now."

Thomas nodded. There was no way they could track *Unicorn*, not from the edge of the infected system. It would be difficult to determine what had happened to the frigate, if she never returned. Thomas wasn't even sure they'd pick up a final signal, before the ship was blown to atoms. It was quite possible that *Unicorn* would simply vanish, presumed lost with all hands. And the first he'd know of the disaster was when the frigate failed to report to the RV point.

"I'll read his report," he said. "Inform me if anything changes."

"Aye, Captain,"

Thomas keyed his console, studying the datapacket as it unfolded. The gas giant was surrounded by enemy installations—he had a feeling the production estimates were definitely on the low side—and would be incredibly difficult to attack, without more ships and starfighters than he had. The mass drivers might prove a headache, if the enemy got a fix on their location. They weren't *designed* to hurl projectiles, but…he shook his head. The virus wouldn't take *that* long to fix that little problem. Hell, compressed and frozen gas would be quite bad enough.

He frowned as he studied the concept. It was clever, he supposed, and not something he would have come up with. Captain Campbell had always been good at spotting the weaknesses within any given system and taking advantage of them. And yet…it would be risky…he snorted in irritation. There was nothing about the entire operation that *wasn't*. He calculated the timing, then keyed the terminal. It might just work.

"Major Craig and Colonel Bagehot, report to my ready room," he ordered. "We have an operation to plan."

"Aye, Captain," Bagehot said.

"On my way," Craig said.

Thomas nodded and sat back in his chair, calling the steward to bring coffee and snacks. He had a nasty habit of not eating when he got busy, although he knew he should. Food just didn't feel *that* appetising when he was deeply involved with something. The hatch bleeped, then hissed open. Bagehot stepped into the compartment, looking tired. Craig followed him, in full combat uniform. The marines had been on standby for the last few hours, ready to intercept any boarding party before it infected the entire ship. Thomas made a mental note to ensure they stood down soon, once the asteroid operation was well underway. They'd need to be well-rested once the enemy started looking for them.

"Captain," Bagehot said.

"Have a seat," Thomas ordered. The steward appeared, poured coffee for the three of them, then retreated. "Captain Campbell has sent us an interesting idea."

He keyed the terminal, displaying a tactical outline. The concept was very simple, perhaps too simple. It was hard to believe that someone—somewhere—hadn't already thought of it. And yet, looking at the idea, it was easy to think that anyone capable of doing it wouldn't *want* to. It would cause no shortage of problems, for very little return. But here… here it might do a great deal of damage instead.

"A relatively simply ploy," Craig observed. "I take it you're not expecting opposition?"

"I don't think so," Thomas said. "There's no sign the mass driver projectiles are actually *manned*."

He frowned, considering it. The fusion plume ships that had carried the early deep space explorers from Earth to Pluto, before drive fields had been invented, had put immense strain on their crews. The constant acceleration had nearly killed them…*would* have killed them, if they hadn't been in suspended animation. The virus, on the other hand, might not be quite so disturbed by high gravity. It was possible it could build host-bodies capable of surviving or simply repair the damage, when the G-forces faded. There was just no way to be sure.

"Better to be careful," he said. "Colonel? What do you think?"

"I think it should be possible, but there would be a risk of being detected," Bagehot said. "If we"—he broke off, studying the trajectories—"if we come in from an angle, it should be possible to minimise the risks."

"Run it through the simulators," Thomas ordered. "If you can work out a way to do it with minimal risks, ask for volunteers. One gunboat, one fire team of marines. I don't want to risk any more than minimal manpower. Once you have the final details lined up, inform me. We'll launch the mission once everything is in place here."

"Aye, Captain," Bagehot said. He finished his coffee and stood. "I'll see to the simulations personally."

"There'll be no shortage of volunteers," Craig predicted. "The lads are getting bored."

Thomas smiled. "Better to be bored than to be shot at," he said. "And the virus will be shooting at us soon enough."

CHAPTER NINETEEN

"I MUST HAVE BEEN OUT OF MY MIND," Tobias subvocalised into the private channel. "What the fuck was I thinking?"

He shook his head in annoyance. He knew *precisely* what he'd been thinking. The command manuals Bagehot had…*encouraged*…him to read had suggested, very strongly, that a commander shouldn't order his men to do something he hadn't done himself. The manuals had been very clear on the point the commander might not understand what he was ordering, something Tobias was rather glad he hadn't realised last year, when there'd been literally no one with experience in flying gunboats or taking them into battle. He hadn't been able to refuse, when Bagehot had asked for volunteers. And yet, it was hard not to feel as though he'd made a mistake.

"I think you had no choice," Marigold said, over the same channel. "And I didn't have a choice either."

Tobias felt another flicker of guilt. The gunboat was in full stealth mode, with sensors set to passive and all weapons powered down, but she wasn't cloaked. There was no way a craft as small as a gunboat could carry a cloaking device, which meant the enemy might just see her coming. It would be easy to catch a sniff of the gunboat's presence, run a passive trace and put a ship in place to block her before she could escape. Tobias had worked his way through a dozen simulations, each one more pessimistic than the last. The good guys had won more often than they'd lost, but...

He tried not to glance into the rear of the gunboat. Colin and two other marines were sitting on the deck, looking calm and composed. One was even asleep, snoring so loudly it was hard to believe the enemy couldn't hear it. The other had spent time cracking jokes about no one being able to hear a scream in space, at least until Colin had told him to shut the fuck up. Colin himself...Tobias felt edgy about having Colin behind him, even though they'd buried the hatchet. And...

His eyes studied the display as they plunged further into the system. They were moving at an immense speed and yet they were practically *crawling* towards their target. The system was just too large, even for something that moved at just below the speed of light. The gunboat couldn't even move at *half* the speed of light. He checked the drives warily, concerned about losing one or more of the nodes. They might manage to limp back to the mothership if they lost one, but not two or more. The flare might be spotted, bringing the entire fleet down on them. And that would be disastrous.

For us, at least, he thought. Their target was steadily coming into sensor range. *The virus would know we didn't cross the tramline alone.*

He frowned. The concept was relatively simple. Why bother constructing interplanetary fuel tankers when you could simply freeze the gas, shape it into a rough cylinder and fire it into the inner system? The mass driver wasn't *quite* aimed at the planet, ensuring the odds of an accidental impact were quite small, while the beacon mounted on the projectile would guarantee a hit if something went wrong and the planetary defences had to vaporise the projectile before it struck the surface. And the mass driver could be turned into a weapon, if an enemy entered the system...Colin felt cold. An enemy *had* entered the system.

"We'll be in position in ten minutes," he said. "Unless something happens..."

He felt his frown grow deeper. The projectile had nothing, save for the constantly-blinking beacon. There were no rockets, no gas jets, no nothing…nothing that could alter course or pose a threat to the gunboat. And yet, he knew the virus could be dangerous. One of the analysts had speculated there might be a live colony of viral matter within the projectile, alive and well and aware of its surroundings despite the ice. Tobias hoped not. If the virus infected the marines, it would take the gunboat itself shortly afterwards.

"*Transformers*," he muttered.

Marigold looked up. "Pardon?"

"I used to watch *Transformers*, when I was a kid," Tobias said. It had been easy enough to locate episodes on the dark web, particularly the ones that had been banned for offending the government. "The whole concept was that simple vehicles could be giant enemy robots in disguise…"

He shook his head. "They were outside context threats," he added. "And the virus is just the same. Anything can be dangerous, even a small animal or the air we breathe."

"That's always been true," Colin said. "It's just…we're more aware of it now."

Tobias jumped. He hadn't realised Colin was listening. "We didn't used to think dogs and cows could be dangerous."

Colin chuckled. "We did," he said. "It's just that *we* grew up in a place where dogs were domesticated and cows were rare. Have you ever *seen* a cow?"

"No." Tobias conceded the point. "Still, you be careful over there."

"I'll scream like a little girl if it turns into a giant robot," Colin assured him. "And you can laugh once you get me out."

"I will," Tobias said. He glanced at the timer. "Five minutes."

The display changed. The cylinder was a giant shadow, barely visible in the inky darkness of space. The virus hadn't seen the need to include running lights, Tobias noted. They were rare, outside shipyards and high orbitals. He was tempted to turn on the gunboat's spotlights, but that would just heighten the risk of detection. The projectile might be midway between the gas giant and the rocky world ahead of them, racing through interstellar space, yet there was no way to know how many eyes were following it. He'd been warned not to take unnecessary risks.

"On your feet, you two," Colin ordered. "Time to take a walk on the wild side."

The marines jumped to their feet, moving with a practiced ease as they collected their helmets and locked them into place. Tobias felt a shiver run down his spine as he saw one of them slip the backpack nuke over his shoulder, as though it was nothing more than an ordinary rucksack. It was hard to believe that the nuke was powerful enough to vaporise a battleship, if it detonated inside the hull. And yet...they were tossing it around as if it were nothing. If it went off...Tobias told himself, firmly, that it wouldn't. The nuke needed an elaborate series of command codes, inputted in the right order, before it went live. Or so he'd been told.

He stood and keyed the airlock controls. "Ready?"

"One at a time," Colin said. He started forward as the inner hatch cycled open. "We'll be back before you know it."

"Joy," Tobias said.

• • •

Colin had been told, when he'd started his training, that the military life was nine-tenths boredom to one-tenth fear. He hadn't really believed it until he'd earned his spurs and been attached to a number of starships, where he'd spent most of his time training and exercising between missions. It made him feel as though he was wasting his time. He'd volunteered for the raid into enemy territory, at least in part, because it was a chance to do something.

A situation can drop into hell at the blink of an eye, he thought, shortly. *And you have to be ready for when it does.*

He stood in the airlock, eyes searching for the gas projectile. He'd expected it to be lit up like something from a cartoon, perhaps the show Tobias had mentioned, and the reality was somewhat disappointing. He wouldn't even have been sure the projectile was even *there* if he hadn't seen it occluding the stars. He hooked a line to the gunboat's hull—missing his target and flying into space would be embarrassing at best and fatal at worst—and then jumped into space. The gravity field vanished, leaving him feeling oddly uneasy as he plunged towards the projectile. His perspective shifted, time and time again, before he slammed into the dull gray cylinder. It felt like just another asteroid.

His HUD scanned the projectile, analysing the beacon's signal. It hadn't changed...not as far as they could tell. The concept of someone actually *stealing* the frozen gas was absurd—space pirates were incredibly rare, the stuff of trashy fiction rather than real life—but the virus knew it had enemies. He inched forward as Private Scott Davies landed behind him, weapon in hand. There was no sign of life, let alone a threat, but they'd been warned not to take chances. The virus could be bubbling under his feet. He looked down at the gray surface and found nothing but ice. The gravity field was effectively non-existent.

He reached the front of the projectile and peered at the beacon. It was nothing more than a simple transmitter, surprisingly primitive by the virus's standards. Colin found it a little odd. Military tech was as simple as possible, to facilitate repair in the field, but the virus could have put together something a little more solid. Perhaps it felt safe, so far from the front lines. Or perhaps it just thought that one gas projectile more or less wouldn't make a difference in the grand scheme of things. It might well be right.

Private Henry Willis landed as Colin turned away from the prow, the nukes strapped to his back. Colin held up a hand, warning Willis to stay back, then knelt and tried to dig into the ice. It didn't work. The ice was just too solid to be broken, even by their armoured hands. Colin had hoped...he shook his head, then pointed to the rear of the projectile. The nuke would have to be emplaced there, hopefully hidden well enough to remain undetected until it was too late. The proximity sensors would ensure no one got close enough to remove or disarm the bomb without detonating it.

Willis unstrapped the bomb and pressed it firmly into place. Colin watched grimly, then keyed in the first set of command codes. The bomb's display turned red, a timer appearing and counting down to zero. Davis input the second set of codes, then stepped back hastily as the timer reset itself. The three marines hesitated, then hurled themselves into space. When the timer reached zero, the proximity sensors would go live. The bomb simply couldn't be defused any longer.

Colin pulled on the rope, flying back towards the gunboat. He hit the hull, made his way to the airlock and stepped inside. The others followed him. He checked his HUD as the airlock cycled, then removed his helmet. The air tasted faintly of too many people in too close proximity, but he'd been in worse places. The locker rooms at school had been so stinky that the pupils had joked one needed a shower, then another shower to recover from the *first* shower. Even Marine Country was something of an improvement.

Tobias glanced at him. "Success?"

"The nuke's in place," Colin said, as the rest of the fire team came through the airlock. "How long until the projectile reaches its destination?"

"Three days, unless something happens," Tobias said. "Are you sure there's nothing they can do about it?"

"If they knew the nuke was there, they could slam a missile into the projectile and vaporise the bomb before it had a chance to detonate," Colin said. The standard practice for dealing with terrorist nukes was to drop a KEW on them, instead of trying to disarm them. It hadn't happened very often, thankfully. "But they would have to know the nuke was there."

He considered it as he leaned against the hull. He'd never been given the *full* rundown on how the border screening worked, but he was fairly sure someone couldn't get a chunk of nuclear material into the country without setting off all sorts of alarms. The bomb material would need to be heavily shielded to prevent detection, which would also attract attention. And yet...could the virus detect the bomb? It was unlikely and yet... what if he was wrong?

We had to try, he told himself. He was fairly sure the nuke would force the virus to start screening everything heading into orbit, even if there wouldn't be any more nukes. Not yet, anyway. It wouldn't be hard to start mining a few more projectiles at random…or let themselves be seen, just long enough to convince the virus that another projectile had been mined. *I'll have to speak to the major about it.*

"I need to rest," he said. It wasn't as if there was anything else to do in the gunboat. He'd brought his e-reader, but he didn't feel like reading. "How long until we get back to the ship?"

"At least ten hours," Tobias said. "We'll have to take the long way out of the system."

"Then I'll sleep now," Colin said. He sat on the deck, leaning against the hull. He'd slept in worse places. The gunboat was paradise, compared to a foxhole in the middle of a battleground. There was no rain, no mud and no sergeants screaming in his ear. "Wake me up when we get there."

Tobias nodded. "Will do."

• • •

Thomas had been on edge ever since the gunboat had been launched into the inner system, taking with it the hopes and fears of the entire battlecruiser. The sensor platforms had barely been able to track the gunboat, despite knowing where to look and what to look for, suggesting the virus wouldn't be able to track it at all…and yet, Thomas couldn't help fearing the worst. The brief laser-beamed signal indicating mission success had relieved him, but…he stood on the bridge, watching the enemy movements as they glided around their system. It only took one mistake, one energy signature in a place where none should be, to alert the enemy. And then all hell would break loose.

He studied the updates from the asteroid crews, in hopes of a distraction. The mass drivers were in place, their firing systems being calibrated and keyed to the targeting data forwarded by *Unicorn*. The pushers were in place, the final preparations being made before the asteroids were hurled at their targets. Thomas hoped the RockRat crews were correct, when they'd bragged the pushers could be removed and reused time and time again. The slightest mistake would result in losing one or more of the pushers, weakening his ability to continue raining death on the enemy system. And then...

"Captain," Donker said. The XO looked disgustingly fresh, for someone who couldn't have had much more sleep than his commanding officer. "The survey team just checked in. They have picked out a number of other firing positions."

"Good." Thomas knew they couldn't stay where they were, not once they started steering asteroids towards the inner system. He'd be surprised if they were allowed the time to throw the remaining rocks into the system before they had to move. The virus could get a handful of fast cruisers out to the cluster within hours. "Move the preliminary teams there. We may as well get a head start on the preparations."

"Aye, Captain," Donker said. "The factory ship reports she has taken up position and started forging kinetic projectiles. We should have more than enough within the next few days."

"Good," Thomas said, again. He kept his doubts to himself. Either the plan worked or it failed. If the latter, the new projectiles would be worse than useless. They'd have to be abandoned while the squadron retreated to human space. "Tell them to keep up the good work."

He turned away from the display. "Has there been any update from *Unicorn*?"

"The last update was four hours ago, in which they said they were ready to start deploying spy platforms, decoys and mines," Donker said. "That was sent five hours ago."

And is therefore nine hours out of date, Thomas reminded himself. To all intents and purposes, Captain Campbell was on his own. He knew the younger man preferred it that way. *It wasn't as if we planned for the operation to go like clockwork.*

He shrugged. "The mined projectile will reach its destination in three days," he said, instead. "We'll launch the asteroids and mass driver projectiles to reach their target just before the nuke. We might not hit anything, not the first time, but we'll make it harder for them to stop the nuke. And that should make them paranoid as hell."

"Aye, Captain," Donker said.

Thomas turned back to the display. The tension was starting to get to him, but...he knew he'd miss it when it was gone. The enemy would spare no expense to drive them into deep space, if they couldn't destroy them. The majority of the enemy fleet might be elsewhere—Thomas wanted to believe it had been destroyed, but he knew better—and yet there were more than enough mobile units in the system to hunt *Lion* down and blow her to atoms. And they couldn't hide forever without giving up the chance to hurt the enemy.

"Captain," Cook said. "Colonel Bagehot's compliments, sir, and he reports that the gunboat has returned to the ship."

"My compliments to her crew," Thomas said, calmly. "Was there any sign they were detected?"

"None, according to the preliminary report," Cook said. "They encountered no opposition."

Thomas allowed himself a smile. "Good," he said. Given time, they could repeat the feat or try to slip a nuke onto another target. Even if it didn't work, it would give the virus a nasty fright. "And now, we wait."

CHAPTER TWENTY

THE PLANET ON THE DISPLAY looked to be surrounded by a small galaxy.

Mitch knew, without false modesty, that he was a seasoned interstellar traveller. He'd been born on Earth and been stationed in a dozen systems, human and alien alike. And yet, Virus-3—Virus Prime—was the most intensely developed planet he'd ever seen. There were so many orbital installations that it looked as if a man could walk around the entire planet, just by jumping from base to base. It was possible to believe a starship could fire a salvo of pellets from a railgun towards the planet and be sure of hitting something—anything—before the pellets flew into the planet's atmosphere and burned up. The sheer *scale* of the orbital installations dwarfed anything he'd seen, anywhere. It would take years for humanity to match the virus's work, if the money was made available. And the cost would be light years out of the human race's budget.

He allowed his eyes to wander over the display, trying to comprehend the sight before him. The planet's equator was practically *laced* with orbital towers and space elevators, the latter connected to asteroid habitats as well as industrial nodes and shipyards. *Unicorn* was lurking a safe distance from the planet—or what he devoutly *hoped* was a safe distance—and yet he could pick out dozens of starships taking shape in the shipyards. It was hard not to feel a flicker of raw terror as he computed the numbers, silently calculating how long it would take the virus to put its new ships into service and resume the offensive. A few months? A year? There was no doubt the war had to be won and won quickly. The virus would soon have the numbers to brush the human navies aside and push its way to Earth.

The planet's atmosphere looked...*weird*. It was hard to be sure—there was no way they could fly a sampling mission through the atmosphere without being detected—but it seemed to be a virtual *sea* of viral matter. The oceans were heaving with virus, with giant blobby sea creatures moving slowly through the poisoned waters; the land was so heavily infected, he thought, that the entire planet was practically one mind. He hoped—prayed—that an asteroid strike would be enough to stun the virus, the force of the impact enough to disorient even a planet-sized mind. It would have to, wouldn't it? A human could be brought down by a relatively weak blow, if the blow landed in the right place. Surely, the virus couldn't be that alien...

He was grimly aware of the silence pervading the bridge as more and more data flowed into the sensor displays. His crew were practically holding their breath, for fear of being overheard by listening ears. It was common, he knew, even though he also knew that sound didn't travel through space. His lips quirked in droll amusement. In space, as he'd been told time and time again, no one could hear a scream. He and his crew could be having a drunken student booze-up, complete with loud bagpipe music and hookers, and the virus wouldn't hear a thing. And yet, his crew were silent. It was hard to believe they couldn't be overheard, even though he *knew* it was true. Space, much less the planet in question, was just too big.

And the virus might be working on ways to spread its influence into space itself, he mused. It was hard to believe something biological might survive the cold of space, but...if anything could, it was the virus. The boffins were already speculating that the virus might have infected gas giants, existing in giant clusters of viral matter floating within the clouds. A handful had even speculated that the virus had been *born* in a gas giant, given its completely unprecedented nature. *What if, one day, it envelops the entire galaxy?*

He shook his head to clear it. "Helm, take us to the first checkpoint."

"Aye, Captain." Hinkson sounded stunned, as if someone had slapped him several times. A low hum ran through the ship as she altered course, a flurry of concern flickering through the bridge as the crew heard the sound. "We'll be in position in ten minutes."

Mitch nodded as he studied the sensor display. The virus had assembled a structure that looked like a giant basketball hoop to catch projectiles from the gas giants. It was far too close to some of their orbital installations for comfort, although Mitch had to concede the odds of disaster were very low. The virus had probably run the calculations and decided the slight increase in efficiency was worth the risk. *That* was going to bite them, if Captain Hammond had taken note of Mitch's suggestion and put it into play. Mitch had no idea if he'd done anything of the sort. It was a concept that might have needed to wait until the asteroids started making their way towards Virus Prime.

He waited, grimly, as *Unicorn* kept moving. His ship was cloaked—and all non-essential systems had been powered down—but the odds of detection had never been greater. Virus Prime was practically shrouded in sensor emissions, the virus making no attempt to hide its presence as it filled space with everything from gravity pulses to laser bursts and primitive radar waves. He wouldn't have been surprised to discover it was using *telescopes* too, as well as more advanced optical sensors. The slightest hint of a threat would bring starfighters and gunboats boiling out to investigate, sweeping space with vast numbers until they found and destroyed the threat or convinced themselves it had never really existed. Mitch understood. The planet was so important, in the grand scheme of things, that it had to be defended. It didn't matter how much wear and tear the virus put on its equipment, as long as the planet itself remained safe.

"Captain," Hinkson said. "We have reached the first checkpoint."

Mitch took a breath. "Tactical?"

"No active enemy sensors within detection range," Staci reported. "There's no sign we've been detected."

"Good," Mitch said.

He frowned. He wasn't reassured. *Unicorn* was close enough to the planet to do a basic tactical survey, picking out targets for *Lion*, while remaining distant enough to retreat back into the vastness of interplanetary space if she was challenged. The virus would know it, too. It would have no trouble calculating an intercept vector, then dispatching a flight of cloaked ships to sneak into firing range while pretending to have no idea *Unicorn* was there. There was no time to waste.

"Deploy the first sensor platform," he ordered. "And then activate the tight-beam link."

"Aye, Captain."

The tension on the bridge sharpened as the first platform was released into interplanetary space. The stealthed platforms were meant to be undetectable, practically impossible to locate unless someone stumbled across the platform's position by sheer dumb luck...there were so many starships and starfighters within the system, Mitch noted, that it wasn't entirely impossible. He'd tried to locate the platforms himself, during training exercises, and he'd drawn a blank...he'd only had one starship under his command. The virus could fill space with enough units to search with the naked eye, if it thought it needed to bother. If the cloaking device flickered, just once...

"Platform deployed, Captain," Staci said. "Primary laser link established. Secondary laser link online, ready to deploy."

Mitch nodded, curtly. The platform was designed to transmit its reports to a second platform, which would in turn forward them to *Lion*. In theory, there was no way the virus could detect the laser beam unless a starship accidentally crossed it. In practice...he shook his head as the platform came online completely, deploying a handful of passive sensor arrays to peer down at the enemy planet. It didn't matter. They had to take the chance. Besides—he glanced at the timer—they had only a couple of days before the first wave of projectiles came roaring towards the planet. The virus would have to be stupid not to realise it was under attack. It might be alien, with thought processes that made no sense to the human mind, but it wasn't stupid. Mitch had a nasty feeling the virus's first move would be to sweep local space for unseen eyes.

And if it does find the platform, it shouldn't be able to capture it, he told himself. *Anyone who tries to make contact without the right codes will be blown to hell, when the nuke detonates.*

"All laser links established, Captain," Staci said. "The platform is emplaced and ready."

Mitch smiled. "Helm, take us to the second checkpoint."

He felt his smile grow wider as the frigate glided away from the platform. His sensor crews knew where it was, and yet it was invisible to their passive sensors. They only knew it was there because they'd *placed* it there. Even a full sweep with active sensors, which would reveal their presence to the enemy, wouldn't find the platform unless they were practically on top of it. The boffins—and intelligence officers—had been reluctant to release the platforms, insisting they were top secret as well as expensive. Mitch rolled his eyes at the thought. The platforms would be worthless if humanity lost the war.

The hours ticked on as they glided from checkpoint to checkpoint, emplacing sensor platforms and linking them to the distant units before moving onwards. Sweat beaded on Mitch's back as they flew near enemy starships, shutting down everything they could to avoid emitting even the *slightest* hint of their presence; he felt naked, dangerously exposed, even though he was sure the virus wouldn't have let them just get on with the mission if it had the slightest idea the frigate was there. They glided further from the planet, heading towards the final checkpoint. He took the opportunity to order his primary crew to get some rest. The secondary crew could handle the mission for a few hours.

"David and Matthew have been getting busy," Staci said. She grinned at him, tiredly. "Do you think they'll remember to sleep?"

"They'd better be rested by the time they report to duty or they'll be in deep shit," Mitch said, bluntly. He'd always turned a blind eye to relationships between his subordinates, as long as they didn't infringe upon regulations, but there were limits. There were no secrets on such a tiny ship. He *had* to deal with anything that might become more than a little problematic. "Keep an eye on it."

"Yes, sir," Staci said. "Of course, there's not much else to do right now."

Mitch shrugged as he dismissed her and walked into his cabin. She was right. Everything that wasn't strictly necessary had been powered down, including everything from e-readers to touchy-feely bands. There was no way the crew could watch movies or enter VR sims or even catch up on their reading. He hoped the happy couple would remember to sleep as well as have fun, if only because they'd be needed on duty. He hadn't been joking when he'd said they'd be in trouble. There were very definite limits.

He climbed into his bunk, closed his eyes and slept. The alarm woke him in what felt like seconds. Mitch crawled out of bed, checked the terminal to be sure there hadn't been a horrific mistake, then changed into a fresh uniform and returned to the bridge. The ship was still moving between checkpoints, leaving a network of stealthed platforms in its wake. Their sensors were already putting together a more comprehensive picture of the virus's activities. It was starting to look as though the whole system was *littered* with multiple redundancies.

"Captain," Staci said. She looked as though she hadn't slept very well, either. "That's the last of the platforms in position."

"We'll move to deploy the mines now," Mitch said. "Are they ready?"

"Yes, Captain," Staci said. "And the sensor decoys are ready for deployment as well."

Mitch rubbed his eyes. He'd drunk a cup of navy-grade coffee—the navy's contractors insisted it was as black as the inky darkness of space itself—but he didn't feel awake. He made a mental note to ensure his crew got a few moments of—relative—freedom, as soon as they emplaced the minefields and sensor decoys. They could pull back until they were well clear of the planet, then allow the crew to use their electronic gadgets without fear of detection. They should have the time, if the minefield was laid without problems.

"Take us to the final checkpoint," he ordered. They'd planned the mission carefully, during the long voyage from Earth, but they'd had to concede they might have had to alter the plans on short notice. He was relieved to note they didn't *have* to do anything of the sort, something that bothered him. His experience had taught him that a plan that was going perfectly was one certain to fail. "And prepare to deploy the mines."

He smiled, coldly, as the ship picked up speed. The virus had turned mines into a potent threat, simply by laying them in a location it *knew* the human race would have to deploy its ships. Mitch had to concede the tactic had worked, if only because the various human navies didn't have any real mine-sweeping experience. They might as well have practiced tactics against submarines or wooden sailing ships...his lips quirked in amusement. Primitive wet-navy ships were hardly the threats the space-faring navy expected to face.

And we always assumed mines would be effectively worthless, he reminded himself. *The virus had a better idea.*

He let out a breath as they reached the final checkpoint. "Tactical, begin deploying the minefield," he ordered. "Helm, follow the planned pattern."

"Aye, Captain."

The tension on the bridge sharpened, again, as the first of the mines was unloaded into interplanetary space. They were difficult to detect, in theory, and yet there was a risk of having the field spotted before it was too late. Mitch had picked the location with a certain degree of malice aforethought—and he'd checked his original plans against the sensor records, as they glided closer to Virus Prime—but there was just no way to be sure. They couldn't afford to wait to deploy the minefield, yet leaving it in place meant accepting the risk of losing it before zero hour. It was only a couple of days, he told himself. The field should remain undetected unless the virus changed its patterns and patrol routes without warning.

And they'd only do that if they caught a sniff of our presence, he thought. His instructors had cautioned him to make his patrol routes unpredictable, just to ensure no watching eyes picked out a pattern and took advantage of it, but the virus seemed to have different ideas. Mitch had no idea if it didn't realise the danger, or if it thought the risks didn't matter, or if it had something else on its collective mind. *The brainships might be too busy plotting the next attack on Earth to be concerned with their own defence.*

"Captain, the last of the mines has been deployed," Staci said. "I request permission to deploy the sensor decoys."

"Granted," Mitch said. They were committed now…he shook his head. They'd been committed from the moment they'd accepted the mission. "Helm, take us into position."

"Aye, Captain."

Staci smiled, grimly, as she worked her console. "Do you think they'll take the bait?"

"I hope so, or all our efforts here will be worse than useless," Mitch said. He'd calculated that the virus would *have* to take the bait, but…he hadn't realised just how many defences the virus had put into place. It was just possible the virus would calculate it could afford to ignore the bait. "Inform me the moment you have put the last of the sensor decoys in place."

He sat back in his chair, feeling a thrill of excitement. He'd never liked boredom, even though he'd been a serving officer long enough to know he should be glad of being bored. One way or the other, he wouldn't be bored for much longer. The virus would know they were there. It was going to come looking for them. It was stupid, he knew, but part of him just couldn't wait. He'd always liked the excitement of testing himself against the best the enemy had to offer.

"Captain," Staci said. She looked up from her console, her face composed. "The last sensor decoy has been deployed. They are all ready for activation on your command."

"Helm, move us away from the planet," Mitch ordered. He keyed his console, designating a waypoint. They would remain close enough to the planet to query the network of sensor platforms, while minimising the risk of being detected. They should have more than enough warning if the virus spotted *Unicorn* and sent a fleet to kill her. "Communications, signal *Lion*. Inform her that stage one is now completed."

"Aye, Captain."

Mitch allowed himself a smile. He'd feared the worst, when he'd seen the plan, but they'd managed to keep their distance while completing the mission. It wouldn't be so easy the next time…his smile grew wider. They had to keep the virus guessing, keep it jumping at shadows…hell, they had to keep it *shooting* at shadows. The longer they kept it off-balance, the greater the chance of scoring a major hit.

And there's so much crap in orbit it would be difficult not *to hit something, when we start throwing rocks at the planet,* he mused. His lips tightened as an idea occurred to him. *We should be able to take advantage of that if we plan ahead.*

CHAPTER TWENTY-ONE

"CAPTAIN," COMMANDER DONKER SAID. "The RockRats are departing the asteroids now."

Thomas nodded. The live feed from the stealthed platforms was showing the asteroid cluster, the modified asteroids surrounded by green circles to mark them out from their fellows. The RockRats had done a good job. There were few visible clues the asteroids were any different from the remainder of the cluster, certainly none that could be spotted easily. He glanced at the timer, silently relieved that all nine asteroids were ready before the countdown reached zero. The gas projectile was due to reach its destination in eleven hours. The nuclear blast would be more than enough proof that the system had been invaded.

"Begin the countdown as soon as they're clear," he ordered.

He glanced at the mass drivers, positioned very close to the asteroids themselves. They'd built up quite a stockpile of projectiles in the last few days, although it was anyone's guess how many they'd manage to fire before the crews had to dismantle the mass drivers and run for their lives. Thomas and his tactical staff had run the calculations time and time again, concluding it would be at least ten hours before the virus could get a squadron out to the asteroid base, but a lot of their assessments were based on guesswork. If the virus had a ship—or a squadron—considerably nearer their position, the time estimate was going to become wildly optimistic. They'd practiced dismantling the drivers and gotten the time down to an hour, but it wasn't good enough. The plans to mount a driver on a freighter had come to nothing.

We should probably design a dedicated mass driver starship, Thomas mused. It wouldn't be that hard, although the ship wouldn't be able to stand in the line of battle. *And then we could simply move it from system to system.*

The tactical display bleeped. The countdown had begun. Thomas stood, clasping his hands behind his back as he studied the display. *Unicorn* had provided a remarkable amount of targeting data, but it was important to bear in mind that it was at least five hours out of date and that starships and mobile installations could easily move when they saw the rocks coming. It was lucky, Thomas reflected, that the planet itself couldn't be moved. Captain Campbell's last report had suggested the planet was so infected that slamming an asteroid into the surface would be like punching a man in the face. Thomas thought that was wishful thinking, but he knew they needed to test the theory. If it worked...

"Captain," Donker said. He turned to look at his commander. "The first asteroid will be launched in two minutes."

Thomas nodded, wordlessly. The die was about to be cast. They were about to reveal their presence in a manner the virus could not ignore. He shook his head. He'd seen the images from Virus Prime. He'd read the reports that assessed what they meant for humanity. His tiny squadron was a small price to pay for the salvation of the entire human race. He wished, suddenly, he'd been allowed to bring a few more ships. The images from the alien world might convince the various navies they really *had* to strike now or accept eventual defeat.

He frowned. Imperial Japan had felt the same way too, back in 1941. The Japanese had calculated they had to fight and win quickly, or accept eventual defeat. And yet, the Japanese had been unable to destroy either America or Britain's ability to replace their losses and return to the fight.

Midway had been called the battle that doomed Japan, but—in truth—Japan had been doomed by the decision to fight. And yet...he shook his head. The space navies could and would strike at their enemy's homeworld, destroying its industrial base and half-built starships before they could take flight. He just hoped they could do enough damage to buy time, if they didn't win outright. The human race was constantly developing newer and better weapons. Who knew what new war-winning weapons would emerge from the labs, given time? And who knew what changes they'd bring in their wake?

There's no such thing as a silver bullet, he reminded himself. The navy had spent billions on newer and better weapons, but none had ever given it such an advantage that victory had suddenly become easy. *We develop something new and, by the time we work out the kinks in the system, they've developed it for themselves too.*

"Twenty seconds," Donker said. "Ten..."

Thomas's eyes found the asteroid as it hung in space, seemingly motionless. The pusher was a tiny structure, positioned neatly at the rear of the asteroid. It was hardly the first time the RockRats had moved an asteroid, but...the pusher was largely untested technology. Thomas suspected it wasn't as useful as the RockRats had hoped, when they'd developed it. Stopping an asteroid moving at half the speed of light wouldn't be easy. The pusher was really nothing more than a terror weapon.

The asteroid seemed to shimmer as the drive field enveloped it. Thomas had the inescapable sense of a rock skipping across a pond, an instant before the pusher disconnected and whirled away into interplanetary space. The asteroid should have crashed to a halt—he knew what happened when a drive field failed—but instead it kept going, hurtling towards its target at an unbelievable speed. Thomas felt an icy sensation trickling down his back. The asteroid wasn't quite unstoppable, not if the virus saw it coming, but...it was only a matter of time before the virus developed pushers for itself. And if it decided to bombard Earth...

"Telemetry indicates the asteroid is now falling towards its target at

0.45C," Donker reported, grimly. "The gee-forces were immense. We're lucky the pusher itself wasn't smashed flat."

"Detach a gunboat to recover the pusher, then have it fixed to another asteroid," Thomas ordered. 0.45C. That wasn't quite what he'd been promised, but it was good enough. "And then launch the remaining asteroids, one by one."

He felt his hands grow damp with sweat as the second asteroid was launched, reaching a velocity of 0.5C before the pusher ran out of power and ejected itself into space. The third asteroid barely matched the first, the fourth and fifth reaching half the speed of light before their pushers were released. The virus was going to have to deflect or smash the asteroids one by one, the latter option ensuring a tidal wave of rocky debris crashing into the high orbitals. Thomas gritted his teeth. It was going to be easy—very easy—for anyone who knew what had happened to deduce how the pusher worked, then duplicate it. There were RockRat factions that loathed Earth, that wanted to be permanently free of its influence. How long would it be before they started hurling rocks at Earth, too?

Hopefully, everyone will realise the folly of starting such a war, he thought. *But when have humans ever been wise enough to think of the consequences?*

"Captain," Donker said. "The final asteroid is *en route*."

"Signal the mass drivers," Thomas ordered. "They are to commence firing and continue firing as long as possible."

He forced himself to sit down. The mass drivers were known technology, if scaled up by several orders of magnitude. It wouldn't be *hard* to accelerate a projectile and spit it right across the alien system. They'd arrive while the virus was still recovering from the asteroids...Thomas hoped. It was easy to calculate the precise transit time, but harder to guess what they might hit...if anything. The projectiles were tough, yet they weren't designed to punch their way through a planet's atmosphere and hit the surface. Hitting the planet itself might be a matter of luck, rather than design.

The display updated. The projectiles were difficult to spot, although they weren't stealthed. The virus would have no trouble spotting and destroying them...as long as its sensor network remained online. Thomas smiled, coldly. There was a reasonable chance the steady pounding, and sensor decoys, would degrade the enemy's sensor network over the next few days. The longer the bombardment continued, the greater the chance of one or more projectiles getting through the defences and hitting something vital.

He frowned. The virus *might* have picked up the pushers, even if it didn't know what they were. Their signature was unmistakably artificial. The gravity waves would have twanged local space, in the navy's wonderfully imprecise terminology, and alerted the virus to the squadron's presence. How long would it be, really, before the enemy deployed their ships to intercept the human squadron? Thomas felt tired, tired and exposed. A normal engagement was little more than a quick in and out, a battle that would be decided relatively quickly. This one wouldn't be decided for weeks.

Unless we get very unlucky, he reflected. *And that would be the end.*

"You have the bridge," he said, standing. "Keep an eye on the mass drivers. They are to continue firing as long as possible, replacing overheated or overstressed components if necessary. And alert me the moment you see the enemy respond."

"Aye, Captain," Donker said.

Thomas stepped into his ready room, the hatch closing behind him. It felt weird to be firing blind, even though he was sure they'd hit the planet if nothing else. They'd been a handful of petty skirmishes when humanity first climbed into space, long drawn-out engagements that had been so ruefully imprecise that they'd effectively ended in stalemates. Those days had been over long before humanity had fought its first real interstellar war. And yet...normally, a starship commander would know very quickly if he'd hit something or not. Now, it would be eleven hours—more or less—before the first of the asteroids reached its target and a further five hours before he knew what he'd hit. If anything. The virus would have to deflect or destroy the asteroids…

Get some rest, he told himself. It felt wrong to be sleeping in the middle of an engagement, but there was nothing he could do. There was nothing *anyone* could do until the virus came calling. *You'll be glad of it soon enough.*

• • •

Mitch jerked awake as the alarms blared, one hand reaching for the pistol he kept beside his bunk before his dulled mind realised the ship probably wasn't being boarded. The tactical display was blinking orange, not red. He sat upright and frowned as he checked the terminal. The virus was hastily bringing the remainder of its tactical sensors online, filling space with sensor pulses…all pointing towards the edge of the solar system. Mitch stared at it for a moment, then nodded in understanding. The virus had seen the incoming asteroids. It was getting ready to do something about them.

He glanced at the timer as he poured himself a cup of coffee. The planners hadn't been able to say *precisely* when the asteroids would reach their targets. They'd admitted—when pushed—that the pusher wasn't always predictable. They *had* been sure the incoming asteroids would be detected, that the virus would have its own version of the GATO Deep Space Monitoring Network. Mitch hadn't been able to disagree with their logic. A number of asteroids had come far too close to hitting Earth over the last four hundred years for him to believe the virus wouldn't watch for space junk. It certainly had the technical skill to detect an incoming asteroid and the starships necessary to push it to one side, if not blow it to dust and atoms. He was mildly surprised the virus hadn't noticed the incoming asteroids sooner. It certainly *should* have spotted the overpowered drive fields on the edge of the system.

Unless it thinks something went wrong, he mused. *It might not have figured out the connection between the drive field bursts and the incoming asteroids.*

The intercom bleeped. "Captain," Staci said. "The virus is deploying its ships to meet the threat."

"Understood," Mitch said. He'd be astonished if the virus let an asteroid strike the planet, not as long as the orbital defence network remained intact, but they'd learn a great deal by watching how the virus chose to handle the threat. "I'm on my way."

He finished his coffee, then checked the timer again. The brief update from *Lion* had indicated that the mined gas projectile was due in two hours, shortly after the asteroids were timed to strike the planet. It would be interesting to see if the orbital defences fired on the gas projectile as well as the asteroids themselves, he noted. The virus should have no reason to think it was a threat, but it was probably feeling a little paranoid. It might have realised there was an entire stream of mass driver projectiles heading towards the planet, too.

And that would be ironic, he mused. *It would save itself from the most insidious threat without ever realising it.*

He donned his jacket, then strode onto the bridge. The crew looked more relaxed, now that the operation had finally begun. Mitch hid his amusement as he took his chair and checked the live feed from the network of sensor platforms. The virus was pumping out so many sensor pulses that he doubted the cloaking device could hide them, if they'd been caught within the sensor focus. The virus was putting one hell of a lot of wear and tear on its equipment, but it didn't really have a choice. The asteroids might shatter, if they were struck by missiles. Perversely, it would make the incoming threat worse.

We can take advantage of that, he thought. *But we're going to have to wear them down a little more first.*

His mind raced as he considered the virus's possible options. What could it do? Did it have a deflection crew on standby? Earth did, something that might have saved the planet on a couple of occasions. The beancounters still bitched about the cost...he frowned. Dealing with one asteroid would be a piece of cake, but nine? Did the virus have *nine* deflection crews on permanent standby? Or would it try to use a missile to deflect or destroy the asteroid, gambling it could deal with any pieces of space junk before they reached the high orbitals. Or…why not both? There was nothing to be gained by staking everything on a single option.

"Missile separation," Staci snapped. "I say again, missile separation!"

Mitch leaned forward. The virus seemed to have decided to try to deflect the lead asteroid. It was hard to be sure, but—given the flight path—it looked as though the missile was going to slam into the side of the asteroid and knock it off course. Mitch ran the calculations and frowned. Unless something went badly wrong, the asteroid's altered course would be enough to send it plunging past the planet and into the primary star. The asteroid might shatter…

He watched, grimly, as the missile struck home. The asteroid tilted and rolled off course. Mitch shook his head, turning his attention to the second asteroid. It was smaller, clearly nowhere near as solid as the first. That actually worked in humanity's favour. It shattered into a cloud of smaller rocks when it was hit, several hundred continuing their flight towards the planet. Mitch nodded to himself as the planet's active defences went live, blasting the incoming rocks into dust. They wouldn't get through, he decided, but at least they'd told him more about the enemy defences. His crew was starting to get a very good idea of just how much firepower the virus had assembled to protect its core systems.

"Asteroid Seven is going to miss the planet," Staci reported. She didn't look up from her console, but Mitch could hear the irritation in her voice. The more asteroids that missed the planet outright, the more resources the virus could divert to protecting the planet from the asteroids that wouldn't. "I think they'll just ignore it."

"Blast," Mitch said. He'd have to twit Captain Hammond about the miss, although he knew it wasn't particularly fair. A tiny error—a millimetre or two—could easily grow into a few million kilometres by the time the asteroid reached the planet. He checked the vectors, then shook his head in annoyance. The asteroid was going to miss by a comfortable margin and hit the star. "We'll have to suggest modifying their targeting protocols."

He sat back in his chair as the strange engagement continued. The first wave of mass driver projectiles appeared right on time, shortly after the last of the asteroid chunks had been blasted into vapour. The virus reacted sharply, directing starfighters to target and destroy the tiny rocks before they reached their targets. Mitch wondered, idly, if that was a good idea on their part. The projectiles might be solid enough to shrug off a plasma bolt. But it seemed to work.

We'll have to do something about that, he mused. A starfighter could blow another starfighter to vapour, but it wouldn't have a hope of burning through a starship's armour...not since the First Interstellar War had taught the human race that starships needed heavy armour as well as speed. *Perhaps we can make the projectiles hard enough to withstand a plasma strike...*

"Captain," Staci said. She looked up as the display focused on the basketball hoop. "The gas giant projectile is approaching the hoop."

"How nice of the virus to provide a beacon for us to track," Mitch said. The virus hadn't tried to target the gas projectile, not entirely to his surprise. It *knew* the frozen gas was harmless. "Let's see what happens when they try to catch it."

"Aye, Captain," Staci said. "We have a platform in place to watch the show."

CHAPTER TWENTY-TWO

THE SENSOR PLATFORM HAD NO NAME, just a serial number that had been noted by the navy's bureaucrats and filed away, then forgotten. It had no real awareness of itself, or indeed anything beyond its operational instructions. The highly-restricted learning program that governed the platform's operations wasn't designed to do anything more than follow orders, unless one of a number of specific conditions were met. The fact that some of those orders were effectively suicidal was of no concern to the platform. It didn't have the intellect to understand.

It drifted in a rough position between a larger object and a slightly smaller one. It didn't know or care that one of those objects was a planet and the other a moon, nor did it care that the gravity interaction between the two bodies would eventually push the platform into a balance point between the two or send it flying towards one or the other. All its awareness, such as it was, was focused on two things. Monitoring the giant structure hanging in the balance point between the planet and the moon and signalling its findings to the communications network nearby. Where the signals went after that was of no concern to the platform. It didn't expect any reply. It didn't have the wit to be concerned about that, either.

The platform had quietly watched as the giant hoop caught incoming projectiles from the gas giant, slowed them with magnetic fields and then allowed shuttles to capture the frozen gas and steer them towards the industrial facilities. It didn't have the capability to judge what the facilities did with the projectiles, merely to note the ebb and flow of the energy emissions and report them to its distant superiors. The latest frozen projectile was noted and logged as it appeared from deep space, racing towards the hoop. It seemed as unconcerned by the incoming asteroids as the platform itself...

There was a flash of energy. A number of sensors went dead. The platform hastily activated its self-repair functions, even as it hastily forwarded its last sensor records to its masters in case it had been discovered. The functions rapidly established that all sensors watching the hoop had been blinded, which was evident, and they were beyond the platform's capability to fix. It considered the last set of orders very briefly, then rotated in space to bring its surviving sensors to bear on the hoop. It was gone. A number of neighbouring industrial facilities were also gone or badly damaged. The gas projectile was nowhere to be seen.

A human would have whooped in delight. The platform merely reported the updated sensor records to its masters, then continued the silent vigil.

• • •

"Hit!" Mitch grinned as the cheer ran around the bridge. "We hit the bastards!"

He felt his smile grow wider as more and more information flowed into the display. The basketball hoop had been blown to atoms. It wouldn't have been a very sturdy structure, but still...it was gone. The facilities near the hoop had been crippled or destroyed, leaving the virus unable to catch the oncoming projectiles. Even if it did...he wondered if the virus would simply start shooting them down, rather than take the risk of allowing another nuke into striking range. It was a scratch, compared to the sheer immensity of the virus's orbital installations, but it had to hurt. It was a grim reminder that the virus wasn't as safe as it might have hoped.

"Captain," Staci said. "The virus appears to be throwing together a number of squadrons."

Mitch nodded, sobering rapidly. There was no reason to assume the virus had caught a sniff of *Unicorn*, but she wasn't the primary target. Not now. A pair of mass driver projectiles had gotten through the defences in all the confusion, one striking an orbital facility and blowing it to atoms. It would be *Lion*, *Lion* and the big mass drivers, that would be the primary target. The virus would dispatch its fleets to probe the edge of the system, chasing *Lion* whenever she showed herself. It needed to be distracted.

"Establish laser links to the sensor decoys, but don't go live," Mitch ordered. He started to consider how the virus might respond, then dismissed the thought. They'd run hundreds of wargames and simulations, but they'd been nothing more than guesswork. "We don't want them to know we're here until we're ready."

He forced himself to wait as the alien fleets assembled. The virus had to be annoyed. It also had to have deduced the pusher or something along the same lines, given the sheer velocity of the asteroids. The standard nukes used to steer asteroids back home wouldn't have really been *that* fast, not compared to the asteroids they'd hurled at the alien world. The virus might not know the exact trick, but it didn't matter. It knew it had to force *Lion* to retreat, if it didn't run the battlecruiser to ground and blow her away. It would buy time for the ships in the orbital yards to be completed, deployed and pointed at Earth.

This trick will only work once, he thought. *We'd better make damn sure it's worthwhile.*

The display continued to update. The virus seemed oddly confused, as if it couldn't quite decide what ships to send to chase *Lion* and which to keep in orbit. Mitch wondered if it was stunned, although…he shook his head. They hadn't hit anything vital. Perhaps there was just too much viral matter in the system, with plans changing with every clump of viral matter that linked to the collective. Or perhaps it was just unsure if it was being tricked into sending most of its fleet away from the planet.

The orbital defences were tough, but without mobile units to back them up they could be hacked apart from a safe distance.

"I think they've decided on a sizable fleet," Staci said. "One brainship, three battleships, two carriers and a number of cruisers."

"Communications, transmit a warning to *Lion*," Mitch ordered. It would take nearly fifteen hours for the enemy fleet to reach the battlecruiser, assuming they threw caution to the winds, but there was no point in taking chances. The virus might try to be sneaky instead. It would add at least five more hours to their transit time, but as long as they were careful they might get very close before the battlecruiser realised they were coming. "Tactical, do you have the decoy fleet programs ready to run?"

"Yes, Captain," Staci said. "Once the decoys go active, the enemy will see a whole fleet bearing down on them."

Mitch nodded. It would have been difficult to coordinate a *real* fleet to hit the planet shortly after the asteroids, not without a degree of preplanning he would have considered rigid at best and outright dangerous at worst. Such plans rarely worked in the simulators and almost never in real life. But if the decoy drones could be used to convince the virus that the human race had actually pulled it off...

"Go active on my command," he ordered. Timing was everything. The virus could not be allowed to miss its cue...or, for that matter, approach the decoys from the wrong angle. "On my mark...go live!"

"Aye, Captain," Staci said. "Going live...now!"

Mitch smiled. The virus would be in shock. It would be seeing a sizable fleet bearing down on its planet. What would it do? It couldn't risk allowing the human ships to get into firing range. There were just too many possible targets in orbit. And yet, the ships were too far from the planet for starfighters, gunboats and shuttles to be effective. The only real countermeasure was deploying the fleet to intercept the humans or chase them away.

Unless they think of something new, he thought. *He* would never have allowed himself to be pinned against a planet, with so many vulnerable facilities within enemy firing range, but the virus might have other ideas. It wouldn't be the first time it had caught its enemies by surprise. *They might take the risk of sending out another fleet of shuttles…*

He shook his head. It was unlikely. The virus would *need* the shuttles if it wanted to keep its industrial base active. There was no way it could afford to throw every last shuttle into a fleet's defences…he had to smile. It would work out very well for the virus, if it tried, but would it? If it thought it was being conned…who knew?

"Captain," Staci said. "The enemy fleet is leaving orbit. They're heading straight towards the sensor decoys."

"And the mines," Mitch said. The mines were supposed to be stealthy, and the sensor decoys were pumping out enough emissions to confuse the enemy sensors, but it was impossible to tell if the alien fleet would realise the mines were there before it was too late. "If they scan the mines, detonate them at once without waiting for orders. Take out as many of their ships as possible."

Staci's back stiffened. "Aye, sir."

Mitch nodded in grim understanding. The mines were really nothing more than modified bomb-pumped laser warheads, wrapped in a makeshift stealth coating. There hadn't been any time to put together a better design, not when they'd had to leave in a hurry. The laser beams would damage their targets, he was sure, but they wouldn't take out the entire fleet. It would be a minor miracle if they just blunted the enemy advance.

"Target the battleships and carriers first," he ordered. Brainships were technically priority targets, but taking out the advancing ship wouldn't slow the virus down. "Aim to cripple if not to destroy."

"Aye, Captain," Staci said.

Mitch felt sweat bead under his shirt as he silently counted down the seconds. The enemy fleet was gliding closer, filling space with hundreds of thousands of sensor pulses. The decoy platforms were working desperately to spoof the enemy sensors, but it was just a matter of time before the enemy realised the ships simply didn't exist. Mitch wished, suddenly, that they'd had the time to set up a few dozen missile pods. It would have been far more convincing if the illusionary ships had been firing real missiles. If nothing else, it would have forced the virus to concentrate on the illusions and not the real threat.

"They'll be entering the minefield in twenty seconds," Staci said. "The mines are ready to detonate on command."

Come on, you bastards, Mitch thought. A flash of dark humour washed through him. *Don't pay any attention to the man behind the curtain.*

"Ten seconds," Staci said. "Mines locked on target."

"Orient the mines, then fire as soon as they enter the minefield," Mitch ordered. "Helm, be ready to run."

"Aye, Captain."

Mitch watched, praying the boffins had been right. Gas jets were supposed to be undetectable, allowing the mines to target the enemy ships without being spotted, but they were just too *close*. The brainship was layered in sensor nodes as well as point defence weapons. It would just take one glimpse of a gas jet for the brainship to start sweeping mines out of space, blasting them to dust before they could detonate. If that happened...

"They're in the minefield," Staci snapped. "The mines are going live...now!"

The display seemed to explode as the mines detonated, each one blasting a ravenous laser beam into the enemy ships. Mitch watched a handful of battleships stagger out of position, plasma streaming from gashes in their hulls; the carriers were shattered, the laser beams triggering a series of explosions that tore the ships apart. The smaller vessels scattered, as if they feared attack themselves. The brainship cut its drives so quickly it would have smashed a human crew against the bulkhead. Mitch thought, just for a moment, that it might have killed all the host bodies as well as the blobs of viral matter. The virus might be...well, a virus, but it couldn't have found that experience very pleasant.

"Three battleships have been severely damaged," Staci reported. "Two more have taken light damage and are continuing the advance."

Mitch cursed under his breath. He'd hoped the virus would assume the mines had been deployed to soften the fleet up, before the human starships laid into them. It looked as if the virus hadn't been fooled. It was possible it had been stunned, that its individual units were trying to continue the plan even though it had already failed, but…he shrugged. It would have been very welcome indeed, if he'd had a fleet in place to meet them. Instead, he just had a handful of harmless sensor decoys.

"Bother," he said, mildly. "I think we've outstayed our welcome."

He took a breath. "Tactical, ramp up the sensor decoys to maximum power, then prime their self-destruct systems. Helm, sneak us out of here as quietly as you can. We don't want them seeing us if we can avoid it."

"Aye, Captain," Hinkson said.

Mitch rested his hands on his lap as *Unicorn* pulled back. The cloaking device alone should have been enough to conceal their presence, but the sudden barrage of sensor distortions from the decoys would make it impossible for the virus to figure out what was real and what was nothing more than a sensor ghost. The haze would be so bright, he hoped, that even a brainship would have trouble picking the individual sensor decoys out and killing them. Not that it mattered, he reflected sourly. The sensor decoys would have to be destroyed before the enemy had a chance to try to capture one intact. The boffins had made it clear that letting one fall into enemy hands would be the end of his career.

"Their cruisers are starting to sweep the area," Staci warned. "They won't uncover us unless they widen the pattern quite considerably."

"True," Mitch agreed. *Unicorn* was picking up speed. It shouldn't be hard to evade contact long enough for the hornet's nest to die down or dispatch a new fleet to the edge of the system. He'd be able to sneak right back into the enemy lair, perhaps with a new plan to do some real damage. But that would have to wait. "Destroy the sensor decoys."

"Aye, Captain," Staci said. She tapped a button. "They're gone."

Mitch grinned as the icons—and the haze—vanished from the display. "Communications, download an updated set of records from the sensor platforms, then transmit it to *Lion*," he ordered. "Let Commodore Hammond know he's probably going to have company, sooner rather than later."

With at least fifteen hours of warning, his thoughts added silently. The thought would have irked him, under other circumstances. There hadn't been many simulations, let alone real engagements, where the defenders had known the attackers were coming for more than a few hours. *I know defence commanders who'd kill for a single hour of warning.*

"Aye, Captain," Midshipman David Culver said. "I...*Lion* will see them coming, won't she?"

"It depends," Mitch said. He didn't mind the question. It was part of his job to mentor promising young officers, to teach them their skills before they had to use them for real. "If they push their drives as hard as they can, *Lion* will see them coming from right across the system. If they try to sneak up instead, reducing their drives and cloaking their ships, *Lion* will have far less warning."

"And they have enough ships to try to do both," Staci added. Her voice was cool, perfectly composed even as she outlined a scenario that would lead to inevitable disaster. "One squadron to draw *Lion's* attention, another to sneak up behind her and put a knife in her back."

Mitch nodded, keying his console. "Make sure you add that warning to the list," he said, curtly. Hammond would be aware of the dangers, but it was probably a good idea to make sure. The battlecruiser could outrun anything she couldn't outfight, on paper, yet the virus had to know it. Mitch could envisage a dozen schemes to pin the battlecruiser down, then blow her apart. The virus could probably dream them up, too. "We don't want them to be caught unawares."

He smiled, then sobered as he studied the live feed from the sensor network. The virus's homeworld, if indeed it was, was buzzing like an angry nest of wasps. It was deploying more and more starfighters, some blasting incoming mass driver projectiles while others swept space for hidden sensor platforms. There was no way they'd spot *Unicorn* unless they moved much further from the planet, but it was just possible they'd spot a platform. He grimaced. The boffins would not be pleased, even if the self-destruct systems worked as promised. The virus was putting out so many searchers—and sensor pulses—that he doubted a cloaked ship would survive. The platforms...

We'll just have to hope for the best, he told himself. *Yesterday, the virus didn't have the slightest idea we were in the system. Today, it knows.*

"Captain," Staci said. "The virus just cut loose a cruiser squadron. It's heading out of the system at maximum speed."

"Alert *Lion*," Mitch ordered. The battlecruiser would see them coming, as he'd assured Culver, but there was no point in taking chances. Besides, it would be hard to explain a failure to pass along a warning during the post-battle assessment interviews. "And keep a careful eye out for any clues they're sending a force under cloak, too."

But he knew, even as he spoke, that there were so many ships moving around the system that spotting a handful of cloaked vessels would be almost impossible.

CHAPTER TWENTY-THREE

THOMAS TALLIED UP THE RESULTS from the first wave of asteroids with a profound degree of dissatisfaction. He'd seen the simulations, he'd gone through them time and time again to understand what was about to happen, but he was still displeased with the results. He had known that it was unlikely that *one* asteroid, let alone all of them, would make it through the defences…he shook his head in irritation as the next pair of asteroids were hurled towards their target. The constant bombardment from the mass drivers was likely to do a great deal more damage in the long run.

"Captain," Cook said. "We just received an update from *Unicorn*. A flight of enemy cruisers has been launched in our direction."

"Deploy additional sensor platforms," Thomas ordered, as a handful of red icons and a probability cone appeared in front of him. He ran through the calculations as quickly as he could. Assuming the enemy ships maintained a constant velocity, they'd be on his position within ten hours…probably. If there was any known race that could risk redlining the compensators past the point of sanity, it was the virus. "Inform the asteroid crews that we'll be breaking camp in seven hours."

"Aye, Captain," Cook said.

Thomas frowned as the display updated again. *Unicorn* had noted fourteen cruisers, designed more for speed and striking power than armour. *Lion* could take them in a long-range engagement, Thomas was sure, but if they got within energy range the battlecruiser was likely to come off worst. He keyed his console, directing the tactical staff to run a handful of simulations. Assuming the virus's ships stayed together, they were likely to harass *Lion* to the point she couldn't continue the bombardment. That would be enough to ensure mission failure even if the squadron remained intact.

Shame we can't rely on the mass drivers to take out a few of the cruisers, he thought. The ships were tiny on an interplanetary scale. One might as well try to shoot a dust mote with an assault rifle, a dust mote on the other side of the firing range. *There's no hope of catching them by surprise.*

He leaned back in his chair. The gunboats would have to be used. There was no other option. And yet, they'd be flying straight into the teeth of enemy ships *designed* to provide cover to their capital ships. Thomas cursed under his breath. If they lost more than a handful of gunboats, the engagement would be within shouting distance of being lost with them. But there was no choice. They couldn't let the enemy ships drive them further into deep space or back across the tramline. It would give the virus time to repair the gaps in its defences, complete its new ships and resume the offensive. Thomas doubted the human race could endure another year of war.

"Colonel Bagehot," he said, tapping his console. "Report to my ready room. We have a mission to plan."

"Aye, Captain."

Thomas stood, brushing down his uniform. It wasn't hopeless. His crew had come up with a dozen different ideas for hurting the enemy, from using nukes to shoving asteroids towards the alien homeworld to inserting the counter-virus into water-ice asteroids and trying to use them as makeshift biological weapons. Personally, Thomas doubted the latter idea would work, but it would keep the virus off-balance. It was more workable than some of the madder ideas. The plan to turn the gas giants into new stars had floundered on the simple fact no one could figure out how to do it.

And if the virus really was born on a gas giant, Thomas mused, *it might be impossible to destroy it completely.*

"Commander Donker, you have the bridge," he said. "I'll be in my ready room."

"Aye, Captain."

• • •

Tobias couldn't help feeling, as he stood at the front of the briefing compartment, as though he had butterflies in his stomach. He'd been nervous before, with reason, but this was different. The men and women in front of him—he didn't think any of them were out of their teens—were about to follow him into hell, into the teeth of enemy fire. Fear churned in his gut as he indicated the display, a cluster of red icons racing towards their position at breakneck speed. There hadn't been any official word on just how badly they'd hurt the enemy, when they'd started hurling asteroids towards their homeworld, but it was clear they'd kicked the hornet's nest. Tobias hoped that was a good sign.

Umpteen enemy ships coming towards you with murder in their eyes is never a good sign, he thought. The long-range sensors had picked up fourteen cruisers, but that didn't mean there weren't others. They were flying in close formation, their drive fields blurring together to the point it was hard to separate the individual ships. There could easily be three or four additional ships in the formation, their drives concealed by the others. *They'll blow us to atoms if they get a clear shot at us.*

He cleared his throat. "The mission is very simple," he said. "We are to fly into the enemy formation, providing updated targeting information to the battlecruiser's missiles. When we enter torpedo range, we will launch at the enemy ships and then go to full evasive patterns. We are *not* going to risk entering point-blank range. We don't have to. They're going to impale themselves on our torpedoes."

"Like a woman impales herself on a cock," someone said, from the rear.

Tobias scowled. He'd never been quite sure how to react to such comments. It wasn't as if *he'd* ever had the power to do something about it. The mere fact *he* objected to such statements was enough to give them legs...or it had been, back at school. Colin and his cronies hadn't given a shit about Tobias's opinions. If they'd realised such talk bothered him, it would have just made it worse.

"That will do," he said, finally. He hoped he sounded stronger than he felt. "Once we deploy the torpedoes, everyone not on special duties is to deploy decoys and then flee to the RV point. If all goes well, we'll link up with the motherships and reload before the next enemy fleet arrives. If not..."

He shrugged. They could fill in the blanks for themselves.

"To your ships," he ordered. "We launch in ten minutes."

The compartment emptied. He sighed, rubbing his forehead. The pilots had been cooped up for far too long. The manuals had made it clear there would be stresses and strains, that the merest misstep could set off a series of events that ended in a captain's mast, if not outright court-martial. And yet...he looked up. Marigold was waiting. Tobias wished, suddenly, that she'd been promoted instead. Life had been a great deal easier when he'd only been responsible for himself.

"Come on," Marigold said. "We don't want to be late."

Tobias smiled as he stood, squeezed her hand gently and then led the way through the hatch. He wanted to ask how he was doing, but... he wasn't sure he wanted to hear the answer. Instead, he keyed his wrist-com to check the latest updates as they hurried to the launch ring and scrambled into the gunboat. It felt a great deal roomier without Colin and his buddies. Tobias wondered, idly, if they'd be mounting more raids to the mass-driven projectiles. He hadn't heard anything solid on how *that* had worked out, either.

The gunboat hummed to life as they closed the airlock and took their seats. Tobias glanced at the squadron display, hoping and praying that their hours upon hours of constant practice would pay off. He'd insisted on everyone training on the assumption he *wouldn't* be looking over their shoulder the whole time, but…he hoped, desperately, that the squadron had made all the mistakes they were going to make in the simulators. The training exercises might embarrass a careless pilot. They wouldn't get him killed.

"This is Gunboat One," he said, keying his console. The enemy ships were closer now, their drive signatures clearly visible. They weren't making any attempt to hide. "We are ready to depart."

"Roger that, Gunboat One," Bagehot said. "You are cleared to depart. Good hunting."

A low *clunk* echoed through the gunboat as Marigold disconnected the craft from the hatch, then steered her away from the battlecruiser before bringing her drive fields online. Tobias watched the rest of the gunboats carefully, silently relieved he'd spent so much time drilling his personnel. Bringing up the drive fields too early or too late could be dangerous, if not fatal, but…so far, the mission had gone perfectly. He bit his lip in irritation. The mission had barely begun. There was no time to rest on his laurels.

"Take us out," he ordered. "And bring passive sensors online."

The gravity field seemed to shimmer—again—as Marigold steered the gunboat away from the battlecruiser. Tobias forced himself to concentrate, setting up laser links between the gunboats and the mothership as the display filled with red icons. It didn't *look* as though there were more than fourteen enemy targets, but it was impossible to be sure. They'd have to get a great deal closer before they could get solid reads on the ebb and flow of the enemy drive fields. He kept his eyes firmly on the display, trying not to think about the people under his command. It was all too likely that two or more of them wouldn't make it back to the battlecruiser.

He frowned as the enemy drive fields sharpened. "I have solid locks on all fourteen targets," he said. His hands danced over the console, relaying targeting data to *Lion*. "I don't think there are any more."

"Not if they want to keep up with the rest of the squadron," Marigold agreed. "I wonder when they're planning to slow down."

Tobias shrugged. The enemy ships could simply blaze past the human positions, launching missiles as they came, before cutting their drive fields or reversing course. Their cruisers weren't starfighters, able to stop or start on a dime. They'd be putting their own lives at risk if they tried to come to a dead stop…his lips twisted into a grim smile. A *dead* stop. He'd been warned never to try anything of the sort, unless he was desperate. The risk of sudden death was just too high.

"They probably wanted to get a few ships out here as quickly as possible," he said. He hadn't been involved in the high-level mission discussions, naturally, but he'd played enough strategy games to figure out the problems facing both sides. The virus needed to sweep the outer edge of its system, a daunting task given the sheer *size* of the region. "If they have a fleet out here, they can just keep us from setting up bases and launching more asteroids."

His console bleeped. "They're scanning us."

"Noted." Marigold sounded tense. "I'll evade the moment they open fire."

Tobias shivered. The gunboats were closing on the enemy cruisers at terrifying speed. If the enemy opened fire, there wouldn't be much warning between the shot and the impact. The gunboats were tough, for their size, but nowhere near tough enough to survive even a single major hit. The only upside was that the virus might not realise it had hit *anything*.

Which isn't much of an upside, he reflected, grimly. *We'll still be dead.*

• • •

"Captain," Sibley said. "The gunboats are sending back targeting data."

Thomas nodded. The enemy ships weren't making any attempt to slow down. If he was lucky, he'd have a decent chance to take them out before they'd be able to get a solid fix on his location and return fire. It would have been reassuring, if he hadn't been certain the enemy ships had a *rough* idea of where he was. Thankfully, the mass drivers were already on their way to their new location. Thomas had been tempted to sneak away himself, but he needed to take out the enemy ships. They were just too dangerous to be left intact.

"Mark your targets, then open fire," he ordered. "Helm, prepare for evasive action."

"Aye, Captain."

Thomas braced himself as the external pods fired as one. The bean-counters would probably make a fuss about the number of missiles he'd launched, pointing out that he'd effectively wasted at least half of them. For once, they might even have a point. Thomas's crew had crammed as many missiles as they could into the battlecruiser and her tenders, but there was no hope of any replenishments until a relief fleet arrived. Once the missiles were gone, they were gone. He knew he had no choice—the enemy point defence would blow vast holes in the missile clusters—but the knowledge didn't make it any easier to bear. He might fire a missile he'd need later…

"Impact in seven minutes," Sibley said. "Should I deploy sensor decoys?"

"No," Thomas said. There was little hope of confusing the enemy, not now. "We'll hold them in reserve."

"Aye, Captain."

• • •

Tobias watched as the battlecruiser's missiles streaked towards their targets, the closing speed fast enough to do immense damage to the enemy ships even without nuclear-tipped warheads. The enemy ships were starting to evade, launching sensor decoys of their own to confuse the incoming missiles, but the gunboats kept updating the targeting data to ensure the missiles kept targeting the *real* cruisers. A shudder ran through the gunboat as the enemy ships opened fire, aiming to scatter the formation rather than take the individual gunboats out. It was good thinking on their part, Tobias conceded. The odds of actually *hitting* a gunboat were low, but if the enemy gunners could force the formation to scatter they wouldn't have to deal with so many torpedoes.

"Evasive patterns...now," Marigold said. The gunboat lurched as plasma bolts flashed past the cockpit. "They're drawing a bead on us."

Tobias nodded. "Torpedoes online, ready to launch," he said. He braced himself as the range continued to close. "Launching...now!"

The gunboat shuddered, again, as he volley-fired the torpedoes. The enemy ships would see them coming, of course, but they'd have only a very short space of time to do something about it. *Lion's* missiles were lancing into the teeth of their formation, bomb-pumped laser beams stabbing deep into their hulls. A cruiser shattered, disintegrating into a cluster of debris; Tobias guessed the damage had been extensive enough to disrupt the drive field, ripping the ship to pieces. Four more died in quick succession, a fifth falling out of formation with plasma leaking from its drive section. Colin and his buddies would probably want to try to board, Tobias thought. He hoped they did, if the ship survived long enough. *His* share of the prize money would be low, but *low* was a relative term. He might get enough to start his own company or emigrate to an asteroid settlement or *something*.

He gritted his teeth as Marigold yanked the gunboat around, darting out of the enemy formation. The remainder of the gunboats followed suit, punching into clear space. It looked as though the enemy ships had been shattered, although two of them were rapidly altering course and launching long-range missiles towards *Lion*. The battlecruiser should be in no real danger, he thought, but it was impossible to be *sure*. They were so far from home that something that could be mended quickly, in a shipyard, might be lethal in the enemy system. It wasn't a pleasant thought. The gunboats had more life support than a starfighter—they could spend days on patrol, if necessary—but they might not survive long enough to be recovered by *Unicorn* or link up with the fleet tenders. The thought of being stranded was horrifying.

Ice washed through him as he realised Gunboat Nine was gone. He kicked himself, mentally, for not having noticed her disappearance. When had it happened? He'd have to look at the records to see...he swore under his breath, cursing himself for not watching as the gunboat was vaporised. He should have witnessed it, even if he hadn't been able to save the ship and crew. His heart twisted in pain. He'd tried to keep his distance to maintain his sanity—and to maintain the pretence he was somehow suited to command—but it had failed. He knew too much about his crew to feel nothing upon their deaths.

"Jack and Selma are gone," he said. "I...*fuck*."

"It wasn't your fault," Marigold told him. "You did the best you could."

"I know that," Tobias said. He *did*. He'd worked hard, pushing his personnel to the limits. He'd done everything he could think of, then stolen ideas from starfighter training manuals and pilot experiences. They'd been as ready as he could make them, but they were still dead. "I just don't believe it."

He stared at his console for a long moment. Jack and Selma had been good people. He'd liked them. They would have made good friends, if they'd met at school...if they'd been left alone long enough to become friends. He'd thought they might have bonded over the games they loved; they might have become a proper team. And now, they were dead. He was all too aware it was just a matter of time before another gunboat exploded into dust.

"Take us to the RV point," he ordered, stiffly. They'd have to go through the dead crew's possessions and...he groaned. He'd have to write to their families, too. What the hell was he going to say? He told himself, firmly, to worry about it later. They weren't out of the woods yet. "I'll send a complete update to *Lion*."

CHAPTER TWENTY-FOUR

SUSAN DISLIKED POLITICS. It wasn't that it was a dirty business—although it was—so much as it was extremely difficult to get anything done. A country couldn't be run like a warship or a regiment—she had the example of hundreds of military juntas to convince her that it was a recipe for disaster—and she understood that people needed room to breathe, to think, to vent…but it was still frustrating to spend her time trying to convince the government to dispatch a relief fleet, only to be rebuffed every time. The Prime Minister was in a tough spot, she conceded reluctantly, but it was no excuse—in her view—for not helping mend his government had sent into danger. It had been her idea, and she'd known the dangers when she'd put the concept together, but it was still frustrating. Perhaps she should have accompanied the squadron herself. At least she wouldn't be wasting her time tilting at windmills.

She sat in her Earthside office, staring down at a handful of operational plans. They were very simple—the tactical staff hadn't filled in the blanks to make the plans actually workable—but it didn't matter. The British Government—and GATO—had flatly refused to cut loose any capital ships from the home defence formations, citing the threat to humanity's homeworld. Susan found it hard to believe the virus was in any shape to launch a second offensive so quickly—it wasn't completely immune to logistic demands—but it was impossible to convince the governments to gamble. They were terrified of losing Earth. Susan understood, but she'd also seen the assessments of just how quickly the virus could replenish its losses. Leaving it alone, giving it time to repair its damaged ships and bring new ones online, could easily prove fatal.

And we have no way to know what's happening in the alien system, she reflected. It was bitterly ironic that she'd spent so long cursing the flicker network, only to find herself deprived of FTL communications when she needed them the most. *Lion* and *Unicorn* could have had amazing success, or been blown out of space, and she wouldn't have the slightest idea of what had actually happened. *The only thing we know for sure is that the remainder of the alien fleet passed through New Washington and vanished.*

She keyed her console, bringing up a starchart. The war appeared to have stalemated, with human ships keeping the virus at bay, but she knew better. There was no way to keep the virus from mounting a second invasion, from striking humanity's shipyards time and time again until humanity lost the ability to make war...oh, she could understand the PM's concerns. And yet, the virus had the ability to replace its lost ships very quickly. The stalemate would be broken soon, if they didn't take the offensive.

It could shorten the war, she thought. *But perhaps not in the right way.*

The intercom bleeped. "Admiral, Charlotte Hammond's PA just called," Commander Elliot Richardson said. "She's requesting a private meeting, at her club. The Follies."

Susan felt a flicker of irritation. She was no flunkey to be at the beck and call of an aristocratic woman, certainly not one who'd committed adultery and triggered off a scandal that had already been forgotten. Mostly. The media had moved from praising or condemning Lady Charlotte—or both—to moaning about the lack of planetside defences instead, proving—not for the first time—that most reporters didn't have the slightest idea what they were talking about. Planetary defences were largely worthless, certainly against the virus. She hoped the politicians weren't listening. It would be dashed awkward if they were.

She sighed, inwardly. She'd done her level best to avoid non-military aristocrats as much as possible. The military ones usually understood the limits of their power, the non-military ones—particularly the teenagers she'd known at school—thought themselves the lords and masters of the known universe. And Lady Charlotte sounded like the worst of the wretched girls she'd known, even though she was in her late forties. She hadn't really grown up at all…Susan shook her head in annoyance. If there was anyone who knew how badly the media could warp the truth out of all recognition, it was her. She should know better than to take the media too seriously…

"Inform Lady Charlotte that it will be my pleasure," Susan said. If nothing else, the whole affair would be a distraction. "When does she want to meet?"

"Anytime today," Richardson said. "Should I have the car brought 'round?"

"Please," Susan said. She stood, brushing down her uniform. She had no intention of changing into a dress uniform or civilian clothes; she would go as she was. "Inform her I'm on my way."

She donned her wristcom, strapped her terminal and pistol to her belt, then headed out the door. London was supposed to be safe, but there'd been sparks of zombie activity ever since the alien fleet had been beaten off. The security services *still* didn't know how the zombies had gotten into the city, something that worried her. It was hard to believe anyone would take bribes from a zombie, knowing the potential cost. Even the criminal underground ran blood tests before allowing someone into their people-smuggling rings.

The car was waiting, as promised. Susan climbed into the backseat and closed the door behind her, then ordered the driver to take her to the Follies. She wasn't a member, but she'd visited a couple of times. She was surprised Lady Charlotte had been allowed to enter, given that she was on the verge of divorce. But then, she *was* trying to build up a power base by running for office. The club's staff were probably praying the whole matter would resolve itself before Captain Hammond returned from deep space. Susan's lips quirked. It would be embarrassing, to say the least, if they had to choose between the two.

London looked emptier than ever, even in the high-class shopping districts. The population had practically shrunk overnight, with children evacuated to the countryside and everyone who could afford it moving out of the city. Susan didn't blame them, even though it put a lot of stress on the country infrastructure and impeded military activities. If London was hit from orbit, there would be no hope of escape...she sighed. She'd read plans for building vast underground structures to protect the civilian population, entire cities deep below the ground, but she doubted they'd be any real use. The virus could just infect the entire planet and *wait*. It would win eventually. Better to put the resources into starships and deep-space colonies instead. They were all that stood between the human race and certain extinction.

The Follies was strikingly anonymous, just one building among many in central London. The club didn't advertise. If you didn't know the club existed, she'd been told, there was no way in hell you'd ever be considered for membership. And even if you did know, you'd still have to surmount a number of hurdles before being allowed to join. Prospective members were nominated by other members, then carefully vetted before they were even told they were under consideration. To ask to become a member was to be permanently blacklisted. Susan rolled her eyes as the car came to a halt, outside the main entrance. She had the feeling that too many people had simply never grown up.

The doorman—former military, by his bearing—opened the door for her, allowing her into the lobby. It was quiet, the only sound running water from the fountain in the far corner. Susan refused to allow the atmosphere to bother her as she strode across to the welcoming table and nodded politely to the receptionist. She was dressed tastefully, as if the club was really nothing more than a high-priced hotel. It was, in a sense. The members were entitled to room and board, right in the heart of London. But the cost was quite high.

"I'm here to see Lady Charlotte Hammond," Susan said, pressing her ID card against the scanner. "Please show me to her room."

"Of course, My Lady," the receptionist said. She stood, rather than passing the duty to a page. "If you'll come with me...?"

Susan nodded and followed the younger woman through a handful of tastefully-decorated corridors. The Follies had never seen the need to be tasteless, from what she recalled. There were other clubs that indulged the worst instincts of their members, from hunting associations to sexual exploration groups that constantly pressed against the limits of the law. She kept her thoughts to herself as the receptionist stopped outside a small door and opened it, waving for Susan to step inside. The chamber looked like a comfortable sitting room from a bygone age, right down to the fire burning in the grate and animal heads mounted on the walls. She wondered, idly, if any were real. Somehow, she doubted the club would accept fakes.

"Admiral." Lady Charlotte was seated in a massive armchair, as perfectly elegant as the rest of the room. "Thank you, Wendy. That will be all."

Susan studied her thoughtfully as the receptionist departed, closing the door behind her. It was hardly the first time she'd met Lady Charlotte, but she'd never really had the time to study her. She was shorter than Susan, with curly black hair and a round face that looked a little *too* old to be conventionally pretty. She wasn't overweight, but she was very definitely not skin and bones. It was hard to see what Captain Campbell saw in her... Susan scowled inwardly, reminding herself that she—of all people—should know better than to judge by appearances. Lady Charlotte was a woman of many parts. Who knew? Perhaps they could be allies, if not friends. They had too little in common to be friends.

Which might not be a bad thing, Susan reflected. *If we had things in common, we might fall out over them.*

"I'm glad you came so quickly," Lady Charlotte said, seriously. She indicated another armchair. "Would you like tea? Or coffee? Or something stronger?"

Susan had to smile. "Tell me something," she said. "How...how *realistic* is this place?"

"The Follies?" Lady Charlotte made no pretence of being surprised by the question. "It is not...*historically* accurate, of course. They wouldn't let either of us through the doors if they were trying to remain true to history. No women, you see, or people of colour. The clubs for men who like the company of other men"—she winked—"would be somewhere else. But they like to think they've captured something of the essential nature of gentlemen's clubs, even if some of the gentlemen happen to be gentlewomen."

She shrugged. "It's important not to believe the past was all sweetness and light, because it wasn't," she said. "But it's equally important to avoid throwing out the past, too."

"Very true." Susan sat, resting her hands in her lap. "I assume you have a reason for requesting my presence?"

"I've been hearing stories about you trying to convince the government to dispatch a fleet into enemy territory," Lady Charlotte said. She poured two cups of tea—fine bone china, naturally—and passed one to Susan. "Is that true?"

Susan's eyes narrowed as she took the cup. It was so light and fragile she felt as though she was holding a piece of dollhouse furniture, rather than something real. The slightest touch might be enough to shatter it beyond repair. It was all she could do to take a sip. The tea was excellent—and expensive—but not entirely to her taste. Her father had taught her not to develop any expensive tastes.

"Yes," Susan said, flatly. "Might I ask how *you* know?"

"Of course," Lady Charlotte said. "I have contacts at all levels within government. My connections are quite extensive. I've been drawing together strands and calling in favours and everything else I'd need to run for office. My contacts were kind enough to tell me what's going on."

"Really." Susan kept her voice cold. God! She *hated* the Old Boys Network, although it normally had more sense than this. "And why do you wish to talk to *me* about it?"

"I want to offer you my support," Lady Charlotte said. "And perhaps to discuss your future."

"My future?" Susan shook her head. "My future is meaningless if we don't win the war."

She put the cup down before she broke it. "I don't have much time, My Lady. Please, could we get to the point?"

"Cards on the table, then," Lady Charlotte said. "I have a certain interest in seeing my husband return home safely. And so do others."

Susan bit down the urge to point out that Lady Charlotte hadn't shown much regard for her husband in the last few months, if not years. Susan had never been married. She didn't pretend to know what it was like to fall in and out of love with one's partner, with someone one couldn't simply tell to leave. It couldn't be easy for Lady Charlotte. Charlotte's family—and society as a whole—would expect her to stay with her man, unless he was openly abusive. And even then, her reputation would take a hit.

"I'm glad to hear it," she said, finally.

Lady Charlotte frowned, as if she'd heard something Susan *didn't* say. "It's political," she said, putting her annoyance aside. "There are people who are willing to back a relief mission, but without making it obvious. They'll support the mission by not opposing it, if you see what I mean."

"I don't," Susan said.

"They won't try to help you, but they won't stand in your way either," Lady Charlotte said. "And as long as they're not smoked out, they won't do anything to impede you."

Susan shook her head. "They're playing politics with *lives*?"

"Yes." Lady Charlotte finished her cup and put it to one side. "Like I said, it's political."

"I see," Susan said. Her anger bled into her voice. "And is that going to be enough to convince the PM to launch a relief force? Alone? Because

I'd bet good money GATO isn't included in the Old Boys Network..."

"No," Lady Charlotte agreed. "But there are three points in your favour. Britain will be relatively safe from the other human powers, even if most of the Royal Navy is sent away. GATO will be willing to assign ships, once someone steps up and takes the lead. And third, the Tadpoles have dispatched a fleet to assist in the defence of Earth. You should be able to convince them to join a relief fleet instead."

Susan studied her for a long moment. "And what do *you* get out of this?"

"Most people wouldn't ask that question out loud," Lady Charlotte said. "And they certainly wouldn't trust the answer."

She shrugged. "I get to cement my position within the power structure," she said. "If I win the election, great. If not, I still have power and influence I can use to make another bid for election or find a place within the political party's inner circle. And you, Admiral, could run for office, too. Where do you see your career going, after this?"

Susan said nothing for a long moment. "I always imagined I'd retire after the war," she said. "First Space Lord is probably beyond my reach. I thought I'd retire, write the usual collection of memoirs—mostly fictional—and...I don't know. I did think about emigrating."

"You'd be bored within the month," Lady Charlotte said. "If that happens, give me a call."

"Maybe," Susan said. The thought of running for office was...unpleasant. "Do you really think your plan will work?"

Lady Charlotte grinned. "Do you want to know a dark secret about handling negotiations? You decide what you want, then you demand something a great deal higher and let yourself be beaten down to what you actually want. Your opponent thinks he's hammered you down, while *you* know you got what you wanted. Both of you are actually happy. In this case, the political parties—particularly the ones in opposition—think they have to show their opposition, while quietly supporting the government's policy. Does that make sense?"

"No," Susan said, bluntly.

"It does in politics," Lady Charlotte said. "You make another push for a relief fleet. I'll get the ball rolling, politically. And everyone will get what they want."

Susan stood, feeling dirty. "I hope you're right," she said. "Your plan relies on too many people playing along."

Lady Charlotte smiled. "You want to know another dark secret? Everyone is self-interested. The vast majority of people put themselves first and foremost. Even the ones who claim to be altruistic are self-interested, in the sense they're signalling their virtue to anyone who cares to listen. If you want someone to do something for you, work out a way to appeal to their self-interest and they'll do it. They might even talk *you* into letting them do it. All you have to do is determine what they want, and what's in their interest, and they'll do the rest."

"If that were true," Susan said, "the government would have invested even *more* money in the navy before the war."

"It was peacetime," Lady Charlotte said. She stood and held out a hand. "And funding the navy isn't always a vote-getter in peacetime. Their self-interest dictated otherwise."

"I'll take your word for it," Susan said. She shook Charlotte's hand. "And if it works, you'll have my gratitude."

Lady Charlotte nodded. "I don't hate him," she said. "I don't want him to die."

"We'll do everything in our power to bring him back alive," Susan told her. She was surprised Charlotte hadn't mentioned Captain Campbell. "But it won't solve all of your problems, will it?"

CHAPTER TWENTY-FIVE

"I DON'T THINK THEY'RE GOING TO LET US any closer anytime soon," Staci said. "They're mad as hornets over there."

"It looks like it," Mitch agreed. They sat in his cabin, studying the live feed from the sensor platforms. Virus Prime was surrounded by a swarm of angry starfighters, gunboats and shuttlecraft. He had the feeling the latter had been hastily fitted with more advanced sensor systems, as well as plasma cannons and probably torpedoes. The patrolling hordes had come far too close to spotting a handful of sensor platforms, even though they were heavily stealthed. It was just a matter of time before they stumbled across one or more of the platforms. "If we try to get closer, we die."

He frowned. The virus had known the system was under attack for three days. It was an oddly slow-motion battle, the kind of engagement that had been predicted before the development of drive fields and the discovery of the tramlines. *Lion* and her mass drivers were setting up on the edge of the system, firing a stream of projectiles towards the planet and then vanishing into the shadows before they could be hunted down and destroyed. The RockRats, in the meantime, had kept launching full-sized asteroids right across the system, aiming them at a dozen planets and moons. The virus had responded by dispatching several squadrons of smaller ships, while keeping the capital ships in position to deflect or destroy incoming asteroids. Mitch had the feeling it was up to something. It had to know it was just a matter of time before an asteroid or a projectile hit something vital.

"And yet, it'll see anything we launch from a distance," he mused. "Do you think we could cloak an entire asteroid?"

"I doubt it." Staci, as always, was ruthlessly practical. "It's hard enough cloaking a battleship or a fleet carrier. An asteroid would be several orders of magnitude bigger."

Mitch didn't doubt it. The smallest asteroid the RockRats had launched, so far, was easily a *hundred* times the size of a battleship. The cloaking field required to cover it would be staggeringly huge, well beyond the capabilities of any known device…and yet, he found himself considering the possibilities. Could they wrap an asteroid in stealth coating? It wouldn't have to last very long. If they could get the asteroid a little closer to the planet, the virus might find it impossible to deflect before it was too late. It would have to blow the asteroid into dust, which would cause its own problems. The idea was worth considering.

He made a note of the concept and sent it to the data cache, where it would be forwarded to *Lion*, then returned his attention to the holographic display. They'd been staring at it long enough for his eyes to ache, looking for a way to slip a missile through the defences and slam it into an enemy target. It wasn't going to be easy, if it was even possible. The virus was treating all sensor contacts as real, launching starfighters at the first hint of a cloaked ship gliding towards the planet. Mitch had the impression of a boxer, his fists at the ready even as his eyes were hidden behind a blindfold. If the boxer figured out where his opponent actually was, it wouldn't be hard to kick him out of the ring…

"They're not going to let themselves be decoyed away, not this time," he said. It was clear, from *Lion's* tactical data, that the virus had learnt to fear minefields. The analysts thought that was why the virus hadn't dispatched a far larger force to chase *Lion*. It was too concerned about running into another minefield. "I think we're going to have to think of something else."

"We could try mining more gas projectiles," Staci said, doubtfully. "But they're being a great deal more careful with *those*."

"We wouldn't hit anything worth the effort," Mitch agreed. The virus was intercepting the projectiles well short of the planet, checking them carefully before they were forwarded to their destination. Its paranoia wasn't misplaced, but it was bloody inconvenient. "We might need to risk trying to sneak the missiles through on a ballistic trajectory. Or..."

He frowned. The virus was unlikely to believe in the existence of another fleet of sensor ghosts, not unless the ghosts started shooting. They just didn't have the missiles to make it look realistic. And yet... perhaps they could use the sensor ghosts as cover for the real missiles. They might not *distract* the virus, but...if they could convince the virus it was being fooled, that its enemies were trying to fool it. Mitch smiled, his hands dancing over the console as he ran a handful of simulations. It might just work.

"Look at this," he said. "If this works, we might just be able to hit a high-value target."

"If," Staci said. "We've yet to find a single point failure source."

"No," Mitch agreed. "But even a handful of nukes detonating in the high orbitals would give them a nasty fright."

He leaned back in his chair. "We'll launch the missiles on ballistic trajectories, keyed to go live once they reach the high orbitals," he said. It might be possible to obtain a handful of backpack nukes from the marines and start slipping them into orbit, too, but that would require them to link up with *Lion* and make the transfer. He tapped his terminal, sending the concept to *Lion*. "Perhaps we could land a marine on the orbital towers, then climb down the structure into the planet's atmosphere."

Staci chuckled. "You'd be looking at a climb of over two thousand kilometres," she pointed out. "Even if the poor bugger isn't detected, it'll still take a *long* time to get deep enough within the atmosphere to launch the BioBombs."

"We could try using a robot instead," Mitch said. The idea might not work, and the downsides were obvious, but they needed to think of something before they ran out of resources and had to withdraw. "I'll give it some thought."

He shrugged. "You go make the preparations," he added. "I'll join you on the bridge in an hour."

Staci stood. "Aye, Captain."

• • •

Tobias said nothing as he stood with the remainder of the squadron as they listened to Captain Hammond eulogising their dead comrades. Part of him was relieved he wasn't the one giving the speech; part of him felt guilty that he'd allowed the captain to take his place. He knew he could hardly have stood in the man's way, when he'd said he'd lead the service, but… he still felt guilty. He wondered, vaguely, if the captain felt guilty, too. He hadn't spent any time with the gunboat pilots, leaving them with Tobias and Colonel Bagehot. He didn't *know* the people under his command.

There's over a thousand crewmen on this ship, Tobias reminded himself. There'd been over seven hundred pupils at his old school and he didn't know even a small percentage of them. He'd barely known his classmates. *The captain can't know them all.*

He stared at the older man, trying to determine what he was feeling. Captain Hammond sounded regretful at losing two young lives, and their gunboat, but it was hard to be sure. The captain was old enough to be their father. He'd been in the navy longer than Tobias had been alive. He might have attended enough services, over the last two decades, to understand that death was a part of life. Tobias knew it too, but…he'd never lost anyone under his command before. He'd never so much as held a command. And now…he wondered, suddenly, if the parents would blame *him*. He'd been their commanding officer and he hadn't even seen them go.

The captain closed the service book and stared at the gathered pilots. It was traditional for all off-duty personnel to attend services for the dead, but the shuttlebay was largely empty. The captain had ordered the crew to continue their duties, rather than take the time to remember the dead pilots...Tobias understood the logic, he knew they might be called back to action at any moment, but it still burned. His pilots were part of the ship's crew. They damn well should be remembered as part of the crew.

"It is never easy to lose someone," Captain Hammond said. His voice was gentle, yet firm. "It is never easy to accept that someone is gone forever, nor that their body cannot be recovered and returned home. It is never easy to believe that they will never be seen again. I wish I could make it better for you, but there's nothing I can say or do that will. You will have to come to terms with it, in time."

Tobias scowled, then hastily schooled his face into a mask. He knew the captain meant well, as he spoke about one's duty to one's country, but it was hard to believe. They'd known the job was dangerous when they'd taken it...he shook his head as the captain's speech came to an end. His country had helped him and his country had hurt him and now...it had hurt him again, although the virus would do far worse if it got into his system. He told himself that he was being silly. There was no one to blame, not even himself. And yet, he *did* blame himself.

He cleared his throat, as the captain turned and left the compartment. "Marigold and I have to deal with their possessions," he said, curtly. It should have been done at once, as soon as they confirmed they'd lost a gunboat, but they'd had to continue the fight over the last few days. He just hadn't had the time. "Give us an hour. Once we're done, you can return to the sleeping berths."

A dozen suggestions ran through his head, all things he could say...all things he knew would be worse than useless. The squadron had bonded, becoming a unit...it hurt to lose two of their number, two of their most popular members. It was all the harder because their military training was nothing more than a thin veneer, painted over their civilian lives. And there was nothing they could do about it. They just had to hope they could get through.

His heart ached as they made their way back to the sleeping compartment. It wasn't the first time he'd packed a fellow pilot's possessions into a box, as if they were all that were left of them, but...this time, *he* was the commanding officer. Neither of the pilots had had very much, certainly nothing that couldn't be shared out amongst the rest of the squadron...it was easy to believe, all of a sudden, that the handful of things in the box were *all* they'd left behind. He knew it wasn't true and yet he believed it.

"I don't know what I'm going to say," he said. "Do I have to write the letter now?"

"You could probably pass the job to the CAG," Marigold said. "He'd certainly have to take a look at it."

Tobias grimaced. The letter his mother had received, when his father had died, had been little more than *pro forma*. It hadn't told them anything about his father's career, let alone when and where he'd died. The days when the navy could afford to send officers around to break the news in person were long gone. Now...it was just a little letter on official notepaper and a pension that never went far enough. At least the pilots he'd lost hadn't been married with children. They'd barely been old enough to drink!

"I'll do it myself," he said, finally. "If I tell them the truth..."

"If you tell them the truth, there's a very good chance the letter will be censored," Marigold said, bluntly. "You might want to hold back the details until you see them in person."

"... Fuck." Tobias hadn't thought of it. God knew *his* father's commanding officer had never bothered to get in touch, even to offer insincere condolences. Perhaps he'd been killed, too. Tobias had never dared try to find out. "I'll do what I can."

Marigold patted his shoulder. "I'll take the boxes and pack them away," she said. "The rest of their possessions can be shared out."

"I don't want anything," Tobias said. "Do you think anyone will?"

"Someone will," Marigold said. "At least there'll be something of the dead still with us."

• • •

"Drones in position, Captain," Staci said. "They're ready to go live."

Mitch nodded. The last set of mass driver projectiles had appeared out of nowhere and lanced towards the planet, throwing the defenders into another flurry of confusion. They were getting better at shooting down the projectiles, he noted, but they moved so quickly that a lone starfighter would only have one shot at them before they vanished into the distance. The virus had compensated by deploying hundreds of starfighters in an interception formation, one that looked more effective than it actually was. Mitch had the feeling it could be broken easily if they'd had enough ships to take advantage of it.

"Launch the missiles," he ordered. "Activate the drones when the missiles reach Point Hammer."

"Aye, Captain."

Mitch forced himself to relax as the missiles glided away from the ship. Their drive fields had been completely deactivated, ensuring they were extremely difficult to detect. They would trip alarms when they entered the sensor sphere, he was sure, but not until they were a great deal closer. A timer appeared, counting down the seconds until the missiles were sure to be detected. The decoys had to go live shortly before it was too late. or the whole operation would be worse than useless.

"They'll cross the line in nine minutes," Staci reported.

"Good," Mitch said. The enemy defences were slowly returning to normal, now the remainder of the mass driver projectiles had been destroyed. It wasn't a good sign. The virus had started randomising its patrols, making it even *harder* to sneak up on the planet. "Watch for any signs they've been detected earlier."

His eyes narrowed as he spotted a handful of alien starships launching themselves into deep space. They weren't pushing their drives to the max—it would be at least twenty hours before they managed to get anywhere near *Lion* and her mass drivers—but that wasn't a good sign either. The virus was quietly slipping more mobile units out there, trying to make life harder for the bombardiers. Mitch had to admit it was a decent idea. There weren't many other options.

"Three minutes," Staci said. "They're adjusting their sensor pulses."

Mitch hesitated. If he gave the order to trigger the drones now, the missiles might be spotted ahead of time. But if he waited, the missiles might be spotted anyway. He leaned forward, trying to determine what—if anything—had alerted the enemy. There were so many pieces of space junk near the planet now, thanks to the mass drivers, that it was possible a piece of rock had tripped their defences.

"Hold steady," he ordered. "Let them get a little closer."

Sweat beaded on his back as the seconds ticked down to zero. The enemy sensor pulses grew stronger, sweeping out in all directions. There was something about the pattern that nagged at his mind, even though he didn't know why. Something he'd seen, once upon a time. It wasn't focused on *Unicorn*, or even anywhere near her. He wondered, suddenly, if someone else had had the idea of coating an asteroid in stealth paint. Or if another starship was trying to sneak up on the planet. Or...

The timer reached zero. "Activate the drones!"

"Aye, sir," Staci said. "Drones going live...now!"

Mitch leaned forward as the ghostly ships appeared on the display. The virus wouldn't be fooled this time—the ghost ships were about as subtle as a naked pitch invader in the middle of a football game—but hopefully it would be looking in the wrong direction when the missiles went live. The drones were pumping out so much energy, drawing the virus towards it, that the missiles should be easy to miss.

"Activate the missiles in ten seconds," he ordered. The enemy starfighters were already altering course, clearly hoping to snag a drone or two before it was too late. "Tactical, prepare to alter course."

"Aye, sir."

"Missiles going live, sir," Staci reported. Her posture straightened. "Sir, they're already being targeted."

"Shit," Mitch growled. The missiles were powering up, but the mere act of bringing their drives online was enough to make them targets. Their chances of scoring even a single hit were dropping by the second. "Order them to engage the nearest enemy targets."

"Aye, Captain."

"Helm, reverse course," Mitch added. The outcome of the brief engagement no longer mattered. They'd have to find a new approach—and quickly. "Take us back to the RV point."

"Aye, Captain," Hinkson said.

Mitch frowned as the planet started to recede behind them. The missiles were already being engaged. Only one lasted long enough to strike its target, an automated weapons platform...one of hundreds. Mitch knew—there was no way around it—that the virus had come out ahead. They'd definitely have to think of something else, before it was too late.

One platform per ten missiles, he thought, sourly. *It isn't as if we brought a hundred thousand missiles...*

"Captain," Staci said. "Turbulence! Dead ahead!"

"Evasive action," Mitch snapped. A cloaked ship. It had to be a cloaked ship. The virus must have guessed their location, then used their sensor pulses to steer a cloaked ship into their path. "Prepare to launch drones..."

"Incoming fire," Staci snapped. "I say again, incoming fire!"

CHAPTER TWENTY-SIX

"STAND BY POINT DEFENCE," Mitch ordered. "Deploy two decoy drones on my mark."

His mind raced. The alien starship—it looked like a cruiser—had gotten very lucky. Or he'd gotten *very* unlucky. *Unicorn* had been laying stealthed sensor platforms all over the system. There was no reason the virus couldn't do the same. The virus could have easily scattered a few platforms around itself, in hopes of catching a sniff of a cloaked ship. And it had clearly succeeded. The odds of the cruiser stumbling across them by chance were frighteningly low.

We showed them how to do it, Mitch thought. *And they learned their lessons well.*

"Deploy drones," he ordered. The enemy missiles were closing the range rapidly. Mitch doubted the virus expected to blow them out of space with a single volley, but *Unicorn's* point defence fire would pinpoint her position to any watching eyes. "Alter course on my command."

He counted five seconds, then leaned forward. "Alter course."

The display shifted. The enemy cruiser was picking up speed, trying to narrow the range as quickly as possible. Two of its missiles appeared to have been fooled by the decoys, the remainder continuing their suicidal course towards *Unicorn*. Mitch gritted his teeth. The cruiser was just too close to be fooled, if they launched drones in hopes of convincing the enemy that *Unicorn* had fled in one direction while actually fleeing in the other. His mind raced, considering options. They might simply outrun the cruiser, given time, but the enemy ship had a solid lock on them. He was gloomily aware the enemy might already be massing more ships—under cloak—to cut off their retreat. The billions upon billions of cubic kilometres of interplanetary space could hide an entire fleet of enemy ships.

"They'll enter point defence range in thirty seconds," Staci warned. "Point defence locked, ready to fire."

"Fire at will," Mitch ordered, harshly. They dared not try to withstand a blow. The missiles would do immense damage, even if they didn't destroy the frigate outright. "Helm, bring us about…"

His fingers traced a line on the console. They were going to have to run. There was no other choice. And yet, they could be being herded right into a trap. He frowned, considering the possibilities. When had they actually been spotted? When they'd launched the missiles at the planet? Before? Afterwards? How much advance warning had the virus actually had, before it sprung its trap? It couldn't have had *much* warning or it wouldn't have let the frigate get anywhere near the planet. There was no way in hell that any *sane* defender would assume the defences could handle whatever was thrown at them, certainly not to the point of letting it happen.

"Helm, set course for the nearest uninhabited asteroid cluster," Mitch ordered. The idea of luring the enemy ship into a tight space was absurd, the stuff of science-fantasy, but they might be able to power down and pretend to be an asteroid long enough for the enemy to lose interest. Or…a flicker of hope shot through him as he had an idea. "Communications, signal *Lion*. Inform them that we'll do our best to escape, then attach a copy of our final sensor records."

The display updated. "Point defence engaging…now," Staci said. "The enemy ship is firing another salvo."

Mitch nodded, unsurprised. His tracking computers had had all the time they needed to plot out the flight path, then plan their countermeasures.

The missiles had been flying in straight lines…he smiled, despite the situation, as the last of the missiles was blown into vapour. It was good to know his ship could defend itself, even though they'd also given away their exact position. The next salvo would have far more accurate targeting data.

A low *thrumming* ran through the frigate as she picked up speed. Mitch keyed his console, running a course projection. The range would continue to narrow for several minutes, then start to widen again…unless the enemy ship altered course or proved to be faster than any of his projections suggested. If the ship had a higher acceleration curve than he'd realised, the range was going to narrow so sharply they'd practically be at point-blank range. And that would allow the enemy ship to bring its real weapons to bear.

"Signal sent, sir," Culver said. "It'll be nine hours before we get a reply."

Mitch shrugged. He had every confidence Captain Hammond would do everything in his power to assist them, but…there was nothing he could do. By the time *Lion* reached their current location, the battle would be over. *Unicorn* was on her own. He studied the display as the second flight of missiles neared his ship, their drives overloading as they struggled to push the missiles even faster. It didn't *look* as though the cruiser carried variable-drive or multistage missiles, although producing them was relatively simple once you had the general idea. The virus had definitely seen the missiles in action. Mitch hoped it was a sign the ambush had been thrown together in a rush…

His ship lurched. Alarms howled. The display flared with red light. "Report!"

"Direct hit, lower deck," Staci snapped. The red icons started to blink out as the datanet reassessed the situation. "I think they hit us with a bomb-pumped laser."

"And it didn't kill us?" Mitch wasn't so sure. "Did they have a misfire?"

Staci worked her console for a long moment. "Sensor records indicate they triggered a starburst detonation, instead of a single beam. Only one of the beams actually struck us."

The intercom bleeped. "No major damage, Captain," Lieutenant-Commander Brian Wimer reported. The engineer sounded grim. "The armour took most of the blast. We've sealed off the zone, for the moment."

"And if they do the same to somewhere a little more vital, we're fucked," Mitch finished. "Do what you can."

He cursed under his breath as the enemy ship altered course, then fired another salvo of missiles. It was a cruiser. It wouldn't carry many missiles. But its supply base was only a few million kilometres away. The virus couldn't be sure, of course, but it had to have reasoned that there couldn't be *many* human ships in the system. If it managed to take out one, perhaps trading ten ships for one, it would still come out ahead. And the starburst detonation pattern worked in its favour. It didn't have to blow *Unicorn* out of space with a single shot. All it needed to do was cripple the frigate, close the range and finish the job.

Or send boarding parties over to infect us, Mitch thought. He disliked the idea of surrender, even to a civilised foe, but the virus wouldn't treat its captives very well at all. *If that happens, I'll trigger the self-destruct and blow the ship to hell myself.*

"Deploy additional drones," he ordered. "And then fluctuate the cloaking device."

"Aye, Captain," Staci said.

Mitch braced himself as the enemy missiles entered point defence range. Their calculations might be in error. They'd assumed the missiles would want to close the range to the point they could be relatively sure of a hit, but if the enemy was using a starburst pattern they wouldn't *have* to close the range. Probably. The odds of scoring a hit would be low... just not *that* low.

Fluctuating the cloaking device might confuse them, he thought. *But it won't fool them for very long.*

Unicorn lurched again. "Direct hit, rear sector," Staci said. "We've lost a drive node."

Mitch swore. In theory, *Unicorn* could lose two or three nodes without losing speed. In practice…he wasn't so sure. Their acceleration curve had just been cut, sharply. The enemy ship might be able to overhaul them, given time, or simply summon reinforcements. Mitch had no illusions about the outcome, if the virus managed to bring a flight of starfighters into attack range. The frigate would fight to the last, but she would be overwhelmed and destroyed.

"Keep us moving," he ordered. "Launch two recon drones ahead of us."

"Aye, Captain."

Mitch forced himself to relax—slightly—as the range started to open again. They'd have to fly two-thirds of the way across the system to outrun the enemy cruiser completely, but—given time—they could do it. Would they have the time? The situation had reversed itself completely. The inky vastness of space he'd used as a hiding place had suddenly become a deadly threat. An entire fleet could be inching its way into firing range, with him completely unaware of its presence until the fleet opened fire. The virus would have problems coordinating such a movement, but they could be overcome. He was morbidly sure of it.

"Deploy five mines, scatter-burst pattern," he ordered. It was unlikely they'd take out the enemy ship, but it might convince the cruiser to be a little more cautious. "Detonate them as soon as she enters extreme range."

"Aye, Captain," Staci said. "Mines deploying…now."

If we can get a little more distance between us and them, we might be able to decoy them with a drone, Mitch thought. *But right now, they have a solid lock on us.*

His mind raced, calculating possible options. It would take at least seven hours to reach the asteroid cluster, assuming they weren't intercepted well short of their destination. Even then…he mulled his plan over and over in his mind, testing the concept mentally before he loaded it into the simulators. The odds wouldn't be good, but that wasn't a problem. They were already pretty damn bad. He smirked at the thought, despite everything. He'd been in the navy long enough to know that unfavourable odds weren't always a guarantee of defeat. The human—or alien—factor could never be discounted.

The display updated. "The mines detonated, Captain," Staci reported. "No apparent effect."

"Hold the remaining mines," Mitch ordered. "Let's see if she decides to be a little more careful."

He felt sweat prickling down his back as the minutes turned into hours. He knew he should snatch some rest, he knew he should order the beta crews to take their stations, but...he kept a wary eye on the display as the range inched wider and wider. The enemy cruiser wasn't overloading her drives, something that worried him. It suggested the enemy ship was more interested in keeping a lock on his position, rather than trying to kill him, which meant...he frowned as he stared at the endless wastes of interplanetary space. There *had* to be an ambush ahead, waiting for him. And he didn't have the slightest idea where it actually was.

Altering course randomly will just give the bastard behind us a chance to catch up, he thought, coldly. *But not altering course will give them all the time they need to plan their ambush.*

He worked the console for a long moment, but it was pointless. The tactical situation had been reduced to a very simple problem. They had to lose—or destroy—the ship behind them before they flew straight into an ambush. He surveyed the records from the sensor platforms, cursing—not for the first time—the speed-of-light delay. There were hundreds of enemy ships within the system, all of which could have changed course and speed since they'd been spotted and logged by the platform. Their current locations were somewhere within the probability cones, but where? A handful could have moved to intercept his ship without being detected...he shook his head as the recon drones continued to fly into the empty space ahead. He might *just* get enough warning to change course...

"Beta crews, take your stations," he ordered. "XO, get some rest. I'll remain on the bridge."

Staci shot him a look that said, very clearly, *get some rest too* as she stood, handed her console to her relief and headed off the bridge. Mitch ignored it. There was no way he could sleep, not with an enemy ship behind them and an unknown threat ahead. He wanted to believe they could simply outrun their pursuer, or lead it straight to *Lion*, but he knew it wasn't going to be possible. The bloody ship was just too close.

He forced himself to stay alert as the hours ticked on. The asteroid cluster looked deserted. There wasn't even a single *hint* of enemy presence. Mitch would have found it suspicious, if he'd been hunting his fellow humans, but the virus seemed intent on rationalising its exploitation of the system. There was so much junk in the system that the virus didn't *need* to lay claim to each and every single asteroid. Mitch supposed that being a single entity would make that very easy. The more oppressive governments, back on Earth, had discovered—to their horror—that trying to repress asteroid settlers was a recipe for disaster. They could simply slip into the darkness of space and vanish. Rumour had it that there were entire networks of hidden settlements that had no contact with the Belt Alliance, let alone the Great Powers. Mitch believed them.

It was hard, so hard, to remain focused as they steadily closed on the asteroid cluster. His imagination insisted that the enemy cruiser would hit an asteroid when it tried to follow them into the cluster...he shook his head, dismissing the thought as absurd levels of wishful thinking. The cluster might look as if dozens of asteroids had been crammed into a relatively small region, but there was enough space between them to allow a dozen battleships to make transit without any risk at all. And yet... Mitch was tempted to fly through the cluster and try to vanish into deep space, but he knew it would be futile. They *had* to take out the cruiser before it was too late.

"Tactical, stand by to deploy decoys," he ordered hours later, once the alpha crew had returned to the bridge. "Helm, prepare to cut our speed on my mark."

"Aye, Captain," Staci said.

Mitch braced himself as he started the countdown. They'd lost a drive node. There was a very real risk of the drive field destabilising, when they tried to cut speed sharply. The engineers had done their best, but the drive node had been damaged beyond repair. It would have to be pulled out and replaced and…Mitch shook his head. It was academic. Either they'd survive long enough to make the repairs, when they reached the edge of the system and linked up with the rest of the squadron, or they wouldn't. The remainder didn't matter.

"Mark," he commanded.

A low shudder ran through the starship—Mitch was *sure* he heard the hull creak, although he knew he was imagining it—as her speed dropped sharply. The gravity field shimmered and then stabilised. Mitch stared at the display as they glided towards a giant asteroid, easily large enough to conceal their presence while the drones lured the enemy ship away. It wouldn't be fooled for long, if at all, but he should have a few seconds to proceed to the next stage of his plan.

"Deploy the sensor platform and the reprogrammed missile," he ordered. "Detonate the missile on my command."

"Aye, Captain," Staci said.

"Helm, keep us moving around the asteroid," Mitch said. "Let them think we're trying to hide."

"Aye, Captain."

Mitch braced himself, counting down the seconds. The enemy cruiser had cut speed too, but she'd overshot. She hadn't *had* to slam into an asteroid—an extremely unlikely outcome—to lose track of *Unicorn*. The combination of the sudden reduction in speed and the two decoys were enough to confuse her, although she *had* to have a rough idea of the frigate's hiding place. Mitch watched as the cruiser reversed course, prowling towards the asteroid. He felt like a mouse, being chased by a cat. If the cruiser got a clear shot at his ship, they'd be blown to atoms. And yet, it was gliding towards the missile as well. He checked the live feed from the sensor platform. The cruiser wasn't even trying to hide. She was pumping out enough sensor pulses to reveal her position to someone on the other side of the system. If she spotted the missile…

"If she scans the missile, detonate it at once," Mitch ordered, quietly. "If not, detonate the missile when she enters point-blank range."

He waited, feeling ice running down his spine. The cruiser was steadily closing the range…he remembered, suddenly, an old story about a man in a spacesuit who'd evaded a giant battleship by moving around a moon. It might have worked, if *Unicorn* had been a little smaller. The frigate wasn't *that* small…

"Captain," Staci said. "I have three enemy ships lighting up their drives, inbound on our location."

Mitch cursed. The cruiser had called in reinforcements. The newcomers were already piling on the speed. They'd reach the cluster in ten minutes. Perhaps less…

"Detonate the missile," he ordered. There was no time to waste. "Now!"

The missile detonated. A bomb-pumped laser beam stabbed deep into the cruiser's vitals. She seemed to hesitate—for a moment, she looked unharmed—before a series of explosions blew her into atoms. Mitch had no time to savour the victory. There were three more ships bearing down on them. They had to *move*.

"Deploy our remaining decoys," he ordered. "And then cloak us and…"

He broke off as the three icons vanished. He thought, for a second, that the enemy ships had been nothing more than decoys. The cruiser could have tried to use them to frighten him…no, it hadn't been in place to deploy the decoys. It couldn't have…

"Captain," Culver said, as a very familiar signature appeared on the display. "*Lion* is hailing us."

Mitch blinked. *She came to our rescue?*

He cleared his throat. "I think we'd better thank them," he said. "Open channels."

"Aye, Captain."

CHAPTER TWENTY-SEVEN

"MY CREW AND I OWE YOU OUR THANKS," Captain Campbell said. "We weren't expecting you to come to our aid."

"We could hardly leave you to face the enemy alone," Thomas said. It was difficult not to feel as though he'd made a mistake. He wouldn't have taken the risk, if he hadn't already been dismantling the mass drivers and moving them to a new position. Even so, it had been a close-run thing. The virus might not have *intended* to use *Unicorn* as bait to draw *Lion* away from the mass drivers—that would have required precognition—but there was no reason it couldn't take advantage of the distraction. "And the next time, maybe they'll think twice about chasing you."

He allowed himself a tart smile. Captain Campbell had taken out an enemy cruiser. He might have managed to evade the other three ships, given time. But he wouldn't *know* it for sure. Thomas was tempted to indulge in a minor gloat. The enemy ships had been so focused on the frigate that they hadn't spotted an entire battlecruiser sneaking up behind them. If nothing else, it *would* make it difficult for the virus to spread out its units. It wouldn't be able to tell if it was flying straight into a trap until it was too late.

"We thank you," Captain Campbell said. If he was embarrassed by the whole affair, he gave no sign of it. "We still don't know how they spotted us."

Thomas frowned. "Forward all your data to the analysts," he said. "They might be able to figure it out."

His mind raced. Captain Campbell wasn't incompetent, whatever else could be said about him, and his crew was very well trained. *Lion* had run enough tracking exercises on *Unicorn* to be sure the frigate's crew was very capable indeed. And yet, the frigate had been spotted...bad luck? Had they passed too close to a passive sensor array? Or had the enemy calculated what they'd do and deployed ships to take advantage of it? The virus knew the human ships were out there, raining asteroids and space junk on its worlds. It wouldn't have any trouble working out what the humans had to do to win.

"Of course," Captain Campbell said. "If you don't mind, my crew and I need to start repairs."

"And you need to get some rest," Thomas said. The younger man looked as if he was on the verge of falling asleep. "We'll start making our way back to the outer system. Your crew can do the repairs on the way."

Captain Campbell looked irked, but nodded. "Yes, Commodore," he said. "We'll be back on harassment duty before you know it."

He tapped a switch. His face vanished from the display. Thomas snorted. Part of him would always wonder if he'd done the right thing. It would have been easy to leave *Unicorn* on her own, to escape or be destroyed without any help or hindrance...he shook his head. Captain Campbell might be an asshole who'd slept with Thomas's wife, but his crew didn't deserve to die. There was no way in *hell* they deserved to die. And it had been Thomas's duty to go to their aid...

The intercom bleeped. "Captain, this is Tactical," Sibley said. "We've found something you ought to take a look at."

Thomas stood. "I'm on my way."

He strode onto the bridge, frowning. They'd deployed a handful of sensor platforms and drones they could ill spare, just to be sure no one was trying to creep up on them. There were no hints of any incoming ships, not as far as anyone could tell, but he knew from grim experience that could be misleading. The virus knew where they were. It could have dispatched an entire cloaked fleet to kill them. Thomas knew they had to get underway, quickly, before they were pinned down and blown to atoms. And yet…

"We ran a cursory survey of the asteroids, in hopes of locating rocks that could be hurled at the targets," Sibley explained. "We located an asteroid that was suspiciously well-formed, so I ordered one of the drones to take a closer look. This"—he keyed a switch—"is what it found."

Thomas sucked in his breath. There was no way in *hell* that asteroid was natural. It was a sphere, perfectly smooth… it was artificial. It had to be. He glanced at the live feed from the drone and frowned. The asteroid—no, the *base*—was over fifty kilometres in diameter. The surface was unmarked, save for a dark spot that might—or might not—be an entrance. He cursed under his breath. He'd been told to watch for alien structures, for evidence of alien life that might be a great deal more advanced than humanity, but…why did it have to be *here?* They *had* to vacate the asteroid cluster before the virus came calling.

He forced himself to think. The squadron didn't have any real xenospecialists. There'd never seemed to be any need. They already knew all they needed to know about the virus and its technology. And yet…he shook his head as he keyed his wristcom. They *had* to take a look at the station, whatever it was, before the virus swept the asteroid cluster from end to end. The marines would have to slip into the structure and make what recordings they could, before it was too late. Thomas wondered, idly, if there'd be any prize money. They'd found something worth billions, but getting it back home might be a problem.

"Major Craig, Colonel Bagehot," he said. They were going to have to improvise. Again. "Report to my ready room. We have another mission to plan."

"Aye, Captain."

Thomas smiled as a thought occurred to him. "Mr XO, did engineering finish repairing the pusher?"

"Yes, Captain," Donker said. "What do you have in mind?"

"There's a bunch of asteroids here," Thomas said. He briefly considered trying to push the alien structure into deep space, before dismissing it as a waste of time and resources. There was no guarantee they'd be able to slow the structure enough to capture it. "Order engineering to select a suitable asteroid and set up the pusher. It will make one hell of a weapon."

"Aye, Captain."

. . .

Colin liked to think of himself as brave, although—in truth—he was often nervous when an operation began. It was easy to consider oneself brave, he'd been told, when there was no real risk of serious injury or death. Even the most experienced marines felt a twinge of nervousness, if not fear, no matter how extensively they'd trained and practiced. And yet, as the alien structure came into view, he couldn't help feeling as if he was walking into the unknown. What the hell *was* it?

He felt uncomfortably exposed, even though he wore a spacesuit. There was no sign the structure was active, no hint it was doing *anything*, and yet he felt certain he was being watched. Combat instincts he'd built up over the last few years, instincts he'd been warned to take seriously, insisted on just that. He had the impression, as the sphere grew to the point it dominated the skyline, that he was crawling across a vast, unfathomable piece of machinery. He felt like a fly, landing—briefly—on a starship. The fly would have as little understanding of the starship as he had of the alien sphere.

A jolt ran though him as he touched down on the sphere. There was no gravity field. His magnetic boots were unable to lock on. Colin noted that absently, filing away for the report he'd write later. The rest of the fire team had no better luck. He used hand signals to warn them to stay back as he drifted across the surface, steering towards the gash in the hull. The sense of being confronted with something unimaginably alien grew stronger as he reached the gash and looked inside. The darkness pulsed like a living thing.

His mouth was dry. He swallowed hard. "I'm going in," he said, activating his suit's lights. The brilliance drove away the darkness. "One man will remain on the hatch at all times."

He lowered himself into the hatch, spinning around in a wide circle to ensure the recorders caught everything. The room was unnaturally large—he felt like a child, in an adult world—the proportions jarringly alien. It looked…it took him several seconds to put it into words. It looked as if someone had taken a starship and insisted it be scaled up, without taking into account all the changes that would need to be made. The compartments were several times the size they needed to be, immensely huge and wasteful…he found himself wondering just how big the builders had been. The Vesy were the largest race ever encountered and even *they* would have found the compartment oppressively huge.

A shiver ran down his spine. The walls were covered in writing, alien writing, and diagrams. One of them looked like the system, right down to the planets and moons; the others were completely unfamiliar. The walls were a dull brown, resembling clay or brick rather than cold metal. Colin poked it carefully, only to discover it was at least as solid as battle steel. He stepped into the next section and frowned. The walls were no thicker than a sheet of paper. Whatever the metal was, it was tough…and thin. Even a starfighter had a thicker hull.

"This place is deserted," Davis commented. His voice made Colin jump. "Where *is* everyone?"

Colin nodded, thoughtfully. If the sphere, whatever it was, had been abandoned in a hurry, there should have been a *lot* of stuff left behind. He'd worked his way through towns and villages that had been evacuated after the bombardment and then abandoned for decades, and he'd been amazed at how much crap had simply been lying around. It was no wonder that looters had been sneaking through the fences and searching the abandoned homes, picking up everything from cars to family heirlooms. The sphere didn't look as if it had been abandoned in a hurry and yet, if the evacuation had been planned, why hadn't the sphere been pushed into the sun or blown to atoms? Any power capable of building the sphere would be equally capable of destroying it. Why had they just left it in place for the virus to find?

The virus might not have been able to tell it was there, he reminded himself. *If they can hide a structure on an infected surface, they can certainly hide something in the trackless wastes of interplanetary space.*

The thought nagged at him as they continued to explore. There was no way to be sure they were dealing with the same race. Humans and Tadpoles might have evolved in worlds hundreds of light years apart, but on a galactic scale they were practically next-door neighbours. For all he knew, there could be two super-races. The galaxy was old and the universe older still, dating back nearly fourteen *billion* years. Millions upon millions of races could have evolved, climbed into godhood and then vanished before the ancestor of the human race took his first step out of the ocean. Colin wasn't given to philosophising—he was far too focused on the universe surrounding him—but even *he* was daunted by the thought. They could be being watched by intelligences so far beyond them that they had literally nothing in common, no way to relate to each other…

He had a hard time keeping his composure as they made their way through the structure. It tore at his mind, jarring his senses to the point he wondered if he'd been fed a hallucinogenic drug or if he was being bombarded with sonic pulses designed to unsettle him. His air mix seemed fine, but…just looking around the sphere made his eyes hurt, as if an unseen force was poking and prodding at his eyeballs. They moved from room to room, noting the strange combination of empty chambers, wall-mounted diagrams and a complete lack of anything that might tell him anything about the builders and occupants. He'd been taught the importance of cleaning up after himself—he'd been shown how easy it was for someone to go through the remains of an abandoned campsite and deduce things about the people who'd left it behind—but the sphere's builders had taken it to the next level. They'd left the structure behind, yet they'd removed everything else. The walls were as bare as a jail cell .,

"Or are they?" Colin's voice sounded odd, even to himself. "They might have left everything behind, but we just can't recognise it."

Willis coughed. "Colin?"

Colin nearly jumped again, one hand reaching for his pistol before he stopped himself. "I was thinking…"

"Always a terrible habit," Davis put in.

"Hah." Colin shot him a rude sign, then continued. "The old authors, the ones who wrote the first science-fiction books, would they recognise half of our equipment? Would a computer expert from the world before the Troubles have any idea what to do with a modern computer? Would they have even the slightest idea where to begin? We could be surrounded by everything we need to understand the guys who built this…this *thing*… and not know it."

"That's a point," Willis said. "The old computers were boxy pieces of crap. Whoever designed them wouldn't recognise a wristcom or a datapad or a datacore if it came up to them and punched them in the face."

"A marine from the second global war would recognise one of our assault rifles," Davis countered, dryly. "So would a marine from the days of sailing ships. They might not be able to understand how the rifle worked, or how to fire it, but they'd know what it was. Given time, they might even be able to work out how to fire it."

Colin shuddered, adding it to the list of issues he intended to mention in his report. Guns hadn't changed *that* much, at least in appearance, for hundreds of years. Computers very definitely had. He stared at the walls, wondering if he was looking at an alien computer screen. There might be holographic projectors concealed within the bulkheads. The star diagrams might be nothing more than an alien screensaver or decorations. Hell, he'd known marines who'd covered their barracks with everything from softcore porn to images from botanical gardens. For all he knew, whoever had set up the room had just been very fond of starcharts. And…

He shook his head. It was impossible to tell if the builders were humanoid. The virus was the only known race that *wasn't* and even *it* infected humanoid bodies or did its level best to mimic them. He forced himself to take a step back and stare at the door, trying to determine what sort of creature would use it. The effort made his head hurt all the more. He'd been in far larger compartments, from shuttlebays to mess halls, but this… it was just *wrong*. He felt as if he was in a giant's house, as if a giant would come stamping in at any moment, calling for the blood of an Englishman. The scale was just too big.

They found nothing of interest, as far as they could tell, as they swept through the rest of the sphere. The interior was smaller than he'd expected, as if chunks of the hull were sealed off, seemingly inaccessible…he wondered, again, if they were simply missing doors and access points that would be obvious to the original builders. They might have decorated their doors in ways humans couldn't see, if their eyesight reached into parts of the visible spectrum inaccessible to humans…there was just no way to know. The boffins would analyse the recordings, then determine what—if anything—they'd actually uncovered. Colin hoped there'd be time to bring more specialists out from Earth. He wasn't sure they'd get a share of the prize money if the sphere was blown to dust before it could be studied.

"Around two-thirds of the projected interior is sealed off," Willis concluded. "If, of course, it exists at all."

"Yeah," Colin agreed. There was just no way to know. They hadn't been able to take a sample from the walls, nothing that might tell them what the structure was actually made of. The remainder of the sphere could be solid metal, a concealed industrial complex or…or *something*. It would be frustrating as hell to find a door and discover it was just more of the same. "I think we're just rats, running through a maze."

"That's a charming thought," Davis commented. "If you have any more like it, feel free to keep them to yourself."

Colin grinned. "I love to spread the mood," he said. "Who was it who said a problem shared means that two people have a problem?"

"You," Willis said. "Just now."

Colin's radio bleeped before he could think of a retort. "Return to the shuttle," Major Craig said. "We have incoming. I say again, we have incoming."

"Understood." Colin took one last look around the compartment, then headed for the hatch. They might never have a chance to return. If the virus hurled a missile into the sphere, it might be blown to atoms or simply rendered useless before anyone managed to intervene. Colin doubted the virus cared one jot for what it could recover from the sphere, if anything. It might regard the unknown builders as a deadly threat. "We're on our way."

CHAPTER TWENTY-EIGHT

"THE MARINES DID A GOOD JOB," Thomas said. "But it may take years to unlock the sphere's secrets."

He scowled as he glanced at the tactical display. The enemy had dispatched three battleships and a single carrier, as well as a dozen smaller ships, to destroy the human vessels or drive them back into deep space. *Unicorn* was already heading to the edge of the system, despite Captain Campbell's loud protests. The frigate was in no state for a fight and couldn't have added much, if anything, to the coming engagement. Thomas supposed the same was true of *Lion*. The battlecruiser could and would snipe the incoming ships, but she couldn't take them out unless his plan worked.

"Yes, sir," Craig said. "We could leave a party behind, on the sphere…?"

Thomas shook his head. The sphere was technically airtight. It wouldn't be *that* hard to put together a life-support system, a basic tent combined with a shuttle or gunboat, but he suspected it would be futile. There was little hope of discovering something—anything—immediately useful, not when they didn't have any real specialists to deploy to the sphere. They'd just have to hope the virus wouldn't bother to sweep the cluster properly, in the wake of the engagement. In hindsight, they might have been wiser to attach a handful of xenospecialists to the mission.

But that would leave us with the same problem, he mused. *We'd have to abandon the sphere or risk leaving the xenospecialists behind.*

He glanced at Nathan Morrison. "Can you determine anything useful from the marine recordings?"

"No, Captain," the Chief Engineer said. "To all appearances, the structure has been stripped of pretty much everything. The suggestion we simply might not be able to *recognise* alien technology is a good one, but we don't have time to go through the sphere with a fine-toothed comb. As far as we can tell, the sphere is completely inert…there's certainly no physical reason for the sense of unease the marines reported. It may be only in their minds. I've known people who had similar reactions to drive cores, nuclear fusion plants and other pieces of advanced technology."

"And people do become uneasy when they see someone carrying a gun," Major Craig said, sardonically. "Are you suggesting the marines wouldn't feel *anything* if they didn't know where they were?"

"I'm not suggesting anything," Morrison said. "All I can tell is that, as far as we are able to determine, the sphere is nothing more than an abandoned shell. If there's *anything* in the sealed compartments, if indeed there *are* sealed compartments, we are unable to determine what it might be…if it exists at all. The sphere is not going to teach us anything useful in time to matter. All we can do, I think, is mark it down for later attention."

"And it probably won't tell the virus anything useful either," Thomas mused. "There's nothing to find, not unless it *does* get into the sealed compartments."

"It *might*," Craig said. He smiled, rather humourlessly. "The virus is a *virus*. It is composed of millions upon millions of tiny viral particles. All it needs to do is seal the gash, pump an atmosphere into the sphere and then release itself. It'll search all the accessible sections very quickly and, perhaps, find a way into the inaccessible sections. If there's a tiny little gap in the metal, it'll find it."

"Joy." Thomas rubbed his forehead. "We'll leave a handful of sensor platforms behind to keep an eye on things. If it moves to secure the sphere…we'll have to do something about it."

"Yes, sir," Craig said.

"We will learn a great deal from it," Morrison said. "It'll just take longer than we might hope."

Thomas nodded, curtly. He'd been warned, when he'd been briefed on the artefacts they'd taken back to Earth, that it might take years before the research programs produced anything useful. Studying alien tech was always difficult, even when the aliens weren't *that* far ahead of the human race. There were just too many differences, too many unspoken assumptions about the proper way to do things…even something as simple as the measurement standards were different. It might be years before the sphere yielded anything useful, if they managed to land a research team without having to worry about the virus. There was no hope of finding something they could use against the virus.

And someone built the sphere and left it here, he mused. *Why?*

The intercom bleeped. "Captain," Donker said. "You asked to be notified when the alien squadron reached Point Gamma."

Thomas stood. "I'm on my way," he said. "Deploy the drones as planned. Have the remaining marines and engineering crews returned to the ship?"

"They're just returning now," Donker said.

"Once they're all back onboard, activate the drones and bring the cloaking device online," Thomas ordered. "And then we'll spring our trap."

He smiled, coldly, as he stepped though the hatch and onto the bridge. The virus shouldn't have been able to monitor their activities, not since *Lion* had blown its three cruisers out of space. There was certainly no reason to think the asteroid cluster was being monitored, although that might change now the virus knew it had unwelcome guests. It would practically *have* to start monitoring the asteroid clusters now, just to keep the RockRats from turning them into weapons. Unless it thought it was a waste of time…there was so much space junk in the system that monitoring it all would be pretty close to impossible.

And we'd see them doing it, Thomas thought. He took his seat and studied the display. The enemy squadron was closing rapidly. Long-range sensors suggested they were taking no chances. A flight of sensor drones flew ahead of them, sweeping for minefields or starships lying in wait. He couldn't fault their paranoia. It was clear they felt they didn't have the time to try to sneak up on the cluster. *They don't realise it's already too late.*

"Sir," Sibley said. "I have established a secure link to the pusher. Which ship should be the primary target?"

"The carrier," Thomas ordered. The battleships weren't exactly slow-coaches, but their acceleration curves were so low *Lion* could outrun them from a standing start. They'd have enough problems locating the real starship amongst the decoys to make it very hard for them to draw a bead on her before it was too late. The carrier's starfighters, on the other hand, could catch the battlecruiser easily. "Don't worry about hitting any of the other ships."

"Aye, Captain," Sibley said. "Target locked. Ready to fire on your command."

Thomas nodded, silently calculating the perfect moment to trigger the pusher. The incoming squadron would have only a few seconds of warning, if the simulations were accurate. They'd need to react at inhuman speed...no, they'd need to get the hell out of the way. Their point defence was good, but nowhere near *that* good. Even if the whole plan failed, he told himself, the virus would get a nasty fright. It would be a lot more careful about trying to sneak up on human positions.

"If they launch starfighters, trigger the pusher at once," he ordered. "If not, wait for my command."

He smiled, suddenly, as his heart started to race. There'd always been a depressing predictability about space battles, certainly ones fought between capital ships. Both sides could assess the likely outcome and evade combat, if they didn't *have* to fight. Half of tactical planning consisted of devising ways to force the enemy to fight on unfavourable terms. But here...he understood, suddenly, why Captain Campbell liked to take his ship into risky engagements. There was a certain thrill in staking everything on one roll of the dice.

And yet, my ship is too big to risk on a whim, he corrected himself. *If I had a smaller ship, perhaps I'd take more chances.*

"Fire on my mark," he ordered. He silently counted down the last few seconds. "Mark!"

"Pushing...now," Sibley said. "Impact in thirty seconds."

Thomas watched, coldly, as the asteroid shuddered and lurched forward, as if God Himself had stood behind the rock and *pushed*. The asteroid was flying towards the alien carrier at a goodly percentage of the speed of light, advancing hard on the heels of any warning...Thomas thought, just for a second, that it had swatted a recon drone as it flew onwards, the impact barely noticeable as it careened towards its target. It was hard to be sure. The virus had no time to react, beyond a handful of point defence bursts that were worse than useless, before the asteroid slammed into the carrier and vaporised the entire ship. Debris flew in all directions. There were no survivors.

"Tactical, launch the pre-deployed missiles," Thomas snapped. "Helm, get us out of here!"

"Aye, Captain," Sibley said.

Thomas smiled, very slightly. The carrier had been swatted out of existence. The remaining ships would be distracted, just for a few minutes, by the combination of sensor decoys and pre-deployed missiles. They'd think *Lion* was in completely the wrong place, giving him and his crew a chance to make their escape. The virus's battleships were hastily altering course, as if they feared more rocks were going to be coming in their direction. It was almost a pity there were none, Thomas reflected. He'd only had one pusher on hand. The remainder were on the edge of the system.

"Captain," Sibley said. "They don't seem to have spotted us."

That's what Campbell thought, Thomas reminded himself. The analysts had studied the records and concluded, unsurprisingly, that *Unicorn* had simply gotten unlucky. Thomas hoped they were right. The virus might be on its back foot, but it had more than enough resources to make the mission impossible. One more stroke of good luck—bad for the humans—and it might turn the whole situation around. *We have to be very careful.*

"Take us along the pre-planned course," Thomas ordered. They'd make absolutely certain they'd broken contact, or as close to it as they could, before they moved to link up with *Unicorn* and the fleet tenders. They needed to rearm the ships—and replace *Unicorn's* destroyed drive node—before resuming the offensive. "Sensors, keep an eye out for enemy ships."

"Aye, Captain."

Thomas nodded as he returned his attention to the display. Losing the sphere—or at least *access* to the sphere—was annoying, and he was sure someone back home would insist he should have stayed by the alien artefact and fought to defend it, but it was unlikely to give the virus the key to victory. The engineering report had made that clear. The implications of so many strange artefacts left behind were chilling—he was happy to admit as much—but right now it wasn't a major problem. He'd wonder about it after the war was won.

And yet, the thought nagged at him. *If someone is keeping an eye on us, or the virus, why?*

It was hard not to think about it. The sphere was clearly the product of a far more advanced race. Where were they? Why were they monitoring the virus? And had the human race attracted their attention, too? Was there a similar sphere in the solar system? Or somewhere near Tadpole Prime? Or...he shook his head. It seemed unlikely. There were so many asteroid miners in those systems that it was hard to believe a sphere would have gone unnoticed...

He stood. "Commander Donker, you have the bridge," he said. "I'll be in my ready room."

"Aye, Captain."

• • •

Mitch was torn between amusement and irritation as he watched, from a safe distance, as the pusher-driven asteroid smashed an alien carrier into atoms. The asteroid hadn't hit anything else, as far as his long-range sensors could tell, but it hardly mattered. The loss of the carrier would slow the alien response down, particularly if they thought they were about to be hit with an entire *stream* of asteroids. The thought made him smile. The pusher would change the face of war. Again.

He shook his head as he returned his attention to the live feed from engineering. They'd isolated the remains of the disabled—destroyed—drive node and were currently disconnecting the unit from its mounting. They were lucky they were doing it on a frigate, rather than a battleship, or the task would take a great deal longer... if it could be done at all.

His lips quirked, rather sourly, at the thought. A battleship's heavy armour would have shrugged off the laser beam, perhaps without even noticing it had been hit. The starburst laser pattern would have been quite ineffective.

"I think we're clear, Captain," Hinkson said. "There's no sign of enemy contact."

"We can afford to take our time," Mitch said. It was going to take a week, at least, to replace the drive node and perform tests to make sure the replacement would work under combat conditions. Longer, perhaps, to put together plans to hit the enemy again. "The XO and I will be in my cabin. You have the bridge."

Hinkson grinned. "Aye, Captain."

Mitch returned his grin. Hinkson was in line to be XO when Staci was finally promoted to command rank herself. Mitch had no idea when that would happen, but if the navy survived the next year it would be hard to justify *not* promoting her. There was supposed to be an entire *squadron* of battleship-frigate duos coming off the slips, if production hadn't been halted after the attack on Earth. He stood, putting the thought out of his mind. If they didn't survive the next few weeks, the future would be someone else's problem.

"We should get a share in the prize money," Staci said, once they were in his cabin. "If it wasn't for us, the sphere might never have been discovered."

"I hope so," Mitch agreed. The wet-navy crews had prayed that wounds were distributed in equal proportion to prize money. The modern-day navy was a little more civilised, although it would be tricky to calculate how much the prize was worth and then distribute it over the squadron. The navy would need to balance the need to reward the finders with the need to avoid resentment amongst those who hadn't had a chance to earn a reward themselves. "If the reward is as high as it should be, we would all get a reasonable amount."

He shrugged as he keyed his console. "I think they'll make it a great deal harder to get back to their homeworld's orbitals," he said. "And that means we need a new plan."

"Agreed," Staci said. "Do you have something in mind?"

Mitch brought up the sensor logs. "They always deflect the asteroids," he said. "It makes sense, of course. They don't want to risk having their high orbitals showered with debris if they shatter the asteroids. I think we should rig an asteroid to shatter before it can be safely deflected."

He allowed his smile to grow wider. "We make the repairs, then rig the asteroids before sneaking back into the system," he said. "And we can also steal an idea from the RockRats and fill a water-ice asteroid with counter-virus. And…we might just manage to sneak a maintenance robot through the high orbitals and send it crawling down the orbital towers…"

"It would be tricky," Staci pointed out. "They'll have motion sensors, surely."

"Would they?" Mitch wasn't so sure. "We keep forgetting. The virus is a single entity that lives in many bodies. Why should it need security? It would be like one hand putting a security code on your personal datapad because you don't trust the *other* hand. It might not bother to set up a sensor barrier, if only because it *knows* there's no reason to mistrust itself."

"I know addicts who might disagree," Staci said. "They didn't dare trust themselves, Captain. They had to go into care because it was the only way to clear their system to the point they could beat the wretched drugs. Or worse."

She looked away for a second, then shook her head. "If we shower the high orbitals in pieces of debris, Captain, we would do one hell of a lot of damage."

"That's the plan," Mitch agreed. It was a brutally simple plan, yet that was a very definite advantage. The more moving parts in a plan, the greater the chance of outright failure. "They have plenty of point defence around the high orbitals, but we can hit them with so many pieces of junk that *some* of them would be bound to get through. They wouldn't be able to stop them all. And I think…"

He smirked, again, as a thought struck him. "And I think there's another possibility," he added. "But we'll have to run some simulations to be sure."

Staci frowned. "Your idea of trying to cloak an asteroid?"

"It may not be possible, even if we borrow the cloaking device from one of the tenders and fit it on an asteroid," Mitch said. "Even trying to wrap an asteroid in stealth coating is unlikely to work, not unless the virus can be distracted…we might try, if we throw the asteroid right after the shattering asteroids. If the virus misses it long enough for it to get too close… either they shatter the asteroid, showering the high orbitals in even more junk, or the asteroid hits the surface. Either way, we come out ahead."

He shook his head. "But I had a very different idea," he said. It would be risky, and it was possible Commodore Hammond would refuse to go along with it, but it was worth serious consideration. Nothing ventured, nothing gained. "And it might just work."

Keying the terminal, he started to outline the concept.

CHAPTER TWENTY-NINE

SUSAN FELT AS IF SHE'D COME HOME.

HMS *Vanguard* was no longer *her* ship. The battleship had passed through six more commanding officers and a number of refits since she'd completed her term as *Vanguard's* captain, leaving Susan feeling as though something was subtly wrong. It had taken her months of service to get used to the battleship as she'd been and now, after they'd grown apart, it felt strange to stand in the CIC. She'd been tempted to insist on standing on the bridge, but it would have been a severe breach of military etiquette. The bridge was the captain's domain.

She forced herself to remain calm as the relief fleet—forty human starships, seventy alien—made its way across the New Washington system. Lady Charlotte had come through, leaving Susan torn between annoyance and gratitude. The grim awareness that she should be grateful that the aristocratic woman had managed to convince everyone to support the redeployment—partly by not *opposing* it—contrasted oddly with a feeling of disdain for the woman herself. It was hard not to feel as though she'd been used, as though…she shook her head. Getting through to Virus Prime and winning the war was all that mattered. She could worry about the politics—and the prospect of going into politics herself—after the war.

An aide passed her a datapad with the latest set of updates from the fleet. Susan glanced at it, keeping her face under tight control as the full scale of the wear and tear on the fleet's drives became apparent. She'd ordered the fleet to red-line their drives to reach New Washington in record time, as well as crossing the tramlines as close to the primary stars—the anchor stars—as they dared. The risk of accidentally materialising *within* the star—or too close to escape—was disturbingly high, even though she'd minimised it as much as possible. It had worked. They'd cut weeks off the voyage. But she feared the fleet would have to pay a high price for her decision.

We didn't have a choice, she told herself. *The virus has to know we sneaked a force into its home system by now.*

She watched the display as the fleet crawled closer to the tramline, inching forward even through it was travelling at a respectable fraction of the speed of light. The original plan had called for leaving a line of flicker stations as the raiding party made its way into enemy space, but that plan had gone by the wayside when the virus attacked Earth. There was no way to know what was happening two jumps away, let alone on Virus Prime. The Americans had noted the remnants of the virus's fleet making its way through the New Washington system, but where had it gone since it had jumped out? There was just no way to know.

"Admiral," Commander Elliot Richardson said. "USS *Potomac* has lost two of her drive nodes and fallen out of formation. She's requesting permission to divert to New Washington for repairs."

"Granted," Susan said, shortly. *Potomac* wasn't the first starship to find herself unable to keep up with the fleet. Susan had drawn up contingency plans for losing more starships, including her flagship. Transferring her flag to another ship would be embarrassing, but she couldn't let the fleet proceed without her. "Signal New Washington and request they stand ready to reinforce us when we cross the tramline."

She sighed, inwardly. The last update from Earth had made it clear the fleet would be expected to punch its way to Virus Prime, rather than trying to sneak through the enemy systems and only revealing its presence when it hove into range of the planet itself. She understood the logic—hitting the virus's outlying forces might take some pressure off the human defenders, as well as forcing the virus to concentrate on two separate problems— but it felt like a waste of time. They *had* to take out the virus's industrial base. The planners had also ordered her to dust the infected planets with BioBombs, sentencing countless host-bodies to certain death…

Susan grimaced. She'd been in the military long enough to know there was no point in trying to ignore reality. The host-bodies had been infected for so long they were effectively dead. The original personalities were gone. Their bodies were controlled by an alien intelligence intent on turning the bodies against their former friends. She knew the facts. She'd heard them repeated, time and time again, to convince the more hesitant politicians to authorise the operation. And yet, it felt like a failure.

Maybe she had to kill millions of people—people who were already dead—to save the rest of the human race. She didn't have to like it.

"Admiral," Richardson said. "We are approaching the tramline. We'll make transit in twenty minutes."

"Good," Susan said. "Order the fleet to alter course as planned, once we are through the tramline."

It was hard to resist the temptation to issue more orders, to remind her ships and crew of what they had to do. She clasped her hands behind her back, reminding herself—sternly—that there was no point in repeating herself. They'd worked their way through the simulations, wargaming the entire operation time and time again until they knew *precisely* how to handle it. Her lips quirked at the thought. Simulations and wargames were all very well and good, but there was no guarantee the enemy would react as planned. For all she knew, the enemy had a far larger fleet on the other side of the tramline, just waiting for them. She'd ordered the fleet to vary its course, once it entered the New Washington system, but their transit point was still going to be too predictable for her peace of mind. There'd been no way to alter it without adding hours, if not days, to their transit time.

Twenty years ago, it wouldn't have mattered, she thought, as the final seconds ticked down to zero. *Now, the defender can coordinate its ships to ensure it has a fleet waiting for us on the far side of the tramline.*

The battleship made transit. Susan's stomach lurched as the display blanked, then hastily came back to life. There were no ships within engagement range, but there were a sizable number of energy signatures hanging near the planet itself. The system had never been particularly developed—there were no gas giants to help support a spacefaring industry, making the system less valuable than it might seem—and there was little to recommend it, beyond four tramlines and a habitable planet. There'd been a thriving settlement on the planet when the system had fallen, four years ago. She liked to think the settlers might have escaped, before the virus made its first landings, but she feared the worst. The virus was slowly permeating the planet's atmosphere. The slightest mistake might expose the hidden settlements to infection, then certain defeat.

"Admiral," Richardson said. "The enemy fleet is breaking position. They're heading straight for Tramline Two."

Susan frowned. It was unusual for the virus to try to evade combat. She couldn't fault its logic in retreating, in falling back on Virus Prime, but it was still disconcerting. She keyed her console, calculating the vectors. The enemy fleet might *just* make it to the tramline before her ships caught up, although...she allowed her eyes to narrow as the sensors told her things she didn't want to know about the enemy ships. There were enough of them to give her fleet a very hard time, if she caught them. She might not *want* to catch them.

"Order HMS *Manticore* to break off from the fleet and implement Dusting," Susan said. "The remainder of the fleet is to pursue the enemy ships."

Her mind raced as the fleet altered course. The enemy ships ahead of her...were they the ships that had attacked Earth? If so, had they replaced their starfighter complements? The post-battle assessments had made it clear that the enemy fleet had lost most of its starfighters, facing human pilots on their home ground. It was impossible to be sure, but it was possible the enemy fleet barely had enough pilots for even a *light* CSP. If so... she might be able to take the fleet on, in a long-range engagement. But if she was wrong, she was going to be sending her pilots straight into a meatgrinder. A great many young men and women were about to meet their maker.

"Signal the carriers," she ordered. "They are to equip half their starfighters for antishipping strikes, then prepare to launch on my command."

"Aye, Admiral."

Susan forced herself to wait as the two fleets steadily converged. The sensor readings were clear. The virus was redlining its drives too, pushing itself to the absolute limit. Susan hoped that was a good sign. If the virus was feeling the need to conserve its ships, to the point of risking disabling its own units rather than leave them to be shot at, it had to be feeling the pressure. And yet...her eyes narrowed as her recon drones picked up more and more details. If the virus was willing to trade space for time...she wondered, suddenly, if it really understood what it was doing. It had *seen* the BioBombs in action. It knew it was leaving hundreds of thousands of host-bodies to die. It knew...

It doesn't care, she reminded herself, grimly. *It cares as little for its hosts as we do about our nail clippings. Why should it? They're just...skin cells.*

"Admiral," Richardson said. "*Manticore* is deploying the BioBombs now."

Susan nodded. It wasn't *that* easy to insert a biological weapon from orbit. Anything tough enough to survive re-entry would be an easy target, if the planetary defences were on the ball. The virus had tried, more than once, but it had never managed to get a single capsule of viral matter through a planet's atmosphere. Susan had wondered why it kept trying, until she realised it was a low risk and high reward situation. If it failed, the virus hadn't lost anything important; if it succeeded, the virus had won a whole planet. It would certainly force the defenders to act quickly, perhaps even nuking their own positions to take out the viral matter before it had a chance to spread. She wondered, idly, if the virus would start nuking the counter-virus too. It might be its only hope.

She kept an eye on the display as the destroyer commenced its mission. It would take weeks, perhaps months, for the counter-virus to spread, destroy *the* virus and die off. The planet would survive, she thought, but the preliminary reports from Operation Thunder Child suggested the ecosystem would be a mess for years to come. It depended on just how far the virus had spread, before the counter-virus had been deployed. She shuddered. Even if the war was won tomorrow, without any further losses, it would be decades before the human sphere recovered. A number of infected worlds might have to be simply abandoned. It would be cheaper to settle a new world than try to re-terraform a former colony world.

The display bleeped. They'd entered starfighter range. "Signal the carriers," she ordered, calmly. "They are authorised to launch starfighters."

She smiled, coldly, as the starfighters launched from their motherships and raced towards the enemy units. She'd always been a battleship officer—she'd never served on a carrier—and it had taught her a healthy respect for the tiny craft. An individual starfighter might be largely harmless to a battleship, if not their fellow starfighters, but an entire squadron could be extremely dangerous. Their torpedoes packed a punch, while their plasma cannons could hack away at a battleship's point defence and weaken their ability to fend off the next wave of starfighters or long-range missiles. She checked her targeting patterns, updating the orders to her battleships. If the enemy point defence weakened, it might be worth launching missiles in a joint attack with the starfighters.

A handful of red icons appeared on the display. The virus had clearly read humanity's tactical manuals—she reflected, in a flicker of gallows humour, that that might actually be true—and was launching its starfighters, even though they were grossly outnumbered. It was better to have them in space, fighting to defend the fleet, than to have them destroyed when their motherships were blown to atoms. Susan watched as her starfighter pilots adjusted formation, the lighter craft rushing ahead to engage the defenders while the antishipping starfighters fell into attack formation.

They knew what to do. They'd concentrate on disabling, rather than destroying, the enemy ships. Once the targets were disabled, they could be safely ignored.

And they'll burn through their supplies and die, she thought, coldly. Trapped in a deserted star system, the sole inhabited planet infected with counter-virus, there would be no hope of escape. They would have nowhere to go. *There's no need to finish the job.*

"Admiral," Richardson said. "The enemy point defence is proving disturbingly effective."

"Signal the battleships," Susan ordered. "They are to engage the enemy fleet with long-range missiles."

"Aye, Admiral."

Susan gritted her teeth. She could request replacement starfighters from New Washington, if she felt she needed them, but transferring the newcomers to her carriers would take time she didn't have. The enemy *had* to know that something was up, they *had* to know she was coming… it was difficult to tell what sort of intelligence and surveillance networks it might have set up—the virus just didn't *think* like any other known race—but it was hard to believe it hadn't picketed all the stars between Earth and Virus Prime. Royal Navy tactical doctrine insisted on picketing every known system, even if it was apparently useless. Who knew? The system might not be so useless—and uninhabited—as everyone thought. Life could come in some remarkable forms. Humanity's next enemy might be composed of dark matter or something equally strange.

She watched, calmly, as the alien formation started to come apart. The virus had designed its ships to be tough, but there were limits to how many torpedo strikes they could take before their drive sections were shattered beyond repair. Susan quietly logged the locations of the disabled ships—they'd need to be pointed at the local star, once the host-body crews were dead—and then ordered her ships to evade further contact. The remaining enemy ships picked up speed, one of them redlining her drive to the point she suffered a compensator failure and spun madly out of control.

Susan nodded to herself. It was reassuring to know the virus was just as vulnerable to compensator failure as its human enemies. She supposed they should have expected it. If the virus hadn't needed compensators, its ships could have outrun starfighters. And even missiles…

"Admiral, the enemy light units are going to reach the tramline before we can stop them," Richardson reported. "We can't get rearmed starfighters out to them in time."

"Let them go," Susan ordered. She'd have to hastily rearm her starfighters before pressing through the tramline herself. She eyed the tramline. There would be a flicker station somewhere along the line, probably close enough to the primary star to be difficult to spot. It needed to be taken out, but she didn't have the time to search for it. "Detach *Pinafore* and *Ivan*. They are to head down the other tramlines and carry out the dusting protocol."

"Aye, Admiral," Richardson said.

Susan nodded. She didn't want to think about what she'd just ordered. The decision to commit genocide…it wasn't really a genocide, she told herself. The virus had already committed genocide. But it still didn't sit well.

"We'll rearm here, then push onwards," she said. The battle had cost them in both starfighters and time. The enemy had killed at least fifty-seven starfighters…she shook her head, silently noting how many enemy ships they'd killed or disabled. It had been a cheap victory…she cursed under her breath. They still didn't know how many starships the virus had left. "Detach two more destroyers to scout the tramlines, then we'll push further into enemy space."

She looked at the starchart, silently assessing the situation. The virus should have enough warning to redeploy its ships, to try to block them before they reached Virus Prime itself. But would it? There were so many defences around Virus Prime that standing on the defensive might actually be a good idea, forcing her to either lay siege to the planet or bleed her fleet white trying to crack the enemy position. And if there were more worlds like Virus Prime…she shook her head in frustration. They just didn't know, but…

"We hit several of their planets pretty badly during the early days of the war," she reminded herself. She'd seen the records. The virus had taken a beating, with a number of worlds nuked from orbit, and yet it had just kept coming. "And even if it started a massive building program, with all the resources it needed on call, it would still need years to construct the shipyards and start churning out new ships."

Richardson looked up. "Admiral?"

"Take a nap," Susan ordered. She needed a rest, too. It would be at least five hours before the fleet was ready to make the next transit, more like six. She briefly considered requesting more starfighters, but she knew it would be hours—perhaps even a day—before the newcomers could arrive. The Americans wouldn't be keen on detaching an entire carrier and her escorts from their defence formations. Susan understood. She wouldn't be keen on it, either. "Order the beta crews to take control. I'll be in my cabin."

"Aye, Admiral," Richardson said.

CHAPTER THIRTY

MITCH FOUND IT HARD NOT TO SHOW his impatience as the squadron lurked at the edge of the enemy system, carrying out repairs while trying to conceal themselves from prowling enemy starships. The virus had dispatched several more squadrons in their general direction, largely composed of smaller starships, and directed them to search the outer edge of the enemy system. It was a task that would have daunted a human mindset, and probably been dismissed as impossible right from the start, but he had to admit the virus was doing a pretty good job. It had taken a leaf out of *his* book and started to deploy vast numbers of passive sensors, using them to steer its ships towards possible human contacts. And it had proven alarmingly successful.

He stood in the engineering compartment and watched, saying nothing, as his crew put the new drive node through its paces. He'd been reluctant to risk deactivating the drive long enough to insert the new unit, let alone test it. The risk of being caught with his pants down—more accurately, with a broken leg—was just too high. And yet, there'd been no choice. They *needed* all of their drive nodes back in action before they resumed the offensive. It was getting harder, according to the sensor platforms they'd scattered near the planet itself, to sneak closer to the orbital defences. They might be uncovered and forced to run at any moment.

If nothing else, we taught them how to be paranoid, Mitch reflected. The virus had kept most of its capital ships close to the planet, as if it feared losing the high orbitals to an enemy fleet, but it had deployed hundreds of smaller ships to search the outer system. *And we forced them to waste a shitload of resources.*

The thought failed to comfort him. He'd never liked boredom any more than he'd liked the sense of victory slipping away. The operation had stalled. The mass driver crews were constantly setting up, firing a few hundred projectiles towards the enemy's positions and then hastily dismantling their weapons and scurrying away before the hunters could catch them, but they were ineffective. The planet's defences were stopping the projectiles before they could reach their targets. The only upside, as far as he could tell, was that the asteroid settlements and industrial nodes made far better targets. The mass drivers had blown several dozen of *them* out of space. It was just hard, if not impossible, to tell how badly they were actually hurting the enemy. The nasty suspicious part of Mitch's mind had a feeling they weren't doing any real damage.

We should turn our attention to the cloudscoops, he told himself. *If we can cut off their fuel supplies, they'll have to take the time to rebuild or risk their industrial production slowing down...*

"Captain," Lieutenant Commander Brian Wimer said. "The drive node appears to be fully functional. All test cycles have come back positive. We're in the green."

"Good," Mitch said, shortly. It was hard to be sure of anything. A tiny harmonic in a drive node wouldn't be a problem under normal circumstances, but if they tried to redline the drive it would probably end in disaster. "What about the rest of the repairs?"

"We've done all we can," Wimer assured him. "The armour plating could do with another coating, sir, but we can't do that without a shipyard."

"Which isn't likely to happen," Mitch said. The closest shipyard—the closest *human* shipyard—orbited New Washington, several jumps away. "Keep an eye on it, and the drive node. Inform me if anything changes."

"Aye, Captain."

Mitch nodded, then turned and walked slowly back to the bridge. The enforced inactivity had been wearing on the crew, as well as himself. They wanted to get back into action, even if it meant going straight back into danger. The sensor platforms had noted the virus jumping at shadows, firing missiles and energy bursts at targets that simply didn't exist. Mitch would have found it amusing—the virus was clearly not giving any random energy fluctuations the benefit of the doubt—if he hadn't known it would make his mission a great deal harder. A single energy flicker too close to enemy positions might get his ship blown out of space.

And that means we can't go too close to their positions, Mitch mused. *It'll hamper our ability to coordinate missile and asteroid strikes.*

The hatch hissed open. He stepped onto the bridge. Hinkson looked up, then hastily vacated the command chair. Mitch shrugged, taking no offense. He'd known captains who loathed the idea of someone else—anyone else—sitting in their chairs, but it had always struck him as stupid. No starship could afford any confusion over who was in command at any given moment. He nodded to the younger man as he took his chair, then keyed his console. The drones had picked up two more enemy formations, active sensors flaring as they searched the inky darkness of space. Mitch had the uncomfortable feeling there might be more, lurking under cloak. *Lion* could kill the cruisers, given the advantage of surprise. And yet it was quite possible the cruisers were bait.

"Communications," he said. "Did we get a new update from *Lion*?"

"No, Captain," Culver said. "The last update was two hours ago."

Mitch let out his breath, trying not to sigh. There had been no reason to expect an update, but...he shook his head. Captain Hammond and his crew were readying the shattering asteroids, drilling deep within the rocks and inserting nukes...Mitch had to smile at the concept, even though there was no way to be *sure* it would be effective. One simulation had even suggested that the rigged asteroids would be fragile, to the point that shoving them towards the enemy homeworld would cause them to shatter ahead of time. Mitch hoped *that* wasn't true. It would be the height of irony if *Unicorn*—and *Lion*—were taken out by their own weapons.

We should be able to mount missiles on the asteroids, too, he mused. *Or even mass drivers.*

The thought made him smile. He'd already added a note to his report, suggesting the mass production of starship-grade mass drivers. They were nowhere near as powerful as the devices hurling rocks into the inner system, but they would be quite effective if they were mounted on an asteroid plunging towards the alien homeworld. The asteroid would provide a suitable weapons platform even if it *was* deflected away from the planet itself.

But that'll have to wait, he reminded himself. *Right now, we're on our own.*

He keyed the starchart, trying to calculate how long it would be before a relief fleet arrived. It was impossible. He just didn't know when—if—one would be dispatched. The admiral would do everything in her power to get the ball rolling, but…Mitch knew she wouldn't have the final say. It was odd, really, to reflect that—for all her rank—the admiral had to spend most of her time working with politicians rather than making decisions herself. She outranked him, and she had the Order of the Garter to boot, and yet she would never command a warship in combat again. Even as a fleet commander, she'd be a guest on someone else's ship. It was a strange thought. He would sooner die then give up his ship.

Enjoy the break while you can, he told himself. He'd made sure to order all unnecessary crewmen to their bunks, to ensure they got some rest. They were going to need it soon enough. *You'll be back in action before you know it.*

• • •

"I feel like I'm playing an online game," Marigold said. "Do you think we can zip around the asteroid and then let everyone chasing us crash into the rock?"

Tobias smiled. The asteroid dominated the skyline. They were drifting so close to the giant rock that they could see the asteroid miners with the naked eye, picking out flashes of light as they sunk giant boreholes into the dark rock. Tobias had learned a great deal about life on a newly-settled asteroid, just by watching the RockRats as they prepared the rock for its flight into the inner system. They were an odd group, simultaneously individualistic and yet committed to working as part of a team. It was easy to see why the government disliked them. The Belters followed orders, but only up to a certain point. They resisted micromanagement from groundpounders as firmly as they resisted the virus.

Not that it's any of our concern, he thought. The gunboats had been drafted to serve as shuttles, if only because the mining shuttles had been dispatched elsewhere. *Who cares about how the job is done, as long as it is?*

"I think we'd have some problems trying it in real life," he said. He frowned as a thought struck him. "That said, if there's any system in which we could fly through an asteroid field, ducking and dodging all the asteroids as we go, it's this one."

He frowned. The discovery of the alien sphere had been classified, so naturally word had spread from one end of the battlecruiser to the other before the captain had even finished speaking. Tobias didn't hear *that* many rumours, but he'd heard suggestions ranging from the possible to the thoroughly outrageous. The virus had been created by the sphere-builders. The virus was a weapon targeted on the sphere-builders. The system itself was an artefact, with a number of planets casually shattered to provide raw material for...for what? The fact there was no good answer to that question hadn't stopped the rumourmongers from suggesting that the entire system was due to be demolished. Tobias thought the rumours were silly, but...at least they were a distraction. He didn't want his subordinates to have time to brood.

Marigold grinned at him. "It might be fun, after the war," she said. "Buy a few demilitarised gunboats and allow people to fly them through the space junk. There'll be no shortage of takers."

"It might be fun," Tobias agreed. He had no idea where they'd get the money to pay for the gunboats. They were supposed to get a big bonus, for their *tiny* role in discovering the alien sphere, but there'd been no official word on how much they'd be getting. The rumourmongers had suggested amounts that would be a sizable percentage of the national GNP. Tobias had the nasty feeling they were just raising impossible expectations. "Did you ever want to go cloud-flying on Jupiter?"

He smiled at the thought, although it was tinged with a bitterness he knew he'd never be able to lose. Cloud-flying was a billionaire's sport. The cost was so high that very few people were able to book a tour, let alone work on a cloud-flying station. It would be cheaper to ride a rocket shell down to the surface or go on holiday to Mars…and even those trips were well out of his price range. It was nice to think his time in the navy would have given him marketable skills—he knew how to fly shuttles as well as gunboats, which opened up a whole series of new opportunities—but they weren't *that* marketable. Once the war was over, there'd be a whole bunch of newly-unemployed personnel with the same set of skills and limited opportunities. He very much doubted he'd be allowed to stay in the navy.

"There was a boy in my school who bragged he'd take his girlfriend to Jupiter," Marigold said. "He insisted he was rich enough to do it. And then his father lost all his money and everyone dumped him like a hot rock."

Tobias grinned, even though it wasn't funny. He'd met enough people who bragged of their wealth, even if they were poor by the standards of the rich, let alone the super-rich. He'd often dreamed of having their money for himself, or watching as they ran out of money and…he shook his head. It was high time he grew up. His schooling was over. He was an adult now…legally, at least. He wished he felt more like an adult. He was sure there was a moment when he'd feel fully mature, when he'd know what to do whatever the situation…

He winked at her. "We'll have to see what we can do, after the war," he said. Who knew? Perhaps their share of the prize money would be big enough to fund their ambitions. "Or we could…"

There was a tap on the hatch.

"All done here," the chief miner said. The RockRats had their own command structure. It wasn't clear if their chief was appointed or elected.

"Permission to come aboard?"

"Granted," Tobias said. The RockRats were a surprising combination of formal and informal. He didn't quite understand it, but at least he was fairly sure they wouldn't board the gunboat—or enter his personal space—without permission. "We'll take you back to the mining ship, then return to the battlecruiser."

"Please," the miner said. "We could do with a rest."

• • •

"Captain, *Unicorn* is ready to return to the fray," Commander Donker said. "She's right on time."

Thomas nodded, irritated. Captain Campbell had had around thirty ideas, more if one counted the concepts that were just variants on a theme. Only three or four of them were workable, including the shattering asteroids and the BioBomb ice, but he seemed intent on making them all a reality. Thomas had tried to ignore endless messages, each one urging the battlecruiser crew to drop everything—including the last idea—and focus on the *next* idea. It was understandable that Captain Campbell might be feeling a bit surplus to requirements, after his ship had been damaged, but there was no need to panic. He should count himself lucky *Unicorn* hadn't been blown to atoms. His ship had already been repaired.

"Good," Thomas said, finally. He keyed the console. "Are the asteroids ready to blow?"

"Yes, Captain," Donker said. A hologram of nine semi-translucent asteroids appeared in front of them. It was easy to see the nuclear charges buried within the rock, ready to smash the asteroid into thousands of pieces of space junk. "They can be detonated upon command."

Thomas nodded. The simulations had suggested that only a small amount of junk would intersect the planet's atmosphere, but *small* was a relative term. There would be hundreds of thousands of pieces falling towards the planet, hundreds of which would pose a threat to the orbital industries or strike the orbital towers themselves. It was quite possible, he reflected, that some pieces would even make their way to the surface. If they struck the ground, they might even do some real damage.

"The timing might be a problem," he said. "But if we key the bombs to detonate when the virus tries to deflect the asteroids…"

"Yes, sir," Donker said. "The water-ice asteroids are also ready, Captain, but we're unsure if they'll be effective."

"I know." Thomas had seen those simulations, too. The counter-virus might not survive re-entry. A dedicated re-entry capsule would be a great deal more reliable, but…he shook his head. They had to weaken the orbital sensor platforms before they could try to get something a little more solid into the planet's atmosphere. Right now, it would be nothing more than a waste of time and resources. "We can but try."

He studied the display for a long moment. "Did you finish the battlestation simulations?"

"Yes, Captain," Donker said. "It would work, in theory, but…too many things could go wrong."

"It's worth trying," Thomas said. The concept had been one of Captain Campbell's better ideas. At the very least, it would make a suitable diversion. The virus had probably deduced just how *few* human ships were within the system. It was hard to be sure, given the sheer scale of the alien activity, but he had a feeling the virus was steadily redeploying more and more ships towards their position. "Order *Unicorn* to return to Virus Prime. We'll head to Virus-5."

"Aye, Captain," Donker said. "What about the remaining ships?"

"We'll take the mining ship with us," Thomas said. "The rest of the squadron can change position—again—just to ensure they don't stumble across the asteroids before it's too late."

And keep shelling their positions from a distance, Thomas added, in the privacy of his own mind. *We don't want them thinking we've given up.*

He sighed, inwardly. It was difficult to tell just how effective the constant mass driver sniping actually *was*. They'd noted a handful of destroyed targets, but—so far—they hadn't managed to hit anything actually *vital*.

Thomas had a feeling the virus didn't particularly care about free-floating structures. It certainly wasn't making any attempt to defend them from long-range sniping. Instead, it was protecting the planets and marshalling its fleets to hunt down the distant human ships.

I suppose this makes us the terrorists, he thought, numbly. It had been a long time since the Troubles, but the terrorist insurgency was still studied in military colleges right across the world. Even naval cadets had been forced to study the war. *The virus has too many targets to cover. It has to hunt us down, instead of wasting resources trying to cover hundreds out of thousands of possible targets.*

The alarms rang. "Captain," Sibley said. "Long-range sensors are picking up nine enemy cruisers, heading directly towards us."

"Understood," Thomas said. His mind raced. Had they been detected? The cruisers might not *know* they were flying towards the battlecruiser. "I'm on my way."

CHAPTER THIRTY-ONE

"SIGNAL TO UNICORN," Thomas ordered, as he stepped onto the bridge. "She is to proceed to Point Shatter and hold position there, maintaining radio silence as planned."

"Aye, Captain," Cook said.

Thomas took his command chair. Nine enemy cruisers were heading directly towards their position. There was no way in hell it was a coincidence. The virus had been scattering so many sensor platforms around the outer edge of the system that it might well have picked up a tiny flicker of energy and directed the cruisers to investigate. It didn't look as if anything bigger was heading towards him, anything large enough to force him to abandon the asteroids and run, but there was no way to be sure. The cruisers could be trying to pin him down, keeping a sensor lock while they screamed for backup. It was pretty much what the virus had tried to do to *Unicorn*.

And the timing is unfortunate, he thought. They could launch the shattering asteroids now, but it would mean relying on automated systems to trigger the bombs. The odds of scoring hits would be significantly reduced. *Do they know what we've been doing?*

He thought, fast. If they could delay launch by ten hours or so, *Unicorn* would be in position to trigger the bombs manually by the time

301

the asteroids reached their destination. If...he frowned as he considered the risks. The cruisers might not realise the asteroids had already been rigged—the pushers were difficult to detect, as long as they were powered down—but they might just nuke the asteroids in passing anyway. Thomas gritted his teeth. Recovering the pushers would be difficult, even if they weren't destroyed. He'd have to make sure to lure the cruisers away from the asteroids, if they weren't launched at once. And that meant...

"Signal *Pettigrew*," he ordered. The fleet tender was worthless in a fight, but with her drives and sensors powered down she was practically undetectable. "She is to monitor the situation from a distance. If the virus shows any particular interest in the asteroids, she is to launch them at once and then proceed to the RV point."

"Aye, Captain," Cook said.

"Tactical, go live," Thomas ordered. A thrill of excitement ran through him. "Bring active sensors to full power, sweep the entire sector of space. If there is anything lurking under cloak, I want to know about it."

"Aye, Captain," Sibley said.

"Helm, bring us about," Thomas added. The nine cruisers could be bait, but he'd have time to alter course and evade anything big enough to take him on before it was too late. Probably. "Prepare to take us right down their throats."

"Aye, Captain."

Thomas smiled, feeling a flicker of droll amusement. Taking a battlecruiser directly *towards* the enemy was what Captain Campbell would do. Treating a battlecruiser as an oversized frigate was asking for trouble. And yet...he felt his smile grow wider as his ship wheeled about, weapons locking onto her targets. There was something to be said for throwing caution to the winds and chasing the enemy position. If nothing else, it would keep the enemy focused on him. The virus might assume he hadn't had *time* to rig the asteroids.

We can't take that for granted, he reminded himself. *Pettigrew will send the asteroids hurtling towards their target if there's any hint they've been discovered.*

He leaned back in his chair as the display sharpened. There were no cloaked ships sneaking up behind the cruisers, no hints there might be something nasty lurking in their drive shadows. It struck Thomas as odd, although he supposed it might make a certain kind of sense. The virus might assume it had no choice, but to keep its heavier units in position to protect the planet. It could spare a few dozen lighter ships if it meant keeping its homeworld safe.

And a single hit in the wrong place will be enough to pin us down, giving it time to send a stronger force after us, his thoughts added. *If it scores a hit on the drive section, or takes out the cloaking device, game over.*

"Launch gunboats," he ordered. "And prepare to fire missiles."

"Aye, Captain," Sibley said.

Thomas sat back in his command chair. The range was dropping sharply as the battlecruiser picked up speed. *Lion* was going to blaze right *through* the enemy formation, a tactic he would never have dared use against a battleship squadron. The enemy ships would be exposed to his fire as he raced past, while they'd have to alter course to either evade him or bring their own weapons to bear. Or try to ram him...he keyed his console, reminding the tactical staff to watch for ramming attempts. A cruiser would be a small price to pay for taking out the entire battlecruiser. The virus would consider it a bargain.

The display flickered. "Captain, the enemy ships have opened fire," Lieutenant Hannah Avis warned. "Impact in two minutes, thirty seconds."

"Deploy countermeasures," Thomas said, calmly. It was rare for cruisers and smaller ships to carry long-range missiles. Even with the two formations converting at terrifying speed, there was a pretty good chance of the missiles burning out before they reached their targets. The virus must be desperate. He hoped that was a clue a relief fleet was blasting its way towards the system. It would only take one stroke of bad luck to bring the entire mission to a violent end. "As soon as the gunboats are in position, return fire."

"Aye, Captain."

• • •

"The enemy ships have opened fire," Tobias said, as the display sparkled with red icons. He didn't have time to be surprised the enemy ships were carrying missiles. "They're firing on *Lion*."

"The battlecruiser can handle them," Marigold said. "I'm taking us into their formation now."

Tobias nodded. The missiles were probably mounted on external racks, according to the live feed. The virus might not have had time to churn out a squadron of purpose-built missile cruisers. The Royal Navy hadn't found it easy to produce *Unicorn*, from what he'd heard, and *she* was a tiny frigate. Refitting a cruiser with missile tubes would take time...he shook his head, dismissing the thought. The analysts could worry about it later, after the battle. It wasn't his problem.

The range closed at terrifying speed. The cruisers were deploying sensor decoys and drones, but their own drive signatures were making it impossible for them to conceal their precise location. Tobias had the feeling that wasn't a good sign. The cruisers knew what they were facing, knew they were charging towards a missile-heavy battlecruiser. A near-miss wouldn't do any real damage, not in deep space. They'd be well past any warhead before it detonated.

"I have a solid lock on their hull," Tobias snapped. The remainder of the gunboats had also locked onto their targets. "Transmitting...now!"

"Incoming fire," Marigold said. "Evading...now."

Tobias felt his stomach clench as a burst of plasma fire shot past them. The cruisers didn't seem to have a very good lock on the gunboats—he was amused to note that the drive baffles were working well—but it didn't matter. They were pumping out so much fire that scoring a direct hit was just a matter of time. A gunboat might survive a single plasma hit, but even a glancing blow would be enough to force them to bail out—again—before it was too late. And if he...he winced as he saw a gunboat vanish from the display. Two more of his subordinates were dead. It was no consolation, this time, that he'd seen the enemy kill them.

"They're switching fire to the incoming missiles," Marigold said. "Launch torpedoes."

Tobias tapped his console. "Firing...now!"

The enemy cruiser seemed to flinch. The torpedoes were smaller than the missiles, but they'd been fired at very close range. If it diverted its attention to taking them out, the capital missiles from *Lion* were likely to get into attack range before the cruiser could switch its attention back to them. If...Tobias allowed himself a moment of glee as one of his torpedoes struck home. The enemy ship staggered, shooting wildly in all directions. A missile from *Lion* finished her off a moment later.

"Target destroyed," Marigold said. "We're in the clear."

"Not for long," Tobias said. There were three cruisers left. They were ignoring the gunboats, barrelling directly towards the battlecruiser. "Reverse course. They have to be taken out."

But he knew, even as Marigold wrenched the gunboat around, that they might be too late.

• • •

"Switch to rapid fire," Thomas ordered.

The enemy cruisers weren't stopping—or even trying to evade his missiles—as they closed the range. Their point defence was spitting venom towards the missiles, trying to swat them out of space before it was too late. Thomas felt his blood run cold as he realised the cruisers intended to ram. Part of his mind noted it was a good thing, a sign the enemy didn't have any bigger ships within range, but it was small consolation. The battlecruiser could not be lost or the mission, perhaps even the war, would be lost with her.

He stood, clasping his hands behind his back as his missiles punched through the enemy defences and struck home. One cruiser exploded in a flash of plasma, a second rolled out of formation...it was hard to be sure, but her drive field seemed to have destabilised completely. The third kept coming, hurling plasma bolts towards the battlecruiser as she was struck time and time again. Thomas was morbidly impressed as a missile blew her into a cloud of vapour. She'd held together long enough to worry him.

"Captain, we lost one of the gunboats," Donker reported. "The remaining craft are ready to return to the barn."

Thomas nodded. "Recall them, then copy the details of the engagement to *Unicorn* through the secure communications network," he said. The frigate was already outside sensor range, sneaking towards Virus Prime. It would be several hours before she queried the communications platform for an update. "And then compose a message—use an encryption pattern we know the virus has broken. Make it look convincing. We were unable to set up the mass drivers before we were chased away, so we're relocating now. Let me see the message before you send it across the system."

"Aye, Captain." Cook sounded almost gleeful. "I'll put it together now."

Donker blinked. "Captain, do you think the virus will listen? Or believe in a message we might as well have sent in the clear?"

"I don't know," Thomas said. "But it's worth a try."

He smiled. There'd been little point in trying to mislead the enemy in humanity's last two wars with alien powers. Neither the Tadpoles nor the Foxes had ever had the sort of access to humanity's encryption codes that might have allowed them to decrypt messages, let alone the understanding of the human mind that might let them read between the lines. Trying to intercept alien messages was never easy. But the virus might be able to do it. He knew it had certainly been able to use human IFF codes to sneak into missile range. Perhaps it could be misled.

Perhaps.

"Signal to *Pettigrew*," he said. "My previous orders remain in effect. If they see a hint of trouble, they're to launch the asteroids and run."

"Aye, Captain," Cook said.

Thomas's console bleeped as the communications officer forwarded him the draft message. Thomas scanned it thoughtfully, noting how Cook had based it on a real message...merely addressing it to a ship that was supposed to be hundreds of light years away. Captain Campbell wouldn't

be fooled, if by some mischance he picked up the message. The virus...
Thomas frowned. That was an open question. They'd learn something
interesting if the virus took the bait. Did it have the intelligence and insight
to realise it was being conned?

"Transmit the message," he ordered. Did the virus know what he
knew? Did it know the human race had realised the virus had obtained
copies of the encryption system? Did it have the wit to use it? Hell, did
it even know what it had? It was quite possible the poor bastards who'd
been captured and infected had died of rotting brain before their memories
could be extracted and studied. The process was only successful about a
third of the time, the boffins had insisted. "Repeat it once, then go dark."

"Aye, Captain."

"Tactical, deploy one drone to head towards the fake RV point,"
Thomas added. "Take us into cloak as soon as the drone goes live. Helm,
plot a course to Virus-5. Best possible speed, but keep us as far as possible
from any watching eyes."

"Aye, Captain," Fitzgerald said.

Thomas sat back in his chair. It was impossible to be *sure* the virus
knew there was only one battlecruiser in the system, but it had to have a
pretty good idea. The drone would confirm the contents of the fake message, suggesting that *Lion* was heading towards yet another distant cloud
of space junk. The virus would see the battlecruiser even if it didn't manage to intercept and decrypt the message. And yet...there was no way to
be sure what it would do. Or, for that matter, that they wouldn't be trying
to sneak past a stealthed platform. The virus had definitely learned its
lessons well.

"Course ready, Captain," Fitzgerald said.

"The drone has gone live," Sibley added. "Cloaking device engaged."

"Alter course," Thomas ordered, calmly. "ETA?"

The drive grew louder, just for a second. "ETA roughly seven hours,
assuming we don't have to alter course to evade enemy contacts," Fitzgerald
said. "We could shave a couple of hours off our transit time, if we took the

risk of slipping past known enemy sensor platforms…"

Should have targeted them with the railguns, from a safe distance, Thomas thought. The platforms were tiny on an interplanetary scale, but they didn't have any defences beyond their stealth coating. *We could have fired enough pellets to guarantee at least one hit.*

"We'll take the long way," he said. The gas giant wasn't anything like as heavily defended as Virus Prime, but there was quite enough firepower in orbit for him to be reluctant to give up the advantage of surprise. "XO, you have the bridge. I'll be in my ready room."

"Yes, sir."

• • •

"Captain," Staci said. "We're picking up a wide-angle transmission, from *Lion*."

Mitch froze. Broadcasting a wide-angle signal in the middle of an enemy system was practically *asking* the enemy to kill the sender. The message, racing out at the speed of light, would be heard right across the system. Virus Prime would detect the signal in less than three hours and then…what? The only reason he could think of to send such a signal was if the worst had happened, if the battlecruiser's destruction was assured. Captain Hammond might be dead even now…Mitch disliked the older man, but he didn't deserve to die. Not like that…not so far from home.

"Decrypt it," he ordered, harshly. If *Lion* was gone…he'd tried to come up with contingency plans, but most of them were worse than useless. He might have to collect the remains of the squadron, then sneak back to New Washington. "What happened?"

Staci sounded astonished. "It's addressed to HMS *Thunderous*," she said. "And it says *Lion* is heading to Cluster 576."

Mitch blinked, then started to laugh. *Thunderous* wasn't attached to the squadron, but there was no way the *virus* would know it. It would assume the battleship was somewhere within the system, perhaps lurking near the cluster while more teams of RockRats steered rocks towards the alien homeworld. If it assumed the message was real…he shook his head in amusement. If the virus believed the message, it would waste time and energy trying to intercept *Lion* and a battleship that was hundreds of light years away. If it didn't believe the message, or simply never managed to decrypt it, *Lion* and her squadron were no worse off than they already were. The virus had clearly forced *Lion* to relocate, which meant…

"We'll continue as planned," he said. They needed another look at the alien homeworld, even if the shattering asteroids had already been destroyed. There might be an opening they could use to slip something through the defences, perhaps even do real damage. "We'll check in with the communications platforms as we pass, see what's actually happened."

"Understood," Staci said. Her fingers danced over her console. "We'll pass the next platform in an hour."

"Keep an eye on the long-range sensors," Mitch said. The message was halfway across the system by now. It wouldn't be long until it reached the brainships, if not the planet itself. And then…what would the virus do? "It should be interesting to see how the virus reacts. If it does…"

He settled back in his chair. If *he* overheard such a message, what would he do? Would he take it literally? Or would he assume he was being set up? The message hadn't been sent in the clear…humanity knew the virus had presumably broken the encryption code, but did the virus know humanity knew? He snorted in frustration. It was just impossible to predict what the virus would do. It simply didn't think like its human enemies. Hell, it might simply decide that leaving *Lion* alone was the best of a bad set of choices. It would know where the next set of asteroids would be coming from…

Or so it thinks, Mitch thought. *And in the meantime, we can get on with the real plan.*

CHAPTER THIRTY-TWO

THE SILENCE ON THE BRIDGE was almost oppressive.

Thomas found it hard to blame his crew for falling silent, even though he knew it was absurd. Virus-5 was an immense gas giant, nearly as immense as Jupiter herself, and the sheer scale of activity around the massive planet was terrifying. He'd seen the recordings from *Unicorn*, but he hadn't really believed them until he'd seen the planet for himself. Cloudscoops, mining platforms, dozens—perhaps hundreds—of mining colonies…the display just kept growing more and more detailed as the sensor platforms picked out more and more alien targets. The only upside, as far as he could see, was that the majority of the alien warships had been withdrawn to Virus Prime. The remainder were either too slow to catch *Lion* or too weak to bring her down.

Which might not stop them from landing a crippling blow, Thomas thought. The gas giant was so immense that nothing short of a major fleet action would put a dent in the system, but it was unlikely the virus would just sit back and *let* them rain blows on the orbital network. *They might launch their entire fleet of shuttles at us, just to slow us down for their bigger brothers.*

He shuddered as he recalled the flight of shuttles that had been pointed at them during Operation Lightning Strike, then looked at Sibley. "Tactical, do you have a solid network of targets?"

"Aye, Captain," Sibley said. "I'm locating prospective kinetic missiles now, as well as a suitable asteroid."

Thomas leaned forward. "And a suitable target for the marines?"

"I've located an alien battlestation," Sibley said. "It's not in quite the right place, but it will have to do."

"Show me." Thomas frowned as the tactical display focused on a single enemy unit. The battlestation looked disturbingly solid, ready and able to soak up hundreds of nuclear-tipped missile strikes. "Can we move the station without it coming apart?"

Sibley hesitated. "I think so, Captain, but we don't have reliable data on the station's interior design. It could be a paper tiger."

Thomas smiled. It was unlikely, to say the least. Orbital battlestations didn't have to mount anything beyond station-keeping drives. The mass they saved could be devoted to weapons, fusion cores and armour instead. He'd seen battlestations shrug off blows that would have vaporised a battleship. The human race was relatively new to the concept—they'd seemed like giant wastes of resources until next-generation ablative armour had come into service—but he liked to think the various space navies had learnt a thing or two in the last thirty years. He was fairly sure a comparable human design would survive the pusher...

Slowing down might be a problem, he thought, wryly. *But if one doesn't want to slow down...*

"XO, deploy the mining teams," he ordered. "And then order the gunboats to be ready to launch at a moment's notice."

"Aye, sir," Donker said.

Thomas smiled, grimly. The gas giant—and its halo of moons, asteroids and fragments of space dust—was an electromagnetic nightmare. The nearer moons cut across the gas giant's magnetic lines of force, turning the moons into giant electrical generators. It put out so much electromagnetic distortion that the virus would have trouble spotting an entire *fleet* of cloaked ships, as long as they didn't do anything stupid. He was mildly surprised the virus hadn't tried to tap the electric corridor to power its operations, as the Jupiter colonies had done, although he supposed the power collectors would be easy to take out with kinetic strikes. It was hard to believe the virus hadn't thought of the concept. It could certainly have learnt the truth from human databases, if it had bothered to take the time to study them.

He felt his smile grow wider. The system had one glaring weakness, one that the virus had either overlooked or chosen to ignore. There was little hope of picking off the cloudscoops one by one—they'd been heavily defended even before the squadron started hurling asteroids and kinetic projectiles across the system—but they had to lower their scoops into the planet's atmosphere to draw gas from the planet and into orbit. If something happened to the gas giant, the cloudscoops would have to retract the tube-like scoops or lose them. Either way, if the projections were correct, the virus's operations would be significantly delayed.

Particularly if we hit the other gas giants, too, Thomas thought. The planets might be heavily defended—and they were—but the virus had so much space to cover that he was certain *something* would get through the defences. *They'll have to waste their time coming after us, instead of working to produce new ships and put them into action.*

He sobered. He'd done a stint in the Admiralty, as part of his career before returning to starships, and he *knew* how difficult it could be to compensate for lost mining installations and industrial facilities. The war production economy was a roughly-tuned machine, with each and every unit working towards the overall goal. It would be hard enough retuning the production schedules in the middle of a war, let alone replacing the lost or damaged facilities. And yet, there was so much industry in the system that he found it easy to believe they were just kicking and scratching on their way to the gallows. The virus just needed to be lucky *once*. They had to be lucky all the time.

The display flickered and updated as the mining crews continued their tasks. There was no need to waste pushers, not here. Nukes would be more than enough to knock the asteroids out of orbit and send them crashing into the gas giant's atmosphere. They wouldn't be moving at a sizable fraction of the speed of light, but it probably wouldn't matter. Thomas wished, just for a moment, that the plans to ignite a gas giant had actually proven workable. It would have destroyed the enemy position beyond repair if the planet had suddenly turned into a star...he shook his head. He was no astrophysicist, but he'd seen the working papers. The gas giant would need a far stronger gravity field, as well as a great deal more mass, before it collapsed and ignited into a star. The concept was wonderful, but impractical.

He studied the enemy position, feeling time ticking by slowly. There was so much distortion in the surrounding region that it was hard to know what was going on, outside the gas giant's minute system. Had *Unicorn* made it to Virus Prime? Had the shattering asteroids been discovered? Had half of the plan already failed unknown to him? He shook his head, knowing it didn't matter. They had to keep pounding on their targets, poking holes in the enemy defences, until a relief fleet arrived. If, of course, one did. Thomas had spent enough time with politicians to be all too aware that most of them would prefer to do nothing, rather than do something and risk copping the blame...

Idiots, he thought. *If we lose this war, there'll be no one left to point the finger, let alone take the blame.*

"Captain," Donker said. "The first batch of asteroids have been readied. The miners request permission to proceed to the second batch."

Thomas glanced at the timer, then nodded. They hadn't planned a fixed timetable, something that would be asking for trouble on an interplanetary scale. And yet, he wanted—he needed—to get the plan underway before the prowling cruisers stumbled across the shattering asteroids or *Unicorn* was driven away from the planet again...he frowned, wondering—not for the first time—precisely how the virus had stumbled across the frigate. He'd had his tactical staff go through the sensor recordings in clinical detail, at least partly in hopes of finding something he could use to take a swing at Captain Campbell's neck, but they'd found nothing. It might have been simple bad luck. It might have been something more sinister. Thomas simply didn't know.

"Tell them to hurry," he said. In hindsight, they shouldn't have devised a plan with so many variables. It was all well and good to argue that the separate compartments of the plan could be used individually, if necessary, but they might give the enemy a chance to deal with each section in turn. "Are the marines ready to go?"

"They're ready to launch at ten minutes notice," Donker said. "Major Craig insisted on letting them rest, before the shit hits the fan."

Thomas nodded, curtly. There was no point in packing the marines into their shuttles—like sardines—and then waiting for hours before launch. And yet...his instincts insisted they were running out of time. It was quite possible the virus already knew they were there. There was so much electromagnetic distortion that it might well have disrupted the cloaking device itself. He wanted to believe the virus would just ignore an energy flicker in the middle of nowhere—the disturbances and surges between the planet and its moons appeared to be random—but he knew better. The virus wouldn't let anything go. The moment it picked up an energy surge, it would dispatch ships to investigate.

He forced himself to wait as the timer ticked on. The miners were doing good work, targeting asteroids that could be directed towards the gas giant, while the remainder of his crew were readying missiles and sensor decoys. Thomas had no idea how effective the latter would be now—the virus had to be devoting vast amounts of brainpower to finding ways to pick out the decoys before it was too late—but they would hopefully win the assault force a few extra seconds. His tactical staff picked out targets for his railguns, noting enemy defences that could be either vaporised or forced to defend themselves. Thomas hoped they were right. The squadron had crammed its ships to the gunwales with weapons as well as spare parts—they'd requisitioned hundreds of mining nukes from the asteroid mining corporations—and they had a factory ship, but they were running short. It was hard to imagine they could continue operations for much longer without resupply, certainly not at their current tempo. The factory ship simply couldn't keep up with demand.

The tactical display blinked red. "Captain," Sibley said. "I'm picking up a flight of alien starfighters, heading towards us. They'll be within detection range in seven minutes."

Thomas nodded, slowly. There was no point in pretending the virus hadn't already figured out their position. It would be self-deception, nothing more. The starfighters wouldn't have been launched if the virus wasn't already aware of their rough position and just wanted to zero in on them before it dispatched additional starfighters and shuttles to finish the job. It was inconvenient, he noted, but there was nothing they could do about it. They'd prepared most of the asteroids. They'd just have to hope it was enough.

"Recall the mining crews," Thomas ordered. Thankfully, there wasn't *much* to their task beyond bolting the nukes to the asteroids and checking the detonators were primed. "Ready the marines and gunboats for dispatch, then prime the sensor decoys to go live on command."

"Aye, Captain," Sibley said.

"They're not bringing the rest of their defences on line," Donker said. "They haven't realised what we're doing."

"Probably," Thomas agreed. The display bleeped. The marines and gunboats were ready to launch. "Or they might be preparing themselves for the coming onslaught."

He studied the display for a long moment. The virus was a single entity in many disparate parts, but surely even *it* would have trouble maintaining a steady production level if it had to power down its facilities every time something tripped an alarm. Thomas had been told that mid-level managers often hesitated to shut their facilities down, fearing—often rightly—that their superiors would blame them for any subsequent delays. The virus could hardly pass the buck down the chain until it hit the bottom—it *was* a single entity—but the delays would still bite. It might just be reluctant to start shutting things down until there was no other choice.

Not that it will matter, he thought. *We already know where to aim our guns.*

"Tactical, activate the sensor decoys and launch the marine shuttles, then commence railgun engagement," Thomas ordered. The enemy would have no doubt of their presence the moment they started shooting, but it wouldn't matter. They *wanted* the enemy looking at them. "And trigger the nukes as soon as the first railgun pellets reach their targets."

"Aye, Captain."

Thomas waited, counting down the seconds. The railgun pellets would convince the virus that the defences, rather than the cloudscoops, were the priority targets. They were little more than tiny kinetic projectiles, easily deflected or destroyed if the target knew they were coming. He could see a handful of defence platforms already shifting their positions randomly, trying to evade the incoming threat. It was good thinking on their part, he acknowledged. Railgun pellets flew in a straight line. If the target moved after the projectiles were fired, the pellets would miss and plunge straight into the gas giant. Thomas couldn't fault their targets. Based on what it knew, the virus was doing *exactly* what it needed to do.

And it's in for a surprise, Thomas thought. *Because the real threat is elsewhere.*

"Four enemy platforms destroyed or damaged," Sibley reported. "Nukes detonating…now."

Thomas raised his eyebrows. *Four* platforms? He hadn't expected to do anything like as well. The virus had been given—deliberately given—more than enough time to ready itself for the onslaught. Maybe it suspected it was being conned or maybe it hadn't realised just how long the battlecruiser had been watching them. Captain Campbell's first survey of the gas giant had picked up thousands of targets, Thomas's tactical staff had refined the targeting solutions until they could be fairly sure of hitting the targets…unless, of course, they moved.

The display updated, rapidly, as two dozen large asteroids started to move out of orbit and plummet towards the planet below. Thomas noted, absently, that a couple of them were on longer trajectories, giving the enemy plenty of time to blow them to rubble before they reached the gas giant, but even *that* would work in his favour. The virus would have to cope with thousands of pieces of space debris flying in all directions, chunks of rock that would be almost certain to hit *something*. It would need to clear the high orbitals before it could relax and *that* would take more time than it had…he hoped. The remainder of the asteroids had been perfectly primed. They were plummeting straight towards the gas giant itself.

Do you realise what we've done, he silently asked the virus, *or do you think we've just wasted our time?*

His lips quirked as the virus's defences hastily started to switch targets. It wasn't easy. They'd deliberately chosen asteroids that would keep their distance from the orbital battlestations, asteroids the virus would have to stop…but could only stop by leaving its orbital installations uncovered. His smile grew colder as he watched a number of defence platforms vanish, picked off by railgun pellets that couldn't have hoped to hit their targets if the targets hadn't been distracted. There were clearly limits to the virus's ability to react, he noted. The smaller units weren't acting on their own, but waiting for orders. They weren't going to come, not in time.

Two asteroids shattered, chunks of debris flying in all directions. The remainder slammed into the planet with terrifying speed. The gas giant wasn't solid, but—as the sheer force of the impact struck the planet—Thomas could *see* giant shockwaves marching across the world. It was hard to believe, from his distant vantage point, that the waves were moving at unimaginable speed, that they were really big enough to smash a rocky world like Earth. He watched the tidal waves slam into the lower tubes, tearing them away or yanking the cloudscoops into decaying orbits. A handful broke free, cutting their links to the tubes an instant before it was too late. The remainder were shattered, pulled out of orbit and sent falling into the planet's atmosphere. The virus was tough, Thomas knew, but he didn't see how it would survive the fall. The gas giant's interior was implacably hostile.

"Captain, the enemy is deploying additional starfighters," Sibley warned. "Their original squadrons are still heading towards us."

"Launch gunboats," Thomas ordered. They'd done enough damage, he thought, to justify a retreat…but the plan was only half-complete. The marines hadn't reached their destination yet. "Lock missiles on Targets Two through Ten, fire on my command."

"Aye, Captain," Sibley said.

"The tactical staff think we've crippled the production here," Donker commented. "If we do this to the other gas giants…"

Thomas nodded, although he was all too aware the trick would only work once. The virus knew what they'd done. It would prime the remainder of the gas giant mining stations to be ready to drop their tubes, rather than risk being destroyed too. Not, he supposed, that it would stop him from doing it. Even if the operation failed, it wouldn't cost him anything he couldn't afford to lose. If there was one thing the system wasn't short of, it was pieces of space junk.

"Gunboats away, sir," Sibley said. "Missiles ready."

"Firing pattern alpha-three," Thomas said. There was nothing to be gained by shooting themselves dry. They had to keep the enemy defences busy, rather than destroying them outright. As long as they weren't thinking about what was happening, Thomas came out ahead. "Fire at will."

"Aye, Captain."

CHAPTER THIRTY-THREE

COLIN HAD NO IDEA WHAT TO EXPECT, as the marine shuttles glided towards their target.

It wasn't the first time he'd been on a raiding mission, heading towards an enemy installation, but it was the first time he'd been so close to a gas giant. Virus-5 dominated the skyline, casting a baleful orange-red glow over the miniature system orbiting it. Colin had heard that colonists on Io and Ganymede found it difficult to tolerate Jupiter, with the Great Red Spot peering balefully down on the colony domes, but he hadn't really believed it until now. They were over five hundred thousand kilometres from the gas giant and it *still* dominated the surrounding region. He was glad, despite himself, that it didn't have anything resembling the Great Red Spot.

And yet, as he watched, he could see...giant *waves*...spreading through the planet's atmosphere. He knew, intellectually, that the waves were bigger than Earth, that they were spreading at speeds the human mind wasn't designed to comprehend, yet...he found it difficult to understand. He thought he saw flickers of fire within the planet's atmosphere, bursts of energy that made nukes look like firecrackers...it was hard to escape the sense they were flying over a volcano, a volcano that might explode at any second. He'd done a few weeks on Io as part of his training and yet...he shook his head as the shuttle rocked slightly, the gravity field twisting. It was impossible not to fear the entire gas giant was about to explode into a giant supernova.

Which is impossible, he told himself, severely. He'd been given a very basic briefing on astrophysics, when he'd joined the Royal Marines. He didn't pretend to understand the *how* or *why*, but he'd done enough to know the *what. Gas giants don't explode. They simply blink out.*

He shifted, uncomfortably. The latest combat battlesuits were designed to combine comfort with protection and practicality, for a given value of all three. They weren't as cumbersome as the powered combat armour— he supposed someone had had a brainwave and realised powered armour wasn't *that* useful in deep space—and they weren't given to overheating, but they were still uncomfortable. Whoever had designed them probably didn't have to wear them into combat. He would sooner have worn standard urban or rural battledress, except it would have been suicide. Breathing in the viral particles would be an extremely unpleasant way of committing suicide. He'd read the reports. A person in the early stage of infection *could* be saved, but only if they received immediate treatment. He knew it wasn't going to happen. By the time they rushed an infected marine back to the ship, it would be too late.

The shuttle shifted again. "Ten minutes," the pilot said. "Brace yourselves."

Bastard, Colin thought. They were drifting towards an alien battlestation that—in theory—was too distracted to notice ten stealthed shuttles on an intercept vector. If they were spotted, they were dead. The pilot wouldn't have a hope of realising they'd been spotted and evading before it was too late. A single plasma bolt would vaporise the shuttle before the passengers knew they were under attack. *Keep your fucking gob shut, you bastard.*

Sweat trickled down his back as the seconds ticked down to zero. The silence was oppressive, the air hot and humid despite—or perhaps because of—the suit. The mission had sounded like a lark, when they'd been briefed on the concept. Get onto the alien battlestation, blowing their way through airlocks they would normally have tried to keep intact, all the while spreading the counter-virus in hopes of obliterating *the* virus before it could trigger the self-destruct. Colin didn't like the assurances they'd been given, that the virus would react the marines as potential hosts and refrain from trying to blow up the station until it was too late, but he had to accept they had no choice. The battlestation would be very useful if it could be taken intact.

"One minute," the pilot said. "Hull-cutters online, ready to go."

Colin glanced at his platoon. They'd gone through the mission time and time again, although they'd been limits on just how *far* they could simulate the operation. The virus seemed to use the same basic designs for its outer hulls, but didn't seem to standardise the interiors at all. It made a certain kind of sense, according to the spooks, yet—to the marines—it was just a bloody nuisance. What sort of idiot designed two battleships with very different interior designs? He snorted at the thought. The kind of idiot who didn't have to worry about newcomers finding their way around the interior of the ships.

He raised his rifle, performing one last check as the gravity field flickered. A loud whine echoed through the shuttle a moment later as the cutters tore into the alien hull, burning though armour that could shrug off a nuke. Colin stood and hurried to the opening hatch, keying his suit to spray counter-virus as he jumped through the melted bulkhead and into the alien structure. The corridors were a weird angular shape that messed with his mind, lined with slime that turned the deck into a slippery mess. He nearly slipped and fell as he pushed his way into the station, shaking his head in disbelief. He'd heard horror stories about crews that didn't bother to clean their decks, but this...he reminded himself, sharply, that the slime was probably directly linked to the virus. It was already changing colour as the counter-virus started to bite.

And let's hope it kills the rest of the virus before it blows us all to hell, he thought, as the marines advanced down the corridor. He'd done a considerable amount of his field training in the mud, but the slime was something else. He could *feel* it pressing against his suit, trying to find a way in. *There's no way we can take all the virus out in time if we need to sweep the station from end to end.*

He grinned as he spotted an airlock, then nodded to Willis. Normally, they'd try to open the airlock manually, keeping it intact. Now, Willis unslung the plasma cannon and pointed it directly at the heavy door. Colin braced himself as the cannon whined, then spat a burst of white-hot fire towards the airlock. It melted like snow on a hot summer day, torrents of charred viral matter flowing towards them. Colin saw a handful of humanoid creatures beyond, raising weapons. It looked as though they were growing *out* of the slime. Colin had no time to think. He pointed his rifle at the nearest entity and blew it to hell. The remainder fell seconds later.

"Move," he snapped. He keyed his mouthpiece, reporting the contact as they pushed on. The slime pooled around their feet, rapidly turning to brown sludge. Colin was glad they were wearing masks, saving them from smelling the mess. "We need to find an access point."

They blew through three more doors in quick succession, punching their way through the defenders beyond. Colin didn't like what he was seeing. The virus had never really relied on radios, datanet nodes or microburst transmitters, not when it provided its own communications network. Had that changed? Slamming the airlocks closed was a reasonable decision, but…it had cut the virus into a number of separate entities. It would have problems coordinating its reaction if it couldn't talk to itself…he shook his head. The virus had probably found it difficult to plan ahead. He'd been cautioned that *he* might have to cut off his arm to save himself from infection and…he wasn't sure he could go through with it. He wasn't sure he could do it to the rest of his squad, not again.

A pair of techs spotted an access node and slammed a communications processor into it. The planners insisted they could hack the system… Colin wasn't so sure. The virus had no concept of computer security, but it hardly *needed* it. It provided its own command and control system, as if the entire station was run on manual. Colin's lips twitched at the thought as they kept going, leaving the techs behind. The slime was rapidly turning to liquid, droplets of something—he didn't want to think what—dripping from the ceiling. His eyes narrowed as he spotted more liquid draining from pipes, pooling on the deck. The virus was dying and yet…he couldn't shake the feeling it was up to something. It was too much to hope it had simply given up.

He held up a hand to slow the advance as he checked the HUD. The marines were spreading out in a pattern that would have horrified their old instructors, as if they weren't even *trying* to secure the vital compartments and take control of the battlestation. Colin had to admit it looked bad, even though he understood the underlying logic. If the counter-virus killed the virus, they could take control of the station afterwards. If not…a number of marines had argued for opening the station to vacuum instead, pointing out that the cold would freeze the virus, but they'd been overruled. The planners insisted the virus had to be killed—and quickly—before it could mount a response.

Not that it matters, Colin thought. He knew what the planners had in mind for the giant battlestation. *As long as we leave the interior cold and airless, the virus won't be able to stop us.*

The lights started to flicker and fade as they made their way deeper into the station, smashing down airlocks and opening hatches as they moved. Colin would have found it amusing when he'd been younger—he cringed at the mindless vandalism he'd committed, as a teenager—but now it was just worrying. No one in their right mind would just sit back and *let* them spread a killer virus everywhere, not when they could be challenged and stopped. He kept a wary eye on the progress report, noting that the advance forces were steadily making their way towards the fusion cores. The virus didn't really have—or need—a command centre. It was its own command and control system.

Good thing it doesn't trust its electronic servants, Colin thought. *It could have made our life a great deal harder if it had programmed robots to fight us…*

Liquid dripped from above. Colin looked up, an instant before the roof fell in and yellow liquid splashed around them. He stumbled back, kicking himself for forgetting that trick as dark figures charged towards them. A shape crashed into him and sent him falling back, crashing to the deck. His HUD bleeped a warning as he landed, the force of the impact driving the breath from his lungs. The shape—a humanoid creature, wearing a spacesuit—tore at his mask. Colin fought back, only to be repulsed. He was strong, but the zombie was stronger. Colin twisted, his suit screaming in protest. He freed a hand, yanked his dagger from his belt and stabbed up, hitting the zombie in the gut. It didn't stop the creature, not until Colin had cut his suit wide open to ensure the counter-virus got inside. He breathed a sigh of relief as he shoved the dying creature aside, then cursed under his breath. Two of his men had lost their helmets. It wasn't clear what—if anything—they'd breathed. They were hastily raced back to the shuttle and medical isolation as more contact reports came in, noting that the virus was attacking on all fronts.

Tricky bastard, Colin thought. Putting its zombies in spacesuits... obvious, in hindsight, but no one had anticipated the tactic before the virus actually *did* it. *We knew it had spacesuits. We should have seen that one coming.*

He stared down at the zombie who'd nearly killed him. The faceplate was tinted. Colin knelt down and used his knife to cut it away, revealing a reptilian creature with yellow pus leaking out of disturbingly snake-like eyes. He wondered just what the alien had been, before the virus turned it into a zombie. Some poor star traveller, unaware of the threat until it was far too late, or someone born into the virus's service? His stomach churned, bile rising in his throat. The poor bastard had never stood a chance.

The marines regrouped, then pushed on. Colin had the disturbing sense they were entering a tomb, although the splashing liquid reminding him of boating through the caves and underground rivers that had helped prepare him for military service. The liquid kept trickling down...he wondered, suddenly, if the lower levels would wind up completely waterlogged. He smiled. The marines would probably have to pump the poisoned liquid into space, or hurl it towards the gas giant, or...simply leave it. He knew what the squadron intended to do with the station. Loading it with counter-virus might be very useful indeed...

It isn't as if we can't make more, he reminded himself. *And if it works as planned, it will win us the war.*

A flicker of light tore through the air. Colin hurled himself to one side, realising they'd walked right into an ambush. More suited figures were moving ahead, unaware they were showing themselves. Colin guessed, as he unhooked a plasma grenade from his belt and primed it for detonation, that they weren't used to close-quarter combat. The virus had never had to learn. He suspected that would change, if the virus survived long enough to realise what it needed to do. The grenade vibrated in his hand as it went live. Colin shouted a warning, threw the grenade down the corridor and ducked. Catching a grenade and throwing it back was a bad idea, at least without a friendly scriptwriter, but it might work for the infected zombies. They had no sense of self-preservation. The grenade detonated in a flare of brilliant white light, bright enough to hurt his eyes despite the mask. Colin thought he heard someone scream, but it was hard to be sure. It was quite possible he'd simply imagined it.

"I think they're dead, boss," Willis said.

Colin looked along the corridor. The blast had vaporised the zombies. There was nothing left of them, not even a shadow on the walls. The bulkheads were scorched and pitted, scarred by the heat that—for a few short seconds—had exposed the zombies to a miniature sun. The path to the fusion cores lay open.

"I think they're dead, too," he said. "Let's move."

• • •

"Captain," Donker said. "Major Craig reports that stage one is complete. The target is in our hands. All enemy opposition has been quenched and the station has been pumped full of counter-virus."

"Good." Thomas allowed himself a moment of relief. The virus might have managed to figure out what was happening, then do something about it. A nuke wouldn't do much damage to the station, if it hit the outer shell, but a self-destruct system would be enough to render the battlestation completely useless. "Have they locked the battlestation out of the enemy datanet?"

"Yes, sir," Donker assured him. "The battlestation is completely under our control."

Thomas nodded. They'd done a great deal of damage, relatively cheaply. A number of cloudscoops and defence platforms had been destroyed or ruined beyond easy repair, the remaining installations were of no immediate concern, unable to affect matters beyond weapons range. The gas giant's atmosphere was still churning, ensuring the cloudscoops couldn't resume operations until the storms quietened down. Thomas had no idea *just* how badly they'd hurt the virus's economy, but he was pretty sure it had taken notice. Losing the steady stream of fuel from the gas giant would be a major headache.

They'll have contingency plans, he reminded himself. The Royal Navy had contingency plans to continue operations without its cloudscoops, although—thankfully—they'd never been tested. That might change, if—when—the virus stole his idea and started bombing Jupiter and Saturn with asteroids, too. *And they'll certainly have some stockpiles in orbit around Virus Prime.*

"Recall the gunboats and disengage," Thomas ordered. "Helm, take us away from the gas giant, then steer us towards the captured battlestation. Communications, inform *Haddon* that phase one has been completed and they are cleared to begin phase two. Sensors, deploy two more sensor platforms and alert me the moment you detect any mobile units making their way towards us."

"Aye, Captain."

Thomas nodded as he leaned back in his chair. The mission had been a gamble, but—so far—it had worked. The timing hadn't gone as he'd hoped, yet they were still within mission parameters. Perhaps, just perhaps, they'd be able to pull the whole thing off. And then…

He frowned. They'd done a *lot* of damage, for only a tiny price. If they quit while they were ahead, perhaps moved to repeat the asteroid trick at the other gas giants...he grimaced, natural caution warring with the grim reality that they were running out of time. They might be ahead now, but that wouldn't last. There was no way to know when the relief fleet would arrive, if indeed it was even coming. They had to put the boot in before the virus recovered and struck back. And if they ran out of supplies before they managed to land a major blow...he winced. They had to continue the mission.

"Communications, send a burst transmission to *Unicorn*," he added. "Inform Captain Campbell that we have completed phase one, then ask for an update on his status."

"Aye, Captain."

CHAPTER THIRTY-FOUR

"INCOMING FIRE!"

Susan braced herself as the display sparkled with red icons, missiles, gunboats and starfighters hurtling towards her fleet. *Vanguard* and the rest of the lead formation had made transit, only to run straight into an ambush. It was one for the record books, she reflected sourly; there was no historical record of a fleet crossing a tramline and running directly into enemy fire. The virus had pulled off ambushes before, during Operation Lightning Strike, but only well clear of the tramlines. Susan suspected her political enemies wouldn't hesitate to claim the whole incident was a glaring example of incompetence.

She clasped her hands behind her back and waited as her well-trained crews snapped into action, point defence weapons flaring to life even as starfighters were crash-launched from their carriers. If she didn't make it home, it didn't matter what the REMFs said. She'd known the ambush was a possibility, given how frantically she'd blazed her way through the last three systems—she'd only paused long enough to hurl BioBomb missiles and kinetic projectiles towards the planets and moons—and her course couldn't have been more predicable if she'd tried. It might have been safer, she reflected, to send the enemy a signed note detailing her intentions. No enemy in their right mind would have *believed* it. She smiled. It was clever, but in her experience trying to be clever was just asking for trouble. The simpler the tactic, the greater the chance of either carrying it out or being able to withdraw if the engagement went spectacularly wrong.

"Admiral, long-range sensors are picking up a handful of alien capital ships," Richardson reported. "They're holding position on the edge of our sensor range."

Susan frowned as the red icons blinked into existence. The virus's ships were holding the range open, rather than trying to get closer before the remainder of the relief fleet made transit. The ambush could have been a great deal costlier than it had been, if the enemy battleships had slipped closer. Their weapons could have savaged her carriers before she beat them back or retreated through the tramline. And yet, they were playing it safe. It bothered her.

"Launch a pair of sensor probes towards their position," Susan ordered. Did those ships actually exist? The virus's decoy and deception technologies were quite some distance behind humanity's, but they'd been given ample incentive to catch up. They knew what could be done and knowing was half the battle. "If they want to stay out of the fight, we'll let them."

The sense of unease grew as the remainder of her fleet jumped into position. The ambush had hurt—she'd lost four capital ships, as well as thirty-seven starfighters—but it could have been a great deal worse. The boffins had been babbling about drones that could make transit, scan the other side of the tramline and jump back again. She made a mental note to encourage them to try to develop the technology so it could be put into mass production, although she had to admit the virus had gotten lucky. It wouldn't have found it so easy to mount an ambush if she hadn't made it extremely clear where she intended to make transit. The next victim might not be so cooperative.

"The ships appear to be real, or very good fakes," Richardson said. "They're between us and the final tramline."

Susan nodded. The navy had spent the last decade putting together a picture of infected space. It was hard to be sure—the virus had launched

STL ships as well as spreading through the tramlines—but she was fairly certain they had a decent picture of just how many star systems the virus had under its control. Not that it mattered, she reminded herself; they were only one jump short of Virus Prime itself. The fleet blocking their way might be the only deep space force the virus had left.

Don't be so hasty, she reminded herself, sharply. *The virus might have a final trick up its sleeve.*

She snapped orders, directing her squadrons into position while recon drones shot out in all directions. The system was practically empty, save for four tramlines and a tiny cluster of asteroids far too close to the primary for her peace of mind. They would have to be inspected later, just to ensure the virus hadn't infected them. She keyed her console, bringing up a starchart. The tramlines within the system headed around human space, eventually leading to Alien-One and Falkirk...Falkirk, where *Invincible* had set off on the first mission into infected space. The poor bastards hadn't realised what they were facing. Back then, they'd though the virus was just another alien race, just another power that could be reasoned with...she shook her head. It was hard to talk to the Tadpoles or the Foxes or even the Vesy—the dream of starships with crew from many different races could never be realised—but at least they were intelligent. The virus...was a force of nature. It might mimic humans, it might wear their flesh like spacesuits, but it wasn't really intelligent. There was no hope of convincing the virus to change its ways.

"Signal the fleet," she ordered, once the formation had been assembled. "We will proceed directly to Tramline Four."

"Aye, Admiral."

Susan watched as the range started to close. The virus had ample opportunity to break off and retreat, falling back on its fixed defences, but...it was standing its ground. It made no sense. Susan admired bravery—God knew she'd gotten into trouble time and time again simply by allowing her recklessness to guide her—but the virus had nothing to gain. Her eyes narrowed. Did it think it could delay her? Or...

A nasty thought occurred to her. "Ramp active sensors up to full power," she ordered. It would give away their position, but she'd be astonished if the virus didn't already have solid locks on her starships. "I think they're trying to lead us into a minefield."

"Aye, Admiral," Richardson said. "Should we reduce speed?"

"Not yet," Susan said. The mines—if indeed there were any—couldn't be that close to her ships or she would have spotted them already. Or they would have tried to kill her. "Stand by point defence..."

Her mind raced. If it was a minefield...they'd have to go around it. They had neither the time nor the tools to clear it, not without wasting a great deal of time. And yet, altering course would add at least two to three hours to the journey...perhaps more. Did the virus intend to do something with that time? Was it sending reinforcements to the system? It *was* the last chance to stop her fleet, short of Virus Prime itself. *She* wouldn't give up the tramlines so easily. Losing control of the system would effectively cut infected space in half.

But only on paper, she thought. *The virus could still slip ships through if it was prepared to take the time.*

She looked up as alarms started to howl. The display flared with red light. For a horrified moment, she thought she'd run straight into a cloaked fleet of missile carriers...and then she realised the truth. The virus had taken a human idea and copied it. They'd dumped hundreds of missiles into interplanetary space, then lured the human fleet into engagement range. It might have worked, too, Susan noted. She'd expected a minefield, not a barrage of missiles. And yet, in hindsight, she'd made a mistake. She'd *seen* the virus launching entire salvos of missiles in the past, sacrificing hundreds so a few dozen would get through...

"Launch starfighters," she ordered. The fleet was already responding, its datanet snapping to life as it calculating counterbattery fire patterns. She silently thanked GATO for making sure everyone drilled together, cutting their reaction time as sharply as possible. "Point defence, open fire."

"Aye, Admiral," Richardson said. There was a pause. "The enemy fleet is powering up her drives."

Susan nodded. "Signal the carriers," she said. The fleet couldn't be allowed to retreat. "Antishipping starfighters are to make one pass through the missile swarm and then target the enemy capital ships. The remainder of the starfighters are to assume CSP duties."

"Aye, Admiral," Richardson said.

Better not to give the fleet a chance to escape, Susan thought. *Or to come at us, guns blazing.*

Her eyes narrowed as the missiles roared towards her ships. The tactical staff thought the virus had collected several different designs of missiles, given the disparity in performance. Susan had a feeling the virus had kept improving the design, even after it figured out they weren't as effective as it might have hoped. The sheer volume of wasted missiles would daunt the human beancounters, who would never have allowed *her* to expend so many on a forlorn hope, but the virus didn't seem to care. She supposed it was one advantage it had over the other races. It didn't *have* to feed and care for its own people, not beyond the basics. It could devote the entire power of its economy to war.

The missiles started to vanish as they passed through the starfighters. Susan leaned forward, noting just how many missiles were killed... and just how many survived to continue their flight. More than she'd expected...too many. The tactical staff sent a note, warning that the virus had clearly managed to duplicate the sensor distorters *Lion* had used to make it harder for the enemy to lock missiles on their hulls. Susan wasn't surprised. The virus had seen it in action. It would have every reason to try to devise a way to duplicate the tactic for itself.

And it might even have captured samples of working hardware, she reminded herself. *Or someone who knows how it works.*

She put the thought out of her mind and concentrated on projecting an aura of calm as the enemy missiles roared into her point defence zone. There was no point in issuing any further orders. Her crew knew what to do. Their minds couldn't handle the sheer speed of the engagement either, leaving the command and control role in the hands of computers that could spot a microsecond-long opening and put a plasma bolt through it. She watched, numbly, as hundreds of missiles vanished from the display, the remainder surviving long enough to hammer her ships. Slowly, steadily, the damage began to mount.

"Admiral," Richardson said. "*Texas* and *Mao* have been destroyed. *Stalin* has taken heavy damage. *Napoleon* has lost one flight deck and…"

"Understood." Susan cut him off harshly. She didn't have time to worry about it. "Concentrate on the enemy fleet."

Her heart sank as the final missiles were either killed by the point defence or reached their targets, damaging or destroying more of her ships. The virus had tried to cripple her fleet, rather than blowing a handful of capital ships to hell. She wasn't sure she liked the implications, even though it had worked in her favour. If she'd lost more battleships and carriers, she might have had to concede defeat and withdraw as quickly as she'd come. It had a sense of the enemy buying time, which meant…

Damage reports scrolled up in front of her. Nine ships destroyed, seventeen more damaged to the point they needed repairs before they could proceed. A number of others had been hit, but could—they said—continue the fight. She tapped a command into her console, directing her staff to start reallocating resources before she divided the fleet into two sections and left one behind to wait under cloak. They'd need to be recovered when the remainder of the fleet returned from Virus Prime. It wasn't an ideal solution—personally, she would have preferred to send them straight back to New Washington—but it would have to do.

"Signal Admiral Lagos," she said. "He is to take command of the cripples, once we've broken contact with the remaining enemy ships, and remain in the system, under cloak, until we return."

"Aye, Admiral," Richardson said.

Susan allowed herself a tight smile. Admiral Lagos was a far better organiser—and military politician—than a fighter. She would have declined his appointment, if she'd had a choice. But now…he could organise the repairs while lurking under cloak, then sneak back to New Washington if the fleet failed to return. She was all too aware of what would happen if the cripples were caught, but…she had a feeling the virus didn't have time to go hunting. The attempt to slow her fleet, rather than punching out a handful of capital ships, suggested the virus was trying to buy time. It was, she hoped, good news.

She tried to relax as she followed the engagement. The enemy ships fought well, but at a certain remove. They were definitely trying to escape, rather than close the range or simply force her to expend starfighters at an unsustainable rate. Susan kept launching additional recon drones, making sure the enemy fleet wasn't trying to lure them into another trap. It looked clear, but it was impossible to be sure. They couldn't survive another missile barrage, not like that…

"Admiral," Richardson said. He looked up, face twisted into a grim smile. "The enemy fleet has been destroyed."

Susan nodded. There might be other units lurking under cloak, or watching from a safe distance, but—for the moment—the battle was over. There was a palpable sense of relief running through the CIC, a relief the battle was won mingled with a grim awareness it could have easily gone the other way. The CIC crew had been in the odd position of directing a battle without actually fighting it, without actually focusing on a single element of the overall engagement…Susan smiled. It was easy to forget, at times, that the lights on the display represented real capital ships and real starfighters, that when they blinked out they'd taken a number of lives with them. She'd promised herself, when she'd reached flag rank, that she'd never forget. She owed it to the men under her command.

She pushed the thought out of her mind as she studied the post-battle assessments. Admiral Lagos had already assumed command of the cripples, transferring starfighters, marines and supplies to the remainder of the fleet with an open-handedness Susan could only admire. It wasn't entirely disinterested, she supposed. The cripples were doomed if they ran into anything bigger than a corvette, perhaps even a destroyer. Better to let them hide in the inky darkness of interstellar space than risk an engagement that would end in disaster. Admiral Lagos would do a good job, she was sure. She keyed her console, opening a private channel. Admiral Lagos's face appeared in front of her.

"Admiral," he said.

"Admiral," Susan echoed. The admiral already had his orders, but she knew she had to make them clear. "Stay out of sight. Avoid all contact. If you have to make your way home, head to the edge of the system and make transit there. We'll signal when we return, of course, but verify the signal before decloaking."

"Understood," Admiral Lagos said. If he had any qualms about his orders, he kept them to himself. He might not be a fighter, but he understood the needs of war. They were too far from home for ideal solutions. "Do you want us to take any messages home?"

"No," Susan said. Her crew was too busy to record any final messages. They should have done *that* while they were leaving Earth. She could record one for herself, but...she shook her head. It wasn't *right* for her to record anything personal, not when her crew didn't have the time to do it. "I'll copy my engagement reports to you. You can forward them to GATO when you get home, if we don't link up with you again."

"Of course," Admiral Lagos said. He raised a hand in salute. "Good luck, Admiral."

Susan nodded, taking her seat as the image vanished. Admiral Lagos might have the easier mission. All *he* had to do was remain hidden. *She* had to break into the most heavily-industrialised and defended system in known space, link up with the *Lion* and the *Unicorn* and then finish the task of rendering the system completely harmless. It might be only one jump away, but she was all too aware the system was ready for her. The missiles had to come from somewhere and the system up ahead was the only realistic source. She hoped it was a good sign they hadn't backed the missiles with something else, like a much bigger fleet. They could have stopped the relief fleet in its tracks.

We'll be there as soon as possible, she told herself. They needed a few hours to rearm their ships and make what repairs they could, then they'd resume their course towards the alien system. *And then we'll put an end to the threat once and for all.*

CHAPTER THIRTY-FIVE

THE INTERCOM BLEEPED. "CAPTAIN?"

Mitch opened his eyes. He hadn't been asleep, but…he'd been halfway between sleep and waking. *Unicorn* was too far from the planet to run an op, yet too close for his peace of mind. The virus had been busy, scattering more and more sensor platforms—backed up by starfighters and capital ships—around its homeworld. Mitch hoped—prayed—it really *was* the virus's homeworld. He would have hated to discover, after they'd finally ground down the planet's defences and rendered it a radioactive wasteland, that the enemy fleet could simply withdraw to another world.

He rubbed his forehead as he sat up. "Report."

"Passive sensors are picking up increased enemy activity," Staci said. "They're concentrating their mobile units."

"I see." Mitch glanced at the timer. It was hard to coordinate operations on an interplanetary scale—perversely, it was a little easier to coordinate on an *interstellar* scale—but *Lion* should have hit the gas giant a scant few hours ago. The virus might *just* have heard that something had gone wrong. "Are they headed to Virus-5?"

"It's unclear, Captain," Staci told him. "They're concentrating their forces on the wrong side of the planet."

Which is pretty meaningless, when you consider how fast starships can move, Mitch thought, dryly. It would only add a few minutes to a flight that would take upwards of ten hours, assuming the ships travelled on a least-time course. The battle over the gas giant would be decided, one way or the other, before the enemy fleet reached its destination. *Unless something happened to* Lion...

"Keep an eye on it," he ordered. "Did we pick up any messages from *Lion*?"

"No, Captain," Staci said. "No wide-band transmissions, no nothing. Do you want to query the nearest platform?"

Mitch frowned. The absence of a wide-band transmission—particularly one that wasn't obviously meant to be misleading—was a good sign. Probably. *Lion* would have maintained radio silence, only communicating through tight-beam lasers, unless her destruction was certain. She'd have screamed her distress to the entire system if she *knew* she was doomed, just to make certain *Unicorn* knew she'd lost her partner. No, *Lion* was intact...unless she'd been crippled. The virus might be deploying ships to finish her off before she could make repairs and vanish back into cloak.

"Yes," he said, finally. "Maintain passive sensor watch. I'll be on the bridge in ten minutes."

He stood, checked the terminal to be sure there were no enemy ships within striking distance, then stripped off his clothes and stepped into the shower. It had been an odd night. He'd fallen in and out of wakefulness, half-convinced he was lying in bed with Charlotte...he shook his head in irritation as the water washed the sweat from his body. He had no idea how that was going to work out, when they made their way back to Earth. Who knew? Charlotte might have found someone else by then, or simply decided to concentrate on her planned career. Mitch glanced at the terminal again as he stepped out of the shower, towelled off and dressed in a clean uniform. By now, the by-election would have come and gone. Charlotte would either be an MP or licking her wounds before returning to the fray. Mitch smiled at the thought, then put it aside. Who knew how things would go, when the thrill of cheating on one's husband—and cuck-olding one's superior—began to fade? It wasn't as if they had *that* much in common, beyond a desire to be famous.

I guess we succeeded, he thought. *But not for the right reasons.*

He stepped through the hatch and walked onto the bridge. The display was glowing with light, the planet surrounded by a small galaxy of red icons. It was terrifying to realise that some of the mass driver projectiles had found targets, smashing industrial platforms and mining stations with casual ease, only to have very little effect on the planetary halo. There were always more stations and defence platforms, ready to take up the slack. Mitch cursed under his breath. He was always looking for ways to hurt the enemy, even if it meant getting hurt himself, but he could read a supply table as well as anyone else. They could only afford one last attack before falling back for resupply. They *had* to make it count.

"We haven't picked up anything new from *Lion*," Staci informed him, as he took the command chair. "The enemy fleet hasn't moved from orbit."

Mitch frowned. The virus was behaving oddly. He studied the display, considering possible explanations, but drew a blank. If the virus wanted to reinforce the gas giant's defences, or hunt down *Lion*, it should have dispatched the fleet by now. If the virus had caught a sniff of *Unicorn*... Mitch shook his head. The virus knew better than to just leave the frig-ate alone, once they got a lock on her location. The enemy ships should be trying to sneak up on the frigate, not hanging back...unless they were trying to distract him while the *real* threat crept up from behind. And yet, there was nothing creeping up on his position...

The display shifted. Red icons—seventy red icons—glided out of orbit and set course for deep space. Mitch blinked as the projections rapidly updated. The enemy fleet was heading straight for Tramline One. It made no sense. The virus *knew* its system was under heavy attack. It had to know *Lion* and *Unicorn* were still searching for weak points. It had to assume it was just a matter of time before the remaining gas giants were hammered too. And yet, it was dispatching enough ships to lay waste to a heavily-defended world. It made no sense.

It clicked, suddenly. "The relief fleet is here!"

"It's possible," Staci said. "They'd certainly want to intercept the relief fleet well short of the planet itself."

Mitch nodded. The virus could fall back on the planet, linking its fleet to the fixed defences, but it had to know the planet itself was a target. A single missile striking the surface would make one hell of a mess...a single missile, crammed with counter-virus, would destroy the virus's entire population. He smiled, coldly. The virus was *finally* scared. His imagination filled the enemy ships with fearful blobs, all too aware that they *had* to stop the human fleet before it broke into the system. And they were running out of options. His smile grew wider as he realised the deeper implications. Virus Prime might be the virus's last bastion against a universe that wanted it dead.

He told himself, firmly, not to get too excited. The virus could be using sensor decoys to lure them into a trap. There were so many installations orbiting the planet that the virus could conceal its entire fleet amongst the halo and no one would notice, not until it was too late. It might be hoping for a clear shot at his ship...he tapped his console, calculating the probability vectors. If the departing ships were real, they'd have a perfect window to hit the planet *hard*.

"Tactical, launch two drones to assess the departing ships," Mitch ordered. "I want to confirm they're *real*."

"Aye, Captain," Staci said.

Mitch waited, telling himself not to get too hopeful. He didn't *know* what had happened at the gas giant. *Lion* could have been destroyed, her final signal lost in the haze. The virus might be feeling secure, secure enough to dispatch its ships to resume the offensive. For all he knew, they were wrong. The relief fleet might have been destroyed, if it had ever been launched at all. He trusted the admiral to do everything in her power to get the fleet underway, but...

"Captain," Culver said. "I just queried the platform and downloaded an update from *Lion*. She reports mission success. The enemy battlestation is in our hands."

"Good." Mitch allowed himself a smile. Captain Hammond had just hit the virus where it hurt. "Tactical, do we have a clear image on those departing ships?"

"I think they're real, Captain," Staci said. "They're putting out one hell of a lot of drive field energy. Either most of them are real or the virus has managed to jump several light years ahead of us in deception technology."

Mitch frowned. "Pity we can't force them to open fire," he said. "I wonder…"

He forced himself to think. If the enemy ships, or most of them, were real, they were leaving the planet uncovered. Not undefended—there was still enough orbital firepower to stand off most of the navy—but with a shortage of mobile units to patrol the outer reaches of the defence network. The humans would never have a better chance to hit the planet and hit it hard, hopefully crippling the virus beyond repair. And yet, if it was a trick…they had no choice. They *had* to take the bait.

And they hopefully won't realise what we've been planning, he thought. *They won't see the water-ice asteroids coming…*

"Communications, record for *Lion*," Mitch said. "Commodore Hammond. The enemy has dispatched a fleet to the first tramline, apparently to stand off the relief fleet. Our window is opening. We must attack now. I propose timing the offensive to hit the enemy homeworld at"—he glanced at the display—"1700. *Unicorn* will move to the waypoint and assume overwatch duties. See you on the flip side."

He smiled, thinly. "Attach a copy of our sensor records, then transmit," he added. The die was about to be cast. Mitch had proposed a little leeway, a little room for friction, but Captain Hammond would have to move fast if he wanted to make the deadline. He wasn't going to be too pleased, even though he'd *known* it was coming. "Helm, move us into overwatch position."

"Aye, Captain."

Mitch grinned as he settled back into his chair. One way or the other, the virus was about to take one hell of a pounding. If the plan worked as he expected, the planet was about to be hammered flat. Even if it didn't... he smirked. They were going to force the virus to concentrate on home defence. It wouldn't have *time* to resume the offensive before the human race destroyed it once and for all.

Then we can all go home, he thought. He wondered, suddenly, if he'd miss the war when it was over. Mopping up the infected colonies wouldn't require major fleet actions, just steady pressure and grim determination. *And who knows what we'll find when we get there?*

. . .

"Signal from *Unicorn*, sir," Cook said. "She reports the enemy fleet has left orbit."

Thomas frowned. The gas giant's remaining defenders had kept their distance from his ship and the captured battlestation. His mining crews had been tipping more rocks towards the surviving installations, hoping to do at least *some* damage before they moved to the final stage of the plan, but results had been minimal. The virus was playing a waiting game, he'd thought; it was waiting for reinforcements before trying to drive the battlecruiser back into interplanetary space or destroy it outright. And yet, if Captain Campbell was correct, the enemy fleet was heading for the *tramline*. It made no sense.

He scanned the report quickly. *Unicorn* believed the human relief fleet was on its way. Thomas knew better than to be too hopeful, but he suspected Campbell was right. The relief fleet could be closer than they dared hope, yet...he scowled as he saw the monumental firepower leaving the alien homeworld and heading to the tramline. The virus might stop the relief fleet in its tracks. And yet, in doing so, it had offered him a chance to strike the killing blow.

"Signal the shattering asteroids," he ordered, finally. He hated being rushed into anything…he snorted at the thought. They were about to discover a whole new meaning to *hurry up and wait*. "They are to aim to strike the planet on or after 1700. After they launch their rocks, they are to recover the remaining pushers and go silent. If we don't link up with them, they are to make their way back to New Washington."

"Aye, Captain."

"XO, signal the marines to prepare to launch as planned," Thomas continued. "Tactical, deploy a sensor drone; helm, prepare to take us to the planet. We want to be there at 1700, right behind the battlestation."

He smiled, grimly. The plan was going to go down in history as one of the shoddiest tactical concepts in the Royal Navy's long history. There were so many guesses worked into the plan that it would be a minor miracle if even half the timing came off as planned. And yet, it might not matter. They had to hit the enemy, and *quickly*. Captain Campbell might assume the enemy fleet wouldn't double back, but Thomas didn't dare take that for granted. The enemy ships might reverse course the moment they realised what was coming.

"Captain," Donker said. "The marines are making the final preparations now."

"We leave in thirty minutes," Thomas said. "Pull off all the marines who aren't strictly necessary for the operation, then remind the remainder to jump ship and head for the RV point. If we don't survive, either *Unicorn* or one of the fleet tenders will pick them up."

"Aye, Captain," Donker said.

"Good." Thomas braced himself. The operation might or might not succeed. Either way, they would have to leave the system to resupply once the rocks stopped falling. "Remind the crew. We leave in thirty minutes."

"Aye, Captain."

• • •

Tobias felt weirdly unsure of himself as he surveyed the remaining gunboat crews. Eighteen crewmen…it was strange to realise that his squadron had done better than many a starfighter squadron. *Their* loss rates were so high that…he forced himself not to think about it as he ran through the mission briefing. It wasn't *that* different than anything they'd done before, over the last few months, but the sheer scale of the alien defences was daunting. Tobias didn't want to *think* about how many starfighters, gunboats and armed shuttles might be coming at them. It was like playing a game where someone had set the enemy numbers as near to *infinite* as possible…

"We'll be entering engagement range in seven hours, assuming everything goes according to plan," Tobias said. The briefing notes had insisted *Lion* would be cloaked, but—reading between the lines—Tobias suspected it wasn't going to matter. The virus would have every incentive to focus its sensors in the battlecruiser's general direction. It might discover her presence through sheer coincidence. "Get some rest, if you can; make sure you get something to eat before we go to our craft. Dismissed."

He groaned inwardly as his pilots stood and left the compartment, wondering if he should have said something more. A rousing speech…he could have simply copied one from a movie—they would have gotten the joke—or tried to come up with one. And yet, he had the feeling it would go over like a lead balloon. He lacked the charisma of the actor who'd played Winston Churchill, as well as the speechwriting skills of the writer who'd put the words in his mouth. The idea of him pumping the air and filling his subordinates with enthusiasm was absurd.

"I feel like an idiot," Tobias said. "I could have fired them up."

"You'd have fired them up with nowhere to go," Marigold pointed out. "We have six hours until we have to get into the craft, unless we run into something that blindsides us. And besides, they would have taken it the wrong way."

Tobias nodded. He'd never liked being forced to listen as sadistic gym teachers—and headmasters—made powerful speeches, urging the players to kick ass on the sports field while trying to have a nice clean game…he snorted, rudely. He wouldn't have enjoyed listening to such a speech—he'd certainly come to loathe the gym teachers he'd been forced to endure—and he doubted his subordinates would either. And yet...he remembered the rest of the briefing and shivered. Captain Hammond had made it clear that the operation was their final hurrah. Win or lose, they'd be leaving the system immediately afterwards. They needed to resupply.

"They probably would have thought I was lying to them," he agreed. He deliberately changed the subject. "Do you think we'll get any leave on New Washington?"

"God knows," Marigold said. She leaned forward and kissed him. Tobias returned the kiss, his hands slipping around her to stroke her back. The kiss deepened, a moment before she broke contact and drew back slightly. "I've taken the liberty of booking one of the privacy tubes. Are you coming?"

Tobias grinned. "Are you kidding? Of course."

She took his hand and pulled him towards the hatch. Tobias felt a stab of guilt, mingled with an awareness that this might be their last chance. They'd survived one emergency exit into deep space, where they could easily have been vaporised by a stray shot or simply died when they ran out of air; the odds were against them surviving a second time. Hell, the odds were against them surviving at all. And...and she wanted to sleep with him. It still struck him as wondrous. A year ago, the idea of a girl giving him the time of day would have been utterly absurd.

Much less one as wonderful as Marigold.

He kissed her again, as soon as they were in the private chamber. There wasn't much time—they needed to sleep, as well as make love—but he intended to use it. And afterwards...

Tobias smiled. The future could take care of itself.

CHAPTER THIRTY-SIX

"YOU KNOW," WILLIS SAID, "I had a thought."

Colin grinned. "Oh, God, we're doomed."

"Stop the presses," Davis added. "Willy had a thought!"

"Hah," Willis said. "Really, guys. I had a thought."

"We'll sell it to the newspapers," Davis said. "Do you think they'll pay us a finder's fee?"

"Only if they can find a way to deduct money from you," Colin teased. He cleared his throat as he leaned against the bulkhead. "What is your thought?"

"Well, this is a spacecraft, right?" Willis waved a hand at the bulkhead, indicating the alien battlestation. "Or it's been converted into one, right? So does that mean we have to call you *captain*?"

"My ego demands you call me *Your Imperial Supremacy*," Colin said, in a perfectly deadpan tone of voice. He'd watched a movie, once, in which the bad guy had demanded increasingly outrageous forms of address. "Why do you ask?"

"Well, you're in command of this ship, which makes you the captain," Willis said. "And when something happens to you, *I* become captain."

"And when something happens to *you*, I become captain," Davis said. "I like the way you think."

"I think you two need to spend more time studying your naval protocols," Colin said, making a show of rolling his eyes. "When this thing gets moving, none of us are going to be onboard."

He tried not to shiver. The alien battlestation was creepy as fuck. They'd gone through the station from top to bottom, discovering a complete lack of datacores, actionable intelligence and anything else they might expect to find in a captured enemy facility. The virus's host-bodies had lived in primitive conditions, conditions that would disgust insurgents on the wrong side of the Security Wall. Colin was no stranger to harsh living conditions—he'd had to sleep in foxholes, during exercises—and yet even *he* had his limits. The virus didn't seem to be invested in the health of its host bodies, to the point it didn't care if they lived or died. It puzzled him. Surely, out of sheer practicality if nothing else, it should take better care of them.

The timer bleeped. He stood, breathing a sigh of relief even though he knew they weren't going to be doing very much. The battlestation's command and control systems were nothing more than mush, but the techs had had no trouble wiring a makeshift control network into the alien systems that—they insisted—would remain operational long enough for the mission to be completed. Colin hoped they were right. The marines had spent four hours loading missile tubes, nuclear weapons and counter-virus dispersal projectiles onto the battlestation. He hated to think they might have wasted all that effort. Thankfully, the virus didn't seem to have heard of computer security. The techs insisted it made sense. The virus no more needed to protect against itself than Colin's right hand put a password on his terminal to spite his *left* hand. It clearly hadn't realised that it could lose the control network without actually losing the weapons systems themselves. The techs had simply plugged the abandoned weapons into a whole new command and control system.

"We have ten minutes," he said. "Are we ready?"

"Yes, corporal," the tech said. She was a short pretty girl with dark hair, the sort of young woman he would have asked out if he'd met her on the streets. Colin had seen enough of her work to know she was *way* out of his league. "The command network is up and running. The pusher is charged, ready to fire."

Colin nodded, hiding his awe. The Royal Marines held the current record for long-range sniping—a marine had shot an enemy from over three kilometres away—but *they* were sniping right across an entire star system. It was hard to believe it would work, even though it had already worked more than once. The techs swore blind the battlestation could take the stresses they were about to put on it, that the command and control network would remain intact and operational…not, Colin supposed, that it mattered *that* much. The battlestation would become a flying rock, as deadly as any of the asteroids, even if its weapons were rendered useless.

"Check the command codes," he ordered, as he recalled his team. Most of the marines had been pulled off before the battlecruiser departed, heading towards the RV point. The remainder would board a shuttle, head into deep space…and, in doing so, take themselves out of the fight. "And make damn sure the timer is ready."

"It's ready," the tech confirmed. "The timer is set."

"Begin the countdown," Colin ordered. He keyed his mouthpiece. "Report to the shuttle now. I say again, report to the shuttle now."

He took one final look around the makeshift command and control station, then followed the techs and marines as they hurried to the shuttle. There hadn't been any time to carry out proper repairs—it wasn't as if the battlestation was going to survive more than a few hours, at best—but they'd gone to some trouble to ensure the station was airtight. It wouldn't do to kill the counter-virus before it could do its job. He pushed through the final airlock, checked to make sure it had sealed automatically, then walked onto the shuttle and performed a quick headcount. The entire team was there.

"Disengage," he ordered, as he took his seat and peered through the porthole. "Get us out of here."

"Aye, sir," the pilot said.

Colin frowned as the shuttle rocked, separating itself from the battlestation. The gas giant came into view quickly, the atmosphere still roiling hours after the asteroids had struck the planet. Colin wondered, morbidly, if they'd invented a new form of art. They'd unleashed more devastation than had ever hit Earth, or any rocky world, and yet...it was weirdly beautiful. The gas giant was just...stunning. It cast an eerie radiance over the scene.

"One minute to launch," the tech said. She counted down the seconds. "Launch!"

Colin had expected to see...*something*, although he wasn't sure what. The battlestation glowing with light perhaps, before vanishing in a flash. Instead...the structure seemed to blur, an instant before it was gone faster than the eye could see. Colin remembered his earlier thought and smiled. They really *were* sniping across the entire system. There was no hope of the target moving, to get out of the line of fire. The virus couldn't hope to evade the incoming threat even if it saw the threat coming.

"It's gone," the tech said.

"And, for us, the war is over," Davis said. "What now?"

"We wait," Colin said. "And hope the rest of the crew makes it out."

• • •

"Captain," Cook said. "We just picked up a signal pulse from Virus-5. The battlestation is on its way."

"Good." Thomas let out a breath. The virus would have picked up the drive field burst, of course, but it couldn't be sure something was coming. It would be several hours before the battlestation—and the shattering asteroids—reached their target. "Pass the alert down the chain, then resume communications silence."

"Aye, Captain," Cook said.

Thomas checked the timer. It was impossible to be completely sure, but—if everything had gone according to plan—the shattering asteroids should arrive just before the battlestation. Or most of them, at least.

Unicorn was much closer to the target, ready to send the signal to detonate the bombs. Thomas hoped it would work...

It will, he told himself. *It isn't as if we can miss.*

"Continue our current course," he ordered. "We'll launch gunboats when we reach the first waypoint."

"Aye, Captain."

. . .

Mitch kept a wary eye on the timer, wondering precisely when the first of the shattering asteroids was going to come into view. The last update insisted that all, but one of the asteroids would reach the planet shortly before the battlestation...yet there were too many variables for him to take it for granted. In hindsight, the plan might have been a little too clever for its own good. It might have been wiser to start launching asteroids from clusters far closer to the enemy homeworld.

Most of which had already been turned into colonies or mined for supplies, he reminded himself, dryly. *They would be under surveillance, even if they weren't inhabited.*

He paced the bridge, sweat trickling down his back as the seconds wore on. The enemy fleet had long since moved out of sensor range. His imagination provided too many possibilities, from the relief fleet being destroyed to the enemy fleet doubling back and vaporising *Lion* and *Unicorn* alike. They should pick up *something*, if the enemy fleet reversed course, but... he smiled, sourly. The virus was giving them a taste of the uncertainty they'd wrecked on its system. It had had problems deciding how to react to the human threat. Now, the humans felt the same way too.

"Captain." Staci looked up from her console. "The first asteroid has just appeared on our sensors."

Mitch took his seat and studied the display. The asteroid was *huge*, two hundred kilometres of rocky death falling towards the planet. If it struck the surface, intact, it would destroy all life on the planet. Even a glancing blow would be utterly disastrous. The virus couldn't take the risk. It would try to deflect the asteroid—and its buddies—as soon as possible. This time, it was going to be rather hard.

"Good." Mitch watched the remaining asteroids come into view. Two of them—not one—were missing. He wondered, idly, what had happened to the second missing asteroid, then shrugged. Perhaps it was simply running late. "Establish links to the detonation system."

"Aye, Captain," Staci said. There was a pause. "I have links to all of the asteroids. Command codes locked in, firing codes ready to go. The asteroids can be detonated on your command."

Mitch nodded, watching the enemy deployments. The virus would almost certainly try to deflect the asteroids, rather than risk unleashing a wave of smaller chunks of rock that would do a hell of a lot of damage... ironic, under the circumstances. It also had a great deal of practice in deflecting rocks. Mitch's sensors had even picked up hints it had rushed something comparable to the pusher into mass production, turning human technology against its makers. The boffins had warned it would happen, probably sooner rather than later. There was nothing particularly *new* in the device, as long as one just wanted to throw an asteroid right across the system. The virus could simply shove the rocks into the star or toss them well away from its facilities. It could worry about where they were going later.

"Let them get as close as possible," he ordered. There was no way to predict where all the debris would go, when the asteroids shattered, but...the closer the asteroids got to the planet before it blew, the greater the chance of the majority of the debris intersecting the high orbitals and smashing them to atoms. "Don't detonate them until the virus tries to land shuttles to shove them away."

He smiled, coldly, as the range continued to close. The virus was scrambling shuttles, directing them towards the asteroids. Mitch guessed they'd been designed to carry a pusher to its target, then trigger it. The gravity backwash would be terrible—the shuttle itself might not survive, let alone the host-bodies—but it would probably work. There'd certainly be no need to set up a proper pusher, if all one wanted to do was throw the rock off-course. The virus didn't have time to do anything else.

"They'll land on the rocks in two minutes," Staci said. "Captain?"

"Detonate at one minute," Mitch ordered. The shuttles might be rigged to trigger their pushers at once. Or…they might just be carrying nukes instead. Either way, there was no point in taking chances. "Detonate *all* the asteroids. We won't get a second chance to blanket their defences."

"Aye, Captain."

Mitch braced himself. Win or lose, the face of warfare was about to change. Again. He wasn't much of a long-term thinker, but even *he* understood how different things were going to be once pusher technology became mainstream. Earth's defences would have to be redesigned, again, before someone used a pusher to smash the planet beyond repair. He shivered. There were RockRats in the Belt who loathed Earth with a passion. Who knew what they'd do if they thought they could blast the homeworld with impunity?

The display flashed red as the asteroids exploded. Hundreds of thousands of pieces of debris shot in all directions, the vast majority racing towards the planet itself. Mitch noted a handful of shuttles vanishing from the display, swatted out of existence before they even knew they were under attack. There were so many pieces of junk that the virus's defences were utterly overwhelmed. They didn't even have time to recalibrate their defences before it was too late.

"Tactical, signal the alpha sensor platforms," Mitch ordered. There was nothing to be gained by holding back now. "They are to switch to distortion mode and go live."

"Aye, Captain."

The beancounters are not going to like that, Mitch thought, with a flash of dark humour. The platforms would burn themselves out very quickly, if they didn't get blown away by the virus's defenders. He doubted they'd last long enough to give the enemy a chance. Given that the cost of each platform was staggeringly high, the bureaucratic screaming would be audible right across the human sphere. *But if it works, they'll help win us the war.*

He smiled as the torrent of debris fell through the high orbitals. The point defence opened fire, blowing hundreds of pieces of rock into dust, but there were always more taking their place. Mitch guessed that even the *dust* would make life difficult for the virus, if it fell into the planet's atmosphere. It hadn't been *that* long since the human race had been trying to create a greenhouse effect on Mars, to heat the planet in order to make it habitable. The virus's homeworld could have worse problems if it started to heat up, too.

"The rocks are ploughing through the high orbitals," Staci reported. "Their installations are taking heavy damage."

"Can we paint an entire planet on our hull?" Hinkson smirked. "Or hundreds upon hundreds of industrial stations?"

Mitch shrugged—he'd worry about bragging rights later, when they returned to Earth—and focused on the display. The planet's industrial halo was orbiting slowly, too slowly. The rocky swarm was starting to fade, shooting past the planet or into the planet's atmosphere...he saw hundreds of thousands of pieces of debris burning up, only a handful surviving long enough to strike the surface. They'd done immense damage, but it wasn't enough. The virus could rebuild, given time. He wasn't sure if the water-ice asteroids had survived long enough to carry their cargo into the planet's atmosphere and release it. There were so many pieces of junk flying around that he'd lost track.

"We took out about a third of their installations," Staci said, as red icons started to blink and vanish from the display. "Possibly more. It's hard to be sure. And we dumped a *lot* of crap into the planet's atmosphere."

Mitch cursed under his breath. Any *normal* enemy would be suing for peace while it still had something to bargain with, something it could use to get terms beyond unconditional surrender. God knew humanity had been pushed to the brink, during the war. He suspected some of the politicians would have discussed surrender, if there had been any hope of a life beyond an enemy victory. And yet, the virus had spent the last few weeks building up its point defence to truly insane levels. The planet had been hit and hit hard and—somehow—it was still in the fight. Mitch would have been impressed if he hadn't known it meant the war wasn't over yet.

"Captain, they're launching their remaining shuttles and starfighters," Staci warned. The display flared with red light. "I think they're planning to take out the active platforms."

"Order them to self-destruct, if the virus tries to grab them," Mitch said. They'd done very well. It would be easy to throw more rocks through the gap in the virus's defences. And yet, it wasn't dead. Not yet. It was still using its shuttles to clear the orbitals as much as possible, shoving debris into the planet's atmosphere or away into deep space. "Signal *Lion*. Copy our sensor records to them, then inform Commodore Hammond that we will remain in position as the battlestation arrives."

"Aye, Captain," Culver said.

Mitch leaned back in his chair. The battlestation was going to approach the planet from a slightly different angle. It was both good and bad, good because it would give the battlestation a shot at undamaged installations and bad because it would give the installations a shot at *it*. The timing was slightly fucked up...he shook his head. They still had cards to play, before they quit the system. Who knew? Maybe the relief fleet would arrive in time to finish the job, if the battlestation couldn't.

"They're starting to sweep towards us," Staci said. The display sharpened. A flight of enemy starfighters were heading on a course that would take them far too close to *Unicorn's* hiding place for comfort. "And they're dispatching a second flight towards *Lion*."

"We'll hold position as long as we can," Mitch said. They had to be close. They couldn't afford any time-delay. "And when they get close we'll cut and run, leaving them to die."

"Aye, Captain."

CHAPTER THIRTY-SEVEN

CAPTAIN CAMPBELL IS GOING TO BE INSUFFERABLE, Thomas thought. He shook his head in disbelief as more and more sensor reports flowed into the main display. *He timed it perfectly. He'd steal all the credit...*

He snorted at the thought as the shattering asteroids pounded the enemy homeworld. It was hard to track each individual piece of space junk, but it hardly mattered. Hundreds of enemy installations were destroyed or damaged, hundreds of pieces of rock fell into the planet's atmosphere...a handful even made it to the surface, wreaking immense damage. The sensors couldn't tell if any of the counter-virus had made it to the surface, let alone survived the trip, but it was just a matter of time. The virus would either have to nuke itself or risk losing what remained of the planet. It didn't have much of a choice.

The display shifted, red icons racing towards their position. The vectors were too close for it to be a coincidence. Thomas suspected the gas giant's remaining defenders had signalled ahead, probably warning their companions on Virus Prime that *Lion* was approaching on a least-time course. Or they'd simply flown too close to a stealthed sensor platform. Ironically, he found himself hoping it was the latter. If the gas giant's defenders had signalled Virus Prime, they'd probably also warned the planet about the incoming battlestation.

"Deploy gunboats," he ordered. He took a breath. "Tactical, configure missiles for long-range ballistic bombardment."

"Aye, Captain," Sibley said. "Missiles switched to bombardment mode, locked on target."

"Fire," Thomas ordered. The missiles would be effectively undetectable as long as they remained in ballistic mode. The planetary defence network had been torn to ribbons. The virus was hastily patching the holes, deploying shuttles and even destroyers in a desperate bid to regain coverage, but it simply didn't have much *time*. "Battlestation ETA?"

"The station should enter detection range in five minutes," Donker said. "Planetary impact in fourteen minutes."

Thomas waited, bracing himself. The concept had sounded insane, when Captain Campbell had proposed it. His first inclination had been to laugh in the younger man's face. It was the sort of idea someone might try in a movie—like hacking the enemy command network or flying a starfighter along a trench to put a tiny missile in a tiny hole—but not in real life. And yet, the more he considered it, the more he realised it might just work. The virus certainly wouldn't see it coming.

He frowned as the display narrowed to focus on the incoming starfighters. He wasn't too worried about a squadron or two, although he was fairly sure he'd be seeing the rest of the enemy starfighters soon enough. It was the rest of the enemy fleet that worried him. It wouldn't remain a threat for long, not given how much damage they'd wrecked on the fleet's support network, but what would it do before lack of resupply rendered it combat ineffective? Thomas wasn't sure. It might return to the planet and try to protect what remained of the planet's industries or...

The display bleeped as the battlestation came into sensor range, hurtling towards the planet at terrifying speed. Thomas noted, as the enemy starfighters hastily shifted position, that they'd slightly screwed up the aiming. He'd hoped the battlestation would have a clear flight to the surface, carrying its cargo of death down safely, but it looked as though it was going to have to fight its way through. The enemy was desperately trying to assemble a blocking force. Thomas would have been impressed, if the virus hadn't been so dangerous. He knew it had to be destroyed.

"Captain," Donker said. "The battlestation is opening fire."

Thomas nodded. They'd bolted every remaining weapon and missile pod to the battlestation, as well as taking control of its own weapons. The battlestation spat missiles and plasma fire in all directions, sweeping through enemy starfighters and defence platforms with casual ease even as it neared the planet's atmosphere. Thomas braced himself, half expecting to see a missile or mass driver projectile strike the battlestation. There was so much junk in orbit that it dawned on him, suddenly, that the battlestation might hit a piece of rock from the earlier asteroids. The irony gnawed at him as the range continued to close. The battlestation was taking damage now, but it wasn't enough. The virus had to destroy or deflect the massive structure before it was too late.

"Captain," Sibley reported. "Our ballistic missiles hit the planet's atmosphere. Three of them made it to dispersal range before they were picked off by the planetside defences. The counter-virus is loose."

It's over, Thomas thought. The planetside virus was about to die. The spaceborn would have to abandon the planet completely, cutting the planetside out of its network, if it wanted to survive. *What have we done?*

He tried not to think about it as the battlestation slipped into the planet's atmosphere and roared towards the surface. It was too big and fast and too heavily armoured to be stopped, now the defences had already been torn to ribbons. Thomas knew, without having to check, that it was already launching more and more dispersal capsules into the planet's atmosphere. The virus was doomed. It was just a matter of time. He forced himself to watch as the battlestation hit the surface, the blast terrifyingly large. The entire planet seemed to shiver as shockwaves raced around the globe, vast amounts of dust thrown up into the upper atmosphere. The poor host-bodies were going to experience a nuclear winter. Thomas shuddered. The virus wouldn't be able to keep them alive long enough to make it through the worst.

"The enemy starfighters are altering course," Sibley reported. "They're coming right at us."

"So are the shuttles," Donker said.

Thomas nodded. The virus's industrial base hadn't been destroyed, not completely, but there was no way the remnants of the virus could rebalance it before reinforcements arrived to finish the job. It would take weeks, even for the virus, to catalogue everything that had been lost and start planning how best to rebuild. Thomas would take his ships back to New Washington and ask the Americans to go on the offensive, if there wasn't already a relief fleet on its way. The remainder of the system would be swept clean, followed by the rest of infected space. It would be years, at best, before the virus was gone completely, but…he had no doubt it would be destroyed. Who knew? Perhaps it would lose enough of its cohesion to come apart completely and die.

Sure, his thoughts mocked him. *And maybe the horse will learn to sing.*

"Signal the mass drivers," he ordered. "Send their crews copies of our sensor records and targeting data, then order them to commence firing and continue until they shoot themselves dry. Once they do, they are to return to the tenders and join us at the final waypoint."

"Aye, Captain," Cook said.

Thomas keyed the display, bringing up the images from the planet. He'd never seen anything like it, even when they'd thrown rocks into the gas giant's atmosphere. The planet seemed to be wrapped in darkness, broken only by fires that had to be hundreds—perhaps thousands—of miles wide. The orbital towers had been shattered, falling to the surface and wreaking devastation; the space elevators had been yanked from orbit, often dragging the low-orbit stations down with them. The remainder of the orbital industries looked shattered, as if the network was coming apart at the seams. Thomas wondered, just for a second, if the virus was stunned. It *was* an immense brain. They'd hit it hard enough to stun it…hadn't they?

"Signal *Unicorn*," Thomas said. "The squadron is to fall back on the final waypoint."

"Aye, Captain," Cook said.

Thomas smiled. "Helm, lay in a course to the first waypoint, then take us out," he ordered. "Best possible speed."

"Aye, Captain."

• • •

Tobias frowned as another wave of enemy starfighters flew towards the gunboats, weapons blazing. The virus seemed to have forgotten everything it knew about space combat, its starfighters flying in straight lines long enough—more than long enough—for the gunboats to pick their targets and blow them out of space. Marigold kept the gunboat moving, never falling into a predictable position as the enemy starfighters and shuttles just kept coming. Tobias had a feeling they were trying to break through and throw themselves on *Lion*, before their life support failed. Their launch bases near the planet might have been wrecked by the shattering asteroids, if not the battlestation or the battlecruiser's missiles.

The datanet updated. "We have to fall back," he said. "The captain wants to leave."

He snapped orders as Marigold yanked the gunboat around, then gunned the engines. The battlecruiser was already rotating, picking up speed as she headed away from the planet. Tobias ran the calculations quickly. The enemy starfighters would only have a few more minutes to hit the battlecruiser before they passed the point of no return...he shook his head. The virus had already passed the point of no return and it knew it. The remainder of the squadron fell into a loose formation beside his gunboat, weapons still blazing. Three of the gunboats were missing. Tobias promised himself he'd mourn later.

The enemy craft kept coming, blazing past the gunboats in a desperate bid to hit the battlecruiser before she made her escape. They didn't even try to engage the gunboats in passing, although Tobias hastily shut down the suggestion the gunboats shouldn't waste their time with evasive manoeuvres. The virus might change its tactics, when it realised it had a chance to take out the gunboats too. Tobias suspected it probably wouldn't make any difference—the gunboats weren't important any longer—but he didn't want to die in the final moments of the war in space. Poor Colin was probably going to have to get down and dirty on what remained of the planet's surface. And then...

They flew into clear space as the last of the enemy craft dropped away. Tobias allowed himself a sigh of relief, then watched as Marigold steered them back towards the battlecruiser. The docking ring had never looked so welcome. His uniform felt drenched with sweat, even though the engagement hadn't lasted *that* long. He wanted to run to his bunk and get some rest, then hold the post-mission debriefing later. Perhaps a year or two later. He wondered, as he checked the remaining gunboats, if they had to even bother with a debriefing. The alien homeworld was in ruins. The remainder of the system was going to wither on the vine. And the rest of infected space would be dosed with the counter-virus, wiping out what remained of the infection. The war was over. The war was over, and he'd survived.

He grinned at Marigold's back. "When we get home, do you want to get married?"

Marigold looked at him. Her face was streaked with sweat and her eyes were tired, as tired as he felt, but he thought she'd never looked more beautiful. So what if she wasn't a perfect babe with a perfect figure, the kind of porn actress he'd drooled over in his younger days? Everyone knew they didn't really exist, even with the finest cosmetic surgery known to man. They were just computer-generated figures...

"If we get home," she said, quietly. "We're not out of the woods yet."

Tobias sobered. She was right.

He keyed his console. "You may disembark from your gunboats, but do not leave Gunboat Country," he ordered. "Remain in the squadron room if possible. We might have to return to the fray."

Marigold winked as Tobias stood. "It's bad luck to ask before we get home," she said. "But ask me when we do."

"I will," Tobias promised.

He smiled as he opened the hatch and headed down to the squadron room. There should be time to grab a quick shower and a bite to eat, then remain ready just in case they had to return to their craft. And then... he allowed himself to think, not for the first time, of what life would be like after the war. He'd be a *bona fide* war hero in a society that respected its heroes, that gave them all the opportunities in the world. And he was owed a chunk of prize money, too. And...

And if she comes with me, he told himself, *what does it matter? We'll have each other.*

• • •

"*Unicorn* is keeping pace with us on a parallel course," Donker reported. "We've exchanged sensor logs and the tactical staff is studying them now."

Thomas nodded. He couldn't help feeling uneasy. He wanted to believe that the virus had gone crazy, after its homeworld had been bombarded; he wanted to believe they'd hurt the virus so badly it had been lashing out in helpless rage. And yet, Virus Prime wasn't the first infected world to be hammered from orbit. HMS *Invincible* had laid waste to Alien-One, back in the early years of the war, while Operation Lightning Strike had taken out several more. The virus had lost and lost badly, but enough to drive it mad? He doubted it.

He cursed under his breath. They'd stripped the cupboard bare. They'd fired all of their sensor probes, deployed all of their remaining sensor platforms...they were dependent upon their inbuilt passive sensors and *they'd* been badly damaged. The alien starfighters had raked the hull with plasma fire, taking out a bunch of sensor nodes as well as point defence weapons. Thomas refused to believe it was a coincidence. The virus had been trying to soften them up.

"Order engineering to do what they can," he said, tiredly. "And keep me appraised of their progress."

He was tempted to order the duo to head into empty space, in hopes of finding a place they could hide long enough for the relief fleet to arrive, but...he shook his head. The enemy had one last fleet. He wanted to believe, as Captain Campbell had urged, that the enemy fleet had already been destroyed...he knew, all too well, that he didn't *dare* believe it. The fleet might be heading to Earth, in a desperate bid to extract revenge, or it might be returning to the alien homeworld to save what it could. And, perhaps, to smash *Lion* and *Unicorn* to atoms. The virus had never shown anything resembling vengefulness, let alone any awareness of humans as individuals, but...he sighed. They'd just have to sneak onwards and hope for the best.

"Maintain a full sensor watch at all times," he added. "We'll assume the worst and remain concealed, as best as possible, until we encounter friendly ships or return to New Washington."

He keyed the console, looking at the projections without quite seeing them. They were burned into his mind. The virus would presumably have signalled its fleet—or at least it would have *tried* to signal the fleet—the moment it realised the asteroids had been converted into thousands upon thousands of pieces of space junk. How long would it have taken for the message to reach the fleet? Had the fleet made it through the tramline? What would it have decided to do? He needed answers and he didn't have them. His eyes hardened as he calculated the vectors. If the fleet had reversed course at once, his ships would be under its guns by now.

"Signal *Unicorn*," he ordered. "She is to take point and alert us if she picks up any sign of incoming starships."

"Aye, Captain," Cook said.

Thomas grimaced, feeling tired beyond words. Some wanker looking for a hot story was probably going to read the mission logs and accuse him of trying a Uriah Gambit. The military logic was on his side, but what did logic and reason matter in the face of tabloid bullshit? *Unicorn* was far more capable of maintaining a passive sensor watch than her bigger sister, far more capable of evading enemy contact if they flew straight into a trap. And yet…he shook his head. He'd endure the nastiest the tabloids could throw at him if it meant getting his ship and crew home. The Admiralty would have to agree with his logic. Probably.

He forced himself to stay on the bridge as the hours ticked onwards. It would be easy to detach *Unicorn* and send her to pick up the marines, or launch kinetic strikes on the remaining enemy colonies, but there was no time. He needed resupply urgently. He needed to get back through the tramline. He needed…the lack of activity behind them bothered him. The virus wasn't prone to simply giving up. It was up to something. But what?

"Captain, I picked up a pusher drive signature," Sibley said. "It's right on the other side of the system."

Thomas frowned as an icon flickered briefly on the display, then faded. "Did they just hurl an asteroid at us?"

"I don't think so." Sibley sounded doubtful. "Unless they have some way of steering the asteroid, their accuracy would have to improve a great deal before it could be described as terrible. Our course isn't that predictable. We only hit the planet because we knew where it would be when the asteroids reached their target."

"Curious," Thomas mused. "Are they testing the device?"

"It's possible, but we didn't pick up anything beyond the pusher pulse itself," Sibley cautioned. "They might have tried to launch a starship with it…"

The display sparkled with red light. "Incoming missiles! I say again, incoming missiles!"

"Evasive action." Thomas snapped. The enemy ships had sneaked up on them from the side, evading both *Lion* and *Unicorn*. "Point defence, rapid fire!"

But he knew, even as he spoke, that it was too late.

CHAPTER THIRTY-EIGHT

"ENEMY CONTACTS," STACI SNAPPED. "They're materialising near *Lion*!"

Mitch blanched. He'd assumed the enemy fleet would double back, giving *Unicorn* a chance to detect its presence before it was too late. He would have had time to warn *Lion* and evade incoming fire himself, before the range closed to point-blank range. Instead, the enemy fleet had approached from a different angle, allowing them to evade detection until they opened fire. *Unicorn* was badly out of position and *Lion* was under heavy attack. Commodore Hammond was in deep shit.

"Helm, bring us about," Mitch snapped. "Tactical, prepare to engage."

His mind raced. It would be easy to evade contact themselves, to remain under cloak long enough to escape, but he couldn't abandon the battlecruiser. The ship and her crew needed to be saved. And yet…he found himself staring at the display, unable to determine a way for *Lion* to escape. She was trapped. Commodore Hammond would alter course at once, and ramp up his drives to maximum, but there was no way in hell the range would open wide enough for the battlecruiser to flee before she was blown away. The enemy had timed their ambush perfectly. Mitch couldn't help thinking that, in the final months of its existence, the virus had finally learnt how to be spiteful.

"Deploy two stealth drones," he ordered. They were the last on his ship...he snorted. The odds of them getting home to grovel before the beancounters were infinitesimal. "Prepare to launch missiles as we close the range."

His heart sank as more and more enemy ships came into view. A brainship, a handful of battleships, a pair of carriers...it didn't look as if the *entire* enemy fleet had doubled back, but it was quite possible the remainder of the ships were hiding under cloak. There was so much distortion in local space that it was impossible to detect any subtle signs of their presence. He glanced at the long-range passive sensors, hoping to see the relief fleet flying to the rescue, but the display was blank. *Lion* and *Unicorn* remained alone. The fleet tenders weren't designed to stand in the line of battle and even if they had been, they were too far away to help. He tapped a console, sending the tenders strict orders to remain out of sight. They couldn't help and they'd only get blown away if they tried. Better they remained hidden until the relief fleet arrived. It was only a matter of time.

"They're concentrating on *Lion*," Staci reported. "There's no hint they've seen us. Not yet."

"Good." Mitch knew it *wasn't* good. Better to have the virus shooting at the frigate rather than the battlecruiser. Not that it would make much difference, he conceded ruefully. There was so much firepower bearing down on them that both ships would be rapidly obliterated if they didn't escape quickly. "Prepare to deploy our remaining sensor decoys, then set course into the enemy formation."

"Aye, Captain," Staci said. Her hands danced across the console. "Readying the drones now."

Mitch nodded to himself, sensing the frisson of fear and grim resolve flashing around the bridge. The crew knew they could escape, but the price would be leaving *Lion* to the wolves. They were ready to sell their lives dearly, if they couldn't force the enemy to flinch long enough to give both ships a chance to run. It wasn't much of a tactic, Mitch thought, but it was all they had. There was no hope of saving both ships unless they did something desperate.

And if it fails, he thought as he studied the vectors on his console, *we'll have no time to think of something else.*

. . .

"Alter course," Thomas snapped. The tidal wave of enemy missiles was coming towards them at a terrifying rate, but…they could alter course. "Ramp up the drives, maximum speed."

"Aye, Captain," Fitzgerald said.

"Deploy sensor decoys, launch gunboats," Thomas added. It was too late for the gunboats to take the offensive, but they might add enough firepower to the point defence for the battlecruiser to survive. He knew it was wishful thinking…he pushed the thought out of his head. He wasn't going to give up, even if all he could do was kick and scratch on the way to the gallows. "Target the enemy brainship and engage with our remaining missiles. Do not hold anything back."

He groaned as the enemy missiles roared closer. *Lion* was altering course, preparing to show the enemy her rear, but she didn't have *time*. She was going to take one hell of a beating…he cursed, under his breath, as the missiles refused to be decoyed away. The point defence was spitting death and defiance into the teeth of the onslaught, wiping out dozens of missiles, but the remainder were coming closer and closer. His console bleeped, warning him that the gunboat launch had been delayed. There was little hope of getting them into space before…

Lion lurched. Alarms howled. Thomas gripped his command chair as the gravity field flickered, red lights flaring on the status display as enemy weapons stabbed deep into his hull. His ship was dying…. he heard urgent calls for everything from damage control to medical assistance echoing through the communications channels, the marines and engineering crews trying desperately to locate and report the damaged sectors so they could be prioritised for repair. The ship had been hit so badly that they'd even lost sections of the datanet…Thomas's lips curled in a flicker of gallows humour. If nothing else, losing the datanet would tell them which parts of the ship were beyond immediate repair.

"Captain, we took five direct hits," Donker reported. The chief engineer and his time would be trying to cope with the disaster. They didn't have time to report to their commanding officer. "Two drive nodes are gone. The gunboat launching ring has been put out of commission. The gunboats themselves have been destroyed."

That's going to look terrible on my record, Thomas thought. He should have ordered the gunboat crews to stay in their craft, even though they'd *needed* their rest. He'd relaxed and his ship and crew had paid the price for it. He was going to be marched in front of a court-martial when he got home…he told himself firmly that he should count himself lucky to survive long enough to be court-martialled. If he did, his crew would survive too. *It would be a small price to pay for keeping the crew alive.*

He winced as the damage continued to mount. *Lion* still had most of her drive nodes, but if she lost one or two more she was going to lose speed rapidly. The enemy fleet had already built up a considerable speed advantage…hell, they were *continuing* to accelerate. Thomas didn't need the computer simulations to know that, even in the best-case scenario, his ship was going to be within enemy range for at least twenty minutes. His lips quirked. That was at least ten minutes longer than it would take the enemy to blow them to dust. He doubted the virus would try to board his ship. There was nothing to be gained from infecting his crew. He'd blow up the ship himself, rather than let her fall into enemy hands.

The hull shook as missile after missile was launched towards the alien fleet. The tactical staff had reprogrammed them, setting the laser warheads to detonate as soon as they entered range, but they weren't anything like as effective as they *needed* to be. The combination of seeker heads and decoys should have been enough to get them through the enemy defences, but the damned brainship was holding the enemy fleet together and coordinating its point defence. Thomas tried to come up with a plan for taking the brainship out, but nothing came to mind. The brainship was just too heavily defended. He was fairly sure that even reversing course and trying to *ram* the ship would be ineffective. The battleships would blow *Lion* to hell before she got close enough to ram the brainship.

The virus knows the war is over, Thomas thought. It made no sense. The enemy fleet could have fled, snatching up what freighters and mobile industrial units it could before setting course for unexplored regions of space. It would be months, at least, before any sort of pursuit could be organised. *Why is it so determined to revenge itself on us?*

The battlecruiser shuddered again as more enemy missiles struck home. Thomas gritted his teeth as red lights flashed again, a number refusing to fade. The hull was taking a beating. Heavy armour plates had been blown off, leaving gashes in the hull...it was just a matter of time, despite the dodging, before a nuclear warhead exploded *inside* the hull, blowing the ship to hell. Thomas considered ordering his crew to abandon ship, but he knew it would be pointless. The virus would capture the lifepods and infect the crews, or simply blow the pods to dust. There was no time for *Unicorn* to recover the lifepods. Hell, there was no time for the frigate to do much of anything.

Guess you won after all, Campbell, Thomas thought, morbidly. He didn't feel any anger or rage or hatred, merely calm acceptance. *I won't be coming back from this engagement, but you might.*

"Signal to *Unicorn*," he said. "Copy our final logs to her, then order her to break contact and run. I say again, break contact and run."

"Aye," Captain," Cook said.

Thomas gritted his teeth as he looked around the bridge. The battlecruiser was dying. A drive node was flickering orange on the display, suggesting it was on the verge of failing; the missile tubes were running out of missiles to throw at the enemy ships. The point defence was holding, but the weapons blisters and sensor nodes were being picked off one by one. Thomas had seen the pattern before. The enemy was weakening his defences, each hit ensuring more hits...it was just a matter of time until the end. His crew were holding steady, calm and composed, even though they *had* to know the end was near. Thomas felt a surge of pride as another bomb-pumped laser struck his ship, burning through his armour and digging deep into his hull. They deserved better.

We won the war, he told himself. *Even if we lost the battle, we won the war.*

• • •

Tobias had been half-asleep in his bunk when the alarms howled. He'd thrown himself out of bed, grabbing his helmet with one hand and his terminal with the other, an instant before the ship had been hit. The force of the impact had thrown him to the deck, hard enough to hurt. The lights flickered and died, emergency lighting snapping on a moment later. Tobias grunted as someone crashed down beside him, then rolled over and stood. The hatch was sealed. Blinking red lights warned that the compartments beyond had been depressurised.

Panic shot through him as he keyed his wristcom. He should have had a direct connection to Bagehot, if not to the XO himself, but the communications network was down. Tobias switched the wristcom to direct communications, rather than relying on the onboard datanet, yet there was still no response. The sense of panic, of being alone in a dying ship, was almost overwhelming. He wanted to hide under the bed, to curl up into a ball and wait for rescue...he wanted someone else, anyone else, to take the burden from him. But there was no one. It dawned on him, too late, that *he* was in charge.

He tried to raise his voice. "Grab your emergency kits," he ordered. His voice shook as he surveyed the compartment. There were twelve pilots. The remainder of his pilots and the maintenance crews were nowhere to be seen. There was nothing he could do for them. "We may need to move."

"Something's hissing," a pilot said. "The air is going."

"Get your masks into position, but don't turn the oxygen on until you need it," Tobias snapped. He forced himself to think. The shipsuits weren't as capable as regular spacesuits, he'd been warned, but they'd keep their wearers alive in vacuum long enough to reach an emergency shelter. The instructors had been very clear that they had to find emergency supplies—or make it to a shelter—before they ran out of air, or they'd die. They'd been almost brutally blunt. "We have to move."

He tried to think. What would Stellar Star do? No, that was a bad example. *She'd* take off her clothes and have an orgy. What would *Colin* do? He'd try to escape the compartment and find safety, if there was any to be found. There might be sealed compartments designed to serve as shelters, if the battlecruiser came under attack, but they wouldn't provide much protection if the enemy blew the ship to atoms. Tobias knew that—normally—they'd be expected to stay put, to wait for emergency crews to find them. That wasn't going to happen. They had no way of contacting the marines or the engineering crews and the air was running out. They had to move.

"Check your masks and suits," he ordered. The tiny hatch display indicated the corridor beyond was depressurised. "And then we'll move out."

He glanced at Marigold, then checked everyone was ready, slotted his mask into place and keyed the hatch. It opened slowly, the remaining atmosphere within the compartment rushing out into the darkness. Tobias silently blessed the navy's paranoia as he switched on his flashlight. The corridor beyond was dark, dark and silent. Tobias thought, for a horrified moment, that they'd somehow gotten really lost. The bulkheads were torn and broken, the gunboat launching ring shattered...he could see *stars* beyond, spinning madly as the ship rotated. They were under attack. He swallowed—his mouth was suddenly dry—and led the way down the ruined corridor. It wasn't easy. He knew where he was—where they had to be—and yet everything had changed. The lights and displays were gone. The bulkheads, shattered and ruined. He had the sudden impression they were alone, hunted by aliens from humanity's nightmares. The shadows seemed to move, shapes within them moving menacingly at the corner of his eye. He wished, suddenly, for a pistol. If they'd been boarded...

Tobias stumbled, nearly tripping over something on the deck. He looked down and saw a blackened shape. It was so badly burned it took him a moment to realise it was a body. He couldn't tell if it was male or female, human or alien…he felt his gorge rise and looked away hastily. Throwing up in a spacesuit was bad enough, he'd been warned, but vomiting in a breather mask was the worst. He would be lucky if he didn't suffocate. He forced himself to push on, leaving the body behind. A hatch loomed up in front of him, locked solid. Tobias keyed the controls, but nothing happened. He sagged, then forced his crew to keep moving. There were other hatches. There were other ways to reach safety.

Another humanoid shape appeared in front of them. Tobias flinched, one hand reaching for the pistol he wasn't carrying. He froze instead, ice trickling down his spine. If the ship had been boarded…he breathed a sigh of relief as he spied the marine combat suit. The marine nodded to them, then pointed to a distant hatch. Tobias nodded back, wondering if it was Colin behind the tinted helmet. Who knew?

They stepped through the airlock, into a chamber of horrors. The corridor beyond looked to have been scorched. Fires were burning, the heat searing his skin. Tobias saw the marines at the far end, trying to dampen the blaze. They could simply open the airlock and vent the entire passageway, depriving the fire of oxygen…he forced himself to run on, waving to the marines. The entire ship heaved again, the impact nearly throwing him into the inferno. He hurried past the marines and further down the corridor. It was hard to tell who, if anyone, was in command. The marines seemed cut off from the rest of the ship.

A mid-ranking officer greeted them as they reached the lower compartment. "Good to see you," he said. "If you're injured, report to the medics. If not, stay here. There's shit to do here."

Tobias removed his mask. "Yes, sir."

• • •

Thomas knew it was just a matter of time before the end. His ship was dying. His sensors were badly weakened, crippling what remained of the point defence. The damage was mounting up too rapidly for the damage control teams to handle. He'd already ordered a number of compartments to be sealed off and abandoned while the damage control teams focused on the drive nodes and internal datanets. He was all too aware he'd probably sacrificed a number of his crewmen, leaving them to die in isolated sections that had been separated from the greater whole, yet…what choice did he have?

The thought was agony. What choice did he have?

"Captain," Sibley said. "We're firing the last salvo now."

"Noted," Thomas said. It didn't matter. The virus wasn't being remotely deterred by *Lion's* desperate flailing. The range was steadily closing. The enemy ships would start slamming plasma bolts into his ship's hull soon enough. And then…his ship would be blown to atoms. "Have you copied our last records to *Unicorn*?"

"Yes, Captain," Cook said. "She hasn't acknowledged."

Thomas blinked as the display updated, then flashed with green icons. "What the fuck is she doing?"

CHAPTER THIRTY-NINE

MITCH KNEW HE WAS ABOUT TO DISOBEY ORDERS— that, in a sense, he was *already* disobeying orders—but he found it hard to care. *Lion* carried over a thousand crewmen. She couldn't be abandoned without due cause, even if he'd been *ordered* to turn his back and run. Honour demanded he make an attempt to save her. He owed it to the navy he loved. And besides, he didn't know how he'd handle peacetime.

Charlotte was talking about a political career for me, he thought. *But it would be as boring as fuck.*

"Activate the drones, then take us in after them," he ordered. "Take us right down their throats."

"Aye, Captain," Staci said. "Drones going online...now."

Mitch leaned forward. The virus either hadn't noticed *Unicorn* or had chosen to ignore her. They hadn't even spared a pair of cruisers to chase her away, perhaps believing her meagre firepower was irrelevant to a clash of the titans. Mitch had to admit the virus was probably right to ignore the little frigate, but there was no way it could ignore the drones. It looked as if an entire fleet had decloaked, aiming to slam right into the enemy formation. The virus *needed* to take evasive action. And if it did, *Lion* would have a chance to escape.

"Captain," Culver said. "Signal from *Lion*!"

"Ignore it," Mitch ordered. If the plan worked, the court-martial would be nothing more than a hasty whitewash. The Admiralty couldn't afford to court-martial a naval hero who'd saved a battlecruiser from certain destruction. If the plan failed...there wouldn't be enough of him left to pick up with a pair of tweezers, let alone be put in front of a Board of Inquiry. "Helm, continue on our current course."

Sweat poured down his back as the range started to close. The virus *had* to have seen the drones coming. They were *designed* to be noticed. Mitch was fairly sure most of the enemy ships were undamaged. *Lion* had fought like—his lips twisted into a grim smile—a lion, but she hadn't been able to do more than buy a few seconds of time. The enemy shouldn't have any trouble whatsoever seeing the incoming fleet of ghosts, let alone deciding what to do about it. They had to assume the fleet was real and take evasive action. It was the only sensible course.

His eyes narrowed. The virus wasn't responding. It hadn't even swept the drones with active sensors, let alone altered course to close or widen the range. Mitch shivered. It looked as if an entire fleet was about to slam straight into the virus's flanks. It *had* to take the bait.

It isn't taking the bait, Mitch thought, numbly. The virus was simply ignoring the drones. Of *course* it was. It had been fooled so often it was determined not to be fooled again. As long as the ghost ships didn't open fire—and they couldn't—they could be safely ignored. The virus knew he was bluffing. *It isn't working.*

Staci put it into words. "Captain, they're not altering course."

Mitch stared at the display. *Lion's* drive field was starting to flicker. It wouldn't be long before she started to lose speed, ensuring her destruction. He could obey orders—he could break off and run—and yet that would mean leaving the battlecruiser to his fate. And...what did he have to live for, in the post-war world? He was likely to be discharged from the navy as soon as it became politically possible. He certainly wouldn't be allowed to keep his ship.

A thought crossed his mind. Did he dare...?

He smiled. Of *course* he dared.

"Helm, continue on our current course," he ordered. "XO, declare a stage-two evacuation."

Staci blinked, then smiled. "Aye, Captain."

Mitch leaned forward. "Switch helm and tactical control to my console," he added. "And then order the remaining crew to the lifepods."

"Sir?"

"You heard me," Mitch said. He dug into his pocket, looking for the three recordings he'd made. One for Charlotte, one for the admiral, one for Staci herself. "Go."

• • •

There were times, Thomas knew, when an officer had a duty to disobey orders. There were certain orders that should never be given, he'd been taught, and others that had been issued in ignorance of the true situation. And yet, the navy was reluctant to rubberstamp outright disobedience. There was *always* a court-martial, even if it was nothing more than official confirmation of what everyone already knew to be true. Captain Campbell would be in deep shit if he ever got home.

And yet...Thomas silently gave him points for trying. Deploying his remaining drones in a bid to frighten the enemy was good thinking, even though it had clearly failed. Thomas wasn't surprised. The virus hadn't *needed* to see through the decoys to guess the fleet was nothing more than sensor ghosts. The fleet was already close enough to start launching missiles and starfighters into the enemy formation. The absence of incoming fire told the virus everything it needed to know. The incoming fleet simply didn't exist.

"Signal to *Unicorn*," he grated. The virus would blow the frigate out of space if she got any closer. A single salvo of plasma bursts would reduce the ship to atoms. "She is to alter course and depart at once."

"No response, sir," Cook said.

"Damn him," Thomas said. The battlecruiser was doomed. There was nothing to be gained by hurling the frigate into the fire. It wouldn't make any real difference, beyond ensuring that two ships would be lost instead of one. "Order him to..."

He broke off as the display updated. *Unicorn* was launching lifepods. Thomas stared. It was madness. The lifepods were being launched right in the middle of an engagement. They would be picked off by the virus... they would be...a thought crossed his mind, sending a shiver running through him. Was Captain Campbell insane? Or was he crazy like a fox?

The vectors converged rapidly. It was too late for the frigate to escape.

• • •

"Captain," Staci said. "You should..."

"I told you to go," Mitch said. He shoved the datachips into her hand. "That's an order."

Staci hesitated. Mitch had to smile. He was expecting her to follow orders from her superior while *he* was ignoring orders from *his* superior. The messages from *Lion* had tailed off as the range continued to close, perhaps showing a grim awareness that the frigate was now doomed unless the enemy continued to ignore her. Mitch would settle for a few more minutes. The virus had decided the ghosts didn't exist. It was almost right.

"Go," he said. "Tell Charlotte to live well."

"It's been an honour," Staci said. She saluted, then turned away. "Good luck, sir."

Mitch watched her run from the bridge—the last escape pod was only a few short metres away—and turned his attention back to the display. It was impossible for one man to control an entire starship by himself for long, but he wouldn't have to do it for more than a handful of minutes. The automatics could handle everything, as long as the enemy didn't open fire. Mitch had a healthy respect for the massive plasma cannons on the battleships, weapons designed for hammering other battleships. *Unicorn* wouldn't stand up to their fire for more than a second or two. A single hit would be enough to knock her out of the engagement once and for all.

He programmed the firing sequence into his terminal as the range continued to close. The virus was ignoring him. It had to be feeling very sure of itself, he noted; it had reason to think the incoming fleet was nothing more than sensor ghosts. No incoming fleet, under a sane commander, would hold its fire. The fleet could have devastated the alien ships if it had opened fire.

If the fleet was real, he thought. *But only one of the incoming ships is anything more than a sensor ghost.*

The virus's brainship was growing larger and larger on the display. Mitch finished the firing sequence, then braced himself and keyed the drive to maximum. The frigate lurched and shot forward violently, red lights flickering on the display as the drive nodes threatened to overload. Mitch ignored the warnings. There was no hope of escape. The missiles started to launch, laser warheads detonating almost as soon as they cleared their launch tubes...well within danger range. The brainship staggered under their fire. Beside it, the battleships staggered as well. It was too late to bring their point defence to bear.

Mitch watched, calmly, as the range fell to zero. His life flashed in front of his eyes. It had been a good life, he supposed. He'd commanded starships, he'd led men into battle, he'd been a success in his chosen career...he'd die, like Nelson, before time could wash away his victories and leave him exposed to his enemies. Charlotte would go on without him, he thought. The loss of her lover might even work in her favour. Mitch silently wished her well. And her husband, too. They didn't *need* to destroy each other...

The frigate slammed into the brainship with staggering force. There were no survivors.

• • •

Thomas stared as the brainship was wiped from existence, the enemy formation staggering under the completely unexpected attack. Captain Campbell had timed it well, he noted. He'd held his fire right up until the last moment. A frigate was normally no threat to a battleship, but the missiles had been fired and detonated from point-blank range. And the explosion had been violent enough to damage the enemy command and control network beyond repair. He had a chance to escape...

"Direct all remaining power to the drives," he ordered. If they could get out of immediate range, they might just be able to shut down everything and go doggo until the relief fleet finally arrived. It wasn't the best plan in the navy's long history, and trying to recover the lifepods would risk detection once again, but he couldn't think of anything better. In hindsight, he shouldn't have fired his remaining missiles. He could have given the alien fleet a hammering before it could recover from the lost brainship. "Get us out of here!"

"Aye, Captain."

Thomas allowed himself a moment of hope as the range started to open once again. The enemy ships seemed confused, some continuing the pursuit while others held back as if they were unsure what to do. Thomas hoped the virus wouldn't be able to link up again in a hurry. It was hard to imagine how it worked, how the different collections of viral matter determined who was in charge...he prayed, silently, there'd be enough confusion to give them a chance to make it back. God knew it wasn't always easy for the Royal Navy to determine who should be in command, when the enemy missiles started exploding and the chain of command shattered under their fire. There'd been engagements where a junior officer had assumed command, in the honest belief he was the highest-ranking survivor. He had the nasty feeling the virus would find it a little easier...

"Captain, the enemy ships are forming up again," Sibley reported. "They're accelerating."

Thomas shook his head. The virus's ships seemed to have lost the elegance the brainships brought to its formation, but it hardly mattered. The tactical equation was very simple. All they had to do was chase down *Lion* and batter her to scrap. And they were likely to succeed. He didn't have anything left to throw at them, not even the kitchen sink. His mind raced, trying to think of ways to dump makeshift mines in their path, but there was nothing. His ship and crew had already been crippled. They didn't have the time to recover before it was too late.

"Continue on our current course," he ordered. The enemy fleet would expend a great deal of irreplaceable weapons and drive components catching up with him. They would wither on the vine, unable to resupply before the relief fleet finished the job. "And continue to divert power to the drives."

"Aye, Captain."

Thomas reached for his console, then stopped himself. What could he say to his crew? Tell them they were doomed? Tell them that their one moment of hope hadn't lasted long enough for them to realise it had even existed? Tell them...he knew, all too well, that they already knew. His crew wasn't composed of children. They were naval officers and crew who *knew* their luck had finally run out. They wouldn't escape. They would never see their homes and families again. And their only consolation was that the virus had been broken. It would be a long, hard slog to clean up the mess, to purge and resettle the infected worlds, but it would be done. The war in space was effectively over.

A shudder ran through his ship. The virus disagreed.

Thomas shook his head. Captain Campbell was dead. His trick had brought *Lion* a few more seconds, but...Thomas sighed. It would have been easier, perhaps, if he could have hated the younger man. God knew his marriage had been in trouble well before he'd invited Captain Campbell into his home. He'd never liked Campbell, but...there wasn't any point in dwelling on it. The man was—had been—the sum of his actions, not just *one* action. The navy would probably be quietly relieved he'd died bravely. It would honour his name, perhaps even raise a statue in his honour, then try to forget his failings...

A dull thud echoed through the compartment. The gravity field flickered, threatening to die. Thomas didn't have to look at the displays to know they'd reached the end of the line. Two drive nodes were gone, destroyed by enemy missiles or overwork. The drive field was failing. They were losing speed rapidly, so rapidly there was a very real prospect of the enemy overshooting them. Thomas would have been gratified, if he'd had the weapons to take advantage of it. Instead…

"Thank you, all of you," he said. "It's been an honour."

The display updated, again. "Incoming missiles! Incoming missiles!"

Thomas blinked as green icons flared to life. They were firing on the enemy ships…the virus had been ambushed, as surely as it had ambushed *Lion* earlier. Hope washed through him as the newcomers pounded the enemy ship, hurling salvo after salvo of missiles into their formation… and, behind them, hundreds of starfighters. The virus's ships seemed to hesitate, then altered course…too late. Thomas let out a breath he hadn't realised he'd been holding. The newcomers had saved them in the nick of time.

"Captain," Cook said. "We're being hailed."

"Put them through," Thomas ordered.

Admiral Onarina's face appeared in front of him. "I'm sorry we're late."

Thomas had to smile. "You're just in time," he said. "They had us."

"We crept up on them while they were focused on you," Admiral Onarina said. "Do you require medical or engineering assistance?"

"I'm afraid so, Admiral," Thomas said. He checked the latest damage report. His ship had been shot full of holes. He had the uncomfortable feeling she was going to be scrapped when she returned home. If she ever did…it might be deemed cost-effective to simply abandon her in the alien system, perhaps converting her into a research station near the alien sphere. "I'll forward my report to you."

"I look forward to speaking to you in person, once we have finished the job here," Admiral Onarina said. "And help will be on the way shortly."

Her image vanished. Thomas sat back in his chair, letting out a long sigh of relief. The newcomers had finished off the remaining enemy capital ships and were now exterminating the cruisers. The fight was over. And he'd survived. He took a moment to enjoy the sense of just being *alive*, then stood and keyed his console. His ship was in a terrible state. If the

Admiral wanted to be piped onboard, it was going to be hellishly difficult.

She'll understand, Thomas told himself. Admiral Onarina was a fighting admiral who'd worked her way up through the ranks. She wouldn't be offended by the lack of a formal welcome. She'd understand that *Lion's* crew were too busy trying to save the wounded, patching up the hull and keeping their vessel alive as long as possible. *Of course she'll understand.*

"XO, take command of the recovery efforts," he ordered. "Keep me informed."

"Aye, Captain," Donker said.

Thomas nodded as he studied the reports. They were going to limp home. It wasn't going to be easy, but...he frowned. They could do it. He wasn't going to abandon his ship, not unless there was no other choice. And once they got home...

"Captain," Cook said. "Admiral Onarina's compliments, sir, and she requests permission to board along with the relief shuttles."

"Granted," Thomas said. He could hardly have said *no*. Technically, sure, but it would have been career suicide. "Order her shuttle to dock at the forward airlock. I'll meet her there."

His console bleeped. "Captain, this is Troy in Tactical," a female voice said. "I have something you really should look at."

Thomas frowned. "I have to greet Admiral Onarina," he said. He vaguely remembered Hannah Troy, one of the tactical analysts who was more interested in her field than promotion. She had little sense of the social graces...he grimaced, recalling cautionary tales of analysts who couldn't be allowed to speak directly to flag officers. "Can it wait?"

"The admiral should see it, too," Hannah said. She sounded surprisingly insistent. "This is important."

"Is it?" Thomas scowled. The ship was a wreck, at least a third of the crew were dead or seriously injured...it better *had* be important. "Report to my Ready Room in thirty minutes. You can show it to both of us."

"Aye, Captain," Hannah said.

CHAPTER FORTY

"YOU ARE SURE OF THIS?" Admiral Onarina looked thoroughly displeased. "There's no room for mistakes?"

"Yes, Admiral," Hannah said. She was a slight woman, with an air of perpetual disconnection from the world. "I was able to confirm it through long-range optical sensors on the remaining platforms. There is no doubt."

Thomas swore under his breath. "That's why they attacked us," he said. He'd *wondered* about that. The virus wasn't normally spiteful. "They wanted to make sure word didn't reach the rest of the human sphere."

"I believe so, Captain," Hannah said. "They clearly assumed the worst."

"Yes." Thomas looked down at the sensor images. The virus had worked overtime, putting pushers into production and fitting them onto asteroids. Instead of hurling the asteroids at his ship, they'd launched them into interstellar space at terrifying speed. Thomas could figure out the rest for himself. The virus had crammed itself into the asteroids, relying on its base cells to survive the sudden burst of acceleration. "How do they intend to slow down when they reach their destination?"

"They would have installed a second pusher," Hannah said. "We never bothered, sir, because we wanted the asteroids to hit the planet at speed. The virus will have to slow down before it plunges into an alien star. There's no other way to do it."

Thomas shook his head. He should have expected it. The first contact with the virus—although no one had realised the truth until it was too late—had been through a STL colony ship. Why would it not rely on something similar to save itself from total defeat? He cursed under his breath as he studied the starchart. The virus's asteroids were already well out of interception range. There was little hope of catching them…they'd have to send ships through the tramlines, deep into unexplored space, in hopes of arranging a welcoming committee. And if they missed a single asteroid, and if that asteroid found a civilisation it could infect…

"Our descendants may find themselves refighting the war," he mused. "Unless…can we hit them with mass drivers?"

"It's possible," Hannah said. "But we might never *know* we'd succeeded."

"I think that's a problem for later," Admiral Onarina said. "Right now, we have other problems."

Thomas nodded. "Dismissed," he said. "Report back to the tactical department and wait."

He watched Hannah go, then looked at the admiral. "You saved our bacon."

"Thank your wife." The admiral's lips curved into something that might—charitably—have been called a smile. "She helped get the politics in order."

"Good for her." Thomas was too tired to feel much of anything. "I'm sure she'll do well for herself."

"Quite." Admiral Onarina leaned back in her chair. "We punched out from New Washington and made our way here, taking the time to hit the infected worlds along the way and cut loose destroyers to deal with the planets off the beaten track. We're cataloguing the remaining infected systems and facilities now, in hopes of completing the job—or as much of it as possible—before the virus tries to recover. Our lords and masters may wish to leave a lone colony intact, for further study, but until we receive specific orders to spare one we'll continue with the destruction. We don't want another outbreak."

And you don't want someone trying to convert the virus into a weapon, Thomas added, silently. *The risks of losing control are just too high.*

"My ships can handle that," the admiral continued. "Your engineer appears to believe your ship can make her own way home, once a couple of drive nodes are replaced and the hull is patched. If that's the case, I have no objection to attaching *Lion* to the squadron that will be returning to New Washington, picking up the other damaged ships along the way. Once you get there, you can proceed to Earth as you see fit. Don't be ashamed to ask for a tow if you need it. Your ship was badly damaged. Some of the damage may not become evident until you get back underway."

"Yes, Admiral," Thomas said. "I'm sure we can make it home."

"I hope so," the admiral agreed. "You'll have to give some thought to your future, of course."

"Of course," Thomas echoed. He was fairly sure he'd be offered a promotion to admiral. He was more than just a war hero. He'd been in command of the operation that had won the war. And...he sighed, inwardly. Perhaps he could find another command instead. He didn't really *want* to leave the navy. "We'll see how things go."

"And try not to be too hard on your wife," Admiral Onarina added. "Let her go."

"I wasn't planning to do otherwise," Thomas said. "I..."

He snorted. Captain Campbell was dead. Thomas would have to think of something nice to say at the man's funeral. The tabloids were going to have a field day. Perhaps he'd strike a Marc Antony pose and praise Captain Campbell as an honourable man...he shook his head in amused annoyance. The media would claim Captain Campbell as a war hero, as a man who had died in the final moments of the war...a man who had fallen at the hour of his greatest victory. It would take time for the truth to muddy the man's reputation and by then...who'd care? England had thrown Lady Hamilton aside as soon as Lord Nelson, her lover, was dead and enshrined in myth. Perhaps it would do the same to Charlotte.

It can do whatever it pleases, Thomas thought. *I will do nothing.*

The admiral stood. "You did well, Captain. Earth will be grateful."

"Thank you," Thomas said. "And I hope it won't forget the cost."

He glanced at his terminal. Three hundred and seven crewmen had died on *Lion*. Only one person had died on *Unicorn*—the remainder of the frigate's crew had been ignored by the virus and rescued by the relief fleet—but it was still a high price. Captain Campbell had died bravely, yet…he hadn't deserved to die. Or had he? Thomas wondered, idly, if he'd ever know. The man would go down in history as a hero. Thomas would have been a great deal more accepting of that if he hadn't also been sleeping with Thomas's wife.

He's dead, he thought, as he stood to escort the admiral back to her shuttle. *You are not. Live.*

• • •

"You have a choice," Bagehot said, once Tobias and Marigold had joined him in his battered office. "You two can be on the first ship heading back to Earth, probably to an early discharge—an honourable discharge—and civilian life. There is an outside chance you'll be asked to serve a term at the academy, using your experience to teach newcomers how to handle themselves, but I can't make any promises. We barely know what's happening, on a day-to-day basis, so you might just be given your final pay packet and told to get lost."

"Ouch," Tobias said. "What's the other choice?"

"You stay here, in this system." Bagehot said. "You know how to fly shuttles. There's going to be a major military presence in this system for quite some time, both to finish the task of wiping out the infection and studying the alien sphere. The admiral is already assigning ships to the task and, I've been told, a shipload of xenospecialists is already on its way. You might be more…suited…for the task than the average shuttle pilot."

"Thanks." Tobias hesitated. "How long do we have to decide?"

"I think a week, at best," Bagehot said. "The engineers swear blind the ship will be ready to head home in five days, but Captain Hammond insisted on working some leeway into the schedule. I may be wrong about that"—his eyes narrowed—"so the longer you delay, the greater the chance someone will make the choice for you. Personally, I think you should consider what you two intend to do with your lives and then make up your mind. If you want to stay in the navy, staying here might be your best choice."

"And there's no guarantee of anything when we get home," Tobias mused.

"No," Bagehot agreed. "Sure, you can probably find work in the civilian sector. Or you could release your own version of *How I Won the War All By My Lonesome*, as is traditional. Or"—he shrugged—"point is, right now you and yours are surplus to requirements. Your squadron is effectively defunct. It might be put back into service or, in the post-war world, it might be used, praised and discarded. The navy may decide that rebuilding the squadron from scratch might be a waste of resources."

Tobias swallowed. He'd never been a big fan of the *idea* of a squadron. The idea of working in a team...he'd never had *that*, not until he'd joined the navy. He'd thought he had no emotional connection to the squadron, no real concern for his legacy...and yet, the idea of disbanding the squadron bothered him. He wasn't sure why.

"Discuss it amongst yourselves," Bagehot said. "Let me know as soon as possible, once you've made up your minds. I'll try and make sure you have the chance to choose freely."

"Thank you, sir," Tobias said. "We'll let you know."

Marigold said nothing until they were outside. "I wouldn't mind going home," she said. "But I don't want to be discharged, either. There might be fewer opportunities than we think."

Tobias nodded. There was always work for space pilots, but...there were also a *lot* of fully-trained pilots. Most of them would have more experience than either of them. And yet...it would be nice to see his mother and sister again. He assumed Marigold felt the same way. Her family was nice. Strict, but nice.

Marigold's wristcom bleeped. "I have to check in with the doctor," she said. "See you later?"

"Sure," Tobias said. "Be careful."

He felt oddly unsure of himself as he wandered the decks. A third of the crew was dead. Another third had been reassigned to fill empty billets on the relief fleet. The remainder...Tobias grimaced. He'd been a pilot and then a squadron leader and now...he wasn't quite sure *what* he was. His remaining pilots had already been reassigned. Most of them would probably be on their way home in a week or two.

"Hey," a familiar voice said. "What's up?"

Tobias blinked. His feet had carried him to the firing range. Colin was standing in the antechamber, inspecting a piece of lethal hardware. He looked surprisingly well, for someone who'd spent four days on a cramped shuttle. Tobias didn't envy him. The shuttle's life support had been on the verge of failing when they'd been picked up by the relief fleet. The marines had come very close to choking to death on their own farts. *That* would have been embarrassing.

And a few years ago, it would have seemed a suitable fate, Tobias reflected. *Colin would have deserved it and worse.*

"I've been offered a choice between going home and staying," Tobias said. "What would you advise?"

"I've been told I can stay here, as a big fish in a small pond, or I can go back home and get inserted back into a regular formation," Colin said. "I think I'll be staying."

Tobias lifted his eyebrows. "So far from Earth?"

Colin shrugged. "What's for me back there?"

"Good thought," Tobias agreed. Colin had grown up far too close to him. He probably had fewer prospects, now the war was over. There would be no shortage of former soldiers seeking employment. "Do you think you'll see any action here?"

"I don't know," Colin said. "But if we find a few more alien artefacts..."

Tobias had to laugh. "Money," he said. Colin was right. If they found more alien artefacts, the prize money would make them millionaires. "I take your point."

He grinned, realising—despite himself—that he'd already made up his mind.

$$\bullet \ \bullet \ \bullet$$

Susan had never been very religious. She'd never really cared for her school's aggressive form of Christianity—it hadn't helped that some of the snottier girls had asked her about pagan religions that neither Susan nor her distant ancestors had ever followed—and she'd rarely found herself praying after she'd graduated with honours. And yet, she was tempted to drop to her knees in thanks as she surveyed the final after-action report. *Lion* had been very lucky. She'd not only survived the war, but she'd ensured the human race knew they hadn't won completely. The virus was still out there.

She put the thought aside as she studied the preliminary report from the alien sphere. It was a strange piece of work, the researchers had noted; they'd been at pains to point out the limitations of their equipment. Susan had already sent for a proper team of xenospecialists, as well as alien technology experts from the NGW programme. It was unlikely they'd produce results quickly—she feared it would be decades, perhaps centuries, before they produced much of anything—but she was confident the sphere would be understood one day.

And we need to figure out why it was left here, Susan thought. The sphere might be beyond their understanding, at least for the moment, but the mere fact it existed was clear proof the system had been visited by an advanced alien race. Susan didn't like the implications. Had the mystery race created the virus? Or merely chosen to keep an eye on it from a safe distance? Or...or what? It was hard enough guessing what the known aliens were thinking. How could she even *guess* at the motivations of a completely unknown race? *What were they doing here?*

She frowned as she studied the starcharts from the sphere. They were alien...alien, but recognisable. Given time, they could be matched to human starcharts. And then...would they reveal the alien homeworld? Could a ship be sent there? *Should* a ship be sent there? Susan was a career military officer. She had always believed it was better to know the worst at once, rather than be stabbed in the back by an unknown threat, but her superiors might feel differently. The Virus War had been the costliest war humanity had ever fought, claiming the lives of millions of humans and billions of host-bodies. God alone knew how much cultural diversity had been wiped from the universe, when the virus had infected world after world and turned their inhabitants into zombies. If an advanced race had watched that and done nothing…what did that say about them?

Susan gritted her teeth. One way or another, the human race had to find out. And soon.

• • •

THE END
of *The Lion and the Unicorn Series.*

The *Ark Royal* Universe
Will Return Soon.

AFTERWORD

BACK IN 2013, I PUT TOGETHER A NOVEL that—somewhat to my surprise—took off like a rocket. *Ark Royal*, as I called it, is perhaps the most successful novel I've ever written, selling more copies than almost anything else and giving birth—quickly—to two sequels. The success of *Ark Royal* actually presented me with a curious problem. I wanted to continue the series—it sold very well—and yet I didn't want it to get stale. How, I asked myself, was this to be done?

I decided it would be simplest to write a series of trilogies, each one focused on a different starship. *Ark Royal* was followed by HMS *Warspite*, then HMS *Vanguard,* then, HMS *Invincible* and finally the HMS *Lion* and HMS *Unicorn* duo. This would allow me to introduce new characters with every trilogy, showing how technology advanced as the universe grew older and bring back characters from older novels in the higher positions they'd earned. I hoped this would keep the universe fresh for a little longer, rather than staying with a single ship.

It also allowed me to focus on the characters. I wanted *real* people, people with flaws and foibles that could bring them down or, if they worked to overcome them, raise them up. I designed Theodore Smith as a drunkard because it was something he could overcome, if he had a reason to try. I used the same thinking when, several books down the line, I crafted Thomas and Mitch as two very different characters who would—inevitably—clash.

That said, I was half-convinced, when I plotted the original draft for *The Lion and the Unicorn* trilogy, that it would be the last. I have gone from a carrier to a cruiser to a battleship to an assault carrier to a battlecruiser/frigate combo. I have also written an event story—*The Longest Day*, which covers the first Battle of Earth—and *The Cruel Stars*, which couldn't really be expanded into a trilogy. There aren't many more ships to cover, certainly not ones that can carry a whole story. But I have one more in mind. The seeds of contact with a far more advanced race, sown in this novel, will blossom in the next. And HMS *Endeavour*, a deep-space survey ship, will take the lead.

(If you have any ideas for other ship classes, feel free to forward them to me.)

I was asked, once, if the *Ark Royal* universe is a utopia or a dystopia. I think the answer is, much like our own world, *both*. It has wonders and it has terrors, it has deep space colonies and messy politics, it has brave heroes and cringing cowards…it is both good and bad and the people who live in it are often aware of it. You might think it is a better world than ours or a worse world. To the inhabitants, it is just their world.

And now I've written that, I have a favour to ask.

It's getting harder to make a living as an independent author. If you purchased this book and enjoyed it, please leave a review and share the title with your friends. Please join my mailing list, follow my blog and newsletter; believe me, every little helps.

Thank you.
Christopher G. Nuttall
Edinburgh, 2021

APPENDIX
GLOSSARY OF UK
TERMS AND SLANG

[Author's Note: I've tried to define every incident of specifically UK slang (and a handful of military phases/acronyms) in this glossary, but I can't promise to have spotted everything. If you spot something I've missed, please let me know and it will be included.]

Aggro—slang term for aggression or trouble, as in 'I don't want any aggro.'

Beasting/Beasted—military slang for anything from a chewing out by one's commander to outright corporal punishment or hazing. The latter two are now officially banned.

Beat Feet—Run, make a hasty departure.

Binned—SAS slang for a prospective recruit being kicked from the course, then returned to unit (RTU).

Boffin—Scientist

Bootnecks—slang for Royal Marines. Loosely comparable to 'Jarhead.'

Bottle—slang for nerve, as in 'lost his bottle.'

Borstal—a school/prison for young offenders.

Combined Cadet Force (CCF)—school/youth clubs for teenagers who might be interested in joining the military when they become adults.

Compo—British army slang for improvised stews and suchlike made from rations and sauces.

COBRA (Cabinet Office Briefing Room A)—UK Government Emergency Response Committee.

CSP—Combat Space Patrol.

Donkey Wallopers—slang for the Royal Horse Artillery.

DORA—Defence of the Realm Act.

Fortnight—two weeks. (Hence the terrible pun, courtesy of the *Goon Show*, that Fort Knight cannot possibly last three weeks.)

GATO—Global Alliance Treaty Organisation

'Get stuck into'—'start fighting.'

Head Sheds—SAS slang for senior officers.

'I should coco'—'you're damned right.'

Jobsworth—a bureaucrat who upholds petty rules even at the expense of humanity or common sense.

Kip—sleep.

Levies—native troops. The Ghurkhas are the last remnants of native troops from British India.

Lorries—trucks.

Matelots—Royal Marine slang for sailors.

Mocktail/Mocktails—non-alcoholic cocktails.

MOD—Ministry of Defence. (The UK's Pentagon.)

Order of the Garter—the highest order of chivalry (knighthood) and the third most prestigious honour (inferior only to the Victoria Cross and George Cross) in the United Kingdom. By law, there can be only twenty-four non-royal members of the order at any single time.

Panda Cola—Coke as supplied by the British Army to the troops.

RFA—Royal Fleet Auxiliary

Rumbled—discovered/spotted.

SAS—Special Air Service.

SBS—Special Boat Service

Spotted Dick—a traditional fruity sponge pudding with suet, citrus zest and currants served in thick slices with hot custard. The name always caused a snigger.

Squaddies—slang for British soldiers.

Stag—guard duty.

STUFT—'Ships Taken Up From Trade,' civilian ships requisitioned for government use.

TAB (tab/tabbing)—Tactical Advance to Battle.

Tearaway—boisterous/badly behaved child, normally a teenager.

UKADR—United Kingdom Air Defence Region.

Walt—Poser, i.e. someone who claims to have served in the military and/ or a very famous regiment. There's a joke about 22 SAS being the largest regiment in the British Army—it must be, because of all the people who claim to have served in it.

Wanker—Masturbator (jerk-off). Commonly used as an insult.

Wank/Wanking—Masturbating.

Yank/Yankee—Americans

HOW TO FOLLOW

Basic Mailing List—http://orion.crucis.net/mailman/listinfo/chrishanger-list
Nothing, but announcements of new books.

Newsletter—https://gmail.us1.list-manage.com/subscribe?u=c8f9f7391e5bfa369a9b1e76c&id=55fc83a213
New books releases, new audio releases, maybe a handful of other things of interest.

Blog—https://chrishanger.wordpress.com/
Everything from new books to reviews, commentary on things that interest me, etc.

Facebook Fan Page—https://www.facebook.com/ChristopherGNuttall
New books releases, new audio releases, maybe a handful of other things of interest.

Website—http://chrishanger.net/
New books releases, new audio releases, free samples (plus some older books free to anyone who wants a quick read)

Forums—https://authornuttall.com
Book discussions—new, but I hope to expand.

Amazon Author Page—https://www.amazon.com/
Christopher-G-Nuttall/e/B008L9Q4ES
My books on Amazon.

Books2Read—https://books2read.com/author/christopher-g-nuttall/
subscribe/19723/
*Notifications of new books (normally on Amazon too, but not included in
B2R notifications.*

Twitter—@chrisgnuttall
*New books releases, new audio releases—definitely nothing beyond (no poli-
tics or culture war stuff).*

BONUS PREVIEW

AND NOW, CHECK OUT A SAMPLE of *Pompeius Magnus* by Leo Champion:

The secessionist light cruiser Pompeius Magnus is the last survivor of her squadron—torn to pieces in a disastrous strike on their oppressors' home system. Her primary weapons are wrecked, her enginers are crippled, life-support is on tertiary backup, and more than half her crew are dead.

Captain Delaney is a lifelong pilot, a veteran who has repeatedly refused promotion so as to stay in the fight. Lieutenant Shan is an activist turned wartime spacer motivated by a fanatic's fire.

Orders are orders. It doesn't matter that Earth's defenses were engineered to stop fleets, let alone single ships – let alone crippled ones.

They're going in anyway.

And they will change history.

https://www.amazon.com/dp/B094VLZKV5

CHAPTER ONE

20 July, 2337; 8:20 pm Earth GMT.

Gravspace. With a juddering hum, the battered ship eased into hyperspace, and the vision turned from star-specked darkness to a deeper black, dotted with faint and distant green glows.

Commander James Delaney let himself relax slightly. Only slightly, as he leaned back into the chair. It had been three hours since the start of the engagement. Slightly more than two weeks since Admiral Lettow's *point-less* strike had began. Drive Earth to the negotiating table, yes. Achieve it by a futile stab at the impossible, *no!* How much of the fleet had been destroyed, how many killed? The *Clodius* was gone. So were the *Annius Milo*, the *Tullius Cicero*, the *Licinius Crassus* and the *Gaius Julius*; every other ship of their squadron. Lettow's own flagship, the *Thomas Paine*, had been crippled – perhaps destroyed, Lettow wounded and conceivably dead. To say nothing of the rest of the fleet.

Billions of dollars worth of ships, some of the Senate's finest, along with more than two thousand lives, lost. Men who had fought at Trenton six weeks ago, whose skill and bravery had helped win the largest battle in human history. Men whose lives had been thrown away now like so much popcorn: the Senate's best, wasted in a futile gesture.

He would have seethed. He had seethed the night before, in a private conference with the other squadron captains and the squadron commander. Captain Jameson had told him she disliked it herself, but orders were orders.

Orders are suicide, he thought as he stood up. Lieutenant-Commander Jennifer Wang, ship weapons officer, was coming towards him. A coldly beautiful Eurasian woman, her face was cut open and covered in blood; her right hand was missing, severed between the wrist and the elbow. A plainly-cauterized wound less than an hour old.

"What's the status, Wang?"

The artificial gravity fluttered again, and both officers flinched. Wang's once-white uniform, Delaney noticed, was covered in blood. Filthy with it. Not just her own.

"We were lucky, *very* lucky. If that nuke had been just a *fraction* closer, it would have overwhelmed shielding. Casualties were light anyway. Seven more dead, nine critically injured, another eleven wounded but capable of limited emergency functions. Sir."

Seven plus nine plus eleven plus eighteen. Delaney had calculated the horrifying arithmetic before Wang finished her sentence. "Seventeen remain from sixty-two," he said. "More than seventy percent of our crew are casualties."

"With respect, sir, not all of those are full casualties. We have twenty-six effectives. Including myself, sir," said Wang. She dabbed at the blood on her face with an already-sodden bandage, flinching as she did so. For a moment the wound itself was exposed. A *horrible* one; a deep cut from her right ear down to her mouth, a fleeting glimpse of bone.

"Have you anaesthetized that, Wang?"

"Sufficiently, sir. There's a finite amount of the locals left."

Again, Delaney nodded. He'd been cut in a half-dozen places, but they weren't even relevant flesh wounds. Imploding panels caused by electronic disruptions; the pain hurt, but was insignificant. If anything, it kept him alert.

Thirty-two of my people dead. We're not going to get to a hospital for a week. For two weeks. God. My God. Why are we doing this?

"What about the ship – what's our current status?"

"Primary weapons are all gone, sir. Direct railgun hit critically damaged main upper, laser burns and another shell wrecked main lower, and the nuke's pulse crippled the others except for the aft antimissile, which is damaged but operational. Engines are limping but functional. Gravspace is obviously online. Torpedoes, we have three tac-nukes that read as nonfunctional, probably jizzed up by that EMP, and a dozen guided incendiaries that were better-shielded and read as functional. Life support is damaged, but secondary backup is working. Art-grav holds, but navigation is damaged. And external comms are mostly destroyed."

Wang took a deep breath.

"OK. Stand down and get something to eat. Do something for those poor incapacitated bastards, if you can."

For a moment Delaney was tempted to tell her *and let them know I'm sorry. So sorry.* But that would have revealed weakness, the one thing he could not possibly afford to show right now. Not at all. His ship had nearly been destroyed; thirty-two dead was a miracle, it should have been more, would have been everyone if the lasers had backflashed. The survivors were shaken, and if their captain lost his cool...

They'd never survive.

• • •

Senior Lieutenant Francois Shan, assistant weapons officer and acting in lieu of the dead navigator, was sitting in front of a burned-out console playing with a calculator. A numerical calculator the size of two playing cards; he was absently playing calculus, toying with vectors and intercepts, when Delaney approached him. He was a handsome Asian with short, dark hair and a heavily-drugged left arm; an electric backflash from one of the wrecked aft lasers had nearly killed him.

"What's the status?"

"I've got us on course," said Shan. "Primary's gone, but secondary's mostly functional. At this present velocity – not high, as you can imagine, but we've got enough distance from the outer planets – we should drop out by the Sphere influence in about five hours. Sir."

"The Sphere influence?" Delaney asked. Confused for a moment – the Sphere was *in*, was near Earth, not away and toward safety. Then, with dulled shock, he realized: Duty. His men were important, but so was the mission, since men existed for a mission and missions required men.

The objectives. Yes, the objective. They'd come in for a purpose. They were still going in. Of course. The orders. He gave a curt, forced nod and wondered if the other man had noticed his hesitation.

"Good. I want us as far from Mars as possible. Interception is going to be at its tightest near there. And of course as far from any gates as possible."

"Already planned, sir. Our course puts us fifty-eight degrees from the nearest gate, and two hundred thirty-two from Mars."

The Sphere. Delaney closed his eyes again. Suicidal. Absurd. Impassable. Necessary. Thirty-six capital ships, Lettow's fleet, might have had a chance at forcing their way through one of the gates. One damaged ship, half its crew dead, wouldn't have a prayer. They'd have to go *through* the Sphere. Which was like charging a brick wall. God.

No. It was the objective. It was unavoidable. It would be difficult, but James Delaney was a pilot. A pilot all his life, and the son of a pilot. *Dammit*, he thought, pushing aside the fear that was rising inside him. He was a pilot and an officer and a citizen of the Free Planets. *And I have to. This is my duty. To try my best and fail gloriously. And maybe other lives, good lives, will be saved in the end because of this.*

. . .

Shan watched the captain walk away. The pain in his arm had numbed, with the help of the drugs; there was still an occasional spasm, but not the ripping, tingling pain across his body that he'd suffered before.

Bastards.

Vermin.

And they were going to kill them. Here he was, on a ship, heading inbound – not to some goddamned loyalist colony, or a planet occupied by the vermin, or a concentration of the fucks in hyper, but *in*. In to Earth. The bastards. The scum.

Five hundred years ago – on Earth – there had been a similar war to this. It had started the nation that Senator Jefferson Caesar had called 'the Second Republic', the first having been the Great Roman one. Ironic that the nation it had created had become one of the leading oppressors of the Free Planets.

During his childhood on New California, Shan had read about that war, daydreamed about battling redcoated soldiers across the eastern coast of North America. Or about its failed successor, the Rising thirty-two years ago that had ended with his grandfather dead; shot without trial by Coalition political-police, simply for being an executive in a corporation that had supported the secessionists. His father, imprisoned through his teenaged years for the crime of having the wrong relatives.

Shan had been thirteen when he'd fired his first gun – an ancient sniping rifle, hidden by one of his grandfather's associates at the end of the Rising, using ammunition stolen from an occupying garrison. At sixteen, he'd done his first combat: a guerilla ambush in the Sacramentan mountains, seventeen Resistance men against a two-car Coalition patrol.

In his mind, a framed and glorious memory: crouching over a Coalition man, a dead Chinese, who he'd hit in the chest from a hundred and twenty metres as he was jumping out of his burning truck. The body a little bit scorched, with flames and other men moving around, stripping the destroyed vehicle and the intact one for everything they could take. Shan had gotten the man's weapons, his pistol and his rifle, his knife and his ammunition.

The next year, Shan had finished High and gone to college on Medici, where the resistance movement was even stronger than on New California. It had been Medici, after all, where the Hevlov and Thatcher massacres had taken place; nearly six hundred people killed by trigger-happy uber-Saharan occupiers. When rebellion had broken out again across the free colonies, Shan had been in his second year of a history degree, with an uncredited minor in politics and organizing.

He'd fought in the first anti-Earth riots, organizing blockades, commanding an impromptu student platoon that had grown to company size, then decided that the war would be influenced on the ground but decided in space and joined the naval militia. His experience as an organizer had gotten him an ensign's commission on a hastily-converted freighter, and almost immediately he'd seen his first action – destroying unarmed troop transports that were trying to reinforce the surviving occupation garrisons. Easy kills that had soon become a hell of a lot harder as the Earthers figured out space combat for themselves and learned to protect their transports.

Four years and two promotions later. Shan found himself smiling despite the pain. High Trenton had been fun. This was going to be better. They were going to hit the vermin at *home*.

CHAPTER TWO

20 July, 2337. 9:18 pm, Earth GMT.

"So we're going to see Earth," said Gunner Second-Class Wyeng Maslow to the man at the defunct missile-tracker next to him.

"Never thought it'd happen," replied Gunner First-Class Ramirez. He was muscular, dark, and bloody from an anaesthetised cut to his thigh. Shrapnel. He'd lost a lot of blood, but the gun officer had patched him up. Two litres from the ship's intravenous depository. The wound hurt badly, but he was alive and at his station. He added, "`course, during all that shit, I never figured *anything*'d happen again."

Maslow tried to grin. His blond hair was shaved, and his uniform coat and tunic were gone. Burn marks were on his bare back, but the pain had been anesthetized away.

"Gonna see Earth," he repeated. "My grand-daddy came from there."

"Why'd he leave?"

"Oppression," said Maslow. "Some corporation said they'd tax him only twenty percent if he promised to farm for at least ten years on one of their worlds. They were taxing him, like, fifty percent in Poland and they didn't let him have free speech. So when they offer him it, he takes it. My great-grand-parents were from there as well."

"*All* our ancestors were from there," Ramirez said. He closed his eyes for a moment. "Wish I knew why we were going to go bomb it."

"'ppression. They were 'ppressing people over there, and people left, and the governments couldn't control 'em any more or tax 'em. So they tried to extend their 'ppression into space. And we rebelled. And they cracked down and sent in garrisons. And then we rebelled again and it became war."

"And now we gotta bomb them just so they can leave us alone. Right?"

"Yeah, that's how I figure it." Ramirez took a water canteen from his hip pocket, wet a bandage, and dabbed it against the slash on his exposed thigh. The anaesthetic wasn't total, and the cut – from a bit of metal that had ricocheted loose when a missile had hit amidships early in the fight – caused a nagging, constant pain. He took a swig of water and offered the flask to Maslow, who took it gratefully.

• • •

The ship co-pilot was a short man named Senior Lieutenant Cody Tenengo. Dark hair in a ponytail, and a dark, scarred complexion. His uniform was spattered with blood, and there was a white bandage tied over his left hand and fore-arm, concealing a second-class burn. His right arm was handling the ship's control stick; it felt unfamilar. Four years of flight experience had given him a habit of using him the left hand.

He closed his eyes, and the pulsing darkness of hyper changed to a steadier blackness. His eyes closed, he turned around, stretched his neck, looked up at the ceiling, opened his eyes. A panel had burst, and there was a tangle of rubber-screened wires; their bare metallic ends cut in a sprayed mess.

Next to him on the bridge: The communications officer's seat was empty, his controls mostly wrecked; their violent combustion in his face had killed him. Junior Lieutenant Pieter Dreyfus, the bridge engineer, was seated with his eyes closed, perhaps trying to sleep. Commander Delaney was out of his seat. The acting navigator was in his little enclave, surrounded on two sides by mostly-wrecked terminals and on the third by paper-and-plastic printouts of references.

The bridge aide wasn't present; he'd been caught by the spray of metallic splinters when the comm and navigation panels had blown, and almost died. He was triaged back in the med-rooms now, maybe dead. Sitting at the burnt-out communications panel was the ship's deputy political/intelligence officer, Lieutenant Barnes. An Engineering Sub-Lieutenant called Morenz was on the other side of the room, staring blankly into space.

Tenengo turned back to the main window. Hyper was black, with faint glowing points of light in the distance signifying gravity wells. Saturn was the big one now, and their speed was delayed largely because of the influence that planet's gravity trail had on the ship. The sun was also a factor, and they'd be nearing Jupiter's influence before long. Already their speed was sub-interstellar. Hyper was based largely on the absence of gravity – moving across the vast interstellar gaps where the total gravitational influence was almost zero. Moving inside star systems, with points of gravitational interference closer and stronger, was much more difficult. Older hyperdrives couldn't do it; the *Pompeius* was a new ship, only a year old and with the best technology that cutting-edge corporate industry could produce.

Even so – Tenengo eyed the near-solid line of of fluorescent blips in the distance. Tiny pinpricks now, but they would grow. The Earth Coalition had taken steps to protect their homeworld. Asteroids and giant masses of ice had been maneuvered into position, a near-spherical net of gravitational influence roughly a third of the distance from Jupiter to industrial Mars. Completely impossible to pass through in hyper – and inside the defensive sphere, you were too close to the Sun's influence to easily return to hyper, to re-ascend.

He closed his eyes again. What they were trying to do was impossible. Maybe if the entire fleet, all thirty-six of Lettow's capital ships, had been intact, they could have attacked one of the Gates, the heavily-defended clearways through the sphere. They could have jumped out of hyper, attacked, and in the distraction of the fight… maybe a ship could have made it through those outer defenses. Or maybe they could have thrown enough nukes at the Sphere, shifted enough rocks, to blast a new path through.

They were going to die. Of that, Tenengo was convinced. He didn't care. At the start of Trenton he had cared, when they had come within two hundred and fifty metres – *quarter of a kilometre; within a ten-thousandth of a decimal point* – of colliding with the burned-out shell of an Armstrong-class, he had soiled his pants.

But somewhere through that vicious two-week battle, somewhere through the haze of stress and exhaustion and illicit drug-induced relief, he had stopped caring. Maybe it had simply been too much of the stress-reducing depressant alcomorph. Maybe it had been the news that the six guys who had come above him in the flight class of `31 had all been killed – two of them without warning or glory on the ground when goddamned General Bush had nuked the polar spaceport on Trenton II.

Whatever it had been, Lieutenant Tenengo had not really flinched when the gravitational influence of the Earth interceptors had shocked Lettow's fleet out of hyper and into hell. He'd assisted Delaney during the opening stages, then taken over, and handed the ship back, and taken over when Delaney had gone to assist after that second missile hit, and given the ship back to the Commander just before the ten-megaton bomb that had come within a nanometre of killing them all. He'd noticed things, and he'd acted well, but it had been remote.

He was an officer; it was his duty to live or die for the Executives and the Senate. Duty was a concept you could get your mind around; life was not. He'd tried, but been unable to. In four years of war, three quarters of his flight class had been killed. Two of his five brothers were dead. His uncle and all that uncle's family; an aunt and seven cousins, none of them older than twelve. Shipmates equal to about one and a half times the listed crew strength of the *Pompeius*; he should have been dead at least once himself, statistically. What the hell was the point of life when everyone died anyway?

. . .

Junior Lieutenant Barnes touched his right thigh again. Nothing. No sense, no pain. The medic had splinted it, had bandaged the slashes, given the entire leg a desensory. Broken in three places – one above the knee, two below- and an hour later, he couldn't feel it. His left leg, which had gotten off lucky -a deep cut above his ankle, that had barely touched the bone – was as irrelevant. As blank.

He was a tall, handsome man in his late twenties. *Young*, he thought, to be the surviving intelligence officer for a Tsau-class. And a moment later, another thought: *Lucky, that I wasn't in the upper section when the shell had hit.*

The ship intelligence officer, Senior Lieutenant Hamous, had died with the crew of Gun Alpha, one of the ship's primary weapons. The intelligence department had been in the upper-section of the ship, and Hamous had been at his station when a seeker missile had faked through the defensive lasers, hit weakened, laser-and-nuke-scorched armor, and blown three compartments. Barnes had been with Beta, which had been hit a couple of minutes later. Depressurisation, thankfully, hadn't been instant. He'd survived, despite the shell fragments that had shredded his legs. Six others hadn't.

Combat. He'd asked for it. When the war had started, he had been at a rabbinical seminary on New Israel, starting his final year. The agitations of the final years of peace had reached even that religious planet; some-how a division of Egyptians had come to be stationed there, had behaved as obnoxiously as their Earthside cousins did to the Jews in Earth Israel. When war had broken out, many of the younger men had rushed off; had joined the defensive militias or the offworld combat regiments that were being formed to take the war to the enemy. Many of the younger men had quickly been killed. Earth's occupation troops were well-trained, well-armed, and, by the time the news came to New Israel, ready.

Barnes had felt the call about nine months into the war, when the last of the garrisons that would fall had fallen and Earth had just repelled the first secessionist offensive into still-occupied worlds. He had been about to finish his schooling when the urge to serve had come. To serve under arms, to defend the Jewish keyworld and her allies. The aptitude tests had shown him best suited for staff work, and he'd quickly proven himself a competent intelligence analyst. He'd been comissioned as ensign about two years ago, promoted after Trenton.

After Trenton, he'd asked for a transfer to combat duty. Serving on fleet staff was fine, but he had felt that if he were a soldier, he should be in a fighting unit. The *Pompeius Magnus* had taken losses in the fighting – as had every other ship – and Barnes, the newly-minted junior lieutenant, had been assigned to replace a man whose nerves had broken.

And now, thought Barnes, *I can see why.*

"This story is a smash-mouth bar brawl from beginning to end with characters who struggle to rationalize their humanity in the face of utter, merciless, brutality. They are a crew with a single-minded objective, torn between doing what is right, and what must be done. A crew who wrestle with the fate of their immortal souls and the survival of their people. It is a must-read for anyone who appreciates a dark, gritty tale centered around the morality—and immorality—of man."

Colonel Shane Gries, author of From The Ashes of a Dead World
For more, go to https://www.amazon.com/dp/B094VLZKV5 !

Printed in Great Britain
by Amazon

65077859R00255